No .... Class ....

Author ....COOK, Gloria....

KT-559-252

Title ......Keeping Echoes (L.P. edition)......

KEEPING ECHOES

KEEPING ECHOES

Gloria Cook

Severn House Large Print
London & New York

This first large print edition published in Great Britain 2006 by
SEVERN HOUSE LARGE PRINT BOOKS LTD of
9-15 High Street, Sutton, Surrey, SM1 1DF.
First world regular print edition published 2006 by
Severn House Publishers, London and New York.
This first large print edition published in the USA 2006 by
SEVERN HOUSE PUBLISHERS INC., of
595 Madison Avenue, New York, NY 10022.

British Library Cataloguing in Publication Data

Cook, Gloria
  Keeping echoes. - Large print ed.
  1. Copper mines and mining - England - Cornwall - Fiction
  2. Women - England - Cornwall - Social conditions - 19th
  century - Fiction 3. Cornwall (England) - Social conditions
  - 19th century - Fiction 4. Love stories 5. Large type
  books
  I. Title
  823.9'14[F]

ISBN-13: 9780727875570
ISBN-10: 0727875574

Printed and bound in Great Britain by
MPG Books Ltd, Bodmin, Cornwall.

To my dear grandchildren
Kerenza and Daniel,
with my love

One

'I'll give your brother another ten minutes. If he's not back then, I swear I'll send him to work down the mine!'

Amy Lewarne avoided her father's accusing glare. She was always included in whatever he considered to be her brother's shortcomings which, for poor Toby, was almost everything he did. It was a bad sign for Morton Lewarne to be sitting at the kitchen hearth instead of in the front room on a Sunday afternoon. He had stationed himself where it would be hard for Toby to creep into the house unnoticed. 'I'm sure Toby's not—'

'I don't want to hear your excuses for him!' Morton screwed up his pallid, frowning brow and chafed at his wiry side-whiskers. 'You're as bad as your mother. Turned the wretched boy into a milksop. He's no right to go off and play after chapel and take that wretched dog with him. He's fourteen, time he thought himself a man. A privileged one at that. How many sons round here have gone straight into his father's business? The boy's a dreamer, unreliable. I'll take my belt off to him for this. He's not to have a bite of his dinner when he comes in, do you hear?'

7

'Yes, Father.' Amy wouldn't obey the order. Her father was right about her and her mild-mannered mother indulging Toby, but it was to compensate for Morton's constant unmerited disapproval of the boy. Hiding her irritation, she said, 'Mother's resting. It's time I left to teach Sunday School. I'll see if Sarah's free afterward to go for a walk.'

'You'll stay here. Reverend Longfellow can manage without you today. And you know I don't like you mixing with mining rabble.'

Amy received another accusing glare. Her father knew she would ask her friend, Sarah Hichens, to help her search for Toby and bring him home. Unable to sit still, she put the kettle on the slab to boil for tea, then placed a cup and saucer on the little round table at Morton's side. A master carpenter and cabinetmaker, he had made the table himself. It was more functional than it seemed, cleverly designed to disguise an assortment of drawers and hidey holes, and no one but Morton was permitted to touch it.

Morton never let a vexation rest. 'The boy had better not gone off to the woods with that mongrel, ruining his best suit!'

'I shouldn't think so.' Amy was certain Toby wouldn't have gone near the woods, even with his dog, Stumpy, for company. It was part of Poltraze land, owned by the belligerent squire, Darius Nankervis. Toby was sensitive and shy, too nervous to be caught as a trespasser. Amy glanced up at the mahogany mantel clock. It was two forty-five.

8

She willed Toby to walk in through the back door. He had never been this late back from anywhere before, he had never missed a meal.

'Did your mother eat her dinner?' Morton's hard expression furrowed with further displeasure.

'She ate her beef,' Amy added to herself, 'Just to please you.' Her mother, Sylvia, was laid up with child, pale and weary, her ankles worryingly swollen. Interspersed with numerous miscarriages, she had borne her father two healthy children, although to his mind Toby was disappointingly puny, not at all clever and far too slow at learning his father's craft.

'Waste of time having him. He's going to let the Lewarne name down.' Morton's oft-repeated opinion just as often upset kind-hearted Sylvia and infuriated Amy.

She had prayed in chapel this morning that her mother would be safely delivered of this latest baby and would then never have to suffer the pain and indignity of childbearing again.

Morton drummed his fingers on the arm of his chair. 'I suppose she's doing the right thing, lying about in bed.'

'Of course she is.' Amy found it hard to keep the impatience out of her voice. Why did he consider everyone was lazy if they weren't on their feet? He was getting mean. There was a time when, as in the households of all successful businesses of people aspiring to the middle class, he had employed a part-time gardener and a woman to do the heavy housework, but several months ago he had declared this an extravagance and had dismissed the services of the mineworker and his wife. It was an extra strain on her mother. 'We don't want to lose her as well as another baby.'

'Mind your lip, girl!' Morton gulped his tea. He fell silent. He had said his piece. He was head of his household, a respected member of the community, with a finer residence than the copper miners, mine ancillary workers and farm labourers who inhabited nearby Meryen Village, and he considered his word as the last. He had built the six-bedroom cottage Chy-Henver and its workshop himself and was proud of every brick, slate and well-honed piece of timber.

Keeping her restless hands folded in her lap, Amy watched him covertly. She was rewarded by seeing his eyelids droop. Morton usually dozed all through Sunday afternoons.

When Morton was snoring softly, Amy slipped out to the back kitchen, hoping to see Toby returning. Their father was unlikely to take his belt to him, he rarely used that sort of punishment for he had a squeamish streak to pain even in others, but he'd confine Toby to the workshop and the house for days, and grumble and find fault and make Toby feel small and unloved, and in turn, Toby would fret that he really would be sent to work under grass at the Carn Croft Mine, over a mile away on the downs. Toby was terrified at

10

the thought of being underground, he was terrified of the dark. Her eye caught something and she caught her breath. Stumpy was outside but it seemed he was back alone. The grey wire-haired lurcher was sniffing about the back yard and searching along the garden path. Perhaps Toby had twisted an ankle and was limping home on his own. She crept back to the kitchen. Her father was fast asleep. She would be able to steal away and, pray God, quickly get the dog to lead her to her brother.

When she got outside Stumpy had disappeared, no doubt gone back to meet his young master. He hadn't run off to the back of the property because she would spot him easily if he were following the moorland path or climbing up the low grassy hill that gave shelter, so she dashed to the front gate. She was just in time to see Stumpy heading towards the village. 'Stumpy! Here boy! Wait for me!' It was a waste of time. The dog, the greater part of its tail cut off in an accident by a slammed gate, hence its name, only obeyed orders from Toby. Amy chased after him.

A pony and open carriage came trotting along. Amy halted, amazed that anything as grand should be in the area. It could only be going to Poltraze. Why wasn't it taking the usual route along the turnpike road? Bobbing a curtsey, she looked up to see who the travellers were.

A pale face, framed by a feather-trimmed poke bonnet, turned to her and a white-lace gloved hand was raised in a demure wave.

11

Then the young woman recognized her and leaned forward animatedly. 'Amy! Hello, it's me.' The girl, eighteen years old like Amy, was chided by the other female passenger, her guardian, the estranged Mrs Darius Nankervis, and she turned obediently to sit correctly forward.

'Tara...' Amy muttered. What were Miss Tara Julyan and her aunt doing here after so many years? The trap turned off immediately, in the opposite direction to the moors, rocking over a little-used byway along a rough route that would lead eventually to Poltraze. They obviously wanted their arrival to be circumspect. Soon after Mrs Estelle Nankervis, second wife to the squire, had walked out on him, Tara had written to Amy to inform her, as the only friend – secret friend – she had ever made, that they would never be coming back. Only the self-righteous in Meryen condemned Mrs Nankervis for the desertion. The squire had been unmerciful since the tragic death of his son and heir, as a young man, in the pool at Poltraze. The big house had seen a lot of misery. It was deemed a desolate place.

Amy didn't stop to ponder the mystery. She pursued Stumpy, to the amused laughter of the children filing into the chapel Sunday School room and the few people who were quietly sunning themselves outside their homes; the land rented from the Poltraze estate. The shops and other places of business were dutifully shuttered and still for the

Sabbath.

Stumpy stopped to sniff at the rough garden wall of Moor Cottage, the tiny home of the Hichens family, which was situated uncomfortably close to the Nankervis Arms, one of Meryen's four drinking establishments. Bal-maiden Sarah, the breadwinner of her family, including for her disabled, widowed mother, had sparse time to relax and she was bending the tops of onions over in the patch of garden. Amy called to her friend. 'Sarah. I'm searching for Toby. Has he been here?'

Sarah rose. Her shabby dress did not disguise her pretty dark looks, but as always, she wore an air of being dragged down by life. 'Sorry, Amy. Something wrong?'

'Not really, well I hope not. He hasn't been home since chapel. He must've got separated from Stumpy because the dog's now searching for him. Toby's probably not far away. He's ripped his clothes or the like and is reluctant to show himself to our father.' Amy gave Sarah a smile. Sarah had enough worries of her own without having to consider hers.

Stumpy took off again and Amy ran after him, sighing. The village of Meryen straggled over slopes and in dells, some homes having up to half an acre of ground, for many miners also eked out their meagre living on allotments and as smallholders. Stumpy kept darting in and out of sight. She passed the church, some cottages of cob and thatch and then reached a short row of new stone and

13

killas, slate-roofed cottages; another row, veering off at a right angle, was under construction. She halted, whirling to the left and right. Where was the dog? As well as the main road that led off to Gwennap, there were many dirt tracks and lanes, and worn-down grassy paths over the scrubland of Nansmere Downs. Which way did he go?'

'Stumpy!'

'The beggar's just shot off down Bell Lane, my luvver.' Godley Greep, a heavily bearded mine surface worker, called from his front doorstep. 'He'll be off up Oak Hill and the woods. Won't see he again till he's hungry, I b'lieve.'

Bell Lane led to tenanted farms and the occasional wayside home, and was frequently used as a route to Poltraze for staff who lived out. Amy pictured Stumpy sneaking on to the grounds of the big house, nearly three miles away, and receiving Nankervis's retribution. It would break Toby's heart if Stumpy were shot. She veered off and pounded along the lane, lifting her skirt and petticoat up out of the dried mud, sighing as her best slippers became animal fouled. She would soon be splattered with dirt, and she had come out of the house on a Sunday without her bonnet! As she began the winding ascent of Oak Hill the pins holding up her light brown hair were falling out and the wavy tresses bounced on her shoulders. She was going to be in a lot of trouble when she returned home.

All the land hereabouts belonged to Pol-

14

traze except for a substantial chunk that fell away into a huge enclosed valley. She had covered a mile and a half, was at the top of the hill and had come to Burnt Oak, owned by the strange and formidable Kivell family. While their cattle and sheep grazed freely in their fields, their buildings were surrounded by a square of granite walls, constructed as more than just a wise protection from harsh winter weather. Over the last half century the Kivells, renowned for their remoteness, had fortified the walls higher and higher following a series of food riots by local tin miners at Redruth market. A few ancient trees gave more cover. Inhospitable iron gates in the outer hedge kept out curious passers-by and an identical pair of gates ran parallel in the front wall far below. Amy was dismayed to see Stumpy racing down over the rough cart track towards the distant gate.

Stumpy leapt through the lower bars of the gate. Amy trod out a frustrated little dance. The Kivells had dwelt in the area for as long as the Nankervises. An old legend had it that in 1066 there were two pieces of land, side by side, of a large and a smaller acreage, ready to be claimed by any of the conquering Normans who rode hard and got there first. A Nankervis had celebrated victory of the manor and a Kivell, an arch-rival, got the much smaller portion. The latter was so enraged for taking a stumble off his horse and losing the greater prize, he'd sulked, and jealously built up an insular community, living mainly self-sufficiently and by producing many fine crafts. The Kivells had evolved from the fearsome French warrior breed and nobility, mixing their blood with gypsies and undesirables and they were notorious for smuggling, poaching and instigating drunken brawls. None sought to work down a mine shaft and indeed none would be allowed to. They applied their own codes and rules as ruthlessly as Darius Nankervis ran his concerns.

Amy bit her lip. She ought to give up and go home, leave Stumpy to return when he would, and let Toby face his punishment. But what if Toby was down there at Burnt Oak? Stumpy might be following his scent. The Kivells bred lurchers, supposedly to help them thieve, and Stumpy had come from one of the litters. Toby had bartered with a Kivell child for him, exchanging a nicely detailed drawing, his one accomplishment. It was the one thing that gave Toby confidence, that he had encountered a Kivell and had come out of it not only unscathed but with a better bargain – Sylvia had been forced to do a lot of pleading on Toby's behalf to get Morton to allow him to keep the dog. Amy hated to go to such a dissolute place but she hoped the Kivells wouldn't mind if she inquired if Toby was there.

She hurried down the valley as swiftly as the long grasses, the thistles and the gradient, which dipped sharply in places, allowed. She eased off as she closed in on the veiled property, now feeling herself to be foolhardy, and hid behind the wall. Panting, her heart thudding, the thought sat uncomfortably that while this wall may have been built to keep intruders out, anyone approaching from the higher reaches of the valley could easily be seen. Would the Kivells treat her as a trespasser, and would they be any kinder over the matter than the Nankervises? Any moment now a strapping, long-haired, dark-skinned savage – some of the good people of Meryen called them savages – might demand to know what she was doing here.

Toby, Stumpy, what have you got me into, she thought.

She stayed absolutely still, the only sound her nervous breathing. No one came to challenge her. Apparently, she hadn't been seen. Perhaps the Kivells were taking a Sunday afternoon nap, the same as the civilized world.

She edged along the wall, grazing her hand on the hefty blocks of lichen-covered granite, until she reached the thick wooden gate post. Leaning round it she glanced through the heavy sun-warmed bars. All was quiet. Nothing and no one was stirring. It was as if the world had stopped. She had seen nothing before like these stone and thatched, or slate-roofed buildings before. There were half a dozen situated on each of the three sides of a stone-chipping courtyard, with more, and the farmyard, rambling off behind. The largest house was an impressive three times larger

17

than Chy-Henver, with cross-leaded windows. She caught sight of Stumpy. He was investigating the ground outside of what looked like a workshop. Amy's stomach tightened into knots. Had Stumpy smelled Toby? Was it fanciful to imagine Toby had somehow got into trouble and this vagabond breed had locked him in there? She was scared but she had to find out.

Taking off her long narrow summer scarf to use as a leash for Stumpy, she climbed through the middle bars of the gate, forcing herself not to cry out as she snagged the hem of her dress. Staring about fearfully, hunched over, she crept across the yard, gritting her teeth as each step made a treacherous crunch. Her prayers that Stumpy wouldn't suddenly take off again were answered. He kept sniffing the ground, and she reached out and grabbed him by the scruff of his neck. The dog jumped at her touch but it recognized her and didn't make a noise or try to strain away.

'Stumpy,' she whispered as she tied the red-flowered, yellow cloth through his collar. 'Where's Toby? Is he in there?' She tried the workshop door. It was locked.

'There's no one in there that shouldn't be,' came a loud, gravelly voice.

'Oh!' Amy leapt round and put her back against the workshop door. Her eyes widened in fear. With a host of fretful lurchers at his heels, a man of about her father's age, in homespun cloth and leather, his thick devil-

18

ishly black, silver-streaked hair streaming to his heavy jaw, was staring at her from wild, suspicious eyes. With chills she surmised he had watched her approach and had kept his dogs at bay until now.

'Stealing one of my dogs, eh, missy?' He thrust his face close to hers.

'No! It's my brother's dog. He bartered for him fair and square. I swear on the Good Book I'm telling the truth.'

'Think I believe that?' the man roared. He thumped his hands either side of her against the workshop door, trapping her. 'You're here to steal something. Who are you? Are you from the village?'

'I'm Amy Lewarne. My father is Morton Lewarne, the carpenter. I'm sorry for intruding. I'm out looking for my brother Toby. He's fourteen, small and thin. Have you seen him?'

The man eyed her all over, taking his time. 'I can see by your clothes you're finer than a bal-maiden. Int'resting you should be Morton Lewarne's girl. I need to have a word with he.'

'Are you one of the Kivells?' What did he want with her father? Was it about Toby?

'Who else would I be living here?' She blinked at his thunderous words, which he pitted with obscene language. 'I'm Titus Kivell.' With a sneer, 'I'm very pleased to meet you, Miss Lewarne.'

Amy felt her terror grow. 'Titus...?'

'I see you've heard of me. I like that

19

reaction to my name. Yes. I'm Titus Kivell. Newly out of gaol after five long months of hard labour.'

Amy swallowed. Titus Kivell was the head, and the worst, of the ungovernable family. He had maimed a man in a fight but had somehow escaped a longer, more just, sentence or transportation to the colonies. No one knew he was free or it would have been the talk of the village. She tried to make herself shrink into the hard door she was pressed against. What would he do to her? 'I'm sorry to be a trouble to you. Please, can I take my brother's dog and go?'

'I don't take kindly to people walking all over my land just as they please.'

'I wasn't doing anything wrong. I just wanted to get the dog.' Amy ducked her head to dodge under his arm but he lowered it, keeping her prisoner. He brought his body so close she could smell the tobacco reeking in his clothes and the rum on his breath. With awe and trepidation, she noticed the scars on his unshaven chin. More were flicked across his dark brow and whittled into his cheeks. The result of much fighting and violence. Even so, and with all the weight of his hostility, it was a strange thing to observe he had strong, arresting looks. He had a multitude of children by the three different women he'd taken as wives, only one properly churched. 'Please, I want to go home!'

'Maybe I don't want you to go yet.' A ghastly smile spread across his swarthy features. A smile that chilled Amy to the marrow of her bones. She remembered she was clinging to the scarf she'd tied to Stumpy's collar. Stumpy could protect her, but the dog, sensing a superior authority, was sitting quietly.

Amy was terrified she was about to be subjected to the very worst of fates but suddenly she dredged up some fighting spirit. 'No! Don't you dare do anything to me. Get away!'

'Father, what are you doing? Who's she?'

Titus glanced over his shoulder and to Amy's relief he stepped back from her. 'Sol. Come here, son. Take a good look at Miss Amy Lewarne. Isn't she as fair as a wild lily? As innocent and lovely as the morning dew? Do you see the gold glinting in her sweet pretty hair?'

Sol Kivell was much like his father, although leaner and less intimidating. His hair was pure black and he too wore it free and unruly. He was Titus's eldest son, his only legitimate son. Amy had seen him at a distance, striding across the moors, a shotgun 'broken' and resting insolently on his shoulder, out hunting, or poaching. The Kivells had no need to poach but they were brazen enough to do so in daylight, proving the point that they thought themselves above any law. The local girls giggled that Sol Kivell would make a 'good catch' but every one of them was too scared to try to 'catch' him or any of his kinsmen who frequented the local inns, beer shops or kiddleys. It was with prayers of thanks that the women of the parish

21

considered themselves safe from too much unwanted attention from the Kivells – they usually took up permanently with women further abroad.

Amy remembered that Toby had mentioned Sol Kivell had helped him once, by pulling him out of a dangerous marsh on the moors. He was her only hope. 'I'm here looking for my brother, Toby. I'm worried about him. Please, will you tell your father that this dog is Toby's? See, he has only part of a tail. You can see he's not one of your dogs.'

On sauntering feet, clad in decorated leather boots, Sol Kivell drew in on her. 'Little Toby's sister, eh? I agree, Father, she is as fair as a lily. A little messed up though. Morton's going to be furious with her.'

Amy had not missed that these men were talking as if they knew her father well.

'Walk her back home,' Titus barked, his gaze resting invasively on Amy. Then he stalked off, taking it for granted his order would be obeyed.

'What?' Amy gulped. Her father, who likely was aware by now that she had absconded, would be outraged to have her escorted home by a Kivell, especially in her state of disarray. People would talk. It would bring disgrace to his door. 'Thank you, but that won't be necessary. Please, I really do have to go. My mother's unwell. I need to get back to her.'

'What about Toby?' Sol reached out and pulled the yellow and red scarf out of her hand. Stumpy leapt to his feet, anxious to

22

please this new master.

'Well, it's likely he's home by now.'

'There's only one way to find out.'

'What are you doing?' He was untying the scarf from Stumpy's collar. 'Don't! He might run off again.'

'Well, if he does, he'll go straight to Toby.' Sol let the knots loose then flapped the cloth at Stumpy. He laughed when the lurcher shot off and scrambled away through the bars of the gate. 'Find your master, boy.'

Tossing Sol a reproachful look, Amy stalked off to the gate. Stumpy was tearing up through the valley. At last it seemed he was on the way home. Sol ambled along beside her. She held out her hand for her scarf.

He wound the pretty yellow and red cloth round his big dark hand. 'I'll keep this.'

'You can't!' She reached for it. 'It was a present from my mother. It's special to me.'

He held it up high. 'You'll get it back. When it pleases me.'

'Oh!' Red spots of anger burned on her cheeks. She had been frightened by his father and although it wasn't wise to confront the son she couldn't hold her temper.

As if he hadn't noticed or cared, he drawled, 'Let me open the gate for you. Be a pity to spoil your petticoat any more.'

She passed through the gateway and sighed gratefully when he closed the gate after her. She was going to be spared the humiliation of him accompanying her home. Now she must get there as quickly as she could and face her

23

father's wrath.

When she reached the lane, Stumpy was there, sniffing the ground, agitated and whining. She tried to grasp his collar, hoping to pull him along with her, but he whipped out of her reach. 'Stumpy, no! We must go home.'

With a loud whine, he shot off in the opposite direction, up Oak Hill. 'No! Stumpy!' She'd not go after him again and she marched off for the village, but the sound of Stumpy's whines went with her every step. Unease prickled a cold clammy path inside her. She had to see what was unsettling Stumpy so much. Toby might have had an accident. He might be lying not far away hurt, the reason why he hadn't come home. She had to see. She pursued Stumpy once more, able to keep up with him this time because he was stopping every so often to investigate the ground. He was on to something. All the while her apprehension grew.

They were closing in on the ancient bridle path of the woods. The woods preceded the parkland of Poltraze and were dark and creepy and rumoured to be haunted. Except for the bravest children playing dares and determined courting couples, locals avoided the place. The Kivells were said to steal about the region, seemingly unafraid of any ghosts – there was supposed to be the remains of a burnt oak tree somewhere on their land, used two centuries ago for burning witches. Amy had seen no such ancient monument a short while ago. Had Toby come here for a dare, or,

24

as many a youth did, to spend time alone to prove himself a man, to stop his father making him feel inferior? It was beginning to seem a likely explanation.

Stumpy entered the bridle path, heavy with summer growth, and was soon out of sight. She was hoping he wouldn't go far in. She heard a long sharp whistle and leapt in fright.

Praying it wasn't Poltraze's gamekeeper about to set his dogs and then his gun on Stumpy, she drew cautiously near the trees. Just up ahead there was a man and the dog. For a moment she was gripped with fear for Stumpy, then relieved to see he had been brought safely under control by Mr Joshua Nankervis, the elder son of Poltraze. From Tara Julyan's account of him, Joshua Nankervis was the only family member with a pleasant disposition. He was crouching, laughing and making a fuss of Stumpy.

He rose as Amy came forward. 'Hello. I heard you shouting to him.' His voice was deep and educated, with an inflection as if he cared to linger over his words. Then he became aware of Amy's disarray. 'Oh, my goodness! What's happened to you? Are you in trouble? Miss ... where are you from?'

'I'm Amy Lewarne, sir. From the village.' She dropped a curtsey and explained the reason for her shameful state. 'Pardon me, Mr Nankervis, would you have seen my brother?'

'No, I'm very sorry, I can't help you, Miss Lewarne.' He glanced about rapidly in all

25

directions. 'I doubt very much if he's in the woods.'

Amy was grateful he didn't mind her being here. He seemed kind but she eyed him warily. He was a puzzling individual. Apparently, he wasn't above spending time carousing with the Kivells, particularly a somewhat milder cousin of Titus's, Laketon. His clothes were often more like those of an ordinary working man. Presently, his white shirt was collarless and unfastened at the neck and cuffs, and over this was a well-worn dark green waistcoat. He had no hat on his dark hair and his boots were caked with fresh mud. 'I think I really need to get back, sir.'

'I think that's probably the best idea.' He consulted his silver pocket watch, as if he too, really should be on his way. 'I'll see you safely on your way to the village.'

How could she refuse his offer without seeming impolite? To be seen in the company of this fine gentleman would invoke as much gossip as if Sol Kivell had been her escort. There would be whispers that Mr Joshua Nankervis should remember his higher standing, or perhaps that he'd been 'rewarded' for his consideration. Amy wondered why he wasn't on horseback.

Stumpy got up and strained towards the direction he'd been running in. He started up an insistent whining. 'The dog wants to get off again. I think I have a piece of string about me. I'll lead him, make sure that you get him home and safely tied up.' Joshua Nankervis produced a long, thick piece of string. A strange item for a gentleman to have on his person, Amy thought, as he secured it to Stumpy's collar. 'I'm a keen horticulturist, Miss Lewarne. That's why I have such a thing,' he said. It also explained his dishevelled state.

Stumpy started to bark and pulled so hard on his makeshift lead that not even the danger of choking stopped him. Feelings of disquiet crept up Amy's back. She tried to see what was alarming the dog. 'Something's wrong.'

'I can't think what.'

'Perhaps if he was let off...' Amy said. She was fearful for Toby again. She had to know if he was close by, if he was all right.

'I'm not sure about that. Oh!' With a determined leap forward Stumpy pulled himself free from Joshua Nankervis and shot off as if fired from a cannon.

'Stumpy! What is it?' Amy called out. The dog disappeared along the bridle path. She began to give chase. Joshua Nankervis put himself in her way. 'No. I insist you stay here. There might be some shady character about.'

She had to obey the gentleman here on his father's land, but even so she edged forward anxiously. She had not covered many yards when she saw Joshua Nankervis standing motionless, looking down. Stumpy was visible through a clump of hazel bushes, whining loudly and sniffing something on the mossy ground beneath a beech tree.

'What is it?' she called, suddenly afraid of the answer. Amy felt as if a heavy curtain of darkness was falling on her, cloaking her in warning, preparing her for despair. She saw something down the steep slope towards the stream. 'There! It looks like a cap. Oh dear God, it's Toby's! It's why Stumpy was so upset. What have you seen? Tell me!'

Joshua turned round, his face drained of colour. 'Stay where you are, Miss Lewarne. I'm very sorry. There's nothing we can do. It's a boy. It must be your brother. He's dead.'

Two

'We have a new queen, a slip of a girl called Victoria, on the throne, and the country is entering a new era. It's prompted me, as in a fortnight's time I'm to celebrate my sixty-fifth birthday, into the decision that this family needs new life breathed into it. For a start, I've ordered the staff to plan a ball to mark my age. Here. At Poltraze.' Darius Nankervis' speech, delivered in his domineering, throaty voice, was brief and blunt. With a satisfaction born out of autocracy, that he had stunned his two sons and his daughter-in-law into silence round his grand dining table, he rose, a fat cigar on its way up to his wide, harsh mouth, and he strode away to his study.

'Well, I wasn't expecting that,' Michael Nankervis gasped, moving his neck about inside his high stiff collar. 'When he said he had something to tell us, from his serious expression I thought the price of copper had dropped through the floor devaluing the land leases, or one of the plantations had been overrun by rebels. He's not talked about anything except business or politics for years. There's not been an important occasion held here since before Jeffrey's death.'

'Indeed, we were not allowed to celebrate the two occasions we presented him with granddaughters, and our dear baby son's funeral was more or less overlooked.' An angry snort marred the cool, milk-white features of his wife, Phoebe. 'This is typical of your father's inconsideration. It would take a hard push for me to organize a dinner party in two weeks let alone a ball! And I can only pray to God that his guests don't see how poorly he maintains his house.'

'Hopefully, it won't be a big affair. People won't be free at such short notice. I hope Father changes his mind about it.' Pulling a long face, Michael gulped down the last of his red wine and held up the glass for the butler to refill.

'I'd no doubt you'd say that,' Phoebe snapped at him. 'Biding quietly on Home Farm or dawdling among boring old documents in the library is all you care about. Not a thought do you give to the tedium I suffer every day in this gloomy house. Have you asked your father if we can accompany him up to London after the summer recess? I'd like to socialize again with a few politicians' wives and other ladies of quality.'

'No.' Michael kept his head down. Phoebe had perfected bickering and baiting him to a fine art. He wasn't afraid of her, he merely made every attempt to ignore her. He had no wish to go up to town and witness his high and mighty father's particular approach to socializing, which always included other men's wives.

'You should leave us, Phoebe, and speak to Mrs Benney about the arrangements for the ball.' This was an order from Joshua rather than a suggestion. He was comparing her to Amy Lewarne, the girl he'd met in tragic circumstances this afternoon. A girl uncomplicated and honest, and devoted to her now grieving family. There was not a woman like her in his own circle, more was the pity. His father had ordered him to take a wife, something he didn't want ever, but now he had reached his thirty-fourth year, it was required of him to produce the next heir. The bonny daughters of Michael's were as unimportant to their grandfather as the servants.

Offended at Michael's disregard for her and Joshua's dismissal, Phoebe's pale eyes were like icy particles. She loathed the men of this house. While Darius was like a deadly tiger, and the damnable Joshua, an untroubled, occasionally riotous stag, Michael was an offhand, underachieving *sloth*. She was wasting her life with him and loathed him for it. If she had means of her own she would find the courage of her estranged step-mother-in-law and leave, and make it much farther away than the twenty miles to Penzance. Making a pretence of smoothing her lace-encrusted dinner dress, she almost swallowed her bow-shaped lips as she sought to keep her tension at bay. Nonetheless, she shot Joshua a look of loathing. Of the three men, it was always he who most made her feel a fool. She'd stay at the table a few seconds longer, even though she should dutifully withdraw and leave the men to their smoking and the port – it irritated her husband that she didn't slavishly live to please him, and she certainly wasn't going to meekly obey his brother.

Joshua threw two neat cigars into the middle of the snowy-white damask tablecloth before leaning back in his chair. 'The only thing we should be concerned about is why the old man suddenly wants this party here. He rarely entertained at Poltraze when Mother was alive. What's on his mind? Why has he sent for Estelle and Tara?'

'He's what?' Michael's fingers paused mid-air above a cigar. His seemingly lackadaisical brother, who appeared to care for little beyond botany and his unsavoury nocturnal life, kept ahead of him in all events. 'What makes you say that?'

'I saw them, on their way to the Dower House. Even Mrs Benney was in the dark about it. I sent her to ask them how long they were staying. She reported back that they didn't know. It sent the staff into a whirl making the place suitable for them. Our step-mother's very unhappy, of course, the house was in much need of airing. I'm surprised she hasn't taken off again immediately.'

'Estelle is here?' Phoebe gasped. 'I don't understand. Your father announced that he would never allow her to set foot in Poltraze again.'

'I'd say that for some reason Father wants her and Tara at this ball.' Joshua was concerned what this sudden quirk in his father's habits might mean for him. While he'd been changing for dinner, his father's valet had appeared to inform him that the master demanded an immediate audience with him. Joshua had thrown on his dinner coat and hastened along the oak-planked corridor to the west wing, where his father had his suite of rooms.

His father had been in his bedchamber, gazing out over the fine view of the oak, beech and birch trees at the front of the house, sucking in a lungful of cigar smoke. 'Why were you late coming in?' he'd curled his lip, glancing round.

'I'm sorry, Father.' Joshua took an appreciative look out of the window and down below. He hated the gloomy house and had asked his father for the responsibility of the grounds. It had grown into a passion and he was pleased with himself for keeping its formal features, the terraces and balustrades and ornamental gardens, rather than denuding the front aspect as other great houses had done. It took the eye away from the unpleasing effect of the house itself, a sorry confusion of pre-Tudor origins and uninspiring later additions. The original building had been burned down in the thirteenth century, and there had been other such happenings. Joshua would like to see the eyesore razed to the ground and a temple-like construction put up in its place. Wealthy his family, or rather his father, might be, but there would never be money enough for that, and even he didn't have the inclination for such a huge undertaking. 'I came across the body of a boy in the woods. He fell out of a tree, apparently.'

'Damned inconvenient. Have you done anything yet about securing a bride?'

Joshua sighed inwardly. 'I'm casting my eye around.'

'Liar. Take care that you don't run out of time and my patience.'

A sense of being chewed by worms niggled Joshua's stomach. He had a bride of sorts, and hated the very thought of taking a real one. He hedged, 'If only I could meet someone with the character of Amy Lewarne, daughter of the village carpenter.' Strange, he should snatch at her name, when the love he already had was involved in carpentry.

Darius puffed a cloud of dark smoke over Joshua's head. 'You can take a wife of appropriate birth and still have fun with this village wench.'

33

'Yes, indeed.' It would be a good idea to let his father believe this. 'Father, it was her brother's body I discovered.'

'He shouldn't have been trespassing in my woods,' Darius shrugged.

'Don't you care at all?' The villagers weren't of much importance to Joshua either but he always had difficulty with his father's heartlessness. He moved on to someone else. 'Father, did you know that Titus Kivell is back at Burnt Oak? While I was escorting Amy Lewarne home she told me she'd been there looking for the boy.' He'd actually been told this before he'd met Amy, by a Kivell. Joshua recalled Amy's distress.

Darius hunched up his shoulders as a predator does to look bigger and more threatening. 'Of course, I know about Titus Kivell. I take pains to know of the circumstances of the man who tried to rescue Jeffrey. I sent him many a comfort in gaol. Now there's a man who's produced many fine children.' In the most dominant place in the room, above the serpentine fireplace was a portrait of Jeffrey, painted a few months before his death in the pool. Jeffrey, fine and dark, energetic and remarkably intelligent. He would have been capable of taking up high office at Westminster.

'Ahem,' Joshua cleared his throat to remind his father he was there.

Darius stared at him from his heavily hooded eyes as if rudely interrupted. It was just as well that his second son didn't aspire to the

34

political field. He had inclinations towards Radicalism; educating the masses, abolishing transportation of criminals, that sort of ludicrous thing. He was a bit soft, so soft he didn't even bother to do more than voice his opinions about it.

Joshua stared down at his feet. He and Michael would never succeed in gaining their father's approval, indeed he was often intent on crushing them. It was why Joshua rebelled in many ways against his own class and why Michael held no sights for a public life.

Joshua's thoughts were now batting between how much he hated his father, the sudden appearance of his step-mother and her ward, and how he could use Amy Lewarne.

'I don't like this. Something's going on.' Michael sighed weightily.

'What do you think, Joshua?' Phoebe said.

Joshua reached for a candlestick to break the delay in lighting his cigar. 'I've no idea, but I'm sure we're not going to like it.'

Three

'I don't think I'll ever forgive your father.'
Her words were raw and strangled, Sylvia
Lewarne, tear-ravaged and weak, struggled to
lift her head up from the pillows of her bed.
'It's his fault your brother's dead.'

'Mother, you know you don't mean that,'
Amy replied, her own voice lacking strength.
It seemed she and her mother had cried out a
lifetime of grief. She had brought up a pitcher
of hot water for Sylvia to freshen up.

'Oh, but I do,' Sylvia was vehement as Amy
helped her sit up on the edge of the bed. 'You
and I think alike, Amy, and I know you share
the same thoughts.' Amy did not argue with
this. 'He, and he alone, is responsible for Toby
being taken from us. My poor dear son must
have gone into the woods to prove himself
and ended up with a broken neck. He must
have been terrified when he fell. Oh, Amy, I
don't think I can bear it!'

Sylvia's hand was shaking and Amy squeezed it gently. 'Mother, please don't cry again.
You'll make yourself ill.' She was anxious the
tragedy wouldn't take her mother's life too. If
her labour started now she'd have little
energy to see the ordeal through and it would

be two months too early. She was unlikely to bear the loss of another child.

'I'm sorry, Amy.' Sylvia's eyes were burnt by scalding tears. 'I have to say it. I have to get it all out of my head or I'll go mad. Your father was a brute to Toby, he never gave him a minute's peace. Not once did he offer him a word of encouragement. And what was his first thought when you and Mr Nankervis turned up with the dreadful news? That heartless wretch who's not shed a single tear over the loss of his son? He demanded that Stumpy be killed! He was going to ask Godley Greep to take Stumpy away and throw him down an old mineshaft or drown him in the stream. He planned to ask someone else to do it because he didn't have the courage to do it himself! He's always been a coward and a miserable so-and-so. I found that out early on in our marriage. I dared to quarrel with your father for the very first time yesterday and go against his will. I told him if he dared harm the dog, the only thing I've got left of Toby, I'd never speak a word to him again. I meant it, Amy. Of course, he didn't like that. After all,' she stressed bitterly. 'What would people say if they thought his wife was against him? He couldn't hold his head up so high then.' Then Sylvia's voice grew low and forlorn, and tore at Amy's heart. 'Where's Stumpy now? It's raining outside. The wind's sharp. Toby would hate it if Stumpy was getting wet and cold.'

Amy was fighting not to cry. The dog was

bewildered; he must have been sniffing about when Toby climbed the tree and had then run off to search when he couldn't find him. Now he didn't understand his absence from home. 'He's in the back kitchen ... lying beside Toby's work boots. Father's brought his basket in from the shed.'

'Mmmm.' It was all Sylvia said. Morton had begged her last night to let him make things up to her. He never could, but at least it meant life would be better for the poor dog. Stumpy had been another victim of her husband's harshness, never before had he been allowed inside the house and Morton had begrudged him every scrap of food. It had taken the death of her son to strike her just how callous her husband was.

When Sylvia had washed and was in a clean white nightgown, a black lace, tasselled shawl and a black, beribboned cap covering her hair, she sat up against the pillows, a dignified and composed older version of Amy. Ready to face the ordeal of the expected stream of sympathizers. Sylvia was seized with worry. 'What are we going to do about cake? People will be calling to pay their respects when the coroner lets us have Toby back. And what if Mr Nankervis calls? He was so kind and concerned yesterday. Amy, have we got plenty of tea in the larder?'

'Oh, Mother,' Amy leaned over and kissed her cheek. 'Even in your grief you're thinking about others. Don't worry. Mrs Greep has already popped in with some yeast cake. We may not have any family to rally round us but our friends and neighbours won't let us down. When I go downstairs, I make a start on some scones.'

'Yes, you do that, my love. Doing something as simple as some baking will help see you through.'

'I'll keep slipping up to make sure you're all right. Now, you get some rest.'

It was the custom to keep the curtains closed until after the funeral and Amy had lit candles on the landing and down in the passage below. At first, in the dim light, she didn't see there was someone at the foot of the stairs. 'Oh!' The bowl and pitcher she was carrying shook in her hands and chinked together. Water sloshed over the rim of the bowl and wetted her skirt.

'Didn't mean to alarm you,' came a firm burr.

'What are you doing here?' Amy hissed, keeping her voice low so her mother wouldn't hear. In his high boots and a long dark overcoat, a round-brimmed hat in his hand, Sol Kivell was filling the short passage. He was like someone from a past age, from no particular age. He gave the word intruder an even more ominous meaning. Amy stayed put, reluctant to go near him.

Sol gazed up at her. Amy got the feeling her unease and offence were unimportant to him. 'Staying there all day?'

'You've got a nerve! How dare you come in here like this? How dare you come here at all.

Don't you know what's happened?'

'I do. On behalf of my family I've come to offer our sympathy. The women have been busy for you. I've left it on the kitchen table.'

'What are you talking about?' Amy was furious. Forgetting her disquiet she descended the rest of the stairs and pushed past him. She was brought to a halt in the kitchen. Food, including two hunks of ham, and an assortment of wine bottles and ale flagons, were heaped on the table. For a moment she couldn't speak. Sol Kivell came into the room and headed for the back door. 'What—I mean, why? Why has your family done this?'

He turned round. 'For Toby. He used to come to Burnt Oak as often as he could.'

Amy couldn't take in this new information. She put the bowl and pitcher down. 'I...'

'Find it hard to believe?' Sol was grim and distant. He had a way of holding himself as a superior. 'Don't know as much about your brother as you'd thought, do you? The family were fond of him. He deserved better. We'll be offended if you refuse our offering.' This was said in distinct challenge.

What was she do? Her father would order Sol Kivell to take away the things he had brought, declaring he'd want nothing from a heathen tribe. Her mother would decline the generosity too, although civilly. As for herself, she wanted to learn why Toby had befriended the Kivells and why they had reciprocated. 'I'm surprised. I thought Toby had never kept any secrets from me.'

'There's a lot you don't know about him.'

And never would, she thought, meeting his accusing stare, if she didn't at least accept his family's gifts. She had lied many times for Toby's sake, a lie after his death wouldn't really matter. Her mother was having to keep to her bed, so she wouldn't be placed in the position of revealing where all this food had come from. Hopefully, her father wouldn't come in from the workshop, where he was about the dreadful task of fashioning Toby's coffin, and she could put the food away in the larder. No one need know that Sol Kivell had been here. He had come by way of the moors, riding, with the addition of a packhorse, along the rough track that ran parallel to the stream, which in turn ran along the back of Chy-Henver – she could see the mounts through the window, waiting across from the stepping stones. Thank goodness the doors of the workshop faced away from the house or her father would have seen Kivell's arrival.

Brought to a humiliating humbleness, she said, 'Please pass on my thanks to your family, Mr Kivell. Um, I hope you won't be offended if I ask you to take back the wine and ale. We're Methodists. We don't drink, you see.'

He put sharp eyes on her, eyes of startling blue. Amy got the impression he wanted to say something hard, perhaps insulting. He nodded. Took his time putting on his hat. Gathered up the alcohol in his broad grasp. 'I'm sorry for your loss.' He left.

Rooted to the spot, Amy listened as he said a few soothing words to Stumpy. The room seemed strangely, horribly empty without Sol Kivell's presence. It was like losing Toby again. For Sol Kivell to have come here, to have brought all this food, reinforced the torment that Toby was actually dead. As did the evidence of her surreptitious hunt at Burnt Oak yesterday by the scrap of her yellow and red scarf she had glimpsed at the last moment peeping out of his coat pocket.

Why should he hold on to it? It was vital to have her scarf back, otherwise she couldn't even try to forget the harrowing events of her search for Toby, of seeing his broken body. Finding her feet, she ran after him, out into the rain. 'Wait!'

He stopped, rainwater dripping off his hat. He was holding his load securely, confidently. He looked at her without a trace of inquiry and she could see he was about to move on. She blurted out, 'I want my scarf.'

He shook his head. Went on his way.

Becoming soaked, she cried, 'Please! You've no right to keep it!'

Without glancing back, he drawled, 'You know where to come for it.'

Four

Tara Julyan pattered down the creaky oak stairs of the Dower House and positioned herself at the edge of the parlour doors. 'Good morning, Aunt. I think the sun will soon grace us with an appearance today. I thought I'd slip out for a little while.'

Whichever room Estelle Nankervis happened to be in she always faced the door; it was part of her nature to be prying and suspicious, and she held a need to be in control. 'Do you indeed? It's very early. Why are you skulking, Tara? Come into the room.'

'I'm not skulking, Aunt Estelle.' Tara had no choice but to obey and she went into the dark, shadowy room on slow reluctant steps.

Estelle took her in with one swift glance. 'What are you up to?'

'Nothing, Aunt.' Tara's attempt at appearing innocent was inevitably ruined by a guilty flush. It was impossible to keep anything from her aunt. She believed everyone in the world owned an element of her husband, to be conniving and faithless.

'Then why are you dressed for riding? I take it you're intending to wear a hat? That you were not about to risk spoiling your complexion?' Estelle was passionate about preserving

Tara's genteel looks as well as her own. She had married young, and having not yet reached thirty, did not look much older than Tara. She had a deceptive soft grace and a much desired classical exquisiteness.

'Atkins is bringing my hat down. I fancied a little more exercise than a stroll round the grounds. Please, may I go?'

'The grounds!' Estelle screeched, something she did with alarming alacrity when angry. 'You could not do so even if you desired it. The few strips of garden outside can never lay claim to the description of grounds, anymore than this festering hulk can be known as a house fit for refined company. It's an insult that we have been given this place as accommodation. It was built over a hundred years ago to lock up an aging Mrs Nankervis who was dangerously in the throes of senility. Every window is heavily barred or locked. It's surrounded by brick walls and tall firs. It's like a prison.' She sighed with irritation. Like her screeching it was something she only did in front of servants and Tara, otherwise she wouldn't dream of being so unladylike. 'Oh, have a little fresh air if you must. Goodness knows we've been cooped up in this mausoleum for the past forty-eight hours. Atkins must not let you out of her sight. Do not go far. Remember that neither you nor Atkins are very familiar with the area. Keep away from the mining parts. Do not enter any properties or speak to the villagers. Return within two hours.'

'I will, Aunt Estelle, I promise. What will you do?'

'There is nothing I can do but wait for my husband to condescend to arrive and reveal why he has summoned us here. Enjoy your ride, my dear.' Estelle looked away. She was unreachable now, had shut herself off into her thoughts and broodings.

'Thank you, Aunt.'

A shedlike building housed the sturdy ponies that had pulled the trap. They were not smart mounts but would do for Tara's purpose. She held no concern as her aunt did if things weren't up to top mark. The grey-stone dower house was positioned at some distance, out of sight of the big house. The wooden gates had long ago rotted on rusty hinges and now lay as a pair of forlorn rejects against the inside of the wall. The surrounding gardens, laid out in precise measurement each side of the house, had become wilder-nesses. When Tara had arrived here two days ago she had wanted to jump off the trap and run away. She felt she was meeting more than a lack of hospitality. There was a sense of despair here.

'I'm glad to be leaving the place even for a short while, Miss Tara,' Atkins declared doughtily. Tall and stiff-boned, she required an undignified amount of help from the stable boy to get up on the side saddle.

Freedom. Away from all restraints and gloomy confines, Tara was tempted to raise her face, lift the lace veil on her hat and take a kiss from the late August sun. Not wanting a reprimand, she contented herself with taking a deep breath. The sense of release didn't last. What did the frightening Darius Nankervis want with her aunt? Aunt Estelle wouldn't have come here if not compelled to. It had taken a lot of courage for her to leave Poltraze knowing she could only look forward to a future of being shunned. A wife had no rights except to be dutiful to her husband, to see to his needs, to strive to never let him down. Tara would never forget the last fierce quarrel, when her uncle had returned unexpectedly and discovered Atkins was packing for them. He had made a lot of threats. True, he had not subsequently demanded her aunt return to him as a wife, nor troubled her in the small property of his on the seafront at Penzance, but it was plain to Tara that he retained a terrible hold over his wife. For months Tara had feared every approach and letter to the house, expecting that they would surely be turned out, with nowhere to go. Her aunt had intended their stay at Penzance to be temporary. Something had gone wrong with her plans, something she refused to discuss, although she had stressed that the situation would one day greatly improve, that patience only was needed. Had that day come? Tara thought not, her aunt was much perturbed by her husband's summons.

Tara forced the worries aside and concentrated on the views. She was on the top of

Oak Hill. It was not the most beautiful of countryside, with scrubland and windswept moor, yet there was a sense of space and purpose. During the spring the banks and hedges were prettified by primroses, bright yellow gorse and dabs of pink and blue and white wild flowers. In the near distance, on a rise, was the heavy grey silhouette of the workings of the Carn Croft Mine, and beyond them, the engine houses of neighbouring districts peeped above the undulating skyline. She remembered everything about Meryen and Nansmere Downs, specially the places where she'd enjoyed Amy's company, after a chance meeting by an ancient Celtic Cross, so-named Pixie Cross, for pixies were said to dance around it on moonlit nights. These memories had kept her spirit afloat during all the stifling and boring days she'd spent since then. Sometimes a younger girl had joined them, an angel-faced ragamuffin called Sarah. What had happened to the downtrodden miner's daughter? Children of the poor died in droves, from starvation or diseases. Sarah might be dead. Or orphaned if her bullying father had died in an all-too-often underground accident.

Tara encouraged her pony into a canter, leaving Atkins behind. Atkins, who doubled as governess and lady's maid, was awkward on horseback and would soon seek a shady place to pull up and rest. She was stuffily formal, but her affection for Tara allowed a little indulgence, so Tara chanced that she

47

wouldn't mind her going on alone for a short while. It was good to be free of the pessimistic Atkins. 'You're doomed to be an old maid and her ladyship to be shunned forever. She shouldn't have minded so much,' she had once intoned. 'You're so comely, Miss Tara, but you'll never be able to take advantage of it, never go up to London for the season and win for yourself a good match.' The only time Tara had examined the dismal prophecy she'd concluded that as marriage was the cause of her aunt's misery, then she'd not be disappointed if it was a state that passed her by. She wondered what it was that her aunt shouldn't 'have minded so much'. Perhaps it was better that she never knew.

Tara's pony was now keeping in line with the echoes of Sol Kivell's horses of the day before. She was going this way to avoid being seen, for her aunt would fly into a fury if she discovered she had disobeyed her orders. She dismounted and tied the reins to the same blackthorn bush as Sol Kivell had, then after glancing about hesitantly, she passed over the stepping stones. Feeling an intruder she walked up the Lewarnes' back garden ash path.

With all the curtains drawn it was no good hoping Amy would see her and come out to meet her. Telling herself to be bold, that Amy wouldn't misread her appearance as untimely interference, she tapped on the well-constructed door with her riding crop. While she waited for an answer she looked about warily for the dog she had heard about – her aunt

48

would punish her if she returned covered with dirty paw marks.

All was quiet. She knocked again, a little louder, wishing she had written a note which she could leave if her visit failed, expressing her condolences. Bolts were being pulled on the other side of the door. Tara swallowed her unease. It seemed visitors weren't particularly welcome. The door was opened a crack and a face peeped round it. Then the door was thrown open.

'Miss Tara!' Amy cried apologetically. 'Forgive me for keeping you waiting. Would you like to come in?'

'I would, Amy, if it's not an imposition. I'm afraid I've only got a few moments.'

Amy led the way to the lamp-lit kitchen. Stumpy, now allowed by Morton into these more sanctified surroundings in a bid to please Sylvia, gazed up gloomily from his basket then settled back down to mope. 'Poor dog,' Tara said. 'Oh, Amy, I'm so sorry about your brother. I was mortified when the maid told me. Toby was just a little boy when I last saw him. I had to come. I hope you don't mind.'

'Not at all. It's very thoughtful of you.' Finally the girls shook hands, a shy, formal undertaking. 'You must go through to the front room. Would you like a cup of tea? I'm keeping a pot going for when people come paying their respects.' The table, at which previous callers had sat, before going upstairs for a few minutes with Sylvia, had plates of

49

cake, scones and biscuits on it. Amy's mind was speeding off to the teak tray and best lace cloth.

'Oh, no, thank you. Please don't go to any trouble on my account. How are you, Amy? And your dear mother?'

'We're trying to be brave.' The constant threat of tears and holding them back made Amy's head throb. 'It's so hard to bear. Hard to believe it's really happened. Miss Tara, did you come along the back way?'

'Yes. I'm not really supposed to be here, you understand.'

'Of course. Did you see anyone out there?'

'No. Amy, are you troubled about something? I thought it most unusual that you'd have your door locked.'

'Yesterday, I had an unwelcome visitor. Do you remember the Kivells? One of them came here. He brought food. A kind thought on his family's part, but he just walked into the house. I don't want that happening again. Mother's expecting. I don't want her to be more upset. The coroner's finished with Toby. He's declared his death was an accident, of course. Father will be back soon from collecting Toby from the chapel, where he was taken. He'd be furious if there happened to be a Kivell here. Miss Tara, please don't say anything, no one knows Sol Kivell came.'

'I promise I won't say a word. Did he frighten you?'

'Not exactly. He made me angry.'

'It's awful that you should have had that to

50

put up with. The Kivells have always done whatever they like. I remember the servants at Poltraze whispering that no one should ever dare to cross them. You must be wondering why my aunt and I are here. We don't know ourselves yet. Amy, we must keep in touch. You're the only friend I've ever had. Please, call me Tara, as you did in the old days.'

'Thank you, Tara. It's good to see you again.'

Both girls were lost for words, thinking how the other had turned out to be neat and pretty. Amy considered Tara to have a delicate, fair-haired beauty. She would be greatly sought after as a wife, already promised to someone, if not for her aunt's deed. Tara saw in Amy, that even in her grief, she had poise and confidence. Tara envied Amy her settled home life. The cottage was much smaller than anything she was used to but it was cosy and exuded a sense of belonging.

'I must go, I'm afraid,' Tara said. 'When is the funeral to be?'

'Tomorrow afternoon.'

'I wish I could attend, but my prayers will be with you. I'll write to you in a few days. Goodbye Amy.'

'Thank you, Tara. Your coming here today means a lot.'

Amy saw Tara to the back door. Tara put a light pressure on Amy's arm with her gauntleted hand, an outward expression of friendship and caring. 'Goodbye.'

Amy opened the door. She and Tara gasped to see a man outside.

'Forgive my appearance here, Miss Lewarne—' Joshua Nankervis broke off. 'Tara! This is a surprise.'

Shortly after Tara had left the Dower House, Estelle Nankervis received a visitor. Darius Nankervis tossed the reins of his horse to the stable boy, let himself inside and into the presence of his wife.

Knowing from the thrusting open of the doors and the heavy tread that it was her husband, Estelle sat still and aloof, although she was far from unruffled. 'At last,' she said, as cold as ice, before he got a word out.

Darius set piercing eyes on her. 'Estelle. My dear, Estelle. How handsome you still are.'

'Say what you've come to say. I'm anxious to leave this place.' Anxious to get away from him, the man who despite being old enough to be her father, had stirred, and could still stir, a great many emotions in her. As damnable as he was, and even though she had soon discovered he had tied up all her own money, she had loved him. Before the summons here she had been living anxiously, waiting out the last long years until Tara came of age, when she'd ensure her own fortune would change.

'Stap me,' Darius's voice was bordering on jovial as he gazed about. 'Didn't know the old house had fallen into such a state. It's as morbid as a tomb. You've hardly a stick of furniture, m'dear. Cloth and curtains are a bit mouldy. Is that a spot of damp on the walls?'

'Is it your intention to mock and torture me?' Estelle aimed her sentence with a precision meant to snap about his ears.

'Oh, I'd like to,' his hooded dark eyes gleamed with a certain lechery. 'You know what I like, Estelle. You liked it too. Then you misread me. I never really cared about your barrenness. Didn't I have sons enough? And I don't think you cared as much as you made out about my mistresses. Almost every gentlemen keeps one or two.'

'Sir—'

'Oh, sir, is it?' he cut her off. Cold. Implacable. 'Glad you know your place at last, woman!'

'I will not go over our old disputes,' Estelle called on the courage that had helped her leave him and then endure the long stultifying years of disgrace. 'Tell me precisely why you have insisted I come here?'

'Don't worry, m'dear. I'm not about to cut off your allowance.' He was light-hearted, bouncy again. Estelle followed his every movement, attended to his every tone. He could be at his most dangerous when like this. 'I've come to invite you and the girl to a ball.'

Estelle had heard about his sixty-fifth birthday ball from Atkins, who had gleaned it from servants' gossip. He could mean no other occasion. 'Really?' She made herself appear disinterested, but she was puzzled, nervous. He might be playing a cruel game in which he

53

would cut her off publicly.

'Always the haughty madam, Estelle. It's what I've always liked about you. I care about you a little, you know.'

'Don't be ridiculous!'

'I could have made your life a misery these last five years. Do you not concede that?'

How should she answer? Throughout her desertion she had dreaded every footfall outside her door, but no trouble had come. Her allowance of five hundred pounds a year, although a small sum compared to what she had received as his wife at home, was in the circumstances, and knowing his nature, a generous one. 'I suppose I do.'

'I'll not waste time, Estelle.' Darius lifted his coat tails and took a seat across from her. 'I want you and Tara at the ball. A lot of fine people will be there. Unknown to my sons I'd planned it a long time ago. I shall be making an announcement.' He paused for effect.

'Which is?' Estelle was too worried to make a dramatic pause of her own. He was forcing her to appear in his home as his wife, a wife fetched out of social shame and put on display. In a dull house in which she could hardly bear to be. What torment had he in store for her? And how would this affect Tara?

'A betrothal. Of my son and heir to your ward and niece.'

Estelle shot to her feet. Her legs had little strength and she fell back down again. 'Joshua and Tara! But why? Are you mad?'

'Not as mad as you think I'm stupid,

Estelle,' Darius leaned back, a malicious smile spreading across his bullish features. 'Did you think I'd not look into your background, your fine coalmining family in Yorkshire? That I'd never discover that the pretty Miss Tara had a fortune settled on her by her father, your late brother, which she'll receive at twenty-one years or her earlier marriage? You took a gamble, Estelle, leaving me in such a manner, apparently making the girl unmarriageable. You thought I'd take no more interest in you, that you'd bide your time until you could get your hands on her money. Perhaps you thought you'd take her overseas and wed her to some foreign count. You thought that with her residing solely with you for some years, you'd be her only influence. To be so grateful to you that she'd offer you a home and every comfort till the end of your days Unfortunately for you, when you made your dramatic gesture, your remaining brother thought the same as society and refused to keep you. You had to stay put here in Cornwall and rely on my mercy. Just like you Estelle, I've bided my time. I've been happy to let you suffer years of shame and deprivation.' He continued in sharp snaps, 'Now I want Tara in alliance to my son. I want him to have her money. And I want you to have to rely on Nankervis mercy for the rest of your life.'

Estelle couldn't move or speak. Her face burned with horror then paled with distress.

'I taught you many lessons, Estelle, not least

in the bedroom. But you missed that no one gets the upper hand of me.'

With an effort she cleared her throat. 'Wh—what does this mean for me?'

'I'm not a vindictive man, no, I tell a lie, I am. And I'm proud of it. I'd cast you off, see you in the gutter, but ... mmm.' He grinned to himself.

'But what? Damn you!' Estelle was being tossed between a glimmer of hope and some dreadful fate. Tara would have to marry Joshua Nankervis, neither the girl nor the young man would be able to stand against Darius' wish, and if Tara tried to help Estelle, Darius would see her every attempt was harshly thwarted.

'Come here to me.'

Somehow she made her feet take the necessary steps, each one a humiliation, to stand before him, like a thieving servant about to learn her punishment. 'It's like this, Estelle. You know I prefer to spend my time in and about London. I care little for Poltraze but I suppose it should be run well. It's got a little out of sorts since your day. Michael's wife does it no justice, she's little more than a wailing bitch. When Tara marries Joshua she will take precedence over Phoebe but she's too young and tender for the responsibility. You can come with her. I'll allow you to resume your place as Poltraze's mistress.'

Estelle thought she would swoon with relief at this unexpected concession so soon after the ruination of her plans. 'And ... in return?

56

There must be some stipulation I have to adhere to. What do you require of me?'

'You will run my house but not the lives of my sons. You must return to my bed and never deny me. Do we have an agreement, Estelle?'

Estelle's green eyes shone like agates. The future she had planned had been annihilated but this new proposition meant she was to be reinstated as a wife, able to mix with smart people again, and now without the fear of taunts from Darius at not conceiving a child, something she'd never wanted anyway. Scathing whispers behind fans would be unimportant. Darius spent as little as eight weeks in a year at Poltraze. She would be able to reign, more or less, in her own little kingdom.

For this she swiftly regained her full dignity. 'We do, Darius.'

'Knew you'd see things my way. Have your things packed. You can return to the house today. Send for the dressmaker,' he was gazing from her snow-white throat to her toes, lingering on the upthrust of her corseted breasts, recalling what he knew lay under her petticoats. 'That dress looks good on your fabulous body but it's not grand enough for your station. Do as you will with the house, within Joshua's agreement, of course.'

'Why are you being so generous, Darius?' Estelle's refined features flickered with distrust.

'I very much enjoyed the look of shock and horror on your face just now and I shall enjoy it again on Michael's and Phoebe's. Of course, you haven't seen my granddaughters. I'm hoping your niece will present me next year with a healthy grandson, one to be proud of.'

Estelle considered what this meant for Tara. Life for her would be much the way Estelle had wanted it. Joshua Nankervis figured among the most eligible bachelors in the county. He was the only one of her two step-sons who had shown her any respect. Any hostility that would come her way from Michael and Phoebe did not bother her. Darius's arrangement meant she'd hold a superior position to them, and Darius wasn't the only one who owned a ruthless streak. With her new power she would fight for her rights. 'I'm pleased it's Joshua whom Tara is marrying. I shall tell Tara the news as soon as she comes in.'

'Order her to keep it to herself for now. I'll tell Joshua tonight. I don't want the reason for your return to Poltraze to become fully known until the night of the ball. Do you hear me?'

'As you please, Darius,' Estelle said softly, slipping back into the role of a dutiful wife.

'Good. Where is the girl?'

'She's out for a short ride.'

'Again, good. You are here alone.' He was on his feet and closing in on her. 'Upstairs Estelle. You and I will consummate this agreement now. Take care to show me just how grateful you are.'

Five

The wind and rain up on the high ground of the Carn Croft Mine was sharp and relentless and penetrated Sarah Hichens' hand-me-down, calf-length dress, petticoat, shawl and hessian towser apron and bit into her flesh, adding more misery to her hard life. Her gook, the cotton bonnet which was gathered at her neck and under her chin and had a long flap over her shoulders, offered little shelter. The shed where she and thirty other girls worked had no sides and when she stepped outside of it her cracked leather shoes, an old pair of Amy's, filled with mud and grit. The canvas bands she'd wound round her legs, necessary for protection and decency due to the traditional short length of a bal-maiden's dress, were being breached by the wet and her skin was becoming chaffed. Often, due to the constant cacophony of noise and labour, she went home with an headache.

Bal-maidens worked at the various dressing stages, in different sheds, according to age, toughness and experience. Sarah's job on the dressing floor, after the ore had been broken to fingertip-sized pieces by the cobbers, was to crush it with a bucking iron –

a flat hammer – to small granules on a long table. Bucking was the hardest of the jobs carried out by girls and women. It made their backs, shoulders and arms ache and their hands hurt from the shock of the continuous blows. Suppressing a shiver, finding it hard to believe it was late summer, Sarah pinned the flaps of her gook across her face, leaving only her eyes free to the weather and flying splinters. The hours before the mid-morning croust seemed twice as long today.

She cheered a little at the thought of the hevva cake she had tucked into her canvas bag. Her monthly fifteen shillings wage didn't stretch to every need of her family, her mother, crippled in an accident four years ago, and her siblings. Sometimes there was only the vegetables she grew to eat. Last evening, when she had passed Chy-Henver on the way home, Amy had slipped outside and given her the cake. Amy and Mrs Lewarne's kindness could always be relied on. In the days before Toby's funeral, eight-year-old Arthur, and Tamsyn, a year younger, who both worked on the mine surface for a few pennies a day, had turned up at Chy-Henver and had been fed each time.

Sarah's mood fell again. Amy had given her the leftovers from the wake, enough to feed the family for three days, but Nancy Hichens, also brain-damaged by the runaway ore barrow that had mowed her down, had thrown most of it on the fire in the open hearth. Sarah had turned her back for a minute, to discover too late, that the gift was burning under the broth pot.

'Oh, Mum, what have you done?' Sarah's voice always emerged dry and disheartened when in the cramped, draughty cottage. She blamed herself, even though it was difficult to stop vacant-eyed Nancy making random movements. Nancy panicked easily, understood nothing and made only infantile noises. Sarah also blamed herself for the disappointment and lack of comprehension on Arthur and Tamsyn's little faces as they'd huddled together on the hardwood settle. They appeared ruddy-cheeked and healthy, but that was only because of being exposed five and a half days a week, from dawn to dusk, in all weathers. There was nothing ahead for any of them but hardship and drudgery and the care of an incontinent mother who, for her own safety, in between the times when an elderly aunt looked in on her, needed to be tied to her chair when they went to work. Sometimes Sarah wished Nancy was dead, then she'd feel guilty about it and wish herself dead.

There was a nudge on Sarah's arm. She was so cold she didn't feel it. Then came a sharp dig in the ribs. 'Ow!' Sarah yelped.

'Look to your sister, maid.' The bal-maiden next to her, a lively girl, who had gleefully announced at the start of the shift that she'd given in a month's notice as she was due to be married, pointed to one of the outer sheds. Mouse-like Tamsyn, who'd been busy with the first process of dressing the ore brought to the surface by throwing out the 'deads', was coming Sarah's way, sobbing, with a hand clutched to her face.

Like all the little girls, Tamsyn was dextrous at her job, which required a good eye for picking the waste from the good ore, but she wouldn't have two good eyes if Sarah didn't remove the particle temporarily blinding her. Sarah sighed, wishing she had only herself to think about, then she felt bad for being selfish. Unpinning the flaps of her gook, she left her place, pulled off the thick padded cloth protecting her left hand against the hammer blows, and used her hanky to carefully lift the minute bit of felspar out of Tamsyn's eye. She gave Tamsyn a quick cuddle, kissed her cheek and straightened her little gook. 'It'll stop hurting in a minute. Cheer up. Soon be time for croust.'

Sarah hurried back to her own shed before she was reprimanded. She worked with one of the several tribute teams; each tribute was sub-contracted from the mine adventurers, the tributes tendered on a given area. The women, invariably spinsters and widows, were proud to be supporting themselves and their dependants, and some were religious in a condemning manner, and it mattered to them that the work, set for a two month period, was completed without penalties. Slackers and wasters of God's precious time were despised.

A gangly youth, Jed Greep, son of Godley Greep, the head of Sarah's tribute team and a waggon lander at the shaft, ambled up to Sarah as she picked up her long-handled bucking iron. 'Morning to 'ee, Sarah. How are you then?'

Absorbed in her melancholy, Sarah didn't hear him.

'Maid, are you going deaf?' Peggy Wetter employed her elbow again. 'You're being spoken to.'

'Eh?' Sarah became aware of Jed Greep. He should be hard at work ragging the heaviest masses of ore. He was blushing, and as a chorus of silly remarks and a few innuendoes broke out among the bal-maidens, his un-imaginative, broad face turned from pink to crimson. 'What do you want?'

'Just saying hello, Sarah.' It was lost on Sarah that he was holding his cap politely and that his hair, dripping from the rain, was parted neatly down the centre.

'Well, you've said it. I'm busy.' Sarah turned away from him as if he was an annoying insect.

He hovered about for a few moments then plodded off, disappearing behind the shed where one of the senior bal-maidens was brewing the tea for the croust.

Peggy Wetter faced Sarah. 'Are you mazed, Sarah Hichens? Jed Greep could be the answer to all your prayers. He's sweet on you, he, and a few others, and 'tis no wonder with the lovely face the Good Lord's blessed you with. Jed came here, risking a telling off from his father, because he don't get much chance

63

to see you as you're rarely in chapel or out and about. That was brave of him just now. He's as good as proposed to you! Marry Jed and you'll be able to stay at home and look after your poor mother.'

'Oh yes? Who are you to live my life?' Sarah hurled back. Unlike most girls Sarah did not dream of falling in love and getting married, it was a dream that was bound to end in some sort of nightmare. She was furious with Jed Greep for making her look a fool. 'Marry him? And then what? End up having lots of babies? The mine's a widow-maker, remember. My own father was killed in a rock fall underground. Jed Greep's about to go under grass where he can earn more money. I don't want to be responsible for a lot of brats who'll likely starve to death!'

'All right! All right, Sarah.' Peggy Wetter was outspoken but she had a kindly way. 'I can see your reasoning. But Jed could offer you a good life. He'd build on to your cottage, plant some barley, perhaps keep a pig or two. You and the little ones would have warmth in winter and you wouldn't have to scrabble for every crust. I'm sure Godley won't see any of you go without if the worst happened.'

Sarah reflected, but she was too cynical about fate to see things in a different light. 'Sorry.' She was too weary to say anything more.

The rain suddenly stopped and the wind was easing. The count house bell rang for the ten minute croust. Sarah sent Tamsyn to fetch

64

the canvas bag and mugs of tea, staying put to avoid Jed Greep. Arthur joined them from jigging the crushed ore through a sieve. The sieves were shaken under water and Arthur was wet up to his elbows and Sarah tried to dry his scrawny arms with her towser. While her brother and sister ate and drank, Sarah saw how, despite the hardships, they were content, trusting her to care for them. She dredged up a smile and vowed to always protect them.

The day wore on. The sun shone brightly and the workers' clothes dried out. Peggy started up the singing. The bal-maidens sang nearly every day. Hymns, folk songs, ballads, comical ditties. Sarah sang to forget her troubles. She would try to spend a few minutes with Amy tonight. She brightened at the thought, and had no notion that her finely spaced features and soft brown eyes shone with beauty. A beauty natural and alluring, and it made her fellows pause and gaze and enjoy the sight of her. Godley Greep, checking on the progress, rubbed at the thatch on his chin and thought her a fair bride for his son. Jed would just have to try again.

The bell in the count house tolled the end of the core in the dimming light. Sarah shepherded Tamsyn and Arthur to the shed where their tools, bought from their own pay, were kept. Towsers were swapped for clean white aprons, gooks for coloured cotton bonnets. Sarah hung back from the other bal-maidens and boys on the long trudge home over the scrubland, not wanting to hear comments about Jed Greep, who had tried to catch her attention again before going on ahead with his father.

Tamsyn and Arthur had gathered some energy and they ran off with the other children. Sarah shouted to them to go straight home and not to play on the downs. She wanted to wash their clothes for the following day, which, because they had nothing else to wear, meant they would have to lie naked under their blanket while she dried them. She smiled as they ran off laughing and larking about, a short reprieve in their uneasy existence. 'Be careful! Watch out for rabbit holes.'

Sarah went off the beaten track a short way, to a secluded spot where she could grab a few moments alone. To clear her mind. To feel a person in her own right. Nature had unceremoniously formed the hills and valleys and tumbled the giant boulders of granite in free and easy patterns; an upright slab here and there, in other places a group stacked one of top of the other. On one such stack the top stones were larger than the bottom ones, looking as if collapse was imminent but the formation was eternally set. Sarah took a moment to watch, at a safe distance, just in case it fell. She chose a pair of slabs, one standing high and proud behind a short flat one and forming a useful seat, on which to linger. There was nothing else of particular interest here so it was unlikely she would be disturbed.

66

She closed her eyes. She tried not to think about anything, but Jed Greep's bashful, hopeful face wouldn't go away. Perhaps she should do as the other girls did, dream of marriage, a future. Give Jed a chance. It wouldn't hurt to dream, if only for a minute.

The minute turned into several more. Exhaustion had taken its grip and she awoke to find her back hurting against the stone behind her and her limbs cold and stiff. She shivered. The last heat of the day was bidding goodbye. She sat bolt upright in horror. Tamsyn and Arthur would be worried about her. How were they coping with their mother? It would soon be dark. She edged forward and jumped down off the granite. She must hasten back to the track yet be wary not to take a tumble over a hidden jutting rock. It was imperative she didn't lose her bearings. It wasn't unknown for a badly injured loner to die overnight on the downs, or disappear altogether, perhaps into a patch of marsh – or stolen away by the moor spirits.

Shadows were falling, deeper and deeper, creating strange shapes of the familiar crops of granite, making the paths she knew so well warped and indistinct. Prickles of nervousness made her stomach churn. Her every sense was at its highest pitch. There came a peculiar sound. A dog fox? A goblin? A lost soul? Like many Cornish folk Sarah was superstitious and now she was afraid. She hurried along. Suddenly the grimness of her home, the exhausting battle to care properly

67

for her family, seemed utterly desirable to being here alone ... and yet not alone.

She was back to where she had called to Tamsyn and Arthur. It was a narrow meandering track, with a bank of thorn bushes and tall ferns which fell away down to rough moors where the ground was waterlogged from the earlier rain. It was safe to run along the track. She made a few yards then her foot no longer landed on firm ground. She was over-ended, and despite her struggles, she was falling, tipping over the bank and then crashing down through clumps of hawthorn and ferns. Her hands reached out to grasp something to stop her tumble, but she was rolling over and over, crying out louder and louder. Finally she came to a stop and she scrabbled to get up but she was tangled up in something and sinking into something soft and wet. She was in a marsh! She was about to drown in foul black sludge!

In terror, she clamped her eyes shut, not wanting to see herself founder, see her approaching fate. 'Help! Help me someone!'

Her cry was answered at once, the surprise making her cry out again. 'Keep still,' a deep male voice ordered.

'Get me out! Please!'

'Get you out of what, girl?' The voice was gruff and puzzled.

Sarah opened her eyes. Her panic subsided when she saw that all she was thrashing about in was a wide dip of long wet muddy grass. It was the grass that had wrapped round her legs and tugged at her dress. 'Oh! I thought I was – oh, dear God!' Her terror came rushing back when she saw who it was, bending from the waist towards her. A pair of dead rabbits dangled from one of his hands and a shotgun lay over his arm. Titus Kivell.

'Don't be afeared, missy,' he said, laying the shotgun and his kills down. 'Give me your hands. I'll help you up.'

Her mouth gawping open she tentatively reached up to him. Titus wrapped his hands round hers and in a smooth continuous movement he hauled her to her feet and up out of the dip. She was trembling, breathless, and he supported her firmly. 'Are you hurt?'

'I … I don't know. I don't think so.' Her legs were taking her weight and no pains became apparent. She pulled up a threadbare sleeve. 'Just a few scratches on my arm.'

Titus eased her round in the circle of his arm so he could look into her face. 'You're a long time lagging behind the other bal-maidens. Been meeting a sweetheart?'

'No!' Sarah had never been this close to a man before and she did not like it. The fact that he was the infamous Titus Kivell made it so much worse.

He was gazing at her, searching every angle of her face, peering into her eyes. 'Men are slow round here. Even in this light I can see what a lovely creature you are.'

A new panic rose up inside her. 'Let me go! I have to go! I've got my sister and brother and mother to see to.'

69

Titus let her go. 'No need to worry. It'll be dark before you get to Meryen. Come with me. My mare isn't far from here. She can find her way even if it's pitch black. I'll get you safely home.'

Sarah felt like a reed battered in a storm. Titus Kivell had released her and was speaking in a calm, thoughtful manner, but she didn't trust him and yet she was too afraid to reject his offer. He wasn't a man to be argued with. She could just make him out as he picked up his shotgun and the rabbits. 'Take my hand,' he said. 'Step where I step.'

In this way they climbed to the bottom of the hill, and all the while Sarah's fears were mounting. Where was he taking her? Would he really take her home or was he about to violate her and then serve the ultimate violence on her? In past times at least two Kivells had been hung for murder. Titus encouraged her until they were on flat ground. Sarah felt stones beneath the worn soles of her shoes and reckoned she was standing on a track.

Titus gave a low whistle. She heard hooves. His mare was coming towards them. Sarah waited, her hands clutched together, praying he'd not take her off somewhere and hurt her.

'What's your name?' he asked in a conversational way.

'Sarah,' she whispered, staring at his broad outline in the rapidly dimming light, getting ready to run in case he suddenly leapt on her.

'That all?'

'Hichens.'

'Well, Sarah Hichens. Moonlight's here.'

He was securing his things to the saddle and mounted. She had a new fear, that he was going to leave her stranded. Then she stepped back. Torn what to do. If she slipped away and groped about carefully she might find shelter in the darkness. She could curl up somewhere and survive the night.

'Don't be silly,' Titus said, as if reading her thoughts. 'I've told you not to be afraid. If I was going to hurt you, I'd have done it by now. Give me your hand, Sarah.'

Something in his tone made her decide her best hope was to trust him. Moments later she was up on the mare in front of him, encompassed by his hefty arms as he took the reins. She was instantly warmer, protected from the cold night air by his body. 'I remember who your father was. Amos Hichens. Was crushed to death back in 'thirty-two. Quarrelsome, he was. Couldn't hold his drink. I heard he threw his fists about at home. Then his wife was badly injured at grass. Life must be hard for you.'

Sarah didn't reply. Her father had picked a fight with this man while in a drunken state and Titus had tossed him head first down the village well. It was a wonder he'd survived. 'Could you let me down at Chy-Henver please?'

'I could indeed. What business have you there?'

Sarah was too ashamed to reveal she

wanted to collect food for her family. 'The girl who lives there is my friend.'

'Amy Lewarne. A pleasant girl. A good friend to have, I should think.'

Sarah wondered how he knew Amy. 'She is.'

The mare must have been following short-cuts for within minutes they had arrived at Chy-Henver. Titus reined in. He slid off Moonlight and lifted Sarah down. Given over to safety, she found a little confidence. 'It was very kind of you to help me, Mr Kivell.'

'Not at all, m'dear. Call me Titus. Would you like the rabbits?'

'Don't you want them?' Sarah was astounded that anyone would give away at least half a dozen family-sized meals.

'I wasn't out purposely hunting for food. You're welcome to them, Sarah. If you ever need any help, for anything, at any time, come to Burnt Oak. Come with Amy. She'll be going there soon.'

He swung up into the saddle and rode away, leaving Sarah with her gifts, and burning with curiosity as to why he'd assume Amy had a reason to visit his lawless community.

Six

'I can't stay long,' Morton Lewarne told the two men he joined in an upper room of the Wayfayer's Inn. It was on the main road to Truro, five miles from the parish where they lived. Rain, driven by a cold easterly wind, rapped on the dusty, tiny-paned window, and made him start nervously.

'Afraid someone'll see you?' Titus Kivell jeered, downing half of a tankard of ale in one noisy draught. 'No one from Meryen's likely to come in here. Although you do, and Mr Nankervis and I do. Thought you'd been going far enough away from home to seek your extra pleasures, didn't you, Lewarne? Had no idea that you'd be seen by us.'

'I haven't been back since that day,' Morton said, colouring brightly, not from shame but because it was partly a lie. Most of the girls who worked here as entertainment lived out and he now visited his favourite at her shanty home, near the village of Chacewater. 'Why have you summoned me here? I'm a busy man.' He looked at the squire for his answer.

'Things getting too much for you, Lewarne?' Darius eyed him mockingly. He used the inn as a resting place and for pleasure on his way to and from his town house in Truro.

73

He glanced at the rough-wood bed, antici-pating the company of the prostitute he'd arranged to join him after this meeting. She'd been in here not long ago. Her musky per-fume lingered in the stuffy confines and tantalizingly there were certain tools of her trade. A log fire had been lit. It was going to be cosy for a long while, once this misfit was extricated. 'I've heard it's a struggle getting your orders out on time. Didn't that boy of yours work fast enough for you? Anyway, it isn't I who wants you here.'

Darius raised his glass of rum to Titus. 'Well, my friend. It's good to see you again. People think you should have got the rope, but I was happy to speak up, behind the scenes, for the man whom I forgave for poaching on my land while he tried to save my Jeffrey.'

'God bless you, sir.' Titus reached out and clinked his tankard of ale against the glass. Then he glared at Morton and held him in his sight.

'Please,' Morton pleaded, frightened at being here with such ruthless men. 'Can we get on? I've just buried my son. I shouldn't stay too long away from my wife.'

'Nor would I if I'd married she!' Titus howled lustfully, making a lewd gesture. 'What the hell did a fine piece like her see in you? Daughter of a mine agent, wasn't she? You was only a mine carpenter back then. You've put on airs and graces since you've had your own little concern.' He lifted his leg on the table and pointed to his booted foot, rolling his dark eyes in mock ecstasy. 'What would your prim woman think, eh, if she knew you had a certain fetish?'

'We're not here to discuss Lewarne's appetites,' Darius said, growing impatient, although the discovery, three years ago, that Morton Lewarne occasionally frequented the nefarious Wayfarer's Inn for wenching never failed to please him. Subsequently, Darius had ordered all carpentry work required at Poltraze be given to Morton Lewarne. Lewarne never dared to ask for payment, he knew it would end with his wife becoming aware of his infidelity. It was part of the reason he had pressing money worries.

Titus returned to the enjoyment of watching Morton squirm. 'I hear you're soon to be a father again, Morton. I never saw your son. Mama Tempest and Sol speak well of him. Your daughter's a worthy little piece. Got spirit in her.'

'You've met Amy?' Morton leaned accusingly across the scratched planked table. His moment of attack was halted by a fierce look from Titus. Damn the man! Why couldn't he have died in prison? He'd survived the deprivation and diseases that stalked Bodmin gaol as if he'd never been incarcerated.

Darius joined in the onslaught simply for the fun of it. 'My son, Joshua, was much taken with the girl's dignity when they found your son's body. He would have paid his respects at the funeral if it hadn't been held in the Methodist chapel.'

'My wife and my daughter are none of your business, either of you.' Morton called up some courage for the honour of his women-folk. Both these men trampled over every consideration of women.

'Your business is my business, I'm making it so,' Titus said, alert, looming.

Morton's top lip became wet with nerves. 'What do you mean?'

'Well, the way I see it, Morton,' Titus was deceptively genial, then turned swiftly to hardness. 'You need help in your workshop and I'm going to send you some.'

'Y—you are? W—why? Who?'

'I had a lot of time to think while I was locked up. Times are changing. Life is becoming more settled. Copper's doing well and more mines are being sunk. Meryen is expanding all the time. I don't consider it's good for my family to stay quite so isolated anymore. It's time the Kivells branched out and that's exactly what we're planning to do. Your tragic circumstance has given me an idea. There's no need for you to root an apprentice out of the workhouse. I've got a highly trained craftsman just perfect for your business.'

'You have?' Morton could hardly get the words out past his tight throat. 'Who?'

'My son. Sol.'

'Your son! B—b—but why? No Kivell has worked for anyone outside your community before. Your son could set up his own

76

business.'

'True enough, and he's been trained by a better craftsman than you, my cousin Laketon, who's doing very nicely. But I think it would help if Sol gained some experience with someone else who's recognized and respected in the trade. He can start tomorrow.'

'I—I'll have to think about it.' Morton was appalled and it showed in every thin quivering inch of him. 'My wife wouldn't care for a ... newcomer so soon after Toby...' Sweat streamed down Morton's back, every nerve in his body was at screaming point. He'd nearly said Sylvia wouldn't care for a Kivell in his employment. Titus would have felt insulted and he would have given him a beating. He was in the worst fix of his life. Sylvia was barely speaking to him. She would never forgive him for allowing this. He'd never be able to face the rest of Meryen again.

Titus placed a hand on the table, not loudly, not with force, but it made Morton jump and cower. He was smirking, enjoying his prey and victim game. He glanced at Darius to see if he was listening. Darius was puffing on a cigar, staring from man to man with incredulity. Titus went on as if he was closing a business agreement in the best of lawyers' offices. 'He won't be bound to you. No one binds a Kivell. You'll pay him treble what you gave Toby on account of his advanced skill. Meals to be included and he's to take as many breaks and to come and go as he

77

pleases.'

Morton looked as if he was about to choke. He tugged at his necktie.

'Don't look so worried, man!' Titus roared with mocking jollity. 'Sol's quick and he takes pains with detail. He was chiselling and hammering on bits of wood from the age of three. He'll build up the reputation of your business, get it back on course.' He spat on his meaty, hairy hand. 'Let's shake on it.'

Morton was like a rat cornered by a wolfhound. He was petrified in his chair. Until Titus banged his fist on the table, making the tankard and glass leap and slop drink. A cry of fear strangled and died in Morton's throat. It took the greatest will for him to make his hand reach across the table. It shook as Titus took it in a mighty grip and nearly crushed his fingers.

'Well, that's settled. Now you can bugger off! Whisper to Nellie to send up some bootleg brandy. Tell her that Mr Nankervis and I are ready for the women. Oh, and Morton, you be good to my boy. He's mine and Mama Tempest's favourite. If you're frightened of being on the wrong side of me, you'd come off even worse against my mother! She'll ill-wish you.'

Shaking from head to toe, on legs like boards, Morton shuffled to the door as if he had suddenly gained thirty years and advanced rheumatism. He shut the ill-fitting door after him with a meek lowering of the wonky iron latch.

'Did you hear that door squeak?' Titus cried out maliciously, loud enough for Morton to hear, while grinning at Darius. 'Should have got him to put a drop of oil on it.'

Stunned at the interchange, Darius did not take in that last spiteful jest. He drew on his cigar and let out a plume of smoke. 'Do you really want this arrangement for your son?'

'Course not.' Titus's lips curled in disgust. 'Sol has every intention to travel and see the world, but it won't hurt him to do this for me first. What I want is Lewarne's business. Having Sol there will grind him down and it won't take long to get Lewarne to agree to sell up for a song. My cousin Laketon's got his eye on the business. I hate him, he's an insidious loner, doesn't study the family at all, just his own needs, and that offends me mortally. He can buy it off me for a higher price. It will all be fun. I want Sol to make gutless Lewarne sweat out every moment. I hate the hypocrite. It's come to my ears that he's had a lot to say about me and my family over the years. He hoped I'd get the noose. Now the villagers will soon see the true measure of him. I'll make sure they know about his double standards.'

'If your family are to become respectable businessmen as you want, they'll have to calm down.'

'They will,' Titus said confidently. 'It's what Mama Tempest's wanted for years, and some of the younger ones realize they won't go far if they're always courting strife. Not that I've got any intention of changing myself.' Titus was one Kivell who hadn't taken up a craft or a trade. He preferred to make his living by arranging bare-knuckle fighting, cock-fighting, smuggling runs and by other criminal means. He was reflective for a moment. 'You've been busy making changes too. You've taken your wife back. I'm surprised at that.'

'She won't be at Poltraze for long. I've brought her back for a purpose. After that, I'll soon have her consigned to the asylum.'

They drank on in a friendly manner, although Titus and Darius didn't trust each other at all.

Seven

Wearing a straw sunhat, and with her black skirt hitched up in her apron strings, Amy was pulling carrots and potatoes from the vegetable patch. She straightened up before her basket was full. She couldn't pinpoint it but there was something different, something strange, about the day. Sometimes, when the winds were soughing across the moors they seemed to sing in mournful notes, as if some lost soul was lamenting its fate. Or it might be still and quiet, and she'd fancy an ancient tribesperson, of the earliest people who'd

80

roamed the hills, was whispering a secret and no matter how hard she listened her human ear could not distinguish it. Occasionally, on dark days, the moors seemed to press in all around her, and in odd uneasy moments Amy would feel an intruder in the wildness of nature.

There was no sense of anything of the kind today but she gazed about anyway. There was reason to be cautious. Of late, things had been stolen in the village, the blame put on newcomers. The sky was the palest of blues, the clouds light and cottony and slow-moving. All seemed in order in the garden. The hens were scratching contentedly behind their wire-netting run. At the bottom the stream flowed undisturbed, its path encroached on only by the stepping-stones. Close by, stretched out and sleeping on the wooden bench was the cat, Floss. The sleek tabby sparred most days with Stumpy. Stumpy, who'd followed along after Amy for the last few days, had deserted her today, making her feel the loss of Toby even more. That must be it. She was feeling even more empty, there was more bruising to her heart. She'd have to get used to the fact that life was never going to be the same.

She finished her task quickly, eager to go back inside to her mother, who seemed to be growing weaker every day in her grief. She had fretted at not being to able attend Toby's funeral. 'I've not been able to say a proper goodbye to my son yet,' Sylvia had sobbed from her bed. 'It's all your father's fault. Move his things out of here! He can sleep in the spare room from now on. I can't bear him near me. I can't bear the sight of him.'

Such a course would have been unthinkable before, but Toby's death had changed that. Sylvia had not a scrap of respect left for Morton. He had argued, shouted for a while, but had accepted Sylvia's wishes. 'You're not much use to me at the moment anyway,' he'd barked. Amy had felt no sympathy for him over the banishment, rather, she was beginning to loathe him, and that was an awful feeling.

She made her way towards the house. She stopped on the path and stared at the workshop and listened. Her father spent almost every waking minute in there now. Today he was even busier. That was the difference. There was so much more activity. Even in the early morning, during the migration of workers past the house to the mine, there had been something unusual. A horse. No one in Meryen could afford a horse on which to ride to work. It could have been a stable groom or one of the gentlemen from the big house riding this way for some reason. Mr Joshua Nankervis perhaps. She had wondered if he'd call again after the day he'd turned up when Tara was here. She hoped he would not. He had been kind, but it was embarrassing not knowing what to say to him and how to behave. Now she realized that her father seemed to be dashing from tool to tool. He

82

had behaved strangely this morning, talking to himself, which she'd never known before. Instead of waiting for her to bring him his morning tea and biscuits he had come to the kitchen and asked for two mugs of tea and double the amount of food, saying he had a terrible hunger and thirst today. It was a lie! He had someone with him. He'd taken on an apprentice and hadn't bothered to inform her or her mother. Dropping the basket on the ground she strode off to the workshop.

The long stone building on the far side of the garden, flanked by a wood store and a stable for Morton's pair of workhorses and covered cart, boasted a large sign in Morton's own hand: Morton Lewarne Esq. Master Carpenter & Cabinet Maker. He could have Undertaker on it too and increase his business but he was too faint-hearted to deal with dead bodies. 'You're not much of a man, Father,' Amy said to herself.

The double doors were open. Wood dust hung in the air, caught in a shaft of sunlight. The workbench ran on three sides of the wall. Her father was in his usual place, just inside, where most light was gained, with his back to her. He was cutting mitred dovetails for a flush-top cabinet, his head down and shoulders hunched up, his breathing loud and tense. The sight of his companion, at the other end of the workshop, made the next breath gag in her throat. Side on to her, at the bench, *Toby's bench*, his sleeves rolled up past his elbows, concentration plain on his powerful dark profile, was the towering figure of Sol Kivell. Stumpy was sitting companionably at his feet on the uneven, sawdust strewn, pressed-earth floor.

'What's going on?' She stared from one man to the other.

Morton went rigid with shock. He turned his head round as if his thin neck was on a rusty ratchet.

Sol only had to glance sideways to see her. He kept on sanding the rails of a small square table, the last piece Toby had been working on. From the evidence of the large leather bag on the end of the bench he was using his own tools.

Amy marched up to him. His black hair tumbled across half his face, which looked set in stone. 'Father,' she pointed a finger at Sol. 'What's he doing here?'

Morton swallowed, twisted his hands in his leather apron and hung his head. He was not master of his domain now.

'Is someone going to tell me? Explain, for goodness sake!' She was getting angrier by the second over the silence and the way Sol Kivell was ignoring her. She was obviously as unimportant to him as a speck of sawdust. He was making a habit of intruding into her family's life. Apparently, he was now terrorizing her father – he'd not be here otherwise. But why? It didn't make sense.

Sol studied his work, as if it were the only issue of the moment. 'You really are the biggest of cowards, Morton,' he said, his eyes not leaving his work.

'Don't you speak to my father like that! What are you doing here?' Amy wanted to push him all the way out of the workshop and then push him over, watch him hit the hard stony ground outside with a loud thump. No one had produced such an aggressive need in her before.

Pushing the hair back off his brow in a lazy movement, Sol finally looked at her. He swept his brazen eyes up and down her, giving her a smile that was at first amused then full of contempt. It made Amy recoil.

'Amy, go away,' Morton said, red-faced and pleading. He seemed like a man suddenly shrivelled with old age. 'I'll explain...' he hesitated when Sol swung round to watch him. 'I'll explain later.'

'Is he threatening you?' Her father might have turned to wood pulp but she wasn't about to let Sol Kivell hold sway here.

'No! No, he isn't. It's complicated. Amy, do what you're told!' Morton snapped.

'No, I won't. I don't know what's going on but I'm not just going to leave things as they are. If he doesn't leave right now I'll go in and tell mother.' It wouldn't have been a feasible threat before but she knew her father was keen to regain her mother's esteem. She was popular in Meryen and he was not. If folk discovered he had been thrown out of his own bedroom he would be ridiculed.

'Don't do that! No, Amy, please. I don't want her upset.'

Amy was appalled at how pathetic he was.

'I'm not going anywhere,' Sol said, drawing out papers and a leather tobacco pouch from his trouser pocket. 'Am I, Morton? Not until I want to, that is. What time's dinner? I take it we'll eat in the house, at the table, all nice and proper. What are we having, Amy?'

'I'm Miss Lewarne to you!' Amy realized she was shouting at the top of her voice. She rubbed at her brow. This was getting out of hand. Now she was being bullied and tormented by Sol Kivell and he was enjoying every moment of it, but not in an humorous way. It unsettled her in a way like nothing had before. How could Toby, so timid and naive, have befriended this man?

Her face on fire, she made for the doors.

'Wait!' Morton wailed, beating her to them. 'I'll tell your mother.' He crept away, bowed over, to the house.

There was no way Amy was going to stay here alone with the infiltrator. She went to retrieve the vegetable basket. She looked back at the workshop. Sol had come outside and was leaning against the high natural bank of moorland that gave shelter to the back of the building. He was smoking, one foot crossed casually in front of the other. He inclined his head to her, a distinct sign of one-upmanship.

In the kitchen, Amy winced as she heard her mother's angry and distraught cries. When Morton propelled himself through the room moments later he ignored her and kicked Floss, who was slinking indoors, out of his

86

way.

'Mother! What are you doing?' Amy exclaimed when she went up to Sylvia. Sylvia was getting dressed, her face as hard as hoar frost.

'We're to suffer even more because of your father's spinelessness.' In a dry, bitter tone, Sylvia repeated the words of the arrangement made by Titus Kivell. 'Your father says he's under some kind of obligation to him. I will not abide in my bed while that young rebel flouts himself in my home.'

Downstairs, Sylvia sat in the rocking chair at the kitchen hearth, one hand resting on her swollen belly. Amy fetched a footstool for her. 'I can't believe this is happening. Why are they doing this? The Kivells? Why does Titus want his son to work here? Why is Sol going along with it? He doesn't obey his father in everything.'

Sylvia looked at her sharply. 'How could you possibly know that?'

'I went to Burnt Oak the day I was searching for Toby.' Amy filled her mother in on the details, leaving out the part about Sol keeping her scarf.

Sylvia was quiet for some time. Amy bit her nails. It seemed as if the greater part of her mother had turned to stone. Finally, Sylvia said, 'If the Kivells were good to my Toby then I'd rather have the company of one of them than your father. Set the dinner table for four, Amy.'

The vegetable soup was steaming hot on

top of the slab. A cottage loaf, butter and cheese sat in the middle of the table on a large round board, decorated with a leaf pattern, sculpted by Morton. There were few things of wood in the house that hadn't been made by him. Sylvia was dignified and purse-lipped as she waited at the foot of the table for the men to come in. Amy's back was hurting from the knots in her spine. Not a muscle moved in Sylvia's face as she listened to the men washing their hands in the back kitchen. Amy thought she'd never breathe a breath again that wasn't loaded with grief and tainted with anger. And loathing for her father and his new worker. Sol Kivell had better not upset her mother...

Morton came in silently. The last drop of colour drained from his pinched features when he saw Sylvia in her place. He sat in his own chair, hollow and hunched over.

Sylvia stared straight into Sol's eyes.

He came to the last remaining place at the table. 'It's a pleasure to meet you, Mrs Le-warne. Please accept how sorry I am about Toby.'

Sylvia inhaled a deep disapproving breath. She motioned for him to sit. He did so. Bow-ed his head and folded his hands together. 'You say grace in your house, young man?' If Sylvia was surprised it didn't come across in her bland voice.

He lifted his head. Amy was taken aback to see the respectful gentleness he returned to her mother. 'Grandmama Tempest insists on it, Mrs Lewarne.'

'I'm glad to hear that not all your family's habits are heathen,' Sylvia said. Amy glanced at Sol, afraid he'd been offended, but he seemed unconcerned.

'Morton,' Sylvia said brusquely, raising her hands in prayer. Never before had he needed prompting in his duty to say the grace.

It was an effort for Amy to sit still. It was a day of new beginnings. The power in her home had shifted from her father to her mother.

Morton could manage no more than a couple of spoonfuls of soup and a few crumbs of bread. Sol ate heartily. Sylvia finished most of her meal, more food than she'd eaten for the last few days. Amy ate to show the unwelcome diner that she was not intimidated by his presence, but the food sat like lead in her stomach. Not a word passed across the table.

When Amy put the last washed and dried dish away she wondered if it had actually happened. She knew it hadn't been a dream when Sol collected his horse from the stable at five o'clock and rode away. How were they going to survive this, him coming here every working day? Yet when she looked at Sylvia, gazing into space, her mind filled, no doubt, with wistful memories of Toby, when Amy saw the fight and the life that had returned to her mother, she had to admit there was a reason to be grateful to Sol Kivell.

Sol didn't ride far. He left his horse at the back of the Nankervis Arms. Murky, with dirty windows and bulky, low rafters, the tavern didn't match up to its esteemed name. It was the roughest drinking place in Meryen, its landlord, Dilly Trewin, the mid-Cornwall wrestling champion, was much given to humour of a lewd kind.

Flexing his conquering muscles, Dilly Trewin plonked a tankard of ale at Sol's usual spot, near the door, far across from the cavernous fireplace, where a smelly old black and white mongrel dozed. ''Tis the talk of the village, boy.'

Sol downed a long cool draught, relishing the refreshing of his throat. 'What is?'

Dilly was one of the few folk who wasn't easily browbeaten by the Kivells ever-ready confrontational manner. As did Titus, Sol would fix his eyes on an inquirer with more than a view to hurl back that they'd be better off minding their own business. The uneven table, greatly darkened by tobacco ash, wood smoke, and spilled drink, also bore slashes and pits from Kivell knives and fists. 'What I mean to say is, what're you doing up-along at the Lewarnes? Strikes me as peculiar.'

'My father wants it so. That's all you,' Sol then glared at the other drinkers, a mix of miners not on their core, old men, and one or two farm labourers, 'or anyone else needs to know.'

'A dear young maid lives there.' Dilly winked suggestively. There was a tense hush in the taproom. The drinkers knew Dilly would persist. They also knew that if Sol, who appeared to have begrudged every minute spent at Chy-Henver, grew impatient, he might turn quarrelsome.

Sol looked up at the towering landlord from under his dark lashes. 'I'm not blind.'

There was an outbreak of bawdy laughter. Dilly went to his side of the bar and took wagers on how long it would take Sol to make a favourable impression on pretty Amy Lewarne.

Sol produced the yellow and red-flowered scarf and brought it up to his nose. Amy's tantalizing fragrance was in the delicate fibres. He twisted it round his hand in the same way he wanted to wind her lovely golden brown hair up and down his fingers. Did she know about the female company he kept? One of the serving girls here and some older women who obligingly opened their doors to him while their husbands were at work. Amy probably did know. The argumentative, haughty madam disapproved of every part of him. That didn't bother him one little bit.

Sol was eager to break out into the world but taking over a business in Meryen wasn't broad enough for his horizons. He'd argued with his father there were better ways of acquiring Chy-Henver than planting him there. His grandmother had advised him to go, saying she had 'seen' something to his benefit, and the great love and affection Sol had for Tempest Kivell, who'd come from a wealthy Quaker family in Falmouth, meant he usually went along with her biddings. Titus had ordered him to come home straight-away to report on his first day. He could wait. His disobedience sometimes brought him and Titus close to blows, but otherwise, Titus stressed he was proud of his single-minded-ness, seeing him as a worthy successor. Sol did not hold his father in much regard; Titus was too objectionable.

Cheap scent filled his nostrils as a young, red-haired woman, with a generously expos-ed bosom, sashayed up to his table. 'Enjoying your new job?'

Sol leaned back on his stool, resting his head against the thick stone wall. 'There's only one thing you should be concerned that I enjoy, Lizzie.'

She let out a wicked laugh. Sol followed her to a back room and placed some silver in her grasping hand. She shut the door and pounced on him eagerly. Sol was wild with her. When at last he was lying on his back, his broad chest heaving, she ran a fingertip along a thin scar on his stomach, a trophy he'd got here on the premises after he'd quarrelled with an unwise tinner from Lanner, who'd come off far worse. 'If I didn't know you better I'd think you had something on your mind.'

He put his arm round her shoulders and brought her hot curves down against his body. Whores knew men. He didn't want this one to come to the decision that there was a reason for him to be looking forward to his next working day.

Eight

Tara was in her old, austere room at Poltraze, where the only decoration was one bleak landscape on the faded greenish wallpaper. There wasn't a drape on the half-tester bed, and it was covered with the same old damask counterpane. The air seemed stale, as if filled with the breath of bygone Nankervises, and she missed the freshness of the sea at Penzance. The atmosphere was dull, dull, dull, but she supposed it was marginally better than at the Dower House. Sitting before her dressing table, in her chemise and stiffened petticoats, her left hand strayed to the trinket jars and she chinked her fingertips on the amber glass. She brought the hand up before her eyes. In an hour she would have a three-stone rose diamond engagement ring on it, a Nankervis heirloom. Joshua was going to place it on her finger before they went down together. They were to be the last to make an appearance tonight at the ball.

She tapped on the silver-scrolled handle of her hair brush, making the bristles bounce on the walnut dressing-table. Her life was about to change forever and she'd been given no say in it. While her aunt was ecstatic about the

93

turn in their fortune, Tara was secretly furious. Furious that Estelle had kept the details of her trust fund from her, and that she was to be used as a pawn to further Estelle and Darius Nankervis's selfish plans. She was pleased, however, that marriage and children were now to be included in her life instead of futile years of increasing loneliness. She hadn't had enough time to explore her feelings in regard to Joshua becoming her husband.

They had heard the news of their impending betrothal together, on returning to the Dower House after their visits to Amy. After Joshua had inquired at Chy-Henver if Amy and her mother were bearing up, he had escorted Tara back, both of them speculating over the reason for his father's summons. 'You've grown up to be very charming, if I may say so,' Joshua had said, in the manner of a doting older brother, much like the way he had treated her when she'd lived at Poltraze.

'It was good of you to keep in touch with me each Christmas,' she'd replied.

It was extraordinary for them, shortly afterward, to be staring at each other as two people soon to be married. Mr Nankervis and her aunt had been in the parlour, he seemingly in the throes of some sort of breathless excitement, as if he'd run too far, and she flushed and coy, yet somehow coquettishly grateful towards her husband. Joshua had shot them a look of disapproval and Tara had

94

assumed he was displeased at the decision they had come to without consulting him first. He did not argue about it, his thoughts had been unreadable.

Estelle now breezed into the room. In an off-the-shoulder, puffed short-sleeved, ball gown of pale blue silk, and sapphires on her wrists and at her throat, and a diamond tiara in her hair, she looked exquisite. Atkins and a young maid were with her. Tara braced herself for the torture of being laced into a corset. 'Now, to get our lovely bride-to-be ornamented in all her engagement finery. Oh, don't look so glum, Tara,' Estelle was suddenly impatient. 'You should be excited to bursting point. I'll see about getting every modern convenience in this dreary old house. And I swear that I shall soon oust the others out of it.'

'Miss Tara's bound to be a little overcome, ma'am,' Atkins pointed out carefully, guiding the dreaded corset under Tara's small bosom. Tara didn't need energetic lacing to procure the much desired tiny waist and she wished her aunt away, or Atkins would be ordered to pull and pull on the laces.

'I've told her not to worry.' Estelle was dismissive. 'Married life is a state in which a woman must endure and make sacrifices. Goodness knows I've had to. I'd never thought I'd prefer living here to that awful little house in Penzance. I was a fool before. I shall not be making any such mistakes in the future. Turn her out splendidly, Atkins.' She

95

pushed the maid aside. 'I'm about to go down with my husband.'

'Do you think she'll be all right?' Tara asked, gasping for breath as the whalebone and stiffened material became ever more familiar with her ribs. 'People might hiss at her.'

'You saw her,' Atkins said, bright and full of confidence. She had declared it was beyond her wildest dreams for her mistress to be reinstated to her rightful place. 'She's sparkling. A match for anyone in the county. The house is bursting at the seams, anyone who's anyone is here burning for gossip. But you, my little bud, have youth and innocence on your side. The romantics will be smitten by you, the devil-may-cares brought to rein, and the sanctimonious will believe they're in the company of an angel. No one will give Mrs Estelle a second glance when you glide down the stairs on Mr Joshua's arm.'

Joshua wasn't unsettled about his forth-coming marriage, he couldn't have chosen a better bride himself than the pleasing, pliable Tara. He'd be able to get on with his life much the same as before. The barrage of complaints he was getting from Michael and Phoebe had been very trying though. Now he was about to witness them publicly disasso-ciating themselves from the return of his father's wife.

'Why is Father doing it?' Michael had launched at him before, seeking him out in one of the hothouses. 'Why has he brought

96

that creature back in the house? She'll drag the family's name through the mud.'

'I don't care what people think.' Joshua had not looked up from giving the grape vines a fine spray of water.

'She'll make us a laughing stock.'

'If Father thought that he wouldn't have brought her back.'

'I can't believe this is happening. Estelle's giving me no peace to get on in the library.' He was making new records of the family history, a passion equal to Joshua's for the gardens.

'Stop being so damned dramatic. Things will settle down in time.' Joshua wished he could tell his brother the truth. He and Michael got on well enough when Phoebe wasn't needling either of them. They went their separate ways, desiring their own privacy, and it worked to their satisfaction. It was a pity Michael hadn't chosen a malleable wife.

Phoebe went further and had vented her gall, when his father wasn't present, on Tara and Estelle. One night she had paced the floor, fluttering her feather fan wildly, as if she was about to combust. 'We'll never be able to hold our heads up again. I hardly feel we can go back to St James's Square after the recess.'

'Be sure that you do, Mrs Nankervis,' Estelle had broken in, her green eyes splintered and magnificently icy, as she'd sipped an after dinner coffee. 'There is only one mistress in this house and my husband has given the position to me.'

Joshua saw problems ahead with Estelle, but they wouldn't last long. She was different than before, when she'd been inclined to sulk and throw rages. Now she bossed and bullied. Oh, for a few hours to revel in with the Kivells. Especially Laketon. His dear Laketon. Meetings with his lover had to be carefully arranged, for if his father discovered his true sexuality, he'd turn him out, penniless, and Titus would in all probability kill Laketon. He and Laketon went to great lengths to hide their true relationship, spending time at brothels, but paying well to keep it a secret that it wasn't prostitutes they shared a bed with. It was fortunate that Tara had been with Amy Lewarne the day he had called at Chy-Henver, he'd gone there so as to appear he was interested in her; his bride would never guess where his true desires lay.

Tara waited for Joshua in the upstairs gallery, keeping out of sight of the party-goers as they climbed the well-trod oak stairs to discard their cloaks and wraps in the powder rooms. She watched them covertly as they made their way back down to the Long Corridor, which had been cleared of its clutter for dancing. On every lip, the oddity of Darius Nankervis entertaining here was surpassed by the surprise of her aunt's return.

She studied the portraits, some by Opie and Reynolds, of previous Nankervises. She

98

would soon be a part of this lot, fated to merge into its now uncelebrated history. There had been some great and gifted Nankervises. Nearly two hundred years ago, Henry, resplendent on canvas in cavalier's garb, had fought in the successful Royalist campaign at Boconnoc. In the 1750s Francis, like many Cornish landowners, had made the family fortune by leasing mineral rights to the adventurers. Celia Nankervis, his daughter-in-law, had been a witty scholar and an exalted beauty. The Nankervises were said to have a philistine touch and sadly Poltraze, as it stood now with its featureless remodelling, with no forethought for comfort or style, echoed this truth in its every corner. At least, Joshua had something to be proud of as he showed his peers round the grounds. His father had already commissioned the likenesses of Joshua and herself to be painted. One day her children's might adorn these walls, and in a sudden urge of ambition she desired a son to groom as a man of achievement, who'd rebuild this draughty dark tomb, who'd care about the living conditions of the humblest individual who dwelt on his land and for humanity in general. In a fusion of daring and fear, she wanted to breed a Radical who would stand up and be counted. Her future father-in-law would hate that!

'What are you thinking about, Tara?'

'Oh!' Her hand flew to her heart. 'Joshua...' He was always thoughtful towards her but now he seemed to be admiring her. Tara was heartened. She had realized that while he saw Amy as a desirable woman – Tara thought she was under no illusions as to why he'd used the Lewarnes' grief to call unexpectedly at Chy-Henver – he must find her unworldly and sheltered. It was unlikely he was as willing to enter this marriage as he was making out. It occurred to her that by not attempting explanations she could be a little mysterious to him, and that might bode well for the future. 'Nothing in particular.'

'You look lovely.'

'Thank you.' She felt lovely, Atkins had done her job well. Silk rosebuds decorated the low boat-shaped neckline and waistband of her ivory tulle gown, her hair was arranged smoothly across her brow and held in a chignon behind her ears in a diamond-studded net, and more rosebuds were scattered on the crown of her head. Joshua made a handsome sight in a pleated shirt, tail coat and lavishly embroidered waistcoat. 'Your father has been congratulated on his birthday. I heard the cheers go up.'

'Then it's our turn to take centre stage.' Joshua smiled. Tara really was lovely. Unassuming and enchanting. He liked her, he always had. He was sure she'd always liked him. Their marriage would work. He produced the engagement ring. 'May I?'

Tara gazed at the beautiful rose diamonds twinkling between his thumb and forefinger. She saw the remnants of earth under his nails. His passion for nature's flora endeared

him to her. Her aunt had married a frightening, intransigent, middle-aged man. For herself she was getting Joshua, who was young
and carefree. Her life with him, as protector,
she was sure, from the harridan Phoebe and
the cold Michael, wasn't going to be too bad.
She held out her left hand.

Joshua pushed the ring gently in place. 'It
fits perfectly. Tara, don't be nervous. I believe
you're going to be perfect for me. Well, people
must be wondering where we are. We're
about to be stared at. Ready to go down?'

Tara breathed in nervously and slipped her
arm through his. 'I am.'

The Long Corridor was filled with myriad
lights from the chandeliers and the tall
candles burning on every table, shelf and
windowsill and in the wall sconces. The
orchestra was playing a country dance and as
the ladies hopped and skipped their dresses
were like a paradisiacal garden of moving
colour; embroidered satins and silks; frills,
lace and flounces galore. Their jewels glitter-
ed in every nook and corner.

'Ah, ah!' Darius sang out, drink a little
heavy on him, beckoning to the couple. 'Here
they are, my son and my wife's dear niece.'
With Estelle at his side, he was engaged with
the titled Bassets of Tehidy, the county's most
important mining family, whose country seat
was not many miles away. The elderly, but
boisterous, Sir Luke Pengarron from Mount's
Bay, and a general and a duchess were also
attending him. Michael and Phoebe were not

101

far off, and while pretending to be merry and bright, the pair had him under surveillance. 'Hush! Hush everyone, I must have hush!'

The music stopped. Tara felt her insides shrink. Every eye in the room seemed to be on her and Joshua. He put a reassuring hand over hers. The touching gesture left little use for an official announcement. Tara watched the horror take hold of Phoebe's haughty features and her fight to keep an undignified scowl at bay. Michael quailed. Joshua squeezed Tara's hand, to let her know he'd seen the display too, that he didn't care about it and was even amused. Tara glanced at Estelle. She was holding herself as a queen, a conqueror. This, more than anything, grated on Tara's nerves.

Unused to so many people and such a volume of noise in one space, the evening took off in a blistering whirl for Tara. Congratulations were given and kisses were planted on her hand. She was crowded and jostled. Gentlemen who wouldn't have passed the time of day with her before declared they wanted the honour of a dance with her. Joshua forestalled them by saying that only he was to dance with his lovely bride-to-be.

Darius demanded she take the floor with him. 'You'll make my son a good little wife, won't you?' he pushed his heavy face close to hers.

Trying to follow his forceful steps, Tara wanted to turn away from his alcohol-laden breath. 'I'll do my very best, sir.'

'Sir? You've never referred to me as Uncle Darius. Now you must call me Father. Mind that you do right by Joshua or I'll not only turn you and Estelle out, I'll ruin you both. I want a grandson, the next heir, under this roof next year. Understand?'

What else could she say except for, 'Yes, Father.'

He gazed into her eyes. Tara forced herself to return the look. 'Mmm, I think you'll do us well. Joshua likes you, it's easy to see why. Now find yourself someone to talk to, I want a word with Michael.'

He escorted her to Estelle. Estelle hugged her arm. 'What did he say to you?'

'He was his usual pleasant self,' Tara said off-handedly. She was trying not to be unnerved by his threat. Could he really harm her when she was Joshua's wife? 'He's got something to say to Michael.'

'Michael? Can't think what he's got to say to him.' Estelle lifted her chin and peered around the room as if she were gloating about something. Tara knew she was lying.

Tara found out the reason for the gloat while she was waiting for Joshua to bring her some punch. Phoebe confronted her in a fury of skirts and hissed in her ear. 'Was it her idea, that bitch, your aunt? My father-in-law is turning us out. He won't have us up in London with him anymore and he says this house is too small for everyone. Michael and I have been ordered to move into the Dower House. It's because we have daughters.

Females mean nothing to him. Take warning, girl, produce a healthy son or Darius Nankervis will set an unjust punishment on you. He's served one on me. I'm resigned to stay here forever and rot!'

Tara was left with the uneasy knowledge that she really must take Darius's threat to her seriously. Joshua returned to her. 'Good news, isn't it, that we won't have to put up with carping Phoebe under our roof anymore? The Dower House will suit her very well.'

'It must be awful to feel rejected though. Why doesn't your father want Michael with him at St James's Square?'

'It's not the sort of life Michael enjoys. He has no money of his own and feels like a hanger-on, and Phoebe never ceases to embarrass him by holding up what she perceives as his faults in public. Actually, it was Michael who went to Father and requested he stay on the estate. He's content with a quiet life. He's not happy about living in the Dower House, of course, but he'll be spending a lot of time here in the library, poring over old documents and things. He'll be compensated by being able to get away from Phoebe more often.'

'I'm pleased for Michael that he'll be getting something he wants.' Tara would be more pleased if he and Phoebe were to live miles away from Poltraze.

That night Joshua changed into the clothes he kept for the gardens. The guard dogs were used to his nocturnal wanderings and didn't bark or follow him. He took a route to the side of the house and soon entered the woods. He knew the paths well and only a little care was necessary to make a safe passage deep into the heart of the trees.

He came to a little hut. It was lit inside by the orangey yellow glow of a single lantern. Laketon rushed to him. 'At last! It's been a terrible day for me. Tell me nothing will change.'

Joshua hugged him. 'I've promised you that nothing will. We've known that this day must come for me. I can't get out of marriage like you can.'

Black-haired and of a good build like the Kivell men, but more polished in features and in movement, Laketon searched Joshua's expression. 'I'll hate it when you have to be with her.'

'I'm afraid I'll have to at some time. The old man wants me to produce a son. Tara won't be bothersome. She's simple and pliable and eager to please. An obedient child.'

'You'll have to be careful, Joshua. Is she the puppy-dog sort? Will she trot along after you? If our secret is ever discovered and Titus gets to hear of it he'll kill us both with his bare hands.'

'I promise I'll always be careful. We've both got everything to lose. Laketon, dearest, don't fret.' Joshua took command in the little hut, not a usual occurrence for it was Laketon who tended to be intense, especially when jealous. 'I promised I'd come to you tonight and what a night we will have. Let's not waste a moment of it.'

Nine

Amy heard Stumpy barking excitedly. Pleased to hear him happy again she left the Saturday baking to see what was the cause. Just inches outside the back door she was knocked off her feet. 'Ahh!' Stunned and winded, she lay in an undignified heap on the path.

Before she could call her wits together, strong, gentle hands were lifting her by the shoulders until she was sitting up. 'Amy, are you hurt?'

Blinking hurriedly, she found Sol there. 'What? Stumpy's never done anything like that before.'

'I'm sorry, it wasn't Stumpy. It was my dog, Rip. They're chasing about together. I'll keep them under control.'

Amy became aware of the two dogs barking and leaping over the stepping-stones across the stream. 'I don't want them frightening Floss, my cat,' she said indignantly.

Sol let out a sharp whistle. The barking stopped. The dogs settled with their muzzles down, sniffing their surroundings. 'I'll help you up.'

106

'I can manage.' In between giving Sol chary looks, she got up by herself and brushed the dust off her skirt. She would have bruises on her legs and elsewhere. 'I didn't think to see you here again.' He turned up at the workshop intermittently and not at all for the last three days. She and her parents had hoped not to see him again, although she wished for the chance to find out more about his friendship with Toby. Her mother was hoping to learn more too.

'I'm not tied here.' She expected his answer to be delivered with his usual uncivil, annoying cut-off manner, but he seemed more forthcoming. 'The workshop's padlocked.'

'My father's gone to collect some sandalwood from the timber merchant at Falmouth,' she replied in a lofty tone.

'For the linen chests ordered for the doctor's wife at St Day,' Sol nodded, as if in everyday conversation.

'Oh, you know about that.'

'I know what's in his order book. He's getting hopelessly behind and his timber store is low. He should have got the timber yard to deliver. Morton's work is sought after. He has the feel for wood – it's the only good thing that can be said for him. Where does he keep the key to the workshop?'

'He takes it with him.' Amy was reluctant to answer his questions but she couldn't help meeting the beguiling darkness of his eyes.

A light wind teased the tendrils of her hair falling free at her temples. Sol followed the gentle movements. 'He does have a spare one?'

'Yes.'

'Well, can you fetch it?' He leaned forward, gazing at her directly.

'I don't think he'd want you in there alone.' Amy's attention was caught by the shadows that danced across his strong face.

'Morton's got doors and window frames to make for the new houses under construction. He needs my help.' Sol never backed down from any sort of disagreement and he was enjoying the sparring.

Amy wouldn't have admitted it, but a little part of her was too. 'That's for him to say. And if you are so concerned you shouldn't have taken time off.'

Sol shrugged off the accusation. 'You want his reputation to suffer?'

Amy was vexed with his mixed messages. 'That's not your business.'

'You want your mother to worry when the orders stop because word's got round Morton Lewarne is unreliable?'

'Don't you bring my mother into this!'

He picked up a small square package he had set down on the garden wall and started off for the house. 'I'll ask her what she thinks. I want to see her anyway.'

As fast as her bruised legs would carry her, Amy went after him. 'Why do you want to see my mother? You can't. She's unwell today. She's in bed resting.'

'I'm sorry to hear that. I've got something

for her.' He held up the package.

'What is it?' Amy couldn't hide her interest.

'It's something Toby made at Burnt Oak.'

'Toby...'

Sol lowered his hand. She knew he wouldn't hand it over unless she dropped her protestations. 'You'd better come in for a moment then.' To hold on to a little status, as daughter of his employer, however strange the situation, she added firmly at the door, 'Be sure to wipe your feet.'

Once in the kitchen he put the package into her hands. With emotion climbing up her throat, she carefully unwrapped the leather wrapping and found a four-inch cube of polished wood. With a sense of reverence she lifted the hinged lid. Inside, in circular grooves, sat a set of small wooden balls as men. 'A game of solitaire. It's exquisite.' She touched one of the men. Tears gathered at her eyes. 'Toby made this by himself?'

'The box, the board and the men. He could work with confidence when he wasn't being put down. He left it with one of my younger brothers, Jowan, and he played with it each time he came back. He said that Morton would never believe he'd made it himself.'

The tears slid down Amy's face. 'Solitaire. A game for one person. I never knew he felt so alone. Poor Toby.' Sol was watching her, with a trace of hardness, she felt, as if wondering how sincere she was. The men on the board shook with her trembling and she nearly collapsed with grief, sobbing as if this was the first time she'd cried for her brother. 'Oh my God. Toby felt I let him down, didn't he? I should have done more to protect him.'

Sol took the box from her and put it on the table. Amy searched for her hanky in her apron pocket and wept into it. After a minute she shook herself back into control and dried her eyes. 'Thank you for bringing it. It will mean a lot to my mother.'

He nodded. 'I'm sorry for you both.'

Amy felt she had crossed a bridge with him. On the wrong side of it he had despised her, blaming her as a contributor to Toby's misery. 'Will you tell me what you know about Toby?'

'By and by. I should get to work. You can trust me, Amy. Morton's got some good tools, all neatly in place on hooks on the walls, but I'm not here to steal them. A crafts-man uses his own tools. I've left mine beside the workshop. Will you fetch the key?'

'It's in my father's den. Give me a moment.'

When she returned, Sol was running a hand over the little round table at the side of her father's chair. 'Please don't touch it. My father gets mad if anyone does more than run a duster over it.'

'It's a mighty interesting piece. What my second-cousin Laketon would call a quizzi-cal. Incorporating hidden compartments, with the most important ones most cleverly concealed, no doubt.' He held out his tough brown hand for the key. 'Don't worry, I won't lose it. Croust in a couple of hours?'

Against her will she handed him the key, yet

110

the kindness this wild-eyed young man had shown Toby made her feel that his word could be trusted. The solitaire would bring her mother great comfort and she was grateful for that. However, she gave an impatient sigh, 'Yes, very well.'

She had a mug of strong tea and a thick slice of freshly baked caraway seed cake on a tray ready to take out to him when he appeared once more in the kitchen. The bruises on her legs and posterior were making her move stiffly. 'Oh, I was about to—'

'Thought I'd save your legs. They must be black and blue and swollen from the bump Rip gave you. Are they?' He eyed the area covered by her skirt.

Amy met his insolent grin by pursing her lips. 'That's my business. Sit down.'

Sol chose the head of the table, ignoring her frown. 'You like to give orders. You're a bit like my Grandmama Tempest. You're probably unaware of it but sometimes you lift your chin as if everything else in the world is beneath you. I don't like that sort of cake.'

'I'll get you a saffron bun.' Amy couldn't believe she was waiting on him. Perhaps it was because she had enjoyed cosseting Toby. She wanted Sol to know this. Then she was cross with herself. It wasn't important what he thought of her. She had loved Toby and had sought to protect him from their father's bullying in every way she could. If this man thought otherwise – too bad.

What should she do now? Busy herself with

a few little jobs? Leave him here on his own? She had never been alone with a young man before, and indeed propriety forbade it for a decent girl even when she was engaged to be married. She was powerless to order him out. She must go upstairs to her mother, take the solitaire game to her; when she'd gone up earlier Sylvia had been asleep.

'My family doesn't wear black when one of us dies,' Sol said, munching on the bun.

'I wouldn't expect your family to,' she replied, making a show that she was about to leave the room, as if dismissing him.

'Why?'

'The Kivells seldom show respect.'

'We enjoy life. We celebrate the life of those who have left us.'

'Don't you grieve?'

'Of course. I didn't eat a morsel for a whole month when my mother died. My family aren't totally devil-hearted.' He had a way of raising his brows that invited a conversant to see his point of view.

Amy felt she had been rude to him. 'No, I don't suppose you all are. It was kind of you to bring the solitaire. I'll take it up to my mother.'

'She won't want you eating the midday meal alone with me, and I don't want to disturb her rest. I'll eat outside later. There's a nice spot on the garden wall.'

The mine surface workers finished early today and shortly afterward there was the buzz of chatter and the tread of boots and heavy shoes as they made their way home. Sarah tapped on the kitchen door. 'Hello. I know your father's not here. All right to come in?'

Amy was scrubbing down the table. 'Yes, do. I've got some baking put aside for you. Goodness, Sarah, you look bright. Are you going to the market?'

'No, of course not. I can't leave Mother and the little ones that long. I just fancied a few minutes chat before starting on something at home.'

'Have you agreed to see Jed Greep at last? He'd make you a good husband.'

'I think I could do better than him.' It was said with confidence, without a trace of the usual doldrums Sarah was in, and it made Amy stare at her.

'Who then?'

Twisting her work-roughened hands shyly in front of herself, blushing prettily, and now less bold, Sarah ignored the question. 'See you got that Kivell fellow here again. What's it like? Are you afraid?'

'I'm not happy about it but there's nothing about Sol to be afraid of, I think ... goodness knows how my father is going to explain the situation to Reverend Longfellow in chapel tomorrow. There must be as much talk about us in the village as there is about Tara's engagement to Joshua Nankervis. What are they saying about us up at the mine?'

'No one knows what to make of it, except to say that Mr Lewarne must be scared of the

113

Kivells for some reason,' Sarah said, offering an apologetic smile. The villagers were saying a lot of contemptuous things about Morton Lewarne. A yellow-bellied coward and a cruel father to, 'that poor little boy, God rest un,' the most common ones. Great respect was held for Sylvia Lewarne and there was a fondness for Amy, but even Godley Greep, a man of the stoutest heart, was too afraid to inquire if the Lewarnes needed any support against the Kivells. 'Has your father told you exactly why he's allowing it?'

'No,' Amy sighed, handing over a food parcel wrapped in cheese cloth for Sarah to take home. 'Mother keeps demanding to know but he just clams up.' Sarah's buoyant spirit struck her again. 'That's a pretty bonnet you're wearing.'

'It's a secret gift,' Sarah beamed, proudly patting the crisp cotton bonnet which was the colour of forget-me-nots. Her shiny black hair streamed down below it and her brown eyes gleamed.

Amy had never seen her looking so beautiful. It was good to see her carefree at last. Amy wondered if Sarah had fibbed about Jed Greep – the hardships of her life had made Sarah reluctant to reveal all about her situation. Looking her over, Amy noticed she was wearing new shoes, of strong leather with reinforced toecaps; a necessity for safety during her arduous work, but one Sarah normally was without. Earlier in the year, the Hichens family had been awarded a little Poor Relief,

114

but it would be another year before the Board could be approached again. Obviously, Sarah had a benefactor. Occasionally a chapel goer or a wealthy individual made such gestures. 'Do you mean an anonymous gift, Sarah?'

'Yes. There's been more than one. I didn't tell you at first because I was afraid I'd put a jinx on it.' Sarah rubbed her hands together like an excited little girl. 'Someone's been leaving parcels outside the back door. There's been food and clothes for all of us, and things for the house. Can't tell you what a difference it makes.' The more she went on the more she glowed a healthy pink. Sarah hoped Amy would think it was merely with the delight over her good fortune, but it was because she was sure she knew who was behind it all. Titus Kivell. Jed Greep would never be able to afford such things to impress her on his wages. The first parcel had been left the day after Titus had delivered her safely off the downs. Something inside her told her it was unwise to keep the offerings – if it was Titus, what might he demand in return? But they were things that were needed badly, and she couldn't bring herself to deny her ailing mother and Tamsyn and Arthur. She had lied at the mine about the changes, saying she had received a sudden monetary gift from a kind relative. The only family she had were the ones at home in the small shabby cottage next the Nankervis Arms and her old aunt, Molly Pentewan.

'I'm really pleased for you, Sarah. It's good

to see you happy. Will you stay and eat with me?'

'Thanks, but I'd better get along. I'm going to sit Mother outside so she can get some fresh air. We won't be seeing much more good weather, now autumn's not far off.' Sarah was suddenly wistful. 'Amy, perhaps when your baby brother or sister arrives, and if Aunt Molly will mind Mother and the little ones, we might get a chance like all the other girls and go to Redruth market one Saturday afternoon. Be nice to dress up and parade about like they do, wouldn't it?'

'Show ourselves off to the young men, you mean? So you are feeling differently in that direction?'

Sarah shrugged. Since her meeting with Titus youths like Jed Greep seemed even more unexciting. 'Not really, but it would be good, just once, to do what others take for granted. What about you? Reverend Longfellow's quite young. Not a year above thirty-five. He's quite presentable. I've seen the way he looks at you. And the baker's boy and others, for that matter.'

'I'll have too much to do looking after my mother and the new baby,' Amy replied, as serious as a scholar. She affected gaiety. 'The squire's putting on an ox roast in the field behind the church as part of the celebration for the wedding. I'm sure we could manage to slip along to that together. It'll be something to look forward to, seeing Tara married.'

'It'll be exciting for the little ones anyway.

116

Have you heard from Miss Tara lately?'

'No. She must be very busy. I don't expect there'll ever be the chance for all of us to meet again like we used to.' Putting ham and hard boiled eggs on the plates for the midday meal, Amy glanced out of the window. 'Oh, his lordship's out there, ready and waiting for his dinner to be brought to him.'

Sarah came to her side and saw Sol where he was perched comfortably on the flat top of the stone wall. 'He's very good looking, isn't he? The bal-maidens reckon he's the most handsome man hereabouts. Some of them envy you.'

'There's nothing to envy,' Amy said stiffly.

'Apart from the strangeness of him being here, isn't it rather nice having him all to yourself?' Sarah giggled, for the first time behaving with jollity and being a bit silly like her young work mates.

Amy paused to consider her answer, while trying not to find Sol an arresting sight. He was wearing a well-tailored shirt. There was a neatness about him, the sort that spoke of a man used to being attended by doting women. No doubt, he'd leave the empty tray on the wall for her to collect. She suppressed a gasp when he produced a book and began to read it. None of the Kivells had ever taken advantage of the lessons given in the Sunday schoolroom in the evenings by the Reverend Longfellow. She'd assumed Sol to be someone who would scorn formal learning. 'Well, if that Kivell there is anything to go by, then

117

I'll say they keep you guessing, so they're not exactly boring.'

'And not as fierce and as dangerous as they seem?' Sarah said, gazing into space. 'That's reassuring.'

Halfway through the afternoon, with her father expected home soon, Amy took to wondering what Sol was actually doing in the workshop. Morton didn't like her or Sylvia interrupting him, but he'd be furious with her for not checking up on Sol. She carried out a mug of tea to him as the perfect excuse. On her approach there was silence. No sawing, no use of a plane. Was he lazing the time away? He wasn't inside but he had been busy for there was the strong smell of wood dust. The fine particles floating in the dry air pointed to the job of sanding. A mahogany bookcase, with a curved head, and pendant finials between the stepped curved feet, was standing ready on the covered floor for varnishing. The piece was precision crafted. This quality of work would do no harm to her father's business.

Where was Sol? Putting the tea down, Amy went outside and peered round the corner of the workshop. He was a short distance away on the moor, smoking, throwing sticks for the dogs.

On a sudden thought, she went quickly to his work bench. As she had hoped, his jacket was hanging up on a hook nearby and she rifled through his pockets for her scarf. There was a folded handkerchief, tobacco and

118

papers and some coins. Impressed by the silk lining of the jacket, she pushed her hand into the inside breast pocket.

'Didn't take you for a pickpocket.'

'Oh!' She whirled round, her face on fire, her heart thudding at having been caught out, annoyed to be made to feel guilty. 'I only want back what is rightfully mine.'

Sol came so close there was no possibility of her easing herself away from him. She was hemmed in against the whitewashed wall. 'Your pretty yellow and red scarf is at Burnt Oak. If you want it you only have to go there to get it.'

She gave him a look of scorn. What a cheek! 'Why have you kept it?'

'It pleases me.' He wasn't sure why himself, except that he'd like his grandmother to meet this girl. There was a sweetness about Amy, an alluring fragility, but she was also a fighter.

Part of her wanted to see more of his community and his mysterious relatives. Until recently, the only ones usually to be seen were the men who patronized the inns and the occasional woman, in distinctive finely trimmed, home-dyed clothes, who'd ventured to the shops. 'If I was to go to your home, would you tell me more about Toby? I'd like to learn about the time you rescued him. Would I be safe?'

'You can learn all you want about the times Toby spent with us.' Then, with a patently slow trawl down over her body with his coal-dark eyes and lowering his voice to a husky tone, he went on, 'And you'll be as safe as you want to be.'

As his eyes came back to her face, Amy found it necessary to turn away. His gaze was unacceptably familiar, and unsettling in a way she couldn't define. She was disturbed by him yet drawn to him and she didn't like this range of feelings. 'You said us, as if that includes your family. You often speak as if you're all one entity. You must be very close.' She'd noticed the affection when he spoke of his grandmother, Tempest Kivell. Amy was curious about her. Tempest Kivell was spoken of in the village in whispers. She was rumoured to be able to read thoughts, to see spirits and make predictions. She was a witch, some said, on former witches' land. A shiver ran down Amy's spine. Did Tempest Kivell know she was thinking about her at this moment?

'We've found it necessary over the years to stand firmly together or fall apart.' Leaning against the square trestle, for various fitting jobs, in the middle of the floor, Sol drank his tea. 'You've no kinsmen close by. Why is that? No, don't tell me. I think I know. It's because they all hate Morton. He turned his back on his own family and alienated all of your mother's.'

'Anyone in Meryen could have told you that. That's not quite right, all my mother's family are dead.' Amy was uncomfortable with the knowledge that it was only because of her mother's charitable heart that visitors had dropped into Chy-Henver. Now, because of Morton's dalliance with the Kivells, only Sarah was ever likely to darken the doorstep again. 'Why are you here? It's not because you want a job, that's a ridiculous notion. Have my mother and I anything to fear?'

'You need not be afraid of me, Amy,' Sol said, drifting away in his thoughts for a moment.

She believed him, but she was suddenly nervous. His answer had implied there might be another to be afraid of. Titus, it could be no other.

'You should know, Amy, that I won't be coming here for much longer.' He felt he owed her and her mother this explanation. 'I'm planning to go off and find my own way in the world, you see.'

She didn't feel reassured, as she would have done this morning by the news. She nodded and left the workshop with a troubled heart. It wouldn't be wise, but as soon as her mother had delivered the baby, and before Sol went away, she would seek an opportunity to go to Burnt Oak and try to discover what hold Titus Kivell had over her father.

Ten

Long before dawn put in an appearance on her wedding day, Tara got out of bed and went to the window. There was an autumnal chill and she shivered in her nightgown but she was too numb to reach for a shawl. She was experiencing odd flashes of panic, for apart from her hope that Joshua would prove to be a sympathetic husband, she was feeling dead inside and she welcomed the cold to help her feel alive and that somehow, somewhere, she actually mattered. Everything seemed unreal. Formless. She was just going through the motions of what she was being told she must do and her existence was verging on becoming an unending nightmare. Things were happening too fast, every decision had been made without her involvement, and she felt a spectator rather than a participant in her own preparations.

She closed her eyes and opened them again. Panic turned her insides to pulp and her legs to water – she was still here at Poltraze, trapped in this dark, brooding, musty old house. The mist rising up above the trees made them murky and seem closer than they really were, and like ominously cloaked guards keeping her prisoner. With all her passion she wished herself back in the quiet little house in Penzance. There, she had felt she was shrivelling up inside but it seemed utterly desirable to what now lay ahead, which was to do only what was expected of her, to do only what she was told.

She'd had no say in what her wedding dress was to be like. She was getting a billowing contrivance covered with an outrageous froth of lace and garlands of artificial red rosebuds on the skirt. It had a low decolletage and ribbons all the way down the wrist-length sleeves. All that, and a ridiculously long train! Michael's daughters, Cecily and Jemima, a five-and-four year pair of deceptively looking blonde cherubs, were to be her bridesmaids. The matter of what they were to wear – their dresses too were overstated nonsense – and the flowers they'd all carry had created friction between their mother and her Aunt Estelle. Nothing had been resolved until, thankfully, Joshua had intervened, forcefully and masterfully, and declared the girls would have posies of pink and white rosebuds from his greenhouse, and specimens of iris and lily would make up the bride's bouquet. Tara might as well consist of fresh air – not that there was much fresh air to be found inside Poltraze. If it hadn't already been old and stale, for the windows were never opened for fear of contracting some contagious disease, and cholera was rumoured to be stalking the locality again, the older women's bitchy quarrels would have turned it sour.

She returned to her bed and curled up under the covers. This was the last time she would use this bed. Tonight she would sleep with Joshua. Fear once again wrapped around her. Atkins had hinted that the intimate duties of a wife were terrible, something to be endured. 'Whatever happens, just close your eyes and keep remembering it won't go on forever.' Tara decided that Atkins, as an old maid, knew little or nothing about sex.

Aunt Estelle had not mentioned the wedding night. Tentatively, Tara had asked, 'I will be all right, won't I?'

Estelle had thought she was fretting about the marriage service and had drilled into her how she must keep her head up and stomach in, hold her bouquet just so, put on a bright but demure smile, and not to let the Nankervises down. Now she and Tara had become respectable again, Estelle had written to her brother in Yorkshire and he had agreed to travel down and give Tara away. Tara had seen little of her rotund Uncle George, who looked prosperous in a pompous way and smelled of some strong liniment. It was anathema to her to have to submit to being escorted up the aisle by a relative, who until a short time ago, wouldn't have lifted a finger to keep her out of the gutter.

She closed her eyes and tried to get a few minutes' sleep but it was useless. She held back her tears. If she started to cry she wouldn't be able to stop, on this, what she believed was going to be one of the worse days of her life.

Amy and Sarah, with Tamsyn and Arthur in front of them, joined the crowds on the opposite side of the road of the church to watch the wedding. Most onlookers were Methodists and had only turned up out of nosiness and to take advantage of the ox roast that was to be had immediately after the ceremony. There were grumbles about the squire's orders to the local constables to keep everyone except the guests outside of the heavy iron lychgate, and allow no one to peep over the surrounding stone and natural hedgerows.

'Squire's got no right to exclude anyone from a house of God,' a male onlooker complained.

''Es, squire's too hard,' another bawled out, bravely ignoring a constable, who was a smallholder, and was armed with a cosh and sported an aggressive scowl. 'I pity that poor young maid marrying into that family. What have they ever done for any of we round here? We don't even get a fowl or a blanket at Christmastide. If I was a betting man I'd wager this ox will be a poor beast. Other gentry folk look after their tenants. The Nankervises are a heartless lot, to their eternal shame.'

Amy was vexed that the order meant she had no access to Toby's grave and would have to wait to place on it the flowers she had brought.

Traps and carriages began to arrive. There

125

were oohs and aahs over the attire of the alighting guests, and some snickering over the ones considered to be 'dressed to death'. The chatter turned to a sour note when the woman, whom the villagers loathed and referred to as Mrs Phoebe, turned up. Girls from Meryen who had been taken on as maids at the big house had fallen foul of her pedantic ways and cruel dismissals without being given a character. Some observers remarked that her daughters were like, 'dear little angels, bless 'em'. A heavy, purposeful silence reigned when the squire and his reunited wife came shortly afterward. Estelle, haughty and stunning in shades of green, flounced up the four, long granite steps, through the lychgate, then along the narrow churchyard path, newly cleared of weeds, as if she and her husband were the two most important people in the world.

'Pride cometh before a fall,' Godley Greep intoned, and there was a unanimous murmur of agreement, and the hope it would come true in this case.

A little cheering broke out when the groom and his brother, the best man, pulled up in a beribboned landau. Wreathed in smiles, Joshua waved regally to the people. Michael managed a brief condescending smile.

The bride arrived traditionally late in the Nankervis coach. The crowd clapped and called out best wishes, and speculated on who the gentleman, 'with a face like a trout's backside', was. 'Don't seem happy to be here, does he?' Godley Greep ruminated.

'Who do you think he is?' Sarah, in her new bonnet and a new blue and yellow dress, spoke into Amy's ear to be heard above the hubbub. 'Her dress is a bit too much, don't you think?'

'It must be her uncle from Yorkshire,' Amy replied in Sarah's inclined ear. 'And yes, there must be enough material in that dress to clothe every little girl in the village. Poor Tara.' Poor Tara indeed. She had dreadful relatives and now she was to get dreadful in-laws. Thank goodness her bridegroom appeared to be a thoughtful man.

Tara was heartened to see Amy and gave her a friendly wave.

'God bless you, Miss Tara. Good luck,' Amy called out.

Tara recognized the girl beside Amy. Amy had written about Sarah and her growing beauty. Of herself and Sarah, Tara pondered, as her uncle pulled her along to her fate, which one of them faced the worse future? She, to be constantly overruled by her aunt and stifled at Poltraze, or Sarah, enduring a multitude of hardships?

Tara played her part in the church to perfection, without faltering a word of her vows, giving a mistimed step, or a reduction of appropriate smiles. I'd make an excellent actress, she thought, as she signed the register in the little vestry, I've given nearly as good a performance of being sincere as most of these people whose name I now bear.

When all the guests had gone and with the churchyard empty, Amy made a lone journey to the small mound of earth where Toby lay. When the ground had settled he was to have a headstone, a fine one, for Morton, in the hope that Sylvia would come round to him, had declared nothing would be stinted in giving his son a fitting memorial. Sylvia had been well enough to visit the grave. She'd allowed Sol, to Morton's muted disapproval, to bring a trap over from Burnt Oak and drive her here and back.

'It's just me today,' Amy said, laying down the flowers, talking aloud as she always did, as if Toby could hear her. She told him about the wedding. 'You'd have enjoyed the ox roast that's to come. There's a fair too, with stalls and cheap jacks. Can you hear the noise? People sound happy. It's all going on just on the other side of the wall. Sol knew I was coming here today. He sends his respects. I'm quite looking forward to going to Burnt Oak when I get the chance, to find out for myself why you liked it there so much.'

She was curious to learn if Sol behaved at home in the same manner as he did at Chy-Henver. He was quite a fusion. He worked hard, at other times languorously. He'd whistle, or sing, or swear, or keep silent. He was always considerate to her mother, and nearly always disrespectful to her father, often baiting him, occasionally quite cruelly, and Amy would find herself demanding that he stop it; after all, her father was her father, even though she loathed his mean ways. She and Sol either bickered or talked seriously about Toby. Yesterday he'd told her how Toby had taken to the lurcher puppy who'd lost its tail, and how he'd laid on the floor at his grandmother's feet and drawn a picture of Pixie Cross, complete with pixies at moonlight, which he'd exchanged for Stumpy with his brother, Jowan. She found herself thinking about Sol a lot and told herself it was only in regard to his association with Toby, yet on the days he didn't come to work, Chy-Henver seemed strangely empty.

As she was making to leave and join the festivities, she realized she wasn't the only one in the churchyard.

She left by the back gate and sought out Sarah in the field. It was a bustling scene, with the carts and waggons of tinkers and quack medicine salesmen. There were sideshows, and peddlers and gypsies and performing animals. They got in the queue for a thick slice of spit-roasted beef, pleased it was from a prime animal. The cooking smells were mouth-watering to those, in the majority, who did not often have a full dinner table and the whole prospect of a feast and entertainment was exciting in everyone's usually dull life. Vats of vegetables and trays of bread and butter and mugs of tea were spread out on trestle tables. Darius Nankervis had also supplied half a dozen barrels of beer, and many non-religious people and atheists were well on the way to getting drunk.

As Tamsyn and Arthur were spending the rest of the day with their Aunt Molly, Sarah was alone. 'Despite the fussiness of the dress, Miss Tara really did look as beautiful as any bride could wish,' Sarah said. Her remark was said in a mature matter-of-fact way rather than the dreamy fashion of bride-to-be Peggy Wetter and many of the girls and women. 'Like a princess.'

'And as pale and wan as a heroine from a tragic legend. I hope she'll be all right.'

''Course she will!' Sarah was astonished at the notion. 'She'll have servants and every fine thing that she could possibly want. She's got herself a good looking husband too.'

'I suppose so. And Mr Joshua's young. Some girls of their class are married off to doddering old men.'

'I don't think age should matter.'

'In a husband? That's a curious thing for someone to say who's not even interested in getting married. How have you come up with that?'

'I don't know,' Sarah looked away, becoming evasive. 'It just came to me.'

'Oh, you'll never guess who was in the churchyard just now. A Kivell. Never thought to see one of them there.'

'Which Kivell?' Sarah tried not to sound sharp.

'Laketon. A rather refined individual compared to the rest of his family. He was staring towards the church porch. I got the impression he'd lost something.'

130

'Oh, him,' Sarah said dismissively, her mind going to Titus. She was finding it difficult to get him out of her mind. It had to be his doing, the continuing gifts left on her back doorstep. She could hardly wait to get out of bed each day and see what new things might be there. This morning there had been some florins wedged in the rind of a thick slab of bacon. It meant she and the children had money to spend at the stalls today. Perhaps she'd get her fortune told. She decided against it. She might hear something she didn't want to hear, that this wonderful turn of events might come to an end, although the generosity received so far meant she'd never have to struggle in quite the same way as before. One thing concerned her. What if the benefactor wasn't Titus? The thought was frightening, just as it was that it actually was him. Titus might have saved her from a terrifying night on the downs but the man was someone to be feared. And, whoever it was, why was he, or she for that matter, giving her and her family so many fine things without making himself or herself known?

Suddenly Sarah wished the gifts would stop and to never find out who was behind it all. The shine had been taken off the day and she was glad that she and Amy weren't planning to stay on here after they'd eaten. They had to look after their respective mothers, and today for Sarah, tending the difficult needs of her helpless mother didn't seem such a chore.

Eleven

Although a lot of patrons of the Nankervis Arms were taking advantage of the free beer at the ox roast, there was still some activity at the inn, including some raucous singing, and Sarah walked past it quickly and cautiously. She had been propositioned more than once by drunken louts lurching about over the cobbles. 'What a place to live next to,' she sighed. Others who had lived in Moor Cottage had moved out as soon as they could afford something better. It was unlikely there was a chance of her and her family doing that.

It was unusual to lock doors in the daytime in Meryen, but for her mother's safety, in case she hobbled outside and wandered off, Sarah did so when she went out. It was also necessary to keep Nancy Hichens away from the villagers. The brain damage she had suffered had left her face badly scarred and lop-sided and people, especially children, tended to be afraid of her. Nancy had been chased away and even knocked into a ditch by unsympathetic folk she had chanced upon. To Sarah's anger and dismay stones had been thrown at her too. It was one of the things that had led to Sarah's former inclination to depression.

Now she was having concerns about her mystery benefactor she was fighting the feelings of once more sliding down into the dumps.

Outside the rough planked door of her home, she lifted up a block of granite where she kept the big iron key and let herself in. She put on a smile, deciding she would try to stay positive. 'Mum, it's me! I've bought you something nice to eat. A pasty and a lovely rock bun, your favourites.'

Nancy was in her spindleback chair, her head lolling to the side, dribbling, her twisted left arm hanging down and swinging near the stone floor. Sarah wrinkled her nose. Her mother needed some urgent attention to her hygiene. Before the mysterious bounty that had given Nancy more clothes, it had been a terrible task to find something for her to wear while her clothes were in the wash. 'Don't worry, Mum, I'll soon sort you out.'

Sarah took off her bonnet then laid an old blanket over her mother's bed, which amounted to straw-stuffed sacking on a bench, in the corner of the cottage; at least there was some proper bedding on it now. Like many of the older dwellings there was only one room on the ground floor. There were no proper stairs and the next storey consisted of no more than a platform, called a talfat, reached by a ladder. It was up there, on straw mattresses, that Sarah and her sister and brother slept. Furniture in the cottage was made up of one chair, the settle, a three-legged stool, a small pine table, a leather-strapped trunk, a wonky dresser and a rag mat, all third-or-fourth-hand. Table linen and brightly patterned cups and platters, a jug and a copper kettle, and a glass vase, all recently provided, gave colour and optimism to the dismal place. Even in summer the un-equal walls, which bulged here and there as the cob ominously redistributed itself, felt cold and damp.

After a struggle to get the thin, wasted Nancy, who struggled in panic at being hauled about, up out of the chair and to lie down on the bed, Sarah took off her soiled skirt and petticoat and the rag that served as a nappy. Patiently, she washed and dried her, and tied on a clean rag above the protruding bones of her hips. Then she put her in a nightgown, combed her long tangled hair, and finished off by fitting on a mob cap. 'There, that's better isn't it, Mum? Hope you're comfortable now.'

Nancy drifted off to sleep and Sarah left her in peace. She'd feed her the treats later. After opening the windows wide in the hope of freshening the foul air, she put the soiled things in a tub of soapy water to soak. The soap was a real luxury and smelled of violets; again a gift. Sarah's previous poverty still made her stretch everything to the last ounce or sliver but she didn't stint on the never ending task of trying to make her mother smell nice. Nancy slept for hours at a time, a blessing for it meant she never realized how

134

long she had to spend on her own, and Sarah considered returning to the fair. It was rare to get a chance to mix with others and see a bit of life but it seemed wrong to desert her mother for another long period. She'd sit outside and eat her own pasty, let the sun warm her, take advantage of these precious free moments.

There was a knock on the door. The Hichens rarely had visitors. Sarah frowned and looked out of the small window beside the door. Jed Greep was outside. 'Sarah, hello, it's Jed! Can I speak to you for a minute, please?'

What's the point? Sarah wanted to call back through the door. She didn't feel a spark of anything for the persistent youth, who'd made sheep's eyes at her while she'd been at the ox roast. But he had overcome his shyness and taken the trouble to follow her and ask to see her at her home, so she felt she must at least answer the door.

'Hello Jed,' she said, opening the door a crack. Embarrassed, she hoped Jed wouldn't notice the smells made by her mother's incontinence. 'Shush. My mother's asleep.'

Jed turned his cap round nervously in his long thin hands. His face was bright pink and twitchy. 'Sorry. I was wondering, that is to say, are you going back? To the fair, I mean? We could go together, if you want. I mean, I'd be honoured if you'd walk back with me?'

Sarah felt sorry about spurning him but all she wanted was for him to leave. 'I can't leave my mother again. It wouldn't be right.'

'Well, I understand. It's good of you to think of her.' Jed swallowed and went pale. 'Um, w—would you like some company?'

'Not really,' she half-closed her eyes, hoping he'd received the message.

'Oh, I see. Perhaps another time, eh?'

'Perhaps. Thanks for calling. You go back and enjoy yourself.'

'All right.' His chin drooped and he stepped away reluctantly. As Sarah was closing the door he made one more attempt to capture her attention. 'See you in chapel tomorrow?'

'I don't know. I'll have to see. Goodbye.' She closed the door with some relief. Then knew a moment of unease. Why wasn't she like other girls? Most would fly at the chance to have a pleasant young man like Jed Greep calling on them. Life was complicated, even more so now she had taken in charity and displayed it by wearing the new clothes at work and in the village. She went to the hearth and coaxed the banked-in fire into life and put the kettle on the hook to boil for tea.

A minute later there was another knock on the door. Cross now, thinking Jed had returned, she marched to the door to thrust it open and get rid of him more determinedly. There could never be anything between them and he might as well accept it. 'Oh!' Titus Kivell was standing there, tall, brawny and resolute.

'Hello, Sarah.' He leaned forward, putting his arm against the door frame.

136

'Hello.' Nothing more would come out of her lips. His intense dark eyes fixed her to the spot.

'Was that boy bothering you?'

'What? Jed? No, not at all,' she answered quickly. If Titus thought that, he'd likely frighten Jed off, perhaps do something worse to him.

'Good, I'm glad to hear it. Let me know if anyone ever does bother you and I'll sort things out. Aren't you going to invite me in?'

'I ... yes, if you want to,' she faltered. 'It's not very pleasant in here, I'm afraid. I've just had to tend to my mother.'

'I very much want to see you, Sarah.' Titus advanced on her and she moved aside so he could duck his head under the low portal and enter the cottage. He shut the door after him. He smiled and kept a straight face. If he noticed the unpleasant odours he didn't show it. 'How are you?'

'I'm well, thank you.' She felt small and vulnerable. Should she ask if he was responsible for helping her and the family? She didn't want to seem ungrateful, but if it was someone else, she got the strong idea that he would be jealous, perhaps cause trouble.

'You look less and less troubled as the days go by. I've been watching you.'

Sarah gulped and blood burned a path up over her neck and face all the way to her hairline. 'You have? It was you? Leaving things for us?'

'I thought you'd be pleased to have a few

things to make your life easier. I left them anonymously so as not to embarrass you in case you should feel you ought to refuse. I'll help you in any way I can, Sarah. If you need anything, anything at all, if you ever need any help, don't be afraid to ask.'

Almost too nervous to breathe, awkward and shy, she asked, 'Why are you being so kind to me, to us?'

'It's easy to be kind to you, Sarah. You've had a hard life. You're struggling but you keep on trying. You're brave. You touched my heart that night you fell on the downs.'

'Do you, I ... do you want something back from me?' She felt compelled to ask and was terrified of the answer, trembling all over, shrinking back from him.

'All I ask, Sarah, is that you trust me.' He smiled a deep warm smile and Sarah managed to return it. He looked around the place, squalid, dark and bleak despite the additions from his generosity. 'You shouldn't have to live like this. If you let me, I'll do something about it.'

Sarah saw her home through his eyes and she was ashamed. Tears flooded her eyes. 'It would be nice for the little ones and my mother if we could get out of here.'

'Trust me, Sarah.' He reached out and touched her hair. 'Don't cry. Come here to me.' Before she could make up her mind whether to approach him or not he moved in on her and she found herself nestled in his arms. He was strong and solid and she felt

138

herself to be in a safe place for the first time in her life. Tension drifted from her, she buried her face against his chest and her tears, of past pain and relief, flowed freely.

Titus stroked her hair. 'You've got such pretty hair, Sarah. You're lovely, beautiful.' His sight fell on the gruesome, curled up spectacle of Nancy, slumbering with her mouth wide open, saliva seeping from the corner of her mouth. His eyes turned hard. 'No, my dear one, you shouldn't live like this. I'm going to look after you.'

For some moments he held Sarah against him, caressing her hair, her back and her arms. Then he tilted her head back and gazed at her. He pressed his lips to her cheeks and kissed away her tears. Sarah shivered. 'Don't be afraid. I'll never hurt you.'

She received her first kiss on the lips, the kiss of a man to a woman, and for her it was strange and daunting and wonderful.

Tara lay in Joshua's low post bed, waiting for him to come to her. What was taking him so long? What preparations did a bridegroom need to make for his wedding night?

What a horrible day it had been. She had endured glowers and sarcasm from Phoebe's bitter tongue, and to her fury at her aunt and the stupid dressmaker, the tittering about her dreadful dress. At least some of the servants had seemed more respectful towards her on her arrival back at the house as the second-in-importance Mrs Nankervis. And to her surprise, Michael had been polite and friendly. To escape the tumult of voices baying to be noticed, and the dancing, an exercise virtuously beyond her dense dress, she had slipped away to the library.

The curtains were kept almost closed during the day to prevent the light spoiling the antiquated books, maps and family records. Lanterns illuminated one dark corner and Michael had glanced up from a red leather club chair, where he had a book in his hands. He took off his spectacles. 'Ah, sister-in-law, I don't blame you for feeling the need to get away from the melee.'

'I'm sorry if I'm disturbing you, Michael.'

'You may wander where you will in the house, Tara, but I do appreciate having this room to myself. I hate crowded places. I prefer as much peace as possible. So does the old house. It's complaining at being packed to capacity. I can hear its timbers groaning and whispering to the trees how fortunate they are to be free.'

'You can?' Tara had intended to make an immediate withdrawal but she moved closer to him and stood in front of the fireplace. The surrounding plaster mantelpiece, which reached up to the ceiling, was ugly and had faces of Nankervis children who had not survived infancy or their formative years incorporated in it. Tara thought it tasteless. Here, as in all the family rooms of the house there was a tender likeness of Jeffrey Nankervis.

'I'm the only one who's sensitive to the house. It's an unhappy place, but of course, you know that. Did you know nine men were killed during its various stages of construction? Two fell off scaffolding. One was killed by falling tiles. One architect, a fellow of no account and little inspiration, died of heart failure, a deserved just end, during the raising of the Long Corridor. Septimus Bloombury was his name. He haunts the corridor day and night, it's why even when the house is entertaining there is very little real merriment. Septimus howls during storms, the house keeps the echoes of his voice for days. The house broods. It consumes. Sucks out one's soul. I was livid at first to be consigned to the Dower House, now I'm delighted. It's as dismal as a ditch but there's nothing there that can't be put right with some decoration. Phoebe's nagging me to approach the old man to grant us a few thousand so work can commence.'

Tara had got a strong foreboding during Michael's morbid account. She had often felt the strange sensation of being watched when walking along the Long Corridor but had attributed it to being spied on by human eyes. Ghosts were going to make the company here even less palatable. 'I hope Mr Nankervis allows it. I'm pleased you're happy there, Michael. I was worried about how you felt when your father demanded you live there.'

'I shall always hate him for turning me out,' Michael's long face expressed darkness,

141

giving him a boldness, then he became matter-of-fact. 'Mind you, I've always hated him. He's a man to be hated, and he doesn't care a tinker's cuss that he's hated. I'm sorry, I suppose you only want to hear happy things on your wedding day. If I may say, you don't look very happy.'

'It's a bit of a strain.'

'I understand. Don't let anyone bully you, Tara. Find ways to cope. It's what I do.'

'Thank you, Michael.' She had thanked him because he'd brought her a small measure of comfort, and the hope that she had an ally in the house.

She lay in her marriage bed and listened. Could she hear Poltraze speaking? Was it really as threatening as Michael had stressed? Perhaps Michael was simply just imaginative. He had a studious mind and was a keen novel reader. Would the house grow content tomorrow when all the overnight guests, including her buffoon of an uncle, left? If the house was placated she would certainly feel more at ease. If only her husband would join her and this first night as man and wife would be over.

The clock chimed one o'clock. She was getting ever more irritated. Bridegrooms were supposed to be eager to consummate their vows. Joshua was unfeeling. She studied the brass carriage clock. It was a plain item. Everything in the room was the same, of distinctly undecorated masculine appeal, with no dashes of colour or frivolous lines. She'd have thought someone could have at least put some flowers in the room as a thoughtful welcome to her.

The connecting door of Joshua's dressing room was opened, at last. Tara froze. A surge of shyness overtook her. She wanted to close her eyes and hope he would think her asleep and not disturb her, but she was too driven by demands of duty to try deception. Her eyes followed Joshua as he approached the bed.

'I thought I'd give you time to feel settled.' He slipped off his dressing gown and draped it over a chair and stood, a little uncertainly, Tara thought, in his nightshirt. 'It's been an exhausting day. You must be weary to the bones, poor thing.'

'I can't say I'm sorry it's over.' It took an effort not to choke on the words, now The Moment was nearly upon her.

He went about the room turning out the lamps, then after sliding his feet out of his slippers he got into the bed. He lay down flat, keeping to his own side. 'I've had a word with Estelle. I've told her she must allow you to consult your dressmaker on your own from now on. The wedding dress was bloody awful. Goodness knows what sort of a statement she was trying to make through it. I'm sorry you had to endure wearing such an overdone creation. My dear, I want you to know that if you're worried about anything you only have to come to me. I'm here to protect you.'

Tara had been lying rigidly but his kind words made her move an inch towards him. 'Thank you, Joshua.'

He moved on to his side and edged a bit closer to her, then again, and again, as if he was trying not to rush her. Finally, she could feel his body against hers. He took her hand in his. 'You are quite the sweetest thing, Tara. If we work together, yet allow each other space we'll be happy that way. Do you see?'

'Yes Joshua.' She didn't mind his nearness. He was warm and smelled good. They lay, both breathing heavily, aware of the other's noisy breath. Tara was heartened by the notion that he was nervous too. He made a little apologetic sound. Then bringing his head forward he kissed her cheek. Tara wasn't sure if she should respond or how to. She waited. He took her hand in his, raised it to his lips and kissed it, the merest touch. She could just make out his face in the darkness and saw that he had closed his eyes. She thought it best to close hers. She was nervous but she wanted to become intimate with Joshua, to form this closest bond with him. He was a good man and she wanted their marriage to be a success. She set aside her anxieties and told herself she was lucky to have him, with his good looks and fine qualities, as her husband.

His hand began to travel over her, here and there, lightly, as if timidly, outside of her nightdress. Then as if he was suddenly in a hurry he leaned over her and kissed her lips, with feather-lightness. No more kisses came. Tara thought there should be more kisses. He touched her neck and cupped a hand over her breast, for a second. Tara breathed in deeply. His hand made a tentative journey to her most womanly region. He took it away almost at once and moved to his side of the bed. 'It's been a long trying day for you, my dear. You've had enough to put up with. We'll ... join together another time. You get some sleep. You deserve it. I'm a light sleeper myself. I always rise very early. I might get up through the night. I'll try not to disturb you. You have breakfast in bed tomorrow. I'll see you at luncheon. Goodnight, Tara.' He turned away from her.

'Goodnight Joshua.' She put her back to his back, not sure whether to be pleased about him being sensitive towards her or to be dreadfully disappointed. She was still awake when he got up about an hour later and left the room.

Laketon Kivell was waiting for Joshua in the hut in the woods, lying on the bunk in pitch blackness. He had turned out the lantern, unable to bear to look at the cosy and sumptuous additions Joshua had made to make this meeting place of their very own. Nothing would be the same again now he was bound to that whey-faced girl, now Joshua was no longer exclusively his. Joshua had promised he'd not take her tonight and Laketon believed him, but the very thought of the man he loved sharing a bed with anyone else for even a few minutes tormented him, scourged him, mocked him.

Damn Darius Nankervis and his wishes!

145

Damn life! Damn the order of things that denied him and Joshua the freedom to express their love. He hated sharing anything, Joshua most of all. When Joshua did pierce the girl – and he'd have to continue doing so until she had delivered a living male child, the heir that was demanded – he could then shun his wife, but he'd have a son to pull at his attention then.

In Laketon's grasp was a wine bottle and he lifted it to his full lips and drained the last drop. Then he hurled it across the hut where it smashed loudly against the wall. It was a dangerous, selfish thing to do. Joshua might walk into the splinters in the darkness and hurt himself, but Joshua knew the risks at the beginning when taking up with him, he knew wild and dangerous Kivell blood flowed through his veins. Today Joshua had obeyed his father, and even though he'd had no choice, Laketon considered that it was only him he should answer to.

Twelve

'Can I come in?' Morton hovered at Sylvia's bedroom door. Before she told him to go away, as she always did, he added quickly, 'I told Amy I'd come up and collect your lunch tray. She said you've got an upset tummy.'

'It's just a bit of wind.' Sylvia stared straight ahead, grim and unyielding. 'I've eaten all I want to. You can take the tray downstairs.'

Morton shot to the tray, which Sylvia had set aside on a nearby chair – before this he wouldn't have dreamed of doing anything considered as women's work. 'You've hardly touched your food again, dear. Is the wind bad? I could slip along to the apothecary and get something for you.'

'I'll be fine.' She did not move a muscle but her eyes glinted with irritation that he was there.

Morton lingered. 'Sol Kivell's here today.'

'I know.'

'He's a good worker.'

'I know. Pity you didn't think the same about my son.' Why on earth was he complimenting Sol? Sol was only ever terse and uncooperative with him.

'I do regret the way I treated the boy, Sylvia.

I want you to believe that.'

'My son had a name. Toby.'

Morton gave a silly, unsure laugh. 'Trouble with me, I'm too much of a perfectionist. I should have been more patient with Toby, I can see that now. My father was hard on me. You know how he was. I thought it was how all men behaved with their sons. To get the best out of them.'

'You were hard on Toby because he was small and sensitive. I told you often enough to be kinder to him, to show him the love of the Lord Jesus, but you'd never listen. You were a bully and a tormentor. It's no good trying to get round me.' She was certain he wanted life to return to normal so he could use her in bed again after the birth of the child, and it disgusted her.

Morton loitered in the room, his desperate mind trying to come up with something to break down Sylvia's hostile barrier. He knew she had never loved him but they had been mainly content in the early years – until Toby had been born. Sylvia had called the scrawny boy 'the apple of her eye', and Amy had doted on him. As the series of miscarriages had left him without the kind of son he'd desired, he'd fitted more and more into the character Sylvia had just given him. Now the chances were good of Sylvia giving birth to a live child he hated the thought of being left out of his family for good. 'I know I did wrong. At least, despite Sol being a Kivell, he's someone whom Toby liked and trusted. Toby might have been glad Sol's taken his place.'

Sylvia tightened her lips. It should not have been necessary for anyone else to work at Toby's bench. Whether Titus Kivell would have demanded his son be given a job if Toby had not died was irrelevant to her. 'Sol's not going to be here much longer. Then what?' *Go. Go. Get out of my room. Get out of my life.*

Morton didn't answer. The future, at least for Sylvia and Amy was more uncertain than they thought. 'Sol's mentioned that he's heard the squire's already preparing to leave for London. Things are going to be different round here now, I shouldn't wonder. Might be better.' Morton tried a friendly grin, the way it emerged made him look stupid.

'I know about the squire. And Sol told that to Amy, not you. Don't try to pretend you like the young man.'

Morton's pointed chin fell nearly to his chest. He hated Sol to bursting point, but he needed him. He'd spent too much time with his paramour, a rough-mannered, quick-witted vamp, who was a specialist in her trade. He had thought Marcie Dunn enormous fun and thought himself clever and sharp to be living a double life. He had fallen in with Marcie's wild friends. Drinking and cards was their favourite pastime and the stakes had got out of hand. Morton was a poor player and to keep up – and Marcie's services didn't come cheap – he hadn't paid a bill for over a year. With the unpaid work he'd been forced to do for the wretched squire it meant

149

he was in serious debt. If Sol could be persuaded to come every day, at the worthy pace he worked, and if he, himself, refused to join in any more gambling, Morton saw a glimmer of a way out of his problems. He had been foolish and now he must mend his ways – except for Marcie, he couldn't give up that side of life. And with rage simmering inside him, he had to keep grovelling to his wife. 'Please Sylvia, don't keep on behaving coldly. Please don't keep shutting me out. It's driving me crazy.'

'Good,' Sylvia finally looked at him, with abrasiveness, without pity. His mien was pathetic, she wanted to slap his face. Ignoring the pain in her back she let rip, 'Perhaps you'll understand how you made poor Toby feel! You shut him out of your heart. You made him feel inferior. You made his life hardly worth living. I've had plenty of time to think, laid up in the house, time to think about what happened. Toby could have climbed that tree and jumped! He might have felt it was the only way out. You terrorized him, your own son, Morton Lewarne. You threatened to send him down into the darkness of the mine. It's you who should be suffering darkness. The eternal kind!'

Morton could barely keep himself in check. The woman should know her place, her main duty was to him, no matter what went on inside her silly head. Silly? She was a disobedient, oh-so-respectable bitch. 'Don't go on like this, you'll make yourself ill.'

'You don't care how I feel! You only care about what's good for you. Oh, get out, before I forget myself and throw something at you.' Sylvia searched about the bed looking for something with which to carry out her threat.

'Damn you!' Morton could take no more. All thoughts of wheedling Sol Kivell into full time employment was forgotten and if Kivell wasn't downstairs at this moment he'd slap Sylvia across the mouth. He hoped she'd die giving birth and the baby went with her. Then he'd ask Marcie to marry him and have his comforts always at hand. If Amy didn't like it she could move out. And the village could go to hell for all he cared. In fact, he didn't really have to care that much because he had a way out of his troubles, and if things didn't pick up soon, he'd damn well take it. He stamped out of the room.

'The same to you!' Sylvia shouted after him. 'You didn't even take the tray with you!' She lay back on the pillows and cried. Her beliefs told her it was wrong not to make the effort to forgive Morton but she couldn't. Losing Toby had made life unbearable in her home and the baby inside her was keeping her a prisoner in it. And God forgive her, she didn't want this baby. She was afraid of how she would feel if it survived the birth and she had to rear it. If it wasn't for Amy, she'd wish the confinement would be the end of her.

Before she'd dried her eyes, Amy rushed into the room. 'Oh, Mum, I came up when I

151

heard the raised voices. What did he say to upset you?'

'At first he tried to get back into my good books. I can't stand him...' Sylvia stopped because she felt it wasn't fair to burden her daughter with how she felt about her husband. Sylvia wiped her eyes with her shawl and put on a watery smile. 'Oh, take no notice of me, I'm just being silly, my love. You're such a good girl, Amy. I'm sorry I've been keeping you close to home.'

'That doesn't matter, Mum. Tell me what the tears were about. It might help if you talk about it.'

'I'll be all right when I'm up and about again. Has Sol said anything new about Toby today?'

'I haven't had the chance to talk to him yet. Mum, won't you try to eat something?'

Sylvia shook her head. 'I think I'll try to have a rest.'

Amy took the tray and went downstairs. She doubted if the pain of the wind apparent on her mother's face would allow her to sleep.

Sol was sitting at the lunch table. 'Your father rushed through here like his heels were on fire. He's gone out with the cart. Trouble?'

'Oh, mind your own business!' At times like this when she was anxious she saw this man as an intruder.

Sol leaned back in his chair and stretched his arms up high and then wide, as if he couldn't be more relaxed. 'It's his business you should be concerned about. Someone's due here this afternoon from Poltraze, with a view to giving Morton a commission for work at the Dower House. Perhaps he's gone for that sandalwood he failed to collect the other day. I've a feeling he won't be back for some time.'

Dumping the tray down on the table, Amy placed her hands on her hips. 'Then you can cut your break short and get back to the workshop and make sure everything's in order.'

'I don't take orders from Morton and I'm sure as hell not going to take any from you.' He smiled, amused and smirking.

Amy muttered a sharp retort under her breath. Her father often slipped away for lengthy periods that seemed to have nothing to do with work. If he didn't come back soon a good commission could be lost, making a sizeable dent in his reputation, and he'd never get work at Poltraze again. It was out of the question for Sol to negotiate on her father's behalf. He had no loyalty to the business anyway and would be pleased if Laketon Kivell made a successful deal instead. She would have to ask the Poltraze steward if it was possible he could come back another day and hope he would agree.

Sol took out the makings for a smoke. A letter came with them from his pocket and fell to the floor. Amy glanced down. 'Wait a minute, that's addressed to me!'

He beat her in picking it up. 'Oh, I forgot about this. It was brought over by someone

153

from the big house. I saved him the trouble of bringing it to the door.'

'You had no right! How dare you keep this from me.'

He shrugged as if he didn't care about her indignation. He made for the back door.

Amy put herself in front of it. 'No, you don't. Well?'

'Well, what?'

'I want an explanation.' She waved the letter in front of his eyes.

'I forgot I had the letter.'

'Oh, don't give me that. You're not the sort to forget anything.'

He put his head to the side, making his long hair sweep on his hefty shoulder, and he smiled in a way, Amy decided, that would melt any other girl's heart. 'I intended to give it to you the moment Morton wasn't around. I thought you'd want to keep your own life private from him. I wasn't going to keep it from you, Amy.'

'Oh.' She frowned, unsure if she should feel sorry about her anger, or foolish, or still cross with him for withholding her property.

'Well?'

'Well, what?'

'You owe me an apology.'

'Never on my life!'

He studied her. 'You look really pretty when you're fierce.'

'What? I'll thank you to keep that sort of stupid, insincere talk for the women who frequent the Nankervis Arms!' She tried not

154

to let him see how rattled she was. Her attitude was fully justified, but a part of her was pleased to receive a compliment from him. She stood in the kitchen, her heart racing, listening to him laughing at her, and opening and closing the back door, then whistling merrily as he strode off for his smoke.

Raising her chin in an effort to forget the interchange, after all, compliments to a woman came two a farthing to a roguish womaniser like him, she opened the letter from Tara. It read:

My dear Amy, It was so good to see you, and Sarah Hichens, waiting outside the church on my wedding day. It gave me some much needed courage. It is very strange to be a married woman and it will take time to adjust to all the changes. I am pleased to tell you that Joshua is very understanding. He has agreed with me that I am unlikely to make honest friends among the local ladies and that there will be times when I shall be quite lonely. He has kindly suggested, therefore, that I call on you soon. I do not wish to impose myself on you yet – you and your dear mother will have a lot to do concerning her confinement. Pray, write to me and tell me when it is a convenient time for me to come. I shall be very grateful to receive a reply with all your news. Yours sincerely, Tara.

Amy had no time to delight in the news that she was to keep her friendship with Tara.

'Amy! Amy, come quickly!' It was her mother shouting to her.

Stuffing the letter into her apron pocket she raced up the stairs. Sylvia was leaning forward, wincing and massaging her back. 'Mum, what is it? The baby?'

Sol was suddenly there in the doorway. 'I heard you from outside, Mrs Lewarne. Is there anything I can do?'

Sylvia was calm. The onset of labour had brought her out of her moroseness – at least she wouldn't have to lumber about, keeping at home, for another month or so. She looked from Amy's worried face to Sol's. He was wide-eyed but steady. 'Now I don't want anyone flying into a panic. I've been suspicious about it all day and now I'm certain. My labour's started. It's a bit early but there's no need to be concerned about that. Amy, I shall require a few things, which I'll mention when Sol has left the room. Sol would you be good enough to fetch Frettie Endean? She acts as the midwife round here. She lives next door to the general stores. The house with the window-boxes. She'll fetch Mrs Greep, so I'll have plenty of help. Now, the pair of you, don't look so shocked. You must make haste but there's no need to tear around like mad hounds. It will probably be a few hours before it's all over.'

'I'll be back shortly, Mrs Lewarne,' Sol said.

'Is there anything I can get you?'

'No, thank you. Is my husband in the work-shop?' The mild contraction Sylvia was having was subsiding and she eased herself down. Amy held her hand.

'He's gone out somewhere in the cart. I'll track him down.'

'You will not. I forbid it. I don't want him here. Do you understand, Sol?'

'I do entirely, Mrs Lewarne. I will pray you'll be safely delivered.'

'He'll pray for me?' Sylvia said, after he had gone. 'What a strange young man he is. I've never thought much about Burnt Oak and its people before, but now I'd be curious to go there and see exactly how they live and meet some of the Kivells, specially Sol's grand-mother, Tempest. Amy, dear, I need a clean nightgown, and will you bring the draw sheets. Don't get the crib ready yet...' The crib was in the spare room, where Morton was sleeping. With the high infant mortality rate and the dangers of childbirth Sylvia, like most expectant mothers, thought it was tempting fate to get anything prepared until the confinement was safely over. She had not even made a new garment for this baby.

Amy did these tasks. She was trembling with fear for her mother's safety and the hope of receiving a healthy brother or sister, and excitement at the prospect that she might soon be able to leave the house for a greater length of time and go to Burnt Oak, and do just what her mother had mentioned. 'Mum,

I know about Tempest Kivell's mystic powers. We know how Sol adores her. I suppose her Quaker background is what influences him to pray.'

'Even with the family's remote ways news has always got out about them. Her husband, Garth, tried to make her forget her religion. He was even worse than Titus. He used to beat her, and Titus and their daughter, Eula.' Sylvia warmed to the theme to forget the impending dangers of giving birth. 'Then one day Tempest had suffered enough and she murdered Garth.'

'What?' Amy raised her perfectly arched brows as she bundled up the soiled linen. She was always kept away from the birthing room when her mother was near the end of a labour, but she knew enough about the mysterious and frightening process to know her mother had just had her 'show'.

'Oh, it's true. The constables were certain of it. Garth was shot through the heart, but they were all too scared to proceed with charges. It was all hushed up and put down as an accident. Mind you, the constables were glad, as all decent folk in Meryen were, to see the end of Garth Kivell. He was an unspeakable sinner. He'd wait outside the church or chapel in a drunken state and hurl foul language at everyone, even the children. Tempest was a beautiful, sixteen-year-old heiress when he snatched her off a Falmouth street. Garth kept her locked away at Burnt Oak until she'd conceived, forcing her to marry him – what

158

else could she do? He'd ruined her. She hasn't been seen out since she killed him. Oh, my goodness!'

'Is it another pain?' Amy asked in alarm.

'No. I've been very remiss. With the grief of losing Toby I've not really considered all the implications of Sol working here. He's young but he's already got a poor reputation about certain behaviour. What must people be surmising? I hope you're not spending time alone with him, Amy.'

'Of course I'm not,' Amy blushed, for it was a lie. Nowadays she saw more of Sol than anyone else. 'Tempest Kivell sounds fascinating. She was good to Toby and he liked her. She obviously dotes on Sol.'

'Amy, some of the things said about the Kivells are probably exaggerated and even fanciful. But you will be careful with Sol? Promise me. He's handsome and he can be kind and amusing, but he's hardly to be trusted. You won't ever let your heart be swayed? When the Kivells want a woman they'll resort to any sort of wickedness to get her.'

'Mum,' Amy was amused at her plea. 'I listen to Sol if he mentions Toby, but I'm more likely to exchange cross words with him than anything else. I'm not about to fall under the spell of someone who keeps a string of loose women at his beck and call. You've nothing to worry about. I'm never going to leave you or the baby.'

Sylvia gripped her bulging front as she was

159

gripped by a slightly stronger contraction. 'Don't you think for a minute about sacrificing yourself for me or this child. I want to see you settled. I want to have grandchildren running about my feet. Amy, you mustn't be afraid to cast your eye round. Do you hear?'

'Yes Mum.' She couldn't think of anything else to say, so she asked, 'Want a cup of tea?'

'Yes please, my love. Amy, when your father shows up, you're not to allow him anywhere near this room.'

Amy nodded and went downstairs with the laundry.

When the pain eased Sylvia smoothed at her stomach. 'I hope you're a little girl. I hope we'll both come through and you'll help to ease the grief in my heart.' There had been so many days when she had wanted to be with Toby. Now she wanted to live for Amy's sake, to make sure her daughter did well with her life. A new child couldn't take Toby's place but a baby girl would give her someone to care for. 'Please God...' She made a vow, if she did bear another son she would not allow his father to ruin his life. She spoke to an image, the last horrid, pathetic image she had seen of Morton, 'This child is mine and mine alone.'

Thirteen

Across land at the Wayfarer's Inn, Darius and Titus were in their usual room. All day long, women had come to them and left, and they had drunk themselves into a contented stupor.

'How's your...' Darius waved a cigar about in one thickly veined unsteady hand from the bed he was sprawled on. A poor quality sheet covered his nakedness. 'How's your boy getting on at ... at Chy-Henver?'

'Sol?' Titus slurred. He was on the bed across the room, in the same state of undress. When he was with Darius he drank beer and he was in a good mood, rather than a violent one brought about by spirits. 'I'm going to pull him out. The business is flagging, it's in trouble. Sol says it's obvious Lewarne's got himself into debt,' Titus roared with mirth. 'He'll soon have no choice but to sell up cheap. To me!'

'Then you'll let your cousin, the chap who drinks and whores with my son, buy it at a far higher price?'

'Laketon wants it but I've decided to keep it for Sol. It'll be something to encourage him to come back to after he's sowed his wild oats. I don't want him gone for good. There's other

161

good carpenters at Burnt Oak, there'll be someone to keep it going for him. Another of my sons, Jowan, can continue his training there.'

'So you have it all worked out.' Darius lay staring up at the ceiling. It was rough and patchy, the beams ragged. The place was a dump. He didn't have to tolerate these conditions. 'What are we doing here? I could be whiling away my time in brothels as fine as palaces. Where new girls are taken on every year. I can mix with society and gamble for real money. I've got what –five or ten years left. I've enough wealth to see me out. To look after myself and myself alone.'

'What about your family?'

'I'm not like you. You like producing children. Family isn't everything to me. I had one son who counted to me and now he's gone I'm left with nothing. I've married off Joshua to money. I've done all I can and all I ever want to for him and his brother. I'm going to leave them to it. They all hate me. I hate them. Time we all parted. When I'm sober and able to travel I'll go up to the capital and never come back.' Satisfied with his decision, Darius lit up a celebratory cigar. 'Have you got any plans?'

'I might take another wife.' Titus also smiled in satisfaction, and anticipation. 'Are you still planning to have yours committed to the asylum?'

'It would have been fun but I can't be bothered. I—'

162

'Shush! I can hear a familiar voice. Ah—ah! It's Lewarne and he's with Marcie. So he's got his appetite back. Shall we go and spoil it for him?'

'No. Let him have one last time. Shows how desperate he is if he's come here openly. Titus, my friend, things are going our way.'

Darius drifted off to a noisy snuffling sleep. Titus dressed and reared up over him and whispered, 'I'm not your friend. I didn't try to save your mealy-mouthed son. I heard his screams from the woods but he was dead when I reached him, and if he hadn't been I'd have watched him drown with pleasure.'

Michael was happily ensconced in the library at Poltraze. He was up on the ladder, carefully pulling out old documents from a high corner shelf. Life was good for him. Here in the library he didn't feel the despondency, the sense of the almost sinister as in the rest of the building. The room was once an early Elizabethan dining-room, where no one had suffered an untimely death. He was able to pursue his ambition to record the family's long and varied history, no longer distracted by the draining complaints of Phoebe, or shrieking voices as she clashed with Estelle. Estelle made it plain she did not like him so often in the house, specially when he studied late and slept on the couch, but he paid no heed to her. Or to the disinterested reception he received from his father. The old man would be leaving for London soon. Michael hoped he'd stay there, and quickly wine and dine and whore himself to death.

He heard voices approaching. Two females were coming along the Long Corridor – the library, like most of the downstairs rooms branched off from it. He paused, hoping they would pass by and not enter the short connecting passage and arrive to bother him. He was not blessed with good fortune. He recognized one of the voices, the raised shrill of his wife. Damn it! Phoebe came up from the Dower House twice a week for a family dinner; always a strained affair. What was she doing here today?

'Michael? Michael, are you in there?' He didn't have time to descend the ladder and conceal himself behind the heavy curtains. Phoebe came bursting into the room. 'Oh, so you are here, as if I couldn't have guessed.'

'What is it? You're disturbing me.' Michael had never been afraid of Phoebe, as people whispered about him, he simply found life easier to allow her and others the belief that he was browbeaten. Due to his new contentment, and from his superior height up the ladder, he felt a greater power over her and saw her for the ridiculous cackling woman she was.

'I've come to root you out. I haven't seen you for days.'

'Days?' he replied with scorn.

'Really, Michael. You get so caught up with the silly business in this place you forget the passage of time.' Phoebe threw off her cloak.

'Neither I nor your daughters have had your company for five whole days. Have you been here all this time? When I asked your prissy sister-in-law just now if you were here today, she said she didn't know, and when I said I'd take a look for myself, she was quite rude to me.'

'Tara rude? I find that hard to believe.'

'Are you friendly with that whey-faced snippet?'

'We are polite to each other.' Michael considered for a moment. 'Actually, I do like her. The servants like her too. She's bringing a sense of concord to the house. She's Joshua's wife. You might as well make the effort to get along with her, Phoebe. And Tara's not at all whey-faced, you can't accuse her of being unattractive.'

'Are you taken with her?' Phoebe exploded, advancing on him until she reached the ladder.

'Don't make a fool of yourself, woman.'

'How dare you!'

'Phoebe, I spend a lot of time here because I find the company of the books soothing and entertaining, whereas I can't say the same for yours. I'm sorry I've neglected Cecily and Jemima. I'll drop down to see them before they go to bed.'

Phoebe was blown off course by his attitude, but she was also pleased. Was he getting into the stride of being a man at last? She was always quick to change her mood to best suit her interests. 'Forgive me, my dear,' she

165

lowered her tone to sweetness and cajoling. 'I've been disappointed not to see you. I know I can be a little demanding, but I've missed you. Now we're to have renovations to our home I've been hoping to discuss them with you, to make plans.'

'The craftsmen will know what's best to do. You have a good eye for design, I trust you to choose well to brighten up the house.'

'Thank you. Don't you miss me a little bit?' Phoebe put on the coy, eager look she gave when he approached her to make love. She enjoyed this side of life, he was a sensitive lover and she was missing it.

Michael was torn. With the harassment of the move to the Dower House and his five day stay here he had been two weeks celibate and suddenly his loins burned. Then he heard Tara calling to the lap dogs as they chased about on the lawn. Such a gentle voice, young and kind. She would never try to trap Joshua with sensual inducements to win her own way. He envied Joshua at that moment. Joshua had a honey-tongued, honest-hearted angel for a wife and he had a jealous, manipulative harpy. Phoebe craved a son, not because she wanted another child, but to put it up as some sort of importance. It hadn't sunk into her ambitious mind that his father would take no more notice of his little branch of the family if she produced one. If she did she would never cease to nag him to further their position. His desire evaporated. 'You must excuse me. I'm in the middle of something.

I'll be home to see the girls later.' He turned away from her on the ladder.

Sol had missed the communal dinner at home in the principal house at Burnt Oak, shared by his ten brothers and sisters, his father's two common-law wives, his Aunt Eula and her family, and his grandmother. The individual families separated after dinner – he was pleased to learn tonight that his father was out – and he went straight to his grandmother's sitting room, where she would be alone.

Tempest Kivell put aside the book she was reading and smiled at him. 'Hello, darling. Oh dear, you look worried. What is it?' Her voice was like fluid honey, which toned in with her handsome appearance and simple clothes. Her Quaker background meant she never wore jewellery except her wedding ring, but she didn't need sparkling stones to enhance her natural grace and excellence.

Sol bent and kissed her cheeks. He chewed his lower lip. 'Mrs Lewarne is in labour. Amy is so fearful. I'm not sure she'd cope with another loss. She'd be left with only her wretched father, and hardly anything at all when he's forced to sell the business. Things seem as bad as they could be for her.'

Tempest lifted her head and appeared to gaze into space. Too restless to sit, Sol watched her intently, this woman whom he loved so much, his friend and confidante as well as doting grandmother. She was in her mid-fifties but looked years younger. Her hair was stark black, her own colour, and her eyes the deepest blue. When she called on her gift of second sight, as she was now, she was still as a statue, as if turned to exquisite marble, a regal image.

She rejoined him and smiled. 'Don't worry. There won't be any complications with Mrs Lewarne's confinement. You've said you'll stay at least until after this baby is delivered. Is this still your intention? Are you restless?'

'Not really. There's time enough for me to see the world, and I somehow feel an obligation to Amy and her mother. It unsettled them badly, my going along with Father's plans for Chy-Henver, and I'd like to stay on a little longer for Toby's sake. To all intents I'm keeping the roof over their heads. Morton's got himself into debt. Chy-Henver could be turned round with hard work and dedication, but Morton's getting more and more difficult. He's like a cornered rat and knows it's likely he'll have to sell up soon. I don't really want Father or Laketon to buy the business, but it looks as if Morton will have to let it go for a grossly unfair price. What would Amy think of me if she finds out this was the intention all along?' Sol paced about on the red and blue carpet. 'I can't let Amy and Mrs Lewarne be put out of their home. There would be barely enough to buy a decent house, and although Morton could work for another carpenter, the way he is now, it's unlikely anyone would take him on.

168

It's all such a mess.'

Sol's face was creased with worry. It was the first time Tempest had seen him concerned like this for someone outside the family. He was a young man used to having everything his own way, everything going right for him. It warmed Tempest that he thought so highly of two women who had been strangers to him until a few weeks ago, that he was willing to take responsibility for them. She had known from the moment of his birth that he was not going to inherit the brutal strains of his father and grandfather. He made her life, when she thought what it might have been if not for Garth Kivell, worth living. When, through her religious beliefs, she fell into the throes of guilt at killing her husband, she saw loving and fostering Sol into a worthy man, as her redemption. She reached for his hand and he went forward and grasped hers. 'Listen to your heart, Sol. Listen to the little quiet voice within you. You'll know what to do. I promise you.'

Amy had crossed over the stepping-stones of the little stream and was on the moors, at the summit of the hill which sheltered her home. The sun was beginning to fall, leaving behind rosy glows and dark pinks, which fed into blues and mauves, which in turn defined crops of gorse and bracken and stubby, wind-bent trees, and the distant hills and carns. When Amy was younger she had seen the silhouetted chimneys and engine houses of

169

the mines as mystical castles and fortresses, the smoke rising up out of them as the cooking for banquets or imprisoned fire-breathing dragons. The world had been a safe place back then. Now she knew how hard and dangerous and disfiguring the work at the mines was, how often young people died from accidents and lung diseases. There was no such thing as an old miner. Back then she'd no notion her brother would die before he reached manhood and that her family would be torn apart.

Now it seemed there was a real possibility that she would lose her mother too. The last time she had gone upstairs to the labour room, an hour ago, her mother's cries resounding round the walls, Frettie Endean had ordered her away. ''Tis'nt going to be no quicker for you wishing it, maid. It'll be a while yet. Mrs Greep and I are doing our best for your mother but she's very tired. Go away and pray, that's the best thing you can do for her.'

Unable to stand the grunting and straining sounds from her mother, and the screams, Amy had sought refuge in the timeless land, the ancient landscape, scarred by the stone and brick mineral workings, and the equally ancient criss-cross paths of fox and badger tracks. She'd said prayer after prayer and now she was listening to the echoes of long ago. With her was Stumpy, mournful and watchful, his ears alert, as if he too were searching for echoes, perhaps of Toby's voice. For a snatch of a moment, Amy thought she heard Toby calling her name and she tried to keep it inside her head.

Stumpy suddenly took a few guarded paces forward until he was looking over the drop, which graduated down in sweeps of ledges and rocks. 'What is it, Stumpy?' Probably just a rabbit but she thought it was time she went back. If darkness speeded up or a mist suddenly rose, even though she wasn't far from home, a safe passage wasn't guaranteed.

Then she saw him. Sol. Climbing up to her, swift and athletic. His black hair swept back by the wind. He was like some warrior of old times. He was coming to her by way of the moor, as he'd done the first time. She went to the edge to meet him, and although he didn't need her help, she reached a hand out to him. The warm grasp of his fingers made her feel safe, and a quickness filled her being, as if she had never really been alive until this moment.

'Amy, is there any news?'

In the twilight, she could see the raw energy in his eyes. She felt it surging through his flesh as it held hers. 'Sol, it's good of you to come back. No, Mother's having a difficult time.'

He cupped his other hand round hers and she felt wrapped up in security. 'You mustn't worry. I've spoken to Grandmama Tempest. She says all will be well. We must go while it's safe.'

'You speak about us to your grandmother?' Amy allowed him to lead the way, and

171

Stumpy and Rip brought up the rear, like a couple of guards.

'Grandmama is interested in all I do so of course we talk about you and all at Chy-Henver.' She allowed him to help her climb down over the rocks and point out places where it was safest to put her feet. If not for the pain and risk to her mother she would have wanted the journey to go and on. It was a wonderful experience to be protected and cared for as if she were someone precious, to be attended in this way.

They came to the stream. Amy stopped and listened for sounds, hoping to hear a baby's cry and not the agonized cries of her mother still labouring to give birth. All she could hear was the tinkling of the water over the stony bed, the wind now buffeting all in its path. 'It's gone quiet in the house! It's too quiet. I shouldn't have stayed out so long.'

'I'll get you there quickly.' The granite stepping-stones stood out in the diminishing light and Amy could nimbly step across them, but Sol swept her up in his arms and they were over the stream in a trice. He didn't set her down. He ran with her up all the way up the ash path and to the back door. She had her arms tightly round his neck, anxious for her mother, yet enjoying the sensation of being close to his strong male body. He put her down and she withdrew her arms. He opened the door. 'Can I come in?'

'Yes.' She didn't want him to leave now. If either of the women were downstairs they'd

172

raise their brows at Sol's presence but it didn't seem right to exclude him. Somehow, at least for the time being, he was part of Chy-Henver. And if there were terrible news, she would need him...

In the kitchen, like apprehensive children, they gazed at each other. There was still no noise coming from above. 'What do you think is happening?' Sol whispered.

'I don't know,' her voice was hushed, and her insides tied themselves in knots. They crept along the hall and looked up the stairs. Apart from the sound of an occasional footstep and some low voices overhead there was silence. 'Oh Sol, if anything's happened to Mum...'

He put his arm round her. She was shaking and trying not to cry and she pressed herself against him, while looking fearfully up the stairs.

The door of her mother's bedroom was opened. 'Amy, are you down there?' It was Frettie Endean.

She glanced nervously at Sol and reluctantly left the comfort of his embrace and climbed up a couple of steps. Sol moved back thoughtfully out of sight. 'Yes, I'm here. How's Mum?'

'Twas a bit of a struggle all the way along.' Frettie, stout and forbidding, in a white, blood-spotted apron, appeared on the landing. 'Your mother's worn out. But, my bird, God be praised, we got a little maid in the end. A little sister for you.'

Amy let out a cry of relief. Her mother had survived but she was still doubtful over the baby. 'Why isn't she crying?'

'Aw, she made a squawk or two but she's breathing fine. Tedn't every baby who comes into the world bawling its head off. Put the kettle on, we'm all parched up here, then come up and see them.'

It took a few seconds for the good news to sink in, then, 'Oh, that's wonderful! A sister! That's wonderful! Thank you so much, Mrs Endean. I'll be up in a minute.'

Amy jumped down to the foot of the stairs. Sol emerged from the shadows. 'Did you hear?'

'I did. Congratulations.'

She was so excited she ran to him, about to give him a hug. Sol's arms were reaching out for her. Realizing the full import of what she was about to do, how deep a friendship they had formed, and perhaps even more, she stopped and glanced down at the floor then up at him, shy and full of strange hopes. Then regret, for the moment was lost, and that was just as well, for he would be leaving Meryen altogether soon.

Sol shrugged, his expression straight, giving no clue to what was on his mind. 'It's really wonderful news, Amy. See, you never need doubt Grandmama Tempest's word. I'll see you tomorrow.'

Fourteen

That night Joshua came to Tara in bed, an increasingly rare occasion. 'The old man's just arrived home. He was singing. I've never heard him sing before but he is somewhat in the grip of inebriation. Michael was working late in the library again. Father ordered us to help him upstairs. Then he sent for your aunt, and announced as cool as could be that he's leaving here tomorrow and never coming back. I suppose I need hardly tell you, my dear, how glad I am about that. Life should settle down quite nicely from now on.'

'I hope so,' Tara replied. She wished her Aunt Estelle was leaving with her father-in-law. Estelle crowed over her plans for Poltraze. Mrs Benney, who made it plain that she thought Estelle was beneath serving, would be dismissed, then gradually after that the rest of the staff. Estelle would do everything possible to keep Phoebe down in the Dower House. Michael would be asked to reserve his visits to the library to twice a week. Only a few ladies had left a calling card for Estelle or had been 'at home' to hers. She intended to form a set of these receptive ladies – all of lesser gentry – over which she would reign supreme, and make the set so desirable, with high teas and musical soirées and parties, that other ladies, of higher social significance, would eventually wish to join. Tara was expected to play a full part in this – until she was with child. Estelle pressed her to be quick about producing the next heir, as was the wish of Poltraze's lord and master. Tara knew enough about her husband to be sure Joshua would stamp on many of Estelle's schemes but it meant rocky times ahead. As for the question of the next heir, there was a complication in that department with Joshua so unwilling for intimacy.

Instead of keeping his distance as he'd done on the few times he had slipped in beside her, Joshua shuffled close and put his arm over her. 'What's the matter, my dear? You are so serious. Are you tired?'

'No, not at all.' She moved towards him, bridging the gap between their bodies. She was hopelessly shy about intimacy but she had grown to care for Joshua and was hoping to become his wife fully. The waiting for IT to happen was unnerving. Why was Joshua so reluctant to perform this duty as a husband, a duty men were reputed to seek eagerly? Also, if she didn't conceive a son, Darius Nankervis, residing in London or elsewhere, was vindictive enough to carry out his threat to throw her and her aunt out.

'What is it? I want to know about anything that's troubling you.' Joshua said.

'I wish...'

'You may have anything you desire, Tara.'

He planted a small kiss on her cheek and gentled a finger down it.

Taking a calming breath, Tara put a hand on his shoulder. It seemed at last he was going to become amorous and she would lose her virginity. She was scared, but Joshua was kind and caring. She trusted him and thought she might even fall in love with him. Tiny tremors of delight began to form inside her. 'I'm fine, really.'

'Good.' With that he cupped a hand under her chin and kissed her. Not for a mere second as before, this time he made it last. His hands travelled over her. Tara forgot to breathe. Lovemaking was about to finally happen and she hoped her responses would be all right for Joshua. As best as she could she made herself relax. He tugged at the buttons that journeyed from her throat to her waist on the smooth material of her night-gown. His hands were roughened from gardening activities and the tiny mother-of-pearl buttons were obstacles to him. She manoeuvred her trembling hands through his and undid the buttons, feeling shy and daring. Joshua gave a sigh and pulled the nightgown down off one shoulder and kissed her there, wetting her flesh. He hiked up the hem of the nightgown, lifted his nightshirt out of the way then mounted her. He was shaking and urgent, clumsy and breathing heavily. It seemed he had no idea what he was doing. It must be his first time too. She was given over to fear, not liking the experience at all, but she moved to give him access.

He halted. 'Hold on to me, Tara, try not to be afraid.' His voice was wobbly.

'I'm not,' she whispered, to reassure him.

He fumbled. She felt a probing. A lot of discomfort. She closed her eyes tight, horribly embarrassed in the darkness, and waited. Just a few moments more, then the act of love would be consummated and she would be his and he would be hers.

There was more probing. Tentative and awkward. Tara willed him to go ahead quickly, to get the greatest pain over with. Joshua suddenly rolled off her. Tara lay still. Too stunned to react. He rubbed a hand down her burning face. 'There, there. You were very brave. That's enough for one night.'

She knew a terrible disappointment. Joshua's breathing was at a normal rate, so he hadn't been excited at all. Then it struck her that he was detached from her in some way. There must be much more to the act of love and she began to doubt if Joshua would ever perform it with her. Would the cautious, faltering breaching of her body render her with child? She had no notion and there was no one she could ask. Trying not to give way to tears of disenchantment and humiliation, she waited for him to get up and leave her.

Estelle lay awake long into the small hours. Darius was on his back, snoring like a contented, rumbling steam engine. He was sweaty and smelled of cheap female company

178

– he had declared he would take a bath in the morning then take his immediate departure.

'You won't be missed for one single moment, you old devil!' The instant he stepped into the landau tomorrow for Truro, to catch the next post coach, she would rule the house.

She dozed off and thought she was dreaming. There was someone in the room. It was so real she sat up and moved aside the lace draped from the post. Darius demanded a lamp be kept lit so he'd have no trouble finding his way to the water closet, and she peered through the yellowy gleam. The low light cast many shadows but all was as usual. The huge room was choked with dense walnut furniture, ugly stuff that lent a heavy atmosphere. She would replace it with items on lighter feminine lines. Just a few hours left to endure the perverse hulk at her side and Poltraze would be all hers.

She was about to lie down when the hairs on the back of her neck prickled. She peered about again, instinctively pulling the covers up under her chin. Then she was almost swallowed up by the fear of knowing there really was someone in the room. Someone who was not a servant or a friend. 'Who is it?' She reached out to the bedside cabinet for something she could use as a weapon.

The figure leapt forward and before she could summon up a scream she was struck hard across the face. She came to seconds later to see a small moving light at her side.

179

She could smell tobacco. Stunned for a moment she thought Darius was up and walking round the bed, smoking. A glance in his direction showed he had blood on his head. Then she detected something else. Something unbelievable. Something deadly. Lantern oil had been splashed all over the bedcover. The next scream died in her throat as she was struck again. She was thrown back on the pillows. In terror she stared up, trying to recognize her assailant. The figure was tall and broad, undoubtedly a man, but who she couldn't tell, he was in black and had his face covered. She made one last attempt to scream but he gripped her by the throat, yanked her up then slammed her head against the headboard before pushing her down. Estelle was barely conscious but to her terror she was aware of him tucking her up tightly in the bedcovers.

Estelle couldn't move. Somehow she made her lips work. 'Who—who are you?'

The whispered answer fed her terror to a frenzy. 'I want you both out of my way.'

As she struggled to free herself and find the strength to scream, he dropped the cigar on the bed. Estelle felt almost immediate agony as tall raging flames ate into her legs. She was able to scream at last. She screamed and screamed, and even as she fought to get away from the bed she was aware of Darius burning beside her. She screamed and howled and shrieked. Long after her final scream ended its echo filled the house.

Fifteen

'Hello Mrs Hichens. I thought I'd pay you a visit.' Titus pulled up a chair beside where Nancy had been left sitting, placing it where he could not look into her twisted, drooling face. 'I saw your relative leave. I suppose she's given you your dinner. I noticed she didn't spend much time here. Probably didn't talk to you much either. I don't suppose anyone does, not even Sarah, that dear, sweet, young daughter of yours.'

Nancy nodded and muttered, as if she was listening and agreeing with him.

'How about I catch you up on all the news? It's two weeks since part of the big house was burnt out. 'Tis reckoned the squire fell asleep smoking one of them grand cigars of his. Burned alive he was, he and his wife. And two others. A pity.' Titus's expression changed from being conversational to dark grimness. 'Pity there hadn't been more dead.' Then back to chattiness. 'Big funeral, of course. Gentry came from all over, to show their faces, that's all. No one will miss that rotten old devil, Darius Nankervis. He deserved a terrible end and that's just what he got. Couldn't have thought of a better end for him myself. If you ask me, there's a sense of justice being done throughout Meryen.

'So, with Darius gone we're moving into new times. Got a new squire. A different individual altogether. People are hopeful he'll do something for Meryen. Can't see it myself. He's got no vision, no backbone. But he's got a dear little wife, as comely as a girl can be. She's friends with young Amy Lewarne, another interesting little piece. I like young girls. Young Mrs Nankervis wouldn't pay no mind to me, and nor would Amy, and anyway, my eldest boy will have Amy, one way or another, so therefore I'm paying special attention to your dear little Sarah. Mind you, don't think for a minute that I believe she to be third best. Not at all. She's the prettiest of the bunch, a beauty. She'll bear fine handsome children, so you can be proud of her, Mrs Hichens.

'Yes, times are changing. There's plans for even more houses to be built. There's people coming in from other parishes to mine the copper and even from across the border. English! That's why my family are coming out from behind our walls. We're going to turn our skills into proper businesses, build our own little empires. People are suspicious, even hostile towards us, those who dare to be! I'd like to see their fears realized, but, well, things have to be done differently now – mostly. One day soon, kin of mine will own the forge, the watchmaker's, the hostelry and other establishments. All bought and paid for at a fair price, mind. Well, more or less. The present owners can stay on and work for us, there'll be plenty of work with all the expansion.

'I'm planning to buy out the carpenter, Lewarne.' Titus fell silent, every muscle in his hard face grew pinched. He was furious Sol had put himself as an obstacle in the way of his plan. They had nearly come to blows in the Nankervis Arms. Titus had reached across the barrel table. 'You'll do as I say! You've started going your own way a little too much and I won't have it! I'm putting a bid to Lewarne and you can't stop me. I want the business for you, for goodness sake!'

Sol had gripped his wrist and thrust his hand away. 'I decide what I want. I only do what Grandmama advises. I want things to stay as they are for now. I certainly haven't considered wanting Chy-Henver as my own.'

'We'll leave it for now,' Titus had growled, hiding how much the close collaboration between his mother and his son rankled with him. 'But if you and Mama have anything to say about it in future I want to hear it. Do you understand?' Titus's boast that he was head of his family had one flaw which never failed to humiliate him. His mother kept control of his excesses by her threat to ill-wish him, to bring him down. She had the 'powers' and he was genuinely afraid she'd use them on him.

Sol had stayed silent, as if he had ended an annoying discussion. That would have brought Titus to a rage with anyone else, but Titus thought it was how a Kivell man should

183

be, in charge, intransigent. Titus had brooded, downing his beer in one noisy draught, slopping it over his chin and chest. 'Are you getting sweet on the Lewarne girl? Is that it?'

'She's just another girl,' Sol had looked at his father levelly, but Titus had never been good at figuring out Sol. 'I respect her mother.'

'Bah! You're getting soft.'

'I am not, but it makes more sense to be hard when you need to be and flexible when it's necessary, rather than go about riding roughshod over everyone. We need to present a softer image if we're going to successfully integrate with the community.'

Titus had got up, sneering at Sol as if he thought his son was going mad. Then he'd vented his ill humour on a drinker by stamping on his foot, accusing him of being clumsy and giving him a thrashing.

'Now Mrs Hichens, I can't stay here much longer so I'll bring the subject back to Sarah. She's told me what a good mother you were before your tragic accident. How you always did what was best for her and the other two. Do you know what? I believe you're a good mother even now and only want what's best for your children.' Titus got up and looked down on Nancy. Her eyelids were fluttering. 'I can see I'm tiring you but you only have to bear with me a little longer. It must be a terrible thing for you, knowing you're bringing Sarah down. Fate hasn't been kind to you. The very sight of you is revolting. None

184

of us wants to exist as some stinking, grotesque hulk, do we? But there's no need for you to worry. I'm going to help you. And Sarah. You're a good mother, Mrs Hichens. You'll understand what I'm about to do.'

He moved behind Nancy, then leaning forward he rolled up the pointed ends of her shawl. With eyes glittering coldly, he pressed the pads of shawl over her nose and face. At once survival instinct gave her feeble arms the strength to fight for her life. Nancy clawed the air and tried to fend off the thing that was suffocating her. Titus pushed her grasping hands away with his forearms.

It took a few minutes to complete his task, the final arrangement to drape her shawl back in place. Nancy looked more gruesome than before. Titus put back the chair he'd sat on. 'Don't worry, Mrs Hichens. You'll be a nice colour by the time Sarah gets home so it won't be too harrowing for her, and I want you to take your eternal rest assured that I will look after her from now on.'

Sixteen

Amy and Sarah were walking along the lanes, two neat attractive figures in black capes and bonnets. They were on their way to Burnt Oak.

'Aunty Molly wouldn't approve of where I'm going and I should feel guilty about lying to her,' Sarah said. 'She's suggested Tamsyn and Arthur stay at her house tonight so I can have a break. Isn't that kind? Lots of people have been kind to me since Mother's sudden passing.'

'That's because you deserve it,' Amy smiled. 'People are impressed by the way you've coped since her accident at the mine and now with her death.' She linked her arm through Sarah's. Not everyone was being kind to her friend. To account for the rise in Sarah's living standard a few nasty-tongued and jealous people had formed the opinion that she must have a well off lover. Amy was sure Sarah knew who her benefactor was but she had fielded off any questions. She hoped Sarah would never get to hear the rumours, and that she wasn't in for some kind of awful disappointment concerning the benefactor and have all her new-found confidence wiped out.

'Aunty Molly says it was a happy release for Mother. I suppose it was, but I wish she hadn't been alone when she died. At least it didn't look as if she suffered, just that she'd stopped breathing.'

'I suppose it all got just too much for her body.' There had been a lot of deaths recently. As well as the tragedy at the big house, eight people had succumbed to cholera, a constant threat due mainly to filthy habits. The villagers were thanking God that it didn't seem they were in for an epidemic. The initial hope that things might improve with a new squire at Poltraze had quickly evaporated. Joshua Nankervis had made no intimations to Meryen that he was about to improve the lot of its people. There was a feeling of gloom everywhere. Amy had reason to feel down and anxious. Since the day of her sister's birth her father was behaving wildly out of character, aggressively – when Sol wasn't there – swearing, and drinking in his den, and staying out overnight. Until, or unless, he returned to his usual self she felt it best not to invite Tara to call.

Now she was undertaking this long awaited excursion – she had been given permission by her mother to go to Burnt Oak today, to learn about Toby's time with the family – she decided to be positive. 'At least things are more settled for you, Sarah, and my mother and baby Hope are strong and well.'

'There's been an amazing change in your mother,' Sarah replied. Of all the changes in

187

Meryen, Morton's moral decline was the most talked about. He had even stopped going to chapel. Sarah had seen the drastic change in his appearance. Huge dark shadows hung under his eyes, eyes that stared out frighteningly, as if there were some madness churning away inside him. The two heavy vertical lines above his nose were now deep grooves and extra wrinkles gathered in his sulky thin lips. His skin was bloated and florid. From being a severely groomed man he was careless with shaving and looked as if he hadn't washed for days. Amy never mentioned the shame and bewilderment she was suffering, so nor did she. If not for Sol Kivell, it seemed her friend would soon be falling on hard times. 'I noticed that your mother seems almost fond of Sol.'

'She's got used to having him around.'

'Have you?'

'He's a good worker.' Amy was always guarded about Sol. While grateful to him for keeping the business afloat, she could never forget that he actually had no right to be there, and when it suited him he would leave.

Apart from the sadness of losing her mother Sarah was content with her own situation. She was excited and her every nerve was on a bouncy spring at the thought of seeing Titus in his home. He had called at Moor Cottage on the night she had found her mother slumped in her chair. Nancy had been laid out for burial and the children had cried themselves to sleep. 'I had a sense that you'd need me,' he'd said. Such a comfort to her he'd been and she had felt honoured. Titus had arranged for Sol to make a pine coffin for her mother, a modest but sensitively crafted affair, and it had been with some pride that she had seen her mother buried decently.

'I'm going to see about getting you somewhere far nicer to live in, my dear love,' Titus had promised. He wouldn't let her down, she trusted him. All she cared about was Titus. She must be in love with him for she felt empty when he wasn't around and she ached to see him again. What would Amy say – and she was shortly about to find out – that she already had a connection at Burnt Oak? That it was with Titus, a man who was feared and loathed, a man old enough to be her father? Sarah hoped to convince Amy that the man who had threatened her the day she'd searched for Toby had many good qualities.

'Is Sol going to be there?' Sarah asked, skirting round a dead bramble thicket hanging out from the hedge. 'Did he turn up for work this morning?'

'He comes every day now.' Amy smiled faintly. Despite her reservations about Sol, he was good to her mother. When he delivered a finished item or made a repair in someone's house he insisted on prompt payment, which he handed over to her mother immediately. She didn't dwell on the fact that he was good to her in many ways too. She didn't want to get to like him. That would be a losing battle. 'He'll be there later. Now the evenings are drawing in it will be dark before we leave Burnt Oak. Mother's permitting him to see that we get back safely. It was his idea.'

'So she trusts him?'

'I suppose she does.'

'Do you? You don't mention him often.'

'Why should I apart from the work he does?' Amy put her shield up again. 'And no, I don't trust him altogether.'

'Because he keeps certain company?'

'That's none of my business.' A horrid feeling dragged down on Amy's heart. Some sort of sense always told her when he'd been with a woman.

'A pity. In many ways he'd make you a perfect husband.'

'Don't be silly!'

'Ah,' Sarah grinned and side-stepped in front of Amy so she could look into her face. 'You've gone all pink and you were too quick with that reply. You do have a fancy for him, don't you?'

'Of course I don't,' Amy was becoming bothered. 'Well, all right, I admit it's hard not to notice how attractive he is.'

'Does he make you feel safe?'

'A little.' Amy's answer was reluctant but when Sol was at Chy-Henver she did feel safe.

'Well, I think the Kivells probably aren't as bad as they're painted. Everyone thought Titus would cause trouble when he came out of gaol but he didn't. The men don't jump into quarrels as often as they used to. The women are seen more often in the village and they're quite friendly. The traders certainly don't mind taking Kivell money. Perhaps gaol had a sobering effect on Titus. I believe everyone should be given a second chance. I, for one, wouldn't be going to Burnt Oak today if I thought I was placing myself in any danger.'

'Sarah!' Amy laughed, cheered at last. 'Where did you come up with all of this? Well, I for one, am both pleased and terrified at the thought of getting a personal invitation to take tea with Tempest Kivell. Her name conjures up a stormy personality. I know Sol's told her a little about me but I can't help getting this uneasy feeling that she knows all there is to know. I'm so glad she said I could bring a friend and you've agreed to come.'

'Come along then,' Sarah picked up the pace, eager to be there as soon as possible. 'She's got the powers. If we're late she might put a spell on us.'

The reception Amy got at Burnt Oak from Titus Kivell was entirely different to the first time. His hair slicked back, in a suit of fine cloth, high collar and silk necktie he was waiting for the girls at the top of the meadow beside the trap. 'Good afternoon Miss Lewarne, Miss Hichens. I hope you've had a pleasant walk. I thought I'd save you the trouble of a rather muddy walk down.'

Amy was stunned and didn't reply. Sarah said brightly, 'It's very thoughtful of you, Mr Kivell.'

With gaiety and chivalry, he helped the girls

191

to climb up into the trap. As the trap shook and jarred on the short downward journey he kept up a cheerful chitchat. He drove through the open gates below into the courtyard and helped the girls alight. They were both overawed to find themselves surrounded by Kivell men and women, who had come out of the workshops and houses to greet them, and children of all ages. Many wore clothes of attractive low-key hues made from vegetable dyes, in tartans and prints, always a mark of the clan's unique identity.

'This is more or less my whole family,' Titus swept a proud hand round the gathering.

The introductions went on until the girls' heads were a whirl of names. There was the oldest member, the hook-nosed, leathery skinned, Uncle Genesis, a blacksmith and farrier in a leather apron, who brandished huge, blackened hands. Tempest's daughter Eula; a mother of seven; a quilter. Cousin Laketon, the carpenter; he was polite and well-spoken, but Amy thought him hard-eyed. There was a new baby boy, Caleb, Titus's first grandchild, to his eldest daughter, Delen. Some in-laws were included but the two common-law wives of Titus were not there. As the girls tried to take in all this information, both were aware they were the objects of avid curiosity and some suspicion. Amy wondered what on earth had got into Titus. Like the villagers, she was afraid the decision of the Kivells to begin mixing in the community would bring trouble. Some traders were being made anxious by the Kivells' efforts to set up their own business premises, leading to a drop in their own trade.

'You might care to take a look around later,' Titus said. 'But first tea with Mama Tempest. She's waiting for you in her sitting room.'

The girls glanced at each other, apprehensive at meeting the formidable woman. Once across the thick stone steps and threshold of the largest house, charmingly named Morn O' May, they joined hands. Titus noticed and chuckled. 'There's no need to be nervous, young ladies.' Another daughter of his, Marthan, aged about twelve, appeared in the hall and took their capes and bonnets. Titus ushered Amy on ahead and she had no notion that he and Sarah were touching and smiling into each other's eyes.

The stairs parted at the top and Amy calculated that eight or nine rooms stretched away on either side, leading off at angles according to the outside appearance, and that another staircase led up to the rooms incorporated in the attic. Even allowing for in-laws and new offspring, there was room enough here for the incumbents not to feel an encroachment on their own space. Where did Titus's so called wives sleep? Would she and Sarah meet them?

'Does your Uncle Genesis live here?' Amy asked in challenge, glancing round at Titus. Why wasn't the older man the head of the family?

''Twas my father's house before mine,'Titus replied. He met the challenge head-on, with narrowed eyes, and Amy shivered. He was being hospitable but in no way had he softened. She had best not do anything to upset him. She hoped Sol would not be long arriving.

Sarah was smiling broadly, entirely comfortable here. She thought the whole of her humble home would fit into one of the rooms she glimpsed into, which was spread with musical instruments.

The wide stone-flagged passage, covered with intricately woven runners, wended its way in turns and branched off into other short passages. Delicious smells came from one direction, indicating the kitchen. The thick walls were adorned with paintings and wood carvings and etchings. A long tapestry, Titus told them, portrayed his family's history, and they caught snatches of a man falling off a horse, a land barren apart from oak trees, of buildings under construction, then busy craft-making scenes and grazing animals. Clocks, including a grandfather clock, side tables, coffer chests, lyre-back chairs, pedestals and mirrors were other additions. Many items began to show a familiar touch, no doubt Kivell crafted, but other obscure things, like silver candle boxes and Chinese urns had likely, down the centuries, come here through dishonest means.

At the extremity of the passage were carved double doors with brass handles. Titus tapped on one door. He waited. 'Come in,' a strong female voice called.

Amy and Sarah traded 'here goes' looks.

Titus opened the doors and went into the room. He pushed out the flat of his hand to tell the girls to wait. 'Mama, the young ladies are here.'

'Usher them in.'

It seemed to Amy and Sarah as if they were about to be granted an audience by an important personage. They momentarily linked hands.

Titus signalled for them to enter the room. 'Mama, let me introduce to you Miss Amy Lewarne and Miss Sarah Hichens.'

Morton was half-heartedly smoothing a long edge true on a piece of pine wood with a jack plane. Every few seconds he stopped and scowled at Sol, who was producing a harmonious sound with a panel saw. This morning the young swine had shown the audacity to tell *him* off for starting late. Morton had not replied. Sol had already ordered him to pull himself together and knuckle down as a husband and father or he'd reckon with him.

Although always nervous of Sol, Morton had worked up the guts to hurl back, 'If you don't like it why don't you take yourself off for good?'

Sol had fronted him, too close for comfort. 'I choose to stay, for now.'

'Why?' Morton hissed, his anger and frustration at being worn down by events making him shake and fume. 'What the hell's in it for you?'

'It pleases me to look out for Mrs Lewarne and Amy, and I'm doing it for Toby. Now, let's get on. Don't you want your business to thrive? You've lost the commission at the Dower House to my second-cousin, Laketon. There's little hope of work at Poltraze when the rebuilding of the burnt-out wing starts. It would have been a lucrative commission.'

It's not my fault! Morton screamed inside his head and rushed outside. *Damn you, Darius Nankervis, you're partly responsible for putting me into debt. I hope you're rotting in hell. Damn you, Titus Kivell! How can I work with your vile spawn here!* It was easy to see what Titus Kivell's game was, to ruin his business and get it off him, and it was succeeding. Morton was in such a frenzy, he missed the fact that Sol was trying to help keep his business going rather than bring it down.

Morton went back to the entrance to the workshop. He often ran out on his work, the only way he could bear his life was to spend time with Marcie Dunn, and Sol, used to working alone, had returned to his job. Morton glared at the powerfully working muscles of Sol's back, wishing he had the guts to plunge a knife into it. *So you're staying here for my wife's sake, are you? My wife, who doesn't tolerate me but dances attendance on you. She shows you preference over me at my own meal table!* Well, he'd had enough. Sylvia was his

196

wife and it was time she remembered her place.

Turning on his heel he strode away from the workshop. Sylvia had made him suffer enough. He would no longer be denied his place as the head of his household and the right to his own bedroom. He burst in through the kitchen and then into the front room.

Sylvia leapt up from her armchair where she was hemming a baby's dress. 'Have you taken leave of your senses, man? How dare you come in here like this and with your boots on.' Morton looked so fierce she was glad that Hope was safely upstairs in the nursery. He had returned the day following the baby's birth in an unkempt state and had not asked about either of them, and since then he had never as much as looked at Hope.

'It's you who's taken leave of your senses and how dare you speak to me like that, you bitch!' Morton curled his fists.

Sylvia was shaken. He had taken to uttering oaths but he had never insulted her before. However, she was not about to let him get the better of her. She lifted her chin. 'Get out.'

'Get out? Of my own house? I don't think so!' He stormed up to her, throwing a high-backed chair out of his way. 'I'm the man here and you'll do as you're bloody told!'

As unwise as she knew it to be, Sylvia spat back, 'A man? You're not a man at all, Morton Lewarne. You're conducting yourself like a villain. You're a weak willed hypocrite!'

Drawing back his hand Morton slapped her hard across the face. Sylvia cried out in pain and was thrown off her feet. She lay huddled, her arms ready to ward off the next blow that was coming, but he was hauled away from her. Sol had him by the back of the collar. He twisted it tight and Morton made choking sounds. He was clearly terrified. 'D—don't hurt me.'

'Don't hurt you?' Sol bawled at him. 'Yet it's all right, is it, for you to hurt your wife? A defenceless woman?' After the abuse his grandmother had suffered at her husband's hands, wife-beating was something he hated and would not tolerate.

'Sylvia ... help me.' Morton's eyes bulged with fear.

Sylvia had got to her feet. Standing resolute, hands clasped together, she stared at her husband for some moments.

'What do you want me to do with him, Mrs Lewarne?' Sol said, shaking Morton as if he was a rat, making him whimper.

Sylvia took a step towards Morton to show she was not afraid of him. 'Get him out of here please, Sol.'

'With pleasure.' To Morton's blubbering wails, Sol dragged him out through the back door, round the side of the house and all the way to the front gate. He threw him down on the road. 'You heard your wife. Get!'

'Get where?' Morton scrabbled about on all fours like a madman. 'Where am I supposed to go?'

'That's for you to decide,' Sol muttered coldly, his eyes blazing. 'Don't ever show up here again.'

'You can't throw me out of my home, my business!' Morton held up imploring hands.

'I've just done it. You're not wanted here. Your wife doesn't want you. You are no use here. None of the villagers will take you in after they learn what you've done to Mrs Lewarne. Don't ever try to come back. I'll be stationing the dogs at the gate, they'll tear you to pieces.'

'But what will I do?' Morton was thinking in rapid fright. 'Amy! Amy won't approve of this. She'll make you let me back in.'

'No, she won't. Amy knows what's best for herself and her mother and sister. And she's making new friends. Do you know where she is at the moment?' With his hands on his hips, Sol leaned forward, mocking, 'She's at Burnt Oak visiting with my grandmother. You're responsible for destroying Toby. And now your wife and Amy have moved on with their lives and they don't want you in it. Leave Meryen today Morton Lewarne. Show your face just once and I swear I'll rip your heart out. Now, go!'

'G—give me a horse. I need a horse.' The only thought in Morton's terrified brain was to ride to Marcie Dunn. He had given the prostitute a whole guinea on his last visit, she owed him at least a bed for the night.

'The business needs the horses. Your disgusting behaviour has forfeited you every-thing.' Sol took a lunge forward. 'Do I have to come to the other side of this gate?'

'No!' Morton squeaked. 'I—I'm going.'

Sol's strong dark features were as cold as a winter's night as he watched Morton, snivelling and crying, get up on rubbery feet and limp off, one weak shambling step at a time.

Sylvia joined him at the gate. 'Where's he going?'

'I sent him away,' Sol replied grimly.

'Morton!' Sylvia called out.

He whirled round. 'Yes? Yes dear?' There was begging in his every stance.

'Send word where you'll be staying. I'll have your things sent there.' With that, she turned and went back inside, on Sol's arm.

Morton fell down in a heap into the dirt. Within seconds Stumpy and Rip were at the gate snarling at him. Scrabbling to his feet again, bent over, Morton trudged on. Spittle ran down his face and he banged his fists against his thighs, and hissed, 'You won't get away with this! I swear on the devil's heart I'll make you all pay!'

Tempest Kivell swept towards the girls on graceful feet. She was tall and slender and regal, with high distinctive cheekbones. Her eyes, like Sol's, were alert, intelligent and jewel-blue. She was the sort of person another couldn't take their eyes off. She wore a dress of lilac, thick with exquisite lace. She was like a queen. Amy and Sarah curtsied as if she really was one. Her private room was lavishly furnished, with glass display cabinets of ornaments and plate, hanging shelves, tabernacle-framed mirrors, jardinères, a spinet and plush stool, and a huge veneered writing desk with a silver ink stand. The curtains were turquoise, opulently draped with swagged pelmets and pleated tails and fringed tie-backs. Amy thought that no room at Poltraze could match this one.

Tempest's redoubtable eyes flicked from the brown-haired girl to the brunette. 'So, you are Amy and you are Sarah?' Her voice was flowing and made Amy think of honey. 'I have heard much about you, Amy, but not your friend. You are both very welcome here. My daughter will bring us tea. Titus, you may leave. Send someone to collect Sarah in half an hour to show her around. Amy and I will discuss Toby privately.'

'Of course, Mama.' He withdrew. Amy noticed Sarah's eyes were on him and his on her. He gave Sarah a long smile.

'Well, sit yourselves down,' Tempest said, pointing to a tapestry cabriole sofa that faced the long windows. She glided to a matching chair where she had a perfect view of a beautifully arranged garden within the perimeter wall. She noticed Amy gazing outside before taking a seat. 'You like the garden, Amy?'

'It's amazing, Mrs Kivell. I've never seen so many different flowers and shrubs.'

'My nephew Laketon is responsible for the landscaping. He has a passion for beauty.'

Tempest took several moments to gaze at each girl in turn. 'I know what you do, Amy. You care for your mother admirably, and I hear the new arrival in the family is thriving. Your mother chose her name as Hope, I understand, because after the tragedy of losing Toby the baby gives her hope for the future. I am pleased for her. Do you feel the same?'

Amy wasn't sure whether to be pleased, annoyed or offended that Sol had obviously repeated so much about her home life to his grandmother. Any hope she had was marred by her father's wanton behaviour. 'Sol was a great help on the day Hope was born. He is full of surprises.'

'Ah,' Tempest said with a meaningful spark in her deep eyes. 'You aren't comfortable with direct questions. Sol has many fine qualities. You will find out more about him. Now Sarah, all I know about you is that you're Amy's closest friend. You live with your parents, I take it?'

'No, Mrs Kivell,' Sarah answered in her best voice, shyly, proudly. 'My parents are dead. I'm a bal-maiden at the Carn Croft Mine, and I'm responsible for my young brother and sister.'

'A mine girl?' Tempest raised her curved eyebrows. 'If I may say, you don't appear as so. You are very well turned out.'

'I—I have a benefactor, Mrs Kivell,' Sarah blushed to the roots of her hair then looked down at her feet, resting on the hand woven carpet.

Amy was embarrassed for Sarah and hoped the woman would not persist with questions. She had wanted to come here for a long time but now wished she had waited for an opportunity when Sol was guaranteed to be here. It was a relief when the door was opened and Eula came in with a tea trolley. A bone china tea service and a tiered floral-patterned china plate heaped with dainty cakes was wheeled across to them. 'Here we are, Mama.'

'Thank you, Eula. Girls, this is Eula Kivell; she married a cousin. Like many here at Burnt Oak she's pleased that we're to make more contact outside of our home. Some of our younger members have been finding things claustrophobic.'

Eula had a glowing smile. 'Some of our people want things to remain as before. I hope Meryen Village will be understanding to all of us. I hope you enjoy your time here today and feel able to go back as ambassadors for us.'

'Yes, indeed,' Sarah replied eagerly. Eula had helped her to relax. She longed to be with Titus again. When Eula left, Sarah hoped it was she who was to show her around.

The talk over the tea drinking and cake nibbling was centred on the garden, a safe subject, an easy subject for the girls to listen to. The tea was delicious, different from anything they had tasted before, and with smuggling rife on both Cornwall's south coast, and the north coast, which wasn't many miles away at Portreath, Amy thought it likely the Kivells indulged in 'freetrading'.

The half hour since Titus had left the room was up. Sarah kept glancing sideways at the mantel clock, keen to get away from Tempest Kivell's penetrating gazes. Although she was paying more mind to Amy, Sarah too was worried the woman could see right into her. Did she know she had an inappropriate relationship with her son? Titus was a widower but he was still involved with two other women. Tempest Kivell would think her a strumpet.

Amy wanted the time to pass quickly too. To talk about Toby and leave. She should never have come here. There was little the woman could tell her about Toby that Sol hadn't mentioned already. Amy wished Sol had never turned up at Chy-Henver, and that her father had taken on another experienced craftsman, someone content to live a normal, everyday life, and that her father was still just a staid and self-righteous misery.

Someone was at the door. Eula? Sarah's head shot round that way. It was Titus who came in. He was all smiles but seemed awkward. 'I thought I'd come for Sarah, Mama.'

'Oh, did you indeed?' Tempest stared at him.

Sarah got to her feet. Amy looked from mother to son, and from their silent communication, hers of disapproval and angry resignation, his of dogged intent but discomfort, she realised that it was a matriarch who ruled here and she did not approve of her son.

'I see,' Tempest said archly. 'Then Sarah had better run along with you.'

When the pair had gone, Tempest fussed with the teapot. It took a full minute before Amy came to the same conclusion as the woman had. Then it all fell into place. Sarah's benefactor was Titus! And he had her firmly in his grasp.

'More tea, Amy?'

'Um, no, no thank you. I think I should take Sarah home.'

'It wouldn't be of any use. I'm afraid she's infatuated with my son.'

'I just can't let her to be alone with him.' Amy stared anxiously at the door. Doubtless it would cause a scene if she tried to get Sarah to leave and Titus might use aggression to stop her, but she couldn't sit tight and allow Sarah to walk into possible danger.

'Amy,' Tempest said in a sad confidential tone. 'Don't you think Sarah has been alone with him many times before?'

Amy brought her hands up to her face. 'Oh, poor Sarah.'

'I'm afraid you can't go against your own fate. There's nothing you can do but remain a friend to her. She may need you. Let's talk about Toby.' Tempest's stern expression moderated into a gentle smile. 'I became very fond of your brother.'

Amy pushed her concern for Sarah to the back of her mind, her mother would want every detail repeated in full. 'I know Sol saved him from the hazards of a marsh. My mother and I wish to thank the women here for looking after him.'

'Dear Toby. When Sol brought him here he was caked in mud. He was wet through, cold, scratched and bruised and sobbing his heart out. He was too afraid to go home. He kept repeating, 'My clothes and shoes are ruined. My father will say I'm a disgrace.' We gave him a bath, washed and dried his clothes and gave him something to eat. My, how that boy ate, plate after plate of lamb stew, as if he'd never had a meal in his life before.'

Amy smiled forlornly, picturing the scene. 'Lamb stew was his favourite.'

'After that I read to him. He told me how you and your mother read to him every night when he was little. I could see he was very unhappy. I pointed out he had a lot to be grateful for. A loving mother and sister. A nice home, food, clothes, an inheritance. He said he was grateful for all that. Then he told me what it was like in the workshop with your father. By the end I wanted to rear up and strike Morton Lewarne across the face. He harangued the boy every minute. He stood over him, rapping on his wrists, banging on his shoulders, cuffing the back of his neck, breathing all over him. He obviously got the poor boy into such a state he could hardly get his hands to work. There were times he could hardly see, he got blinding headaches. He was never excused to make a call of nature and was forced to hold himself for hours.

'I told Toby he could come to Burnt Oak any time he liked. Which he did, as often as he could. One day he went home with Stumpy, exchanging him for a drawing that he made in this very room. He didn't think he'd be allowed to keep him but your mother stepped in and insisted Stumpy stay. Toby told me that his father kicked the dog every chance he could, when only Toby was there to see it. He never told you that he came here, Amy, because he was sure your father tried to listen in on all you and he said together. Toby was afraid that his secret would come out and he'd lose his refuge. He wanted to come here to live. He begged me to let him stay and I said that if things didn't get better that he could. That Sol would ensure your father caused no trouble about it.' Tempest shook her head mournfully. 'It's one of my biggest regrets. I left it too late. I'm so sorry.'

Amy had to produce her handkerchief and wipe away her tears. 'Mother and I knew it was bad for Toby. It sounds so much worse to hear it from someone else's lips. When was the last time he came here?'

'A week before he died. If only he'd come here that day. He often spoke about trying to prove himself. Lingering in the woods must have been his way of doing so, with terrible consequences.'

'Mrs Kivell, people say you have the sight. Why didn't you see Toby was in danger?'

'Amy, sometimes, occasionally, I do get the sense of what is about to happen. I dream

207

dreams that point to future events. The night before that old devil, the squire, died I dreamed about Poltraze. It had black smoke pouring out of the same wing in which he and his valet and his wife and her maid died. I'm sorry, Amy, that I didn't see danger for Toby. I'm sorry you'll never have the comfort of at least knowing how he died. I'm sorry too about your father. He has the darkest heart. He's heading for a terrible downfall.'

'The way things are at the moment,' Amy said, filled with a horrible tension. 'I doubt if a prediction is needed about that.'

Titus allowed Sarah to peep into the music room. It was lined with books where he informed her all the children received lessons four times a week. Then they climbed the stairs and he took her off to the left, passing doors until he showed her into a room with an enormous bed in the centre of it. 'This is my room,' he said. 'Take a look around.'

'It faces south. There's so much light in here.' She touched the bed quilt of hexagonal shapes. 'Did Eula make this? It's beautiful.'

'She did. She could teach you to quilt, if you like.' Titus came up behind her and slipped his arms firmly around her waist. He leaned forward and kissed her cheek and nuzzled her ear. 'Sarah, how would you like to live here, secure, with everything you could ever want? And the little ones? You've seen for yourself how well the Kivells look after their women and children.'

'We could have a room here, you mean? Me, Arthur and Tamsyn?' It was beyond Sarah's greatest dreams. 'And work here?'

'You can work if you want to. Tamsyn and Arthur can share a room until they get older, but you'd sleep in here with me.'

'You mean...? But I couldn't live with you like that!' Sarah was horrified and she tried to get free of him. 'I'm not a trollop! What about your two women?'

Titus kept her within his grip and he turned her round to face him. 'I know you're not loose, darling. I wouldn't be interested in you if you were. We'll get married. As for the other women, I've had enough of them and they've had enough of me. One's left here and the other's moved into Uncle Genesis's house. You love me, don't you? You want to be with me all the time?'

'Get married? You want to marry me?' Sarah shrieked with disbelief.

'It's what people in love do, isn't it?' Titus bracketed his hands either side of her face, stroking her cheeks with his thumbs.

'Yes! Yes. I can't believe this is happening.' Sarah was bubbling with excitement.

Titus played with her hair then ran his hands down her arms, then placed them on her waist. 'You are so beautiful.' His voice dropped to a throbbing husky tone and he brought his face in close for a kiss.

Joyfully, Sarah threw her arms around his neck. She kissed him with every ounce of the love swelling up in her heart.

209

Titus was moving her backwards. She felt her legs come into contact with the bed. Titus kept kissing her, deeper and deeper and more demanding. He was swaying against her and his hands were moving over her, up and down her spine and round to her stomach, then up and up to rest over her breasts. He pulled his mouth away and looked down where his hands were. Sarah shivered as he moved his hands about. He reached round her and began to undo the hooks of her dress. 'Don't be afraid,' he whispered. 'I'm sure you're beautiful all over. You have a woman's body. I want to see it.'

'Titus, we shouldn't be doing this. Amy's downstairs.'

'Mama will keep her occupied for ages. We have time, Sarah. Time to be together.'

Sarah was in love with Titus, her every waking thought was about him. He was offering her everything, but she had been brought up with a different code of what was right and wrong. 'I—I don't know...'

'There's nothing bad about showing love to those we want to be with, darling,' Titus said, smiling at her and giving her tiny soft pecks. 'It'll be all right. You can trust me. In a few weeks we'll be together, always. We'll have a wonderful life. Think how excited the little ones are going to be. You'll all be part of a big, close family. You'll never have a worry again.' Titus had kept his fingers working and Sarah's dress – a dress he had bought for her – was open to her waist. He pulled it down

210

until her shoulders and the swells of her breasts above her corset were exposed. 'You're so beautiful. I must have you.'

With fervency he gathered her in and kissed her with abandon. Sarah's nerves reached breaking point and there came a release of her worries. She loved him and wanted to please him, to repay him for all he'd done for her and to reward him for all he was promising her, and he was filling her with desire. A sensation within the root of her grew hot and fanned out and filled her with exquisite sensations. She allowed Titus to pull her sleeves down and off her arms and unlace her corset. He threw the lace-edged corset, another gift of his, down on the floor. Sarah held her breath as Titus slid her chemise down to her waist but she felt no shyness. He handled her and followed with his lips. 'So beautiful, so beautiful. You'll bear me many fine babies, won't you, Sarah?'

He couldn't wait or linger. He lifted her on to the bed and pushed up her skirt and petticoats. Sarah wriggled with need, a need she had no notion of how exactly would be fulfilled, and Titus weighed himself down on top of her to keep her still enough for him. Then a pain seemed to be tearing her apart and her scream was silenced by Titus placing his hand over her mouth.

Next to Tempest's sitting room was a door that led outside. She and Amy had just passed through it and were strolling down over the

211

well-kept lawn to view the gardens when Sol joined them.

'What is it, dearest?' Tempest said, aware he had travelled here in a rushed state. His black hair was in more than its usual tumbling disarray and a strange light was gleaming in his eyes.

'Excuse me, Grandmama,' he strode up to her and kissed both her cheeks, clasping her hands in his with affection. 'There's been trouble at Chy-Henver. I've come to fetch Amy home.'

'Are my mother and Hope all right?' Amy exclaimed.

'They're fine, Amy, at the moment,' he replied, giving her a smile full of strength and purpose.

Amy turned to her hostess. 'Please, Mrs Kivell, could you send for Sarah?'

'Titus will take Sarah to her home,' Tempest said. 'What's happened Sol?'

Sol frowned over his grandmother's reference to Sarah. He explained briefly why he had come so urgently. 'I'm afraid I need to be at Chy-Henver a lot more, Grandmama. Give me a minute while I pack some things. I will be staying there.'

Tempest stared into space, her august face grim. She looked bereft, as if she was losing the thing most dear to her. She nodded. 'It's as it must be.' She turned her gaze on Amy, who looked as if she was about to argue with Sol's decision. 'It's pointless to say anything. You can't go against your own fate.'

Seventeen

'You have an engagement, Tara?' On light feet, Michael entered Poltraze with the usual intention of making his way to the library. He never failed to stop to share a few words with her. 'It's as well you're wrapped up warmly, it's a bracingly cold day.'

Tara was dressed for travelling, in a fur-trimmed cloak and a small black netted hat. 'I'm on my way to the village to call on a friend,' she smiled, pleased to have received an invitation from Amy.

'You have a friend there? Among the common people?' Michael was bemused. Phoebe wouldn't give the time of day to anyone not high bred.

'I have.' She fastened the jet buttons on her gloves.

'How so? You've hardly left the house since you moved in.'

'I met Amy Lewarne when I lived here as a girl.'

'Lewarne? The name's familiar.' Michael tapped the first knuckle on one hand with a fingertip of the other, a habit of his when thinking. 'Lewarne, the carpenter thrown out by his family. His son died in our woods. Is that right?'

'I thought you knew nothing about the villagers, Michael.' Tara said, picking up a toy, a brightly painted clockwork carousal, off the credenza.

'Oh, I know it seems I'm always poring over old writings but I do listen to what the steward says about local matters. Your friend has had a lot of troubles.' He indicated the toy. 'She is partial to that sort of thing?'

'It's a gift for her new baby sister, a source of some happiness to Amy and her mother.'

'Very thoughtful of you, Tara, my dear, and just as I have come to expect of you.'

It wasn't the first compliment of this kind he'd paid her. Tara always ensured he had refreshment when in the library. Sometimes she went there to inquire if he and Phoebe and the two girls were well, and he'd show her the latest discovery to add to the family records. 'Past events have been jotted down in a most haphazard fashion and stored just about anywhere,' he had said. 'I've found matters of interest in my father's study, on shelves in the drawing room, in cupboards, in chests in the corridors and even up in the attics. It's quite a job getting everything in the right order.'

'But it's a labour of love to you.' She had read the notes about the Mrs Nankervis for whom the Dower House had been built. 'Matilda Nankervis had a tragic life. She lost all her children except one, and had an accident which destroyed the use of her arm.'

'She was highly sensitive and prone to

hysterics. Sadly, she became an embarrassment when senility set in and was banished to a place of her own. It's the first time anyone has been as interested as me in all this. Phoebe thinks only about her social life, or rather the lack of it, and Joshua his precious plants. She's asked Joshua if the Dower House can be renamed, did you know?'

'Yes, he's mentioned it to me. I think it's a good idea. Now the renovations are under way and the gardens are being beautified it will give the place a new lease of life. What name will you chose?'

'I'll leave that to her. Anything to stop her grumbling. No doubt, she'll choose something pretentious in the hope of it giving her a higher standing.'

'I was surprised when Joshua allowed a Kivell to take the commission for the carpentry of your house. I know he keeps company with Laketon Kivell in the inns, but it's different altogether to allow him in the grounds. How's the fellow getting on with the work?'

'Kivell knows the grounds well. Joshua met him a long time ago when he caught him wandering about. They discovered they had a mutual admiration for petals and leaves. Actually, Kivell works very well. Phoebe has no complaints, which is very unusual. She watches all that he and his labourers, all of them younger Kivells, do. I hope she's not getting in the way. My father would never have allowed a Kivell to work for us. Times

215

are changing, Tara. For the better.'

His last sentence was meant to convey that times were better now his father was dead. 'Yes,' Tara agreed with the sentiment, although she still shuddered at the terrible end Darius Nankervis and her aunt had met. She was no longer under pressure to produce an heir, which was just as well, as Joshua had made no second attempt to make love to her. It was easier with her aunt gone and with no more of Atkins's stifling opinions. There was a lightness about Poltraze now. The old house did not seem as heavy, and she had ordered the suffocating curtains to be torn down from every room, and everyone, including the servants, was more at ease. The only sign of mourning was the wearing of black. Michael had given up soothsaying. Joshua had begun to sing about the house. Yes, times were better.

She had taken the opportunity of Joshua's good humour, cornering him as he'd hurried away from his dressing room this morning, to ask about a matter that was normally his or the steward's domain. 'Will Laketon Kivell be responsible for the woodwork in the burnt out wing?'

'I have viewed his work at the Dower House myself and it's satisfactory, therefore his tender will be considered. What a strange thing you're wanting to know, Tara.'

'I was thinking about my friend, Amy Lewarne. Do you remember her?'

'Oh, yes, the carpenter's daughter. What

about her?'

Tara was as disappointed as the villagers that Joshua showed no interest in Meryen. After his earlier thoughtfulness towards Amy and Mrs Lewarne, he seemed to have forgotten they existed. 'Her father's business could do with the work. He's no longer there but there's a young man, another Kivell, as it happens, who's taken over very commendably. Would a tender from there be considered too?'

'Tara,' he had scratched his head, puzzled and amused, too kind to be vexed with her over something that was not her concern. 'I will probably have to hire every local carpentry business and bring in every woodworker on the estate to accomplish the great deal of work required in the west wing. The debris has been removed and the walls are replastered but the site is somewhat dangerous. I don't want you going anywhere near it.'

'That is not my intention.'

'Good,' he had pecked her forehead, a touch of affection that was brotherly. 'I shan't be in for dinner tonight. Good day, m'dear.'

Michael wished her a good day now. Before they went their separate ways, Phoebe arrived. As always when his wife was present, Michael's face tightened and he looked exasperated. As always, Tara secretly sympathized with him. As always, Phoebe had come by trap, considering the walk up the hill out of the question for a lady. 'Oh, Tara, you're about to go out. I was hoping we could take morning coffee together.'

Phoebe had been ingratiating herself with Tara now she was first lady of Poltraze. Tara knew her ploy, to attempt to manipulate her, but she was not about to allow herself to become easy prey. She told Phoebe where she was going. 'You are welcome to join me. I'm sure Miss Lewarne and her mother wouldn't mind.'

Phoebe's attempt to hide her aversion to the invitation was belied by the shift of appalled eyes and a smile that looked sprayed on. 'I wouldn't dream of encroaching on your time together. I'd come to say that the dining room of Wellspring House is completed. It's excellently done.'

'Wellspring?' Michael said, raising his brows.

'Yes. Don't you like it?' Phoebe asked sharply.

'Actually, I do,' he nodded. 'The house is built on the site of an ancient well fed by a spring. An excellent choice.'

For once, Phoebe was delighted with his reaction. 'Tara, you and Joshua simply must come to dine with us soon. Mustn't they, Michael, dear?'

'Indeed they must,' Michael replied, displaying twinkling eyes to Tara above his wife's head.

Tara met his merrymaking with a friendly smile. 'We'd be delighted to, although it will be necessary to pin Joshua down to a particular time. He's always very busy.'

'Well, I am too today, at home, really. I'll call again another time.' Phoebe left on important feet.

'I'd better be on my way too,' Tara said. 'I hope you have a successful day rooting out something interesting for the family annals, Michael.'

'I'll let you know if I do, Tara.' Michael's smile was full of genuine warmth.

'I'd like that.'

He escorted her to the carriage and waved her off. Before leaving the gravelled courtyard Tara turned round to see if he was still there. He was.

Amy sighed at seeing that Sol had left his tobacco on the kitchen table. She snatched up the leather pouch, with his initials S.K. burnt into it, and strode off for the workshop. He had made himself too much at home during the few days he had moved in. She wasn't about to pick up after him in the way he was used to at Burnt Oak. He wasn't just encroaching, he was an encroachment. He behaved as if he was doing her and her mother some great favour. In truth, he was, and it bothered her. She couldn't accept the way her father had been forced to leave. Her mother had no regrets about it, but now she had grasped that her marriage was over she was desperately unhappy. It was a good thing she had Hope to distract her.

Amy bounced the tobacco pouch up and down in her hand. It was full. Sol always had

219

a good supply of everything, he didn't believe in stinting himself. He went out some nights, after stationing the dogs at the doors in case Morton returned to cause trouble, and he came back late. Her mother had been reluctant to hand him his own key to the house but she said he had the right to visit his grandmother. Amy doubted if he spent all his free time at Burnt Oak. Meals were changed to suit his taste and her mother fussed that he had been given enough to eat. He talked about Toby and listened about Toby as if he had as much right to his memory as she and her mother had. He had no right to so many things. She brought the pouch up before her eyes and glared at it. He must stop leaving his things lying about.

As she closed in on the workshop she pulled her face in so tight she threatened to wrinkle her perfect skin. There was much sound of work and singing, from two people. Another Kivell was arriving every day to bother her. Jowan, a cheeky, quick witted individual who often had to be reminded about his language. It irked her that he was of Toby's age. She marched in on the brothers and as always was annoyed to see Sol at her father's workbench and Jowan at Toby's.

The singing broke off. Jowan carried on working, ignoring her and her ill humour. Sol stopped, straightened up and watched her. He waited for her to speak but he formed a sardonic expression. These reactions between the three of them were becoming a habit. 'I've

brought you this,' she tossed the tobacco ◂
pouch at Sol and he caught it deftly. 'I'm expecting a visitor shortly. A lady. I don't want
either of you in the house.'

'What about our tea?' Jowan sang out in his
high-pitched voice.

'I'll see you get it.'

'Mind you don't turn the milk sour.'

'Keep your remarks to yourself.' She turned
on her heel, she wasn't about to bandy words
with an ignorant boy.

She was several steps away when Sol caught
up with her. 'Amy, have you thought about
what I've been saying? About looking at the
account books?'

'Why are you asking me?' she turned on
him. 'You should defer to my mother on any
such decisions.'

He kept a calm, reasonable voice. 'She's got
enough on her mind, and I'm sure she
wouldn't like what she'd see.'

'Why shouldn't she? My father was meticulous about everything. I'm sure the accounts
are in perfect order.'

'Then perhaps you can explain why the
timber merchants and other traders Morton
dealt with are threatening to stop supplies
unless they get prompt payment. I've got
word of this from my second-cousin, Laketon. Amy, don't you realise Morton is in
debt?'

'I beg your pardon?' She had slipped out of
the house without her shawl and shivered in
the biting easterly wind. Spiteful cold rain-

drops were beginning to fall.

'Amy, think carefully, when was the last time anything was delivered here? Morton used to go off for supplies but always came back with an empty cart. He's not been paying his bills. You need to look at the account books as soon as possible.'

'My father's not in debt.' The very idea! Her father had spoken out forcefully against those who did not pay their way.

'He is, and I believe it could add up to several hundred pounds. He may have arranged long credit but he's stretched it too far. It's why I haven't mentioned it to Mrs Lewarne. Would you like me to go over the books with you?'

'No, I would not!' She saw this suggestion as a liberty. 'My father hasn't sent for his things. He may come back any day. He'd be furious if he knew I'd been poking about in his den.'

Sol gazed at her soberly. 'It's time you accepted he's never coming back.'

Her eyes sparked at the harsh announcement, she was shivering but did not feel the cold entering her bones. 'Not while you're here, he'd be too scared. But the business belongs to him and there's nothing anyone can do to prevent him from claiming it. You had no right to turn him out the way you did.'

'You've not said that before.' Sol's face darkened with impatience. He tossed his head to dislodge the hair blown across his face. 'You were pleased he had gone the day you learned he'd hit your mother. He behaved like a savage.'

'And so did you. He had no right to be violent and I hate him for what he did, but it didn't give you the right to take matters into your own hands so brutally. He should have been sent away with his clothes and some money. Goodness knows what he's doing now, how he's living. You Kivells have no heart and you have no morals. You're here to take the business away from us. Why else did you come here? You might not have turned me and my mother out but we'll always be beholden to you. It won't be long before we'll be living like your women, under your thumb, or worse.'

'I'll take against all that,' Sol fumed. 'My father wanted me here and I refused, then I changed my mind because my grandmother suggested it would be a good thing. She has strange notions but I trust her. Now I'm glad I did come, for your mother's sake. I'll make my own way in the world one day and it won't be by ousting another. I thought you'd got to know me. How could you think that of me?'

How dare he become self-righteous? 'You allowed Sarah to be led astray by your rotten father. We should have brought her back with us that day. You Kivells treat women in any way that you care to.'

'Don't presume to think you know everything about all of us,' he raised his voice, leaning towards her. 'There's some very happy marriages, complete partnerships, at Burnt

223

Oak. You don't understand a thing, do you? You know nothing about life yet you dare to stand there and preach at me. I don't approve of the way my father preys on young girls but there was nothing I could do for Sarah. It was too late. She wouldn't have listened to us no matter how much we'd pleaded with her. It's been going on for ages. She's besotted with him. She would have told even you to mind your own business. Anyway, if you had one realistic bone in your body you'd see she's chosen a better life for herself.'

'Better!' Amy shouted, furious that he was justifying Sarah's shame. 'You call being an outcast in the village a better life?'

'It's her life. As least she's got the guts to make her own decisions.'

'What does that mean?' Amy knew she was about to be accused of something and she was ready to fight back.

'It means that she's done what she had to for the best for herself and her family. She's dragged herself up out of deprivation and starvation. She's never known a cosy life hiding behind a mother's apron strings.'

Amy hadn't expected to be derided. She dropped her eyes to the ground. She couldn't bear to see that look in his eyes again, to see that he didn't like her, as on the first day he'd come here. That he thought she was a coward. Perhaps he was right. She had never made plans to leave home and make a life for herself. Perhaps she was scared to face the rigours of life, just like her father was. From

Sol's earliest suggestion that she study the account books she'd had qualms about the financial state of the business and had not wanted to face them. The owner of Meryen's hardware store had hinted that he was owed money.

Her voice surfaced low and dry, dry because she felt the little bit of life left in her since Toby's death had drained away. 'You're wrong about Sarah. She's been led astray from her values. She would never have set out to throw away her reputation. I'll go to the den when my visitor has gone. I'll tell you what I find.'

'Good.' Sol answered grimly. 'And perhaps you'd better arrange for an apprentice. I'll stand Jowan down. And you should start looking for a qualified craftsman. I'll carry on here until I'm no longer required.'

Not knowing if he meant these new arrangements, unable to look at him, she could only nod. She trudged back to the house, tears of shame and despair blinding her. Her old life was gone forever, the future was looking bleak and she had just made things worse. The only thing she had gained in recent months was the return of her yellow and red scarf.

Tara had never driven through the village before. Her Aunt Estelle had forbidden it. With Joshua being so flexible, it was good to be able to please herself on just about anything. People came out of their cottages to see whose horses were making a light clipping trot rather than the heavy rumbling of a workhorse hauling a heavy ore waggon. With mouths gaping in surprise, they touched forelocks and dipped curtseys. Tara looked out each side of the carriage and waved at the windows. Almost to a man, woman and child, after the initial surprise, her waves were returned enthusiastically.

She did as she had planned, familiarized herself with what she saw, for she intended to talk to Joshua about the village. She would make him listen and would not let him humour her. All the little dwellings looked in need of repair or basic amenities. All in all the village looked poor and downtrodden but there were also touches of quaintness and pride. Some dwellings had thick protruding granite window sills, some had mullioned windows. Most had stable doors and most of them needed fresh paint or new hinges. Some were made from cob, some were full or half slate-hung. Roofs here and there were lop-sided. Cottages rambled off in short curving lanes. The newer houses tended to be in spirit-level straight rows. Low thick uneven stone walls divided the gardens; stones were loose here and there and weeds were rife. One cottage had massive buttresses extending nearly out to the road. Another's front door was reached by granite steps, with a rusty iron rail. There was little in the way of pave-ments and those in evidence were of granite slabs or cobbles. Set well back off the road at the far end of the village was the square. Here was where a lot of the trade was carried out; the general stores, a drapery, ironmongery, farm shop, a candle maker, and the mine shop where Tara understood subsist, an advance of wages, was mainly spent. A shop, newly painted, with the sign, *H. Kivell, High Class Greengrocer and Fruiterer*, stuck out like a rose among weeds.

'It was an eye opener,' she told Amy and Sylvia, while drinking tea in the front room. 'I feel it is incumbent on the squire to do something for Meryen. Goodness knows it's been sadly neglected for generations by the Nankervises but I want that to change. You both must know the needs of the villagers, especially the children. Perhaps we could put our heads together and arrive at ways that are helpful, but not at all patronising, to make their lives a little easier.'

'Well, Mrs Nankervis,' Sylvia said, her little finger curled round her best china. She was honoured to have the lady of the big house in her home and she had insisted she and Amy scrub it until everything sparkled. The gifts Tara had brought – sugared almonds as well as the carousal – had been much exclaimed over. 'Meryen has waited long enough for this. Amy and I shall be glad to come up with ideas. For a start it would go a long way if the constables put a stop to the drunkenness outside the public houses. Most inhabitants are God-fearing people but there are those who persist in that sort of unsavoury behaviour

227

which all too often leads to hunger and violence in homes. And, well, it's not a nice subject, I know, but there's filth lying about in certain areas which brings danger of diseases. Something could be done about that.'

'Thank you for your contribution, Mrs Lewarne. I'll speak to my husband about it. Have you any ideas, Amy?' Tara had noticed that Amy was quiet and pale and she took it to be the strain of the family's circumstances.

Amy gave a half-formed smile. The encounter with Sol had left her feeling crushed and she had little energy for the woes of others. Why was life so hard? How could things change so dramatically and sweep away all her security and self-assurance? 'I've often hoped for some more education for the children. The Reverend Longfellow gives lessons twice a week in the evenings in the chapel schoolroom but he does not seem greatly gifted and few children attend, and he doesn't include the girls.' At one time she would have suggested she teach the children herself, she was capable and she would have thought of ways to make the learning fun and interesting, but she had too many concerns here at home for such a consideration.

'Well, that's something to start on,' Tara said. 'Any improvement will inevitably make a difference to people's lives. I shall form a committee to meet once a month. Would you ladies agree to be on it? I mean, it wouldn't work very well without you both. I'd like to suggest we meet at Poltraze, that way our

228

schemes will be taken seriously.'

'We'd both be greatly honoured, Mrs Nan-kervis,' Sylvia said, putting an awed hand to her bosom. 'You and I up at the big house, Amy. Fancy that. Well, I never.' She was too excited to realise Amy was downcast.

Baby Hope began to cry upstairs. Sylvia excused herself to feed her.

'I'd so like to see the baby, if I may,' Tara said.

'I'll bring her down as soon as she's com-fortable,' Sylvia said, scampering out of the room as if half her age.

'Your visit has brightened up my mother. Thank you, Tara,' Amy said. 'More tea?'

Tara declined. 'Apart from what's happen-ed, is there something particularly wrong, Amy? I can see you're very low. You can con-fide in me.'

'Oh, it's just about everything. I've had a quarrel with Sol. I offended him.' She out-lined the details of the angry exchange. 'Now I realize that I don't want him to leave. I should have trusted him. I certainly don't want strangers here.' Her face full of misery, she added, 'He doesn't like me.'

'I'm so sorry you've had such a bad time. Perhaps Sol will come round. It's under-standable that you've been overwhelmed with all that's happened. Is it important that he likes you?'

Amy shrugged. 'Yes and no. I'll try harder to get along with him. If he can help us out of our difficulties then Mother need never know

229

about them.'

'My life seemed to be going nowhere, then it all changed suddenly and I was to marry Joshua and I was scared how I would cope. Then the fire changed things again. I'd do anything to go back and not have Aunt Estelle suffer such a terrible end, of course, but now I'm free to make my own decisions.'

'You think things here might change again for the better?' Amy was almost too weary to cling to a glimmer of hope.

'We never know what lies ahead of us. In the meantime try not to be hard on yourself. We are allowed to be human.'

Amy had heard the last comment before, but often it had an addition. 'But it's the human side of us that gets us into trouble.' She had made trouble for herself with Sol. She hated the sense of desolation it gave her. Witnessing the purpose Tara had in her she made a resolve of her own. To soften her approach with Sol and make him her friend. What ever happened, if it was possible she'd like to always have Sol as a friend.

'Amy, can I have a word, please?' Sol was at the door of the den.

She didn't hear him. She'd spent the last half hour staring into space, having deliberately shut off her thoughts, after a time of horrified and hurt emotions. It had only taken a short while to glean from the account books that no bill had been paid for eighteen months. There were some recent curt letters

230

of demand for settlement. It all tied in with her father's growing harshness and the economies.

'Amy, are you all right?' He stayed put, not wanting to infringe on her. He had not told Jowan about their quarrel. He'd needed to think. Had it been something to do with Amy why he'd agreed to come here? He'd been attracted to her from the moment he'd first seen her, and again when she'd been coming down the stairs here at Chy-Henver carrying china, dressed in black and steeped in grief. The day she'd come to Burnt Oak he'd taken her scarf, something he'd never done before. He'd never wanted anything to remind him of the women he consorted with. But he had kept Amy's scarf, had been reluctant to part with it and had only handed it over the day he'd packed to come here to stay. After the second time she had asked for it back he'd hidden it in his room where he'd occasionally run it through his hands and hold it to his nose to smell Amy's tender scent. He had told himself it meant nothing. Of course, it didn't. He wasn't the romantic sort. The very thought was ridiculous.

Amy. She drifted in and out of his mind all the time. Amy, an uppity young madam – he enjoyed baiting her. Putting her in her place. Sometimes she made him feel uncomfortable and he was sharp with her, for no real reason. Amy … she was … Amy.

He shouldn't have quarrelled with her like that. She had suffered, she was worried and perplexed. He shouldn't have said those severe things to her, it was callous. How small and young and deflated she had looked when she'd walked away from him. Now he wanted to do right by her, he had to put things right. He couldn't leave until everything, one way or another, was settled about Morton and what was to happen to the business.

'Oh, Sol, I'm sorry, I didn't hear you come in.' Amy was at the kneehole desk. She pointed to the only other chair in the room. 'Would you like to join me? We need to talk.'

The den was little bigger than a cupboard and dark, and she had lit lanterns. Morton had kept it locked. Amy had got the brass key from the little round table by his kitchen chair.

Sol joined her, moving sensitively. 'I can see you are shocked. It's how I feared then?'

She shook her head in desperation. 'How am I going to tell Mother? She hasn't a clue this was going on. How are we going to pay for Toby's headstone?'

'Amy, if you let me help you she may never need to know. Look, I shouldn't have gone at you like that before. I'm sorry.'

'I'm sorry too. I should have kept my tongue in check. You're under no obligation to help me, Sol.'

'Yes, I am. I didn't have to force my presence here, and I've no plans to desert you now. I really want to help, Amy. Let's see it as a challenge to make Chy-Henver a well run carpentry business. If your father reappears, well, we'll work that out if or when it happens.'

'I need to know why he ran up these debts. What was behind it? Thanks to you, some of the smaller ones can be paid off. I can think of a few things that can be sold off which won't stir Mother's interest. I'll write to the other creditors and ask for a deferral and hope to convince them that things will be back on track even with my father gone. Sol, I don't really know what there is in the stores. Are they badly run down?'

'I think there's enough seasoned wood, lacquer and stuff to keep things going for a few weeks. Amy, please don't say no to this out of hand. I've got money to buy in new supplies and I'm sure enough remuneration can be made for you and your mother, and I. You could tell the creditors there's a new partner.'

She wouldn't have countenanced such a suggestion a few hours ago. She would even have been offended. But she and her family were at the mercy of the world and she must use any means to try to put things right. In the circumstances it was a kind and touching offer from Sol. 'Well, we will be entering into a form of partnership, won't we?'

'Lewarne and Kivell. Put your hand there.' He stuck his hand out to her.

Amy gazed at the tough, work-marked flesh. Taking a breath, she placed her hand in his. He closed his rough fingers around hers. While they shook they stared into each other's eyes. 'Everything will be fine,' he said, and it came out with the generous measure of emotion he was feeling, a new experience for him. He was trading his carefree life for one that tied him to a promise, a promise he didn't need to make, but the challenge and purpose set before him, entwined to the ones Amy had made, gave him awareness of the greatest sense of adventure. It would do for him for now.

Amy visibly relaxed. The terrible burdens weighing her down for the last few months lifted away and she felt she could face anything. 'We must keep nothing from each other. Sol, I'm sure I could help you and Jowan in small ways. It would help get the orders out. After all, the bal-maidens work hard enough. Actually, I think I'd enjoy it. Mother is able to run the house now. It will be good for her to resume her position.'

'We'll see,' Sol replied, humouring her. 'We'll look after your mother and Hope in every way we can.' He studied her and smiled. 'Pity you don't drink. It would be nice to toast the occasion.'

She opened a bottom drawer and pulled out a near empty bottle of brandy and a glass. 'I found this. My father wasn't keeping it for medicinal purposes. We can share a few sips, cement our new understanding.'

He laughed, a warm chuckling sound. 'I'm enjoying this partnership already.' He opened the bottle and filled the glass halfway. 'You first.'

Smiling with some kind of happiness for the first time in ages, she took the glass, feeling daring. She tasted the brandy with her tongue on her lip. It was warm and soothing. Sol's eyes were on her. She took a big sip, blinked and made a face as she swallowed. 'Mmm, it's nice.'

'I never thought I'd see this.'

Confidently, she took two more sips then passed the glass to him. 'Your grandmother said something to me, that one can't fight their fate. I suppose this was my fate to be going into partnership and drinking brandy with you.'

Sol emptied the glass. 'And who knows what's next.'

Eighteen

'Get a move on, you two. We're going to be late for work,' Sarah said crossly, at breakfast. 'I've never seen you eat so slowly.' It was ironic. Tamsyn and Arthur never went hungry these days but they now had little appetite. They had flesh on their bones and their faces no longer showed thin sharp angles, they didn't suffer so many aches and pains or catch as many infections, but they didn't seem a bit grateful for it.

Wispy haired Tamsyn slowly trudged her

spoon round a bowl of porridge and kept her head bowed. Arthur, with milk teeth missing, was also disinclined to speak.

Sarah glanced from girl to boy, forgetting her irritation, Life would soon give her everything and she had no need to share their gloom, which, she was sure, was because they were missing their mother. 'Do you want some more sugar in it?' Her voice was bright. 'We've plenty to spare.'

'No,' Tamsyn answered, putting a spoonful of the dark brown oats reluctantly to her mouth.

Arthur just shook his head, glum, his lower lip stuck out.

'What is it then?' Sarah didn't look at them. She knew what was really wrong but didn't like to admit it. She went on the defensive, something she'd been doing for some time, in and out of her home. 'For goodness sake what's the matter with the pair of you? You've got no reason to be down in the dumps.'

'We don't want to go to work,' Arthur piped up in his reedy voice.

'Why not?' Sarah tossed her head in challenge.

'You know why,' Tamsyn said, on the verge of tears. 'No one talks to us anymore. They move away when we go near them as if we smell.'

'Take no notice of them!' Sarah blazed. She had got into tempers a lot lately for this reason.

'They call you names,' Arthur wailed. 'A

236

slut, a whore. They're bad names, aren't they? Like the bad women in the inns and the bad women in the Bible.'

'All right!' Sarah jumped up from the table, making the children blink and pucker up their pained little faces. 'There's no need to go on.'

'When are we going to move into this nice house you promised?' Tamsyn sniffed as tears rushed down her chin. 'We want to get away from here.'

'Soon,' Sarah replied airily. Titus had said it would be soon, if all was well – whatever that meant. He had only left Moor Cottage an hour ago after spending the night with her. When sure Tamsyn and Arthur were asleep, they had made love all through the dark hours. After the first awful, painful time, Titus had taught her many things, things she wouldn't have dreamed that a man and woman could, or should, do. Gradually she had overcome her horror, reticence and in-hibitions to reach a place where she enjoyed lying with him and pleasing him. When she was with him she forgot about the rejection and remarks of disgust brought about from her association with him. When she was Mrs Titus Kivell people would have to show her respect, and she didn't care if it came about from fear of Titus. 'Listen, neither of you need go back to the mine again. We've got all we need and your few pence a week doesn't make much difference now. You'd be all right if you stayed at home and tidied up, wouldn't you? Aunty Molly will be glad to see you, it's only me she's refusing to have in her house.' Molly Pentewan had slapped Sarah across the face. 'It's bad enough you've brought shame on your poor mother's memory but to be a whore for that man! How could you? Don't darken my doorstep again until you come to your senses.'

The little girl and boy were a little less strained. 'What have you done, Sarah?' Tamsyn asked. 'Why do people hate you?'

'I've done nothing wrong.' Sarah held her head up haughtily as she put on her cloak and new winter bonnet. 'I've only fallen in love. People are jealous of me, jealous of us. Jealous that we've come up a little in the world, that we've got nicer things than they have, that's all.'

Reassured, Tamsyn finally began on her breakfast. 'Where's this nice house we're going to live in?' she said, as Sarah reached the door.

'It's at Burnt Oak. You'll love it there,' Sarah said, full of enthusiasm. 'There's no need to be scared of the Kivells. Most of them are quite easy to get along with. You'll be able to join the children for lessons, be clever like they are, make something of yourselves. Mother would be proud of that.'

'We saw Sol Kivell yesterday when we ran past Amy's place on the way home from work,' Arthur said, following his sister's example and tucking into his porridge. 'He gave us thruppence each to buy sweets. If all his family are like him then it must be nice at Burnt Oak and not horrible as people say. Hope we don't see much of that big man who comes here though. He's scary.'

'I don't like him. He frightens me,' Tamsyn said, dropping her spoon.

'Don't be silly,' Sarah said sharply. 'He's never said anything to frighten you.'

'He doesn't speak to us at all,' Arthur said, unease making him doubt he wanted his breakfast now.

'Make sure you behave yourselves today.' Sarah left with a bang of the door. It was true that Titus ignored the children but he would grow to like them once they had all moved into his house.

She'd taken to leaving the house early to avoid walking with the workforce. As always she approached Chy-Henver warily. She had only seen Amy once since their joint excursion to Burnt Oak. Amy had turned up at Moor Cottage looking serious and Sarah had made the excuse that she was busy and had no time to talk. Unlike Sarah, Amy had not gone to Burnt Oak again, but Sarah was jealous of the favourable impression her friend had made on Tempest Kivell. The woman who was to be her mother-in-law was polite to her but reserved, seemingly disinterested, and she had hinted that she thought Amy was brave, a girl of honour. Amy was the one person whose disapproval Sarah would not be able to take. If Amy berated her, if she implored her to give Titus up, she'd rise

239

angrily to his defence. She couldn't handle a quarrel and loathing from her only friend.

To her dismay, Amy was out in the lane, shivering in the cold wind in her shawl and bonnet, and it was obvious she was waiting for her. 'Hello Sarah.'

'Hello Amy.' Sarah didn't slow down to enter into a conversation.

'Please don't go past,' Amy said, reaching out a hand. 'You've time to spare. Come inside for a cup of tea. I've got a pot made.'

Sarah hesitated. 'Is this a genuine invitation? I don't want to listen to any moralizing. And what about Mrs Lewarne? She probably doesn't want a fallen woman under her roof.'

'Oh, Sarah, we've got no cause to pass judgment on others after what's happened here. You're my friend, I hope you'll always remain as one. I know what the villagers are saying and I've been worried about you. Come inside. Please.'

'Thanks, Amy.' Sarah was consumed with the need to cry. 'It means a lot that you haven't turned against me.'

Once inside, outer clothes abandoned, the girls sat at the kitchen table and warmed their hands round cups of hot drink.

'Tamsyn and Arthur not going in today?' Amy asked with a smile. She wanted Sarah to be fully relaxed, to prove to her she was a real friend.

'Not today or ever again. Until I give in my notice, there's no need for them to suffer being shunned too.'

'You're leaving the mine?'

'Yes. Of course,' Sarah added, becoming confident and vehement. 'Titus and I are to be married. I know people are saying he's just using me, but they don't know him like I do. He's been so kind to me, so caring.' She told Amy about the time he'd rescued her off the darkening moors. 'He could have tried to have his way with me there and then, and at any time afterward, but he didn't. Nothing happened until the day we went to Burnt Oak, after he'd showed me what was to be my, and the little ones, new home. I love him so much. I can't help the way I feel. I'd do anything for Titus. You'll understand when you fall in love.' She searched Amy's stern expression. 'Do you think like the others, Amy? That I'm heading for a huge fall, for more shame and degradation?'

Amy couldn't accept that Titus Kivell was otherwise but a dangerous brute. Sarah was blind to the true intention of his seeming generosity. It was awful to know she had been innocent until the day they'd gone to Burnt Oak. She painted on a careful look. 'If you want a truthful answer I fear you probably are, but it's not my intention to make you feel uncomfortable. It's your business, Sarah, and I'm your friend and I'll always be here if you want me. Do you really think Titus will marry you?'

'He talks about it all the time,' Sarah replied, eyes dreamy and faraway picturing her future. 'We're going to start a new family.

241

Have lots of children to branch out and spread the Kivell name everywhere. You know how wonderful Burnt Oak is. It's going to be just wonderful living there.'

Amy agreed about the community. Tempest Kivell had extended an invitation to her and her mother to dine at Burnt Oak; Sylvia was considering it. 'I hope it all works out for you.' Amy made the effort to sound sincere.

'It'll be strange being Sol's stepmother.' Sarah bubbled with excitement. 'And just think Amy, if you and he were to marry I'd be your mother-in-law!'

Amy executed a smile that conveyed her reaction: don't get carried away.

Two hours later, after helping Sylvia with some housework, and changing into an old brown wool dress, her stoutest shoes and wearing one of her father's carpentry aprons, Amy went to the workshop. Sol had bought sandalwood, and he was fashioning one of the linen boxes for the St Day doctor's wife and there was the wonderful exotic scent of the wood. He was carving a keel finish, with more flourish to this sort of detail than her father had used.

'This isn't necessary, Amy,' Sol said, running his eyes over her attire, with a long sigh. She had pinned up her hair extra securely. 'You don't have to keep trying to help out here. I'm sure you've got something more pressing to do in the house.'

She was used to this daily opposition. 'Mother's quite happy for me to be here a few hours each day. I'm sorry you don't feel the same way, Sol, but that's how it is.' She looked for the simple dresser shelf she had been spokeshaving the day before. It was gone. It would have been finished off by Sol or Jowan, as had everything else she'd undertaken.

She smiled sweetly straight into Sol's eyes. 'What shall I do today?' The first day she'd asked this question Sol's handsome dark features had stared back in disbelief and the horror of her daring to breach a male sanctuary. His reply had been, 'Are you mad? I didn't think you were serious when you mentioned working in here.' An increasingly heated discussion had ensued, with both of them putting forward every argument on why she should and should not help with the easier, straightforward carpentry tasks. Sol had only admitted defeat when she reminded him it was her family business. 'If you get in the way or hold us up I'll turn you out,' he'd warned. 'And don't expect us to treat you differently because you're a woman.'

Amy knew from her father's day where things were kept, that tools should be scrupulously cleaned or sharpened, that certain substances were potentially hazardous. Sol had scoffed when she'd produced a pair of leather gloves so she worked without them. It had taken him half an hour to find her something to do; he'd either thought he could intimidate her into leaving or thought if he kept her hanging about she would get bored and go

243

away. Her quiet determination had paid off and he'd begrudgingly beckoned her to him. 'You can start off with some sanding but if you make a mess of it I'll make you go back to the house.'

He'd watched her with sighs and heavy stares, but twenty minutes later when he'd stepped up and inspected the piece he'd mumbled, 'It'll do, I suppose.'

She enjoyed working in here, intermittently breaking off to fetch the tea. It gave her something to focus on away from the problems, and they were hopefully getting less. Most of the creditors had agreed to accept small regular payments and Sol had paid off the others, calling it a loan until the business was making profits again.

'I'm not going to change my mind, Sol,' she said today. 'Everything I've done so far has been up to standard so I can't see why you're still putting forward objections.'

'It's strange having a girl about but I'm getting used to her,' Jowan said. He winked at Amy. He made the effort not to swear in her presence, and once or twice when Amy had been perplexed about what to do, he'd mimed instructions to her. 'Let her stay, Sol.'

A few seconds of brooding silence and then he capitulated. 'There are two more shelves for the dresser, but I want you to promise you won't touch anything else. I'm going inside shortly to tidy up, to make my way up to Poltraze for the appointment with the steward about the repair work. All being well I'll win us a very useful commission. It should lift our heads above water and keep us floating.'

'Thank you, Sol. Good luck.'

Together in close proximity for the last few days occasional contact had been unavoidable. It did not seem too much of a liberty when he touched Amy's shoulder, as he said, 'Thanks.'

Amy didn't mind at all.

It was Sampling Day, a two-monthly occurrence at the Carn Croft Mine. The assayers and managers of the smelters arrived at midday in a force of about twenty to sample the ores for quality. The count house was putting on a meal, always a feast by the standards of the mining folk, and every few minutes the delicious whiff of roast beef and mutton was wafted on the wind, masking the choking smells of dust, oil and hot metal. Puddings and bread and cheese would be devoured and wines and brandy drunk in copious amounts.

While some of those hard at their labour appreciated the rich aroma in their nostrils it made many more envious and discontent. It gave Sarah's opponents another opportunity to malign her. The bal-maiden at the table to her left looked round her to the bal-maiden on Sarah's right. 'Hey, Bess, when was the last time you ate two lots of meat in a day?'

'Never, Mary. Be lucky if I see it once a week on my plate.' Bess, short, thick-boned and bluff, made a smarmy face at Sarah and edged in close to her, nudging her hard, putting her off balance so her hammer slipped and juddered on the lump of stone she was bucking. ''Course, Mary, some of us get more than enough. Twice a day and three times on Sundays at least!' Bess wasn't brought up in a religious household and her meaning was lewd.

'Ugh!' Mary, sallow faced and invariably testy, jeered at Sarah's expense. 'Do you mind? You'll put me off that sort of meat for life. Some like it a lot though. Keep going back for more.'

The two girls cackled. Sarah let her hammer droop in her hand and she stared at the gritty ground. She waited for Bess and Mary to lose interest in her then set about the next lump of rock. 'I won't let you get to me,' she mumbled. She coped by reliving the best moments with Titus and looking ahead to a life with him. Each day here was one less to endure and soon there would be no days here at all.

Sometimes men from the business contingent came as individuals or in groups and looked over the women, particularly those of Sarah's age. Half a dozen of the assayers and managers wandered over to her shed on the pretext of watching the work process. The men were in good suits and had pocket watches. Two of them were in their twenties and probably unmarried. Some of the young bal-maidens giggled and threw flirtatious or sly glances, others ignored them, and one or two were offended. Sarah wasn't aware of their presence until Bess pushed her out of line. 'Hey, you lot. If you want a good time then she'll oblige you. She's called Sarah and she's got no morals at all.'

'Shut up!' Sarah shouted, throwing down her hammer and trying to put a hand over Bess's mouth. Bess fended her off and Mary helped her. Sarah's arms were cruelly pinned behind her back. 'She's got a lover, a man more'n twice her age, who keeps her in comforts. I'm sure she'd let you have the same consideration for a shilling or two.'

The men stood and stared, amazed and then embarrassed. Trying to catch the eye of a girl in the hope of a discreet meeting behind a shed or on the downs after the shift was one thing, such a blatant invitation, delivered with malice, degraded them as much as the unfortunate victim. Bess and Mary let go of Sarah and stared at her in spiteful triumph. All work in the shed stopped and all eyes were on Sarah. She stood transfixed in horror. The racket of the rest of the industry died away and she felt she was in the centre of an unnatural hush. There was nothing she could do to limit the damage or regain a scrap of dignity. She couldn't bear to see the accusation or the vilification of the gathering.

She walked away. She expected to receive catcalls and insults at her back but there were none. What the onlookers were doing or thinking, if they had formed a huddle and were talking about her, if Godley Greep had rushed across and ordered them back to work, she had no idea. All she wanted was to get away from here and never come back. To go to Titus.

Numb and as if in the grip of some strange fever she walked and walked, trudging with her beautiful eyes misted over and set ahead, making her way by instinct along the quickest shortcuts over the moors to the man she loved.

There was little activity at Burnt Oak and she reasoned the community would be at lunch. When she got to the courtyard, the lurchers leaping all about her, Kivells began to appear from doorways of homes and business, ordering the dogs off and inquiring if she was all right. She wasn't sure if all family members were ready to accept her but she got the comforting feeling that she, as Titus's intended bride, had these people ready to spring to her defence. She went straight to Morn O' May and let herself in and headed to the dining room.

Titus was there eating beef stew with Tempest, his sister Eula, and five of his older children. Sarah paused in the doorway, windswept and muddy, in her gook, touser and leg wrappings and work shoes. She was unconscious of the fact she had been crying and her eyes were puffy and tear-stained. 'S—sorry, I didn't mean to interrupt...'

Tempest saw Sarah at the same moment as Titus, and they both rose and went to her. Titus wrapped his arms around her. 'Darling, what is it?'

'Are you hurt, Sarah?' Tempest asked, using her fingers to push back the girl's hair as she looked for trauma.

'No,' she rasped, out of breath. 'I ... I...'

'Take her to my sitting-room, Titus,' Tempest said. 'She seems to be in shock. Give her a nip of brandy. Talk to her. I'll come along by and by.'

A feeling of unreality overcame Sarah. She was trembling and weak. Titus lifted her up and carried her out of the room. He set her down on Tempest's sofa and held her close. 'Has someone hurt you?' he demanded, stroking her face.

'No one's hit me or anything like that,' she sobbed softly against him. She filled him in on the day's events. 'Everyone hates me except for Amy. The little ones are so unhappy. I can't go back to the mine, Titus. When are we going to get married? When can I get out of Meryen?'

Titus raised her chin and carefully brushed back the tangled black hair from her face. Even in her distress she was incredibly beautiful. 'You haven't had any women's courses lately, have you?'

'What?' It took a while to comprehend his meaning. What a peculiar thing to ask now. 'No, I, the thing is—'

'Then you must be pregnant,' he cut her off. 'Then I'll tell you exactly what you want to know. You can move in here today, and we'll get married the moment I've set up a date with the vicar. We'll make a wonderful new family together, Sarah. Many more Kivells to spread out and take control of this area.'

'Tamsyn and Arthur can come too? You did say they could.'

'Your family are my family. We'll fetch them and your things as soon as you feel strong enough.'

Sarah couldn't speak through her tears of relief and she clung to him.

Titus gathered her in and rocked her and kissed her hair and said a lot of soothing words, but his eyes were blazing with fury. 'Now, my darling, I want you to tell me exactly who it was who've caused you this misery.'

In a suit of riding clothes as fine as any gentleman's, Sol handed over his horse to a stable boy at Poltraze and left the cobbled yard. He didn't go straight to the back door and ask admittance for his appointment, but took the liberty of going round to the front and gazing up at the charred wing. It was plain to him the blaze had taken hold quickly and that perhaps an investigation should have been called as to its cause, but it was none of his business. If the Nankervis sons were happy to believe their father had burnt himself and three others to death then so be it. The world was better off without the heartless old squire, now deservingly suffering the fires of hell. He ran his eyes along the rest of the grey stone front. No matter what was done to the house it would never bear an inviting prospect, but its unattractiveness could be forgiven for the gardens were magnificent. Even without bloom the avenues of rhododendrons and camellias, the palms and tree ferns, the conifers and climbers, all of prestigious height, and the tasteful ornamentation presented a visual feast. Little wonder that his cousin, Laketon, a lover of the exquisite, had long trespassed over this land and brought back a wide variety of ideas to beautify Burnt Oak.

Sol became aware he had an observer. It was the squire, in his gardening attire. Sol knew him fairly well, he'd drunk and played cards with him and Laketon on a few occasions, and he met his steady gaze without wavering or bowing his head. No one would make Sol humble himself. In the past he had not referred to him by a name or title, but now he had to be polite. 'Pardon me, Mr Nankervis, I was just taking a look at the ruined wing.'

'Sol, you are early for your appointment.' Joshua sounded impressed. He was not displeased to come across this young man. He had always admired Sol's splendid, well sculpted body and strong, handsome face. Never had he seen a man more well put together. His jet black hair fell in sultry tresses. His steely blue eyes were of the sort Joshua could drown in. The presence of the rebel in him, of being his own man, was utterly appealing. He had never thought to be

251

attracted to anyone except Laketon but now he was burning to touch Sol. He offered his hand with a tingling on his flesh. 'I have heard from my wife that you are keeping the Lewarne business on track. A worthy cause, if I may say so. I was involved in the Lewarne tragedy. Mrs Lewarne and her daughter are worthy ladies. All is well there, I hope?'

'Indeed it is, thank you.' The squire's hand was nearly as rough as his own. Sol approved of a gentleman unafraid of good clean dirt.

'Has there been word of the errant carpenter?'

'None. I've asked around but he seems to have vanished off the earth.'

'And you are left responsible for his family. I see little need for an informal interview with you, Sol. I've seen for myself the excellence of the work that Laketon has done at the newly named Wellspring House. I am sure every Kivell can produce work of equal quality.' Joshua was eager to keep Sol talking, to remain alone with him. Laketon had been his first and only love, but with his jealous need to always keep close contact, he'd not had the chance to explore feelings for another. 'As it happens I have a spare half hour. I'll show you over the burnt out wing myself.'

'You are more than generous Mr Nankervis.' Sol allowed a respectful incline of his head, then swept his eyes around the enchanting surroundings. 'The grounds here are a sight worth seeing.'

'Thank you. You must allow me to take you

on a tour.' Joshua took the longest route round the house to stay as long as possible with this gorgeous underling. 'I've an idea. It's my intention to drain and renew the pool, to extend it for more boating. The boathouse needs to be demolished and a grander one put up in its place. You could do that. I'll take you there, and you can tell me if you have any ideas.' All the while, as he set an ambling pace, he studied Sol. He saw Sol was genuinely engrossed; an intelligent, perceptive individual, who appreciated nature and all it could give. Joshua flung out his hands, indicating all that could be seen. 'Everyone knows the gardens are something of an obsession to me. After the pool, I'll show you the shrubberies and take you to the glasshouse, where I have many beautiful specimens of iris and orchid.'

Sol took him at his word, that he was merely proud for just about anyone to view and exclaim compliments over his indulgence. With a commission secured here, to be able to look forward to Amy's delight at the news, he was at ease as he strolled over the shaved lawns and admired the panoramic landscape. 'I can see why Laketon is a devotee of exotic plants.'

'Yes, indeed,' Joshua was thrilled to be holding his attention. 'I allow Laketon the occasional freedom of the grounds. How could I do otherwise? It's a pleasure to converse with someone as knowledgeable as I.' There was a strong hint he would allow Sol the same concession. He knew Sol would never share the same desires as himself, but it would be an intense pleasure to gain his company alone again, just to look at him, to dream ... They were passing the old bath house. A small construction with a steeply sloping slate roof and one small window. It had been stripped of its former use and he had furnished it as another suitable meeting place with Laketon. How wonderful it would be if he could get Sol alone inside and ... he must say something quickly or he might betray himself. 'May I ask, Sol, why you have chosen to work with wood?'

'I haven't chosen it specifically, although it seems at the moment I have arrived at a position where it has chosen me.' He smiled at the picture of Amy happily employed in the Chy-Henver workshop. Life had been cruel to her and she did not smile often. When she did, and when he was the creator of a smile on her lovely face she always captured something from him. He couldn't picture her among all this grandeur, she was a moor girl, wonderfully simple and uncomplicated. The vision of her soulful anxious expression when he'd reached her out in the wild the day of baby Hope's birth was burned into his mind. He'd wanted to take her in to his arms and tell her everything would be all right and he'd always ensure it would be. He should have done. She would have responded to his comfort. She had been open to sharing her feelings with him then, about to cling to him in delight that the baby and her mother had come safely through the labour, but because of his often off-hand ways with her, his well publicized womanizing, she had held back. What would it be like to hold Amy? To hold her very close. He went on, 'I like to do a great many things, to use my hands in many ways.'

'Oh, really?' Joshua felt he was about to turn to jelly. 'Ah, we've come to the pool. It's in a sorry state. I'm afraid we can't get very close.' The basin had some murky rainwater and was overgrown with reeds and weeds and flanked by undisciplined bushes and trees. The boathouse was tumbling down on the west bank. 'My father wouldn't allow anything to be done here after my brother Jeffrey perished in it, but now it can be reclaimed from the wild. I'll get the foliage cleared, and the steps leading down to it.' Joshua set his sight on Sol again.

Up on the high bank, with his hands behind his back, Sol pondered on how different things would be if his father had reached Jeffrey Nankervis in time. The young gentleman would be squire now. Or Darius Nankervis might have lived his life differently and not now be dead. His grandmother's oft repeated words echoed in his mind. 'You can't go against your fate.' Fate had taken him to Chy-Henver, and now here today. He nodded, 'I can see several possibilities. I'll draw up some plans for you to consider.'

'Excellent! I shall be so grateful.'

'Sol! What are you doing here?' a voice demanded gruffly.

Joshua leapt away from Sol, in guilt. It was Laketon. It must have been obvious to him that he had been drooling over Sol in this secluded spot. Laketon was jealous of the time he must inevitably spend with Tara, and questioned him after every night he slept in the house as to whether he had made love to Tara, not believing him when he'd stressed the marriage was not fully consummated. There were rough times ahead. 'Um, Sol arrived to discuss work on the damaged wing. He mentioned your penchant for plants so I was just showing him around. He's going to build a new boathouse for me.'

Sol looked from the squire to his second-cousin, keeping his face straight over the strange interchange. The squire was under no obligation to explain himself to anyone, certainly not a humble craftsman, even if they revelled together. Then the force of the matter hit Sol like a violent gust of wind. Hell's blood! They were deviants. They were lovers. He'd always despised Laketon. Setting aside his sexuality, it was a common consensus among all the Kivells that there was something innately rotten in him. He was quick to take offence and lash out, even against the children. If Titus gained this particular knowledge he'd not hesitate to slit Laketon's throat as a disgrace to the family. It was not going to sit comfortably with Sol that he knew this about Laketon and the squire. He shuddered.

He felt a fool for not realizing the squire's ploy in bringing him somewhere so quiet, and he wanted to thump him for doing so. He would keep his distance from Joshua Nankervis while working here.

Many expressions were vying for supremacy on Laketon's face. 'I see.'

Sol saw the ugly jealousy.

'Well, I must get on,' Joshua pushed back his shoulders and attempted to sound that he was the better here. 'The architect has drawn up the plans for the repairs on the west wing. Details will be sent to you, Laketon. Sol, send your plans for the boathouse to the steward.'

'Of course. Sir,' Sol said in a bland voice, moving back in retreat. 'If I may be excused...'

'Yes, you run along,' Joshua said, on edge.

Sol hastened away. He almost felt sorry for Joshua Nankervis. It was obvious that Laketon was not going to easily excuse his lover.

Nineteen

Late in the morning, in a shanty not far from the Wayside Inn, Morton Lewarne awoke with a thundering headache. He yawned, expelling stale, beery breath, and scratched at the stubbly growth on his chin. Anyone from Meryen witnessing him would be shocked in the further decline of his appearance and appalled at the company he was in.

'Move,' he mumbled, pushing against the naked weight of Marcie Dunn, scrunched up on his arm. Her long greasy hair was spread across his shoulder and for one hungover, befuddled moment, he thought it was Floss, Amy's cat, that had sneaked into his old bedroom, his marital bedroom, at Chy-Henver. He became unbearably aware of his horribly reduced circumstances. That it wasn't Sylvia, his dear, honest to goodness, lovely wife at his side. That he didn't live in a nice, well-furnished house anymore, and have a business – a once thriving business – and a bright, good-natured daughter, the child, if only he had realized it before, he should be proud of. Instead he was existing on uneasy terms with a foul-mouthed, corrupt trollop, in a filthy hovel crawling with lice and cockroaches. Where three mongrel dogs lacking in house training had polluted his boots and used his shirt for tug of war.

He shook his groggy head, bringing himself painfully on full terms with the daylight stealing in through the murky windows, and he maliciously shoved on Marcie's heavy slumbering weight until she was no longer touching him in the narrow contraption of wood and straw-stuffed ticking that served as a bed. His flesh and her flesh were corrupt. They smelled as rotten as a midden. He would have died of shame, if he wasn't past that. Edging past Marcie he got up and dressed in the remnants and rags that were now his clothes.

He peered through pain-lashed eyes for sustenance. 'Damn it! Lazy bitch!' If there was any food the mongrels would have wolfed it down. They were whining at the door and he let them out, tossing a dirty mat after them to discourage them from coming back. He threw an empty battered pewter mug across the single living-room, the only room of the shack. There was no ale left, and not even a drop of water to be found. From a veritable little palace, all spick and span and smelling of beeswax polish and wholesome food, he was starving in a fetid fleapit. When he'd got up of a morning at Chy-Henver, Sylvia or Amy would put oatmeal, topped with milk or cream, and bacon, or ham and eggs, in front of him. There was always a fresh pot of tea to be had. Here, there wasn't even a drop of clean water. His womenfolk had served him without question, moving about quietly and with grace. Now he was lucky if this trollop gave him a crumb to eat, and if he asked for a meal – and it was usually only tea kettle broth – he received abuse from the lazy slut.

'I ain't taken you in to wait on you hand 'n foot,' she'd shriek, putting rouge on in layers, or smoking her dirty clay pipe, or picking at her toenails. 'You said you can get hold of lots of money. 'Tis the only reason I'm putting up with you.' She went on about the money day and night, when she wasn't about her trade at the inn. Trade for her was good, she had enormous expertise at whoring. Thank goodness. At least she wasn't stingy at allowing him the same benefits as when he'd been a generously paying customer.

Marcie stirred, licked her full blotchy lips, stretched her chubby white arms, and rubbed furiously at a flea bite. Her hazy sight cleared and she saw Morton staring down at her, with impatience and disgust. 'Here! Where are you off to?' she trilled, getting ready to make a grab at him, if need be. 'Trying to run out on me? You owe me, Morton Lewarne, and don't you ever forget it. You're a kept man. If you don't do right by me, as you've promised, I'll set my friends on you. And 'tis time you paid up, got hold of this money you're always on about. Or don't it exist?'

Marcie was greedy, grasping and suspicious. And heartless. He'd be thrown out and completely destitute if he didn't make an attempt to pay up soon. 'The money exists,

God's honour.'

'What's He got to do with it? Pray it into my hand, can you?' Sarcasm was another of Marcie's skills. She sat up on the wonky bed, which received much noisy battering when she was about her trade, and struggled into her chemise and reached for her corset. 'Well? Tell me where it is, or you're out on your ear today!'

'I've told you, I've had to lie low for a while. Make people believe I've disappeared for good. When they're confident of that I can slip back and get the money I've secreted away. It adds up to a tidy sum, honest, Marcie. Two hundred pounds. A hundred each. Enough for us to go our separate ways, to keep me going until I can move far away and employ a lawyer to sell my property for me. Then I'll start up something new.'

'Go back, you say?' she clawed her way across the grimy mattress and reared up to the level of his chest, like some fearsome lioness. 'It's hidden in your workshop?'

Morton flinched, afraid she was going to hit him or snatch at his collar. There was a terrible difference between the lashes she gave when she was angry and vindictive and when she was working. 'Y—yes,' he lied. He wasn't about to tell this hell-cat exactly where his nest egg was stashed, the coins he'd put away in case he'd ever needed to make a hasty retreat. He'd also lied about the amount. There was over double what he'd told her. Now, he asked himself, why hadn't he used it

261

to pay off some of his creditors and get himself back on course. If only he had worked up the courage to demand the dues he'd been owned, then he wouldn't have got into such a mess. If only he wasn't so weak and a thorough going coward. 'I'll make my way over there today. Sneak about and see if the coast is clear. Hopefully, Sol Kivell won't be on the lookout for me anymore. If he happens to go out, I'll slip in and get the money.'

'You're shaking like the last leaf on a branch in a gale. Scared, are you?' Marcie jeered. 'Being scared of Sol Kivell is understandable. But I bet you're scared of your wife and daughter too.'

'I'm not! I wouldn't like for them to see me like this, of course.'

'Perhaps I should spy on the place first. I wouldn't mind seeing Sol Kivell for myself,' she fiddled with the curling ends of her hair. 'If he's anything like his father...'

'Yes, you do that, Marcie. Get the lie of the land, so to speak.' Morton was terrified of what Sol would do to him if he was spotted. The dogs would be there and likely they'd sniff him out. The brazen hussy could quickly talk her way out of bother if she was seen. 'Find out what's going on there.'

'I'll do that. It's a lot of money to lose if things go wrong. I hope I don't find the Kivells have taken over the place. That you've lost the place for good. Even the law would have a hard time getting them out.' Marcie looked at him from harsh eyes. Morton quailed, knowing something spiteful was coming. 'Want me to find out how your daughter is? Alice, isn't it? And your pious, don't-do-much-in-bed wife?'

'It's Amy! And don't speak about my wife like that,' Morton exploded. He may have cheated on his family, let them down in the worst possible ways, and beaten Sylvia that last day, but in vile surroundings like these they were sacrosanct to him.

Kneeling on the edge of the bed, putting her hands on her hips, Marcie leered, her pouting mouth twisted and ugly. 'Ah—ah. Hit a tender spot there, did I? So you care about your precious, God-bothering family? Well, that's news to me! You said your daughter was an uppity cow. And you told me your wife was cold in bed, that she was never affectionate. That must be all bleddy lies, you wouldn't care what I thought about them otherwise. Miss Amy and Mrs Sylvia Lewarne will be worth looking at. And your baby. I'll find out when the christening's going to be. You could go in disguise and watch the brat being dunked in holy water.'

'You'll do no such thing. You're not to go near my family, do you hear?' Morton bawled ferociously, donning a manly bearing for the first time in his life.

'Oh, giving orders now, are we? Found a bit of backbone, Morton? Well, it's too damned late for that!' Once Marcie was roused in anger and malice she was unstoppable. 'I'll finish getting dressed and go over there straight away. You'd better be right about this money, or I'll tell Titus where you are. He's been looking for you. He'd be very interested to learn the truth.'

'No!' Morton struck her. One blow across the head. One blow that hurtled Marcie sideways off the bed and propelled her towards the crumbling stones of the makeshift hearth. She didn't make a sound. She didn't get up. 'That'll teach you. Get up, and if you start again you'll get another of the same.' Another first for him, to feel empowered.

He waited. She didn't move. She was playing games. He didn't care. She couldn't intimidate him now. He prodded her with his boot. Then he saw something fanning out on the rough slabbed floor in the region of her head. Something red. Blood! She was bleeding. Hurt. Her head had hit the ragged edge of the hearth. The courage left him as suddenly as it had come. 'Oh God! Marcie! Get up.'

He stared down at her. There was no rising or falling of her body. There seemed to be no breathing. He prodded her again. Kicked her. Then again. He backed away, all the way to the irregular planked door. Panic surged up and flooded him. He stared at Marcie. Move. Move, damn you! The blood had reached her shoulders and was seeping into the cracks on the floor. She must be dead. He'd killed her! And if he was found out he'd hang for it.

His legs gave way and he sank to the floor, crying, blubbering, knees bent up, arms over his face. Minutes ticked by. It could have been an hour. He crawled to a chair, put his shaking hands on the cracked seat and somehow managed to sit on it. He had to think. Try to think.

Bit by bit, he managed to calm himself. If Marcie's friends came here and found she wasn't at home they always assumed she was at the inn, and if she wasn't at the inn, it was thought she was entertaining customers at home. It was possible for her not to be seen for days and no one would realize she was missing. If he got rid of her body. Somewhere. Somehow. He twisted his hands together, mumbled and whined. He'd have to touch her. Touch a dead body. Get blood on him. He bawled like an infant. Shook in fear and gagged on the horror. He had to do it. Do it or swing from the gallows.

Time passed. He had no idea how much. He steeled himself to glance at the body. The bleeding seemed to have stopped spreading. There was a cauldron hanging from a hook in the fireplace. It was rarely used to cook food and was presently empty. He'd find a rag, there was plenty of those about, and mop up the blood and wring it into the cauldron. Then he'd wrap the head in rags, and after that wrap the body in the blankets on the jumbled bed, and put the bloodied rags in with it. He'd strip naked to do all this, and he'd wash his hands thoroughly in the stream, several hundred yards from the shanty. The stream had a small wood behind it, where there was a long drop into a mossy ditch. He'd drag the body there and cover it with leaves. It was late autumn, plenty of fallen leaves about. Even if the body was disturbed by the mongrels or wild animals, hopefully it wouldn't be discovered until he was well away from the area. From the county. Perhaps on a cargo ship leaving the little harbour of Portreath. Or a passenger ship at Falmouth. After he'd been to Chy-Henver and got his money. His only hope.

Sol had finished work for the day, had washed and changed, and was leaving his room. He was brought to a standstill on the landing at the sound of Amy singing. Such a soft, sweet, lilting voice. It was good to hear her happy. The singing wasn't coming from her room, she was in the nursery, laying Hope down for the night, while her mother was out at a chapel meeting. He stole along to them.

Amy was on her knees, rocking the cradle, smiling down on her baby sister with wonder and love. She was singing a lullaby, about how many stars there were in the sky. Sol crept into the little, pale-yellow painted room, and so as not to disturb her, he held his breath. As soon as one song was finished, Amy started another, about Jesus looking after the blessed young. As she rocked the cradle her hair, falling free and tumbling in golden brown curls, rippled over her arms and shoulders. He liked to see her hair hanging loose. It was altogether a beguiling scene.

She was like a gorgeous nymph. Utterly appealing. Enchanting. He wanted to reach out and touch her.

After a while, she knew he was there. She looked up and smiled. He felt a sense of triumph each time she smiled, and felt it a hundredfold when it was he who made her smile.

'I didn't realize you had such a sweet singing voice,' he said.

'It's a pleasure singing this little one off to sleep,' Amy caressed the baby's soft brow. Wispy strands of hair, the same hue as Amy's, were framed around the tiny heart-shaped face; a white, cotton, lace-edged bonnet was tied under her chin. 'She's so good-tempered, you know. She never frets, never seems to get wind. Poor Toby used to suffer terribly from wind. She'll be smiling soon. This time next year she'll be walking, exploring everything. I wonder what things will be like for her, for us, then.'

'I'll make sure all will be well, Amy.' It was easy to make such a promise with her so soft and feminine, and sweet and lovely. He gazed down at the sleeping Hope. 'I don't know much about a baby's development. I've never taken much notice of children. I guess I just take them for granted, there's handfuls of little ones running about Burnt Oak. Hope has the look of you about her.'

'Oh,' Amy leaned over and kissed her sister's cheek tenderly. 'I couldn't have been so beautiful.'

Sol put a light hand on her shoulder, as he did so often now. 'You surely must have been.'

She stared up into his eyes for a moment, saw the appreciative gleam, was pleased and thrilled by it, then dropped her sight shyly. Sometimes he gave her such scrutiny and always she had the same flattered reaction, and would feel a little flustered. He was not yet twenty but had a lot of experience with women, he knew how to flirt and admire, while she had no familiarity at all with romance or relationships. She hoped he genuinely liked her, and found her attractive, and was not playing games or humouring her. 'You're off home now, I suppose.' He always dined with his grandmother on Thursdays.

'No. I've sent Jowan to tell Grandmama Tempest not to expect me.' He was suddenly grave.

Amy got up and ushered him out of the room, pulling the door quietly after them, leaving it slightly ajar in case Hope woke and cried. Her heart beat out a wild tattoo. Had he stayed on to be alone with her? She faced him on the dimly lit landing. 'Why have you changed your mind?' Her emotions were in turmoil as to what would be his answer.

'Don't get nervous, Amy, but I've had this eerie feeling nearly all day that we're being watched. The dogs have been jittery, running about and sniffing. I've looked around a few times but have seen nothing unusual.'

'Oh.' She was terribly disappointed that it

wasn't she on his mind. 'You think it could be my father?'

'It's likely. I think it's inevitable that he'll come back here at some time. Don't you?'

'Yes. Mother does too. It's something we're dreading, yet we want to get matters settled over what's to become of the business, to know if we can stay here for good.' Morton was within his rights to have them all turned out and that could happen at any moment. She didn't want to cast a gloom, not while she had the privilege, and delight, of being alone with Sol. 'Well, I'd better get you something to eat.'

'Thanks.' Sol touched her shoulder again, letting it linger there a few seconds this time. He enjoyed being in close proximity to her. He loved her warm summery perfume, the freshness of her. 'Don't go to any trouble. A slice of cold pie will do.'

They went down to the kitchen. She got him the food, then sat at the table with him and drank tea. In a while he would help himself to porter, mead or cherry brandy. Sylvia did not mind him drinking alcohol in the house as long as neither she nor Amy served it to him.

'Will your mother accept Grandmama Tempest's invitation for you all to come to Sunday lunch?' he said. 'I'll make sure there's someone here to keep an eye on the place.'

'She's thinking about it.' Sylvia was not displeased to be invited there, but she was worried it might not be acceptable to Tara

269

and the other women on the newly formed
Meryen Relief Committee, which was to have
its inaugural meeting at the big house in a few
days time. It would be nice to go to Burnt
Oak again. To see Sarah. She had questioned
Sol about Sarah and he'd said that she and
Tamsyn and Arthur seemed to be happy, but
Amy was sure he didn't take enough interest
in them to really know. The same applied to
Jowan, who had told her the same. Sarah and
Titus's wedding date had been set. She was
invited. It would be one occasion when she
and Sol would be in church together. 'I hope
Mother will say yes.'

'You may go there any time you like, Amy.
Grandmama Tempest took to you. She's
eager to see you again.' There came another
serious look but this one had cajoling in it.

'Yes. I will go along. When I've time. When
things are more settled.'

When he'd finished eating, Sol retired to
Morton's old chair. As he often did, he fell to
examining her father's small circular table.
He ran his broad hands all over it and underneath it. He opened the drawers, and the
drawers he had discovered within them by
use of ingenious hidden springs. And the
nooks he had found. He didn't have to say
that he was convinced the table, the *quizzical*,
held some dark and fascinating secret. Amy
knew her mother would prefer it if she didn't
stay in the room alone with Sol but went
along to the front room, and sewed or read, in
a respectful manner on her own, but she was

enjoying his company, enjoying just watching him, to follow the call of obedience. She took the rocking chair opposite him. She had watched him searching before, avid to know if the table would reveal its riddle. She believed the table would solve the mystery as to why her father had gone so critically off the rails. She had the perfect view to study Sol's well drawn features. The firelight cast exotic and excitingly wicked shadows into each strong angle and chiselled frame, and made his eyes hint of hidden depths.

Suddenly Sol fell down on his knees, his thumb apparently pressing something within the table, while his arm was stretched across the top and a finger was pushing up on something underneath. There was a little click. 'Ah, ah!' He sat back on his heels in triumph.

Amy got down beside him. 'What's happening? What did you do?'

He glanced at her, full of delight. 'If I've got this right, I'll only have to slide off the top.' He did so. And the table was almost miraculously changed into a circle of compartments, eight in all, as if set into a wheel. 'Magnificent! I wonder how he managed to achieve it.'

In each compartment there was a leather, draw-string pouch. Amy lifted one out. 'Feels like there's coins inside.' She undid the loose knot of the draw-string, opened the pouch and tipped out the contents into the compartment. Guineas clinked as they fell speedily one on top of the other, glinting in the light. 'Good heavens! How much is there?'

271

Together, they emptied the other pouches and made a rough count of the money. Seven more piles of shiny coins. About five hundred guineas. 'Father obviously secreted it away in here. He must have been saving it in case of hard times. But why didn't he use it to pay off his debts?'

'Five hundred would have gone only a little way in covering two and a half thousand, Amy,' Sol said. 'Perhaps he was planning to use this if he felt he had to make a run for it. He'd have taken it with him that day if I'd given him the chance. Now, this amount will buy us a lot of good will and ease the debts. I could apply for a loan from the bank on your mother's behalf, the creditors could be paid off and there would just be the loan. Nothing too much to worry about. Things are looking much better, Amy.' He was excited over the find, but especially for Amy. Her eyes were gleaming with optimism and the hope of future opportunities. He was enjoying this partnership with her, helping to get the business back to a respected concern.

It would be better if Morton turned up and sold up. He'd been too hasty with him that day. He should have made him sign a bill of sale to him or to hand ownership over to Mrs Lewarne. Instead, the ownership of Chy-Henver hung over him like a heavy shadow. There was the possibility that Morton was dead. It was being said that a coward such as he, with nowhere to live, no money or prospects, had probably taken his own life. Sol

272

had been beginning to believe this likely, although now there was the question of who had been hanging about the place today. Who better than the wretched man himself, to watch and wait, to be able to nip away and hide and elude him and the dogs. He hoped it was Morton and he would soon show himself.

Right now, it was a joy seeing Amy happy. A joy to be with her. 'Mother's going to be pleased about this,' she said. 'Although everything relating to my father and his miserable and deceitful ways is always a source of anger and sadness to her.' She was enjoying the excited boyishness in Sol, such a contrast to his usual manly, shrewd self.

Of a sudden thought, he frowned, 'Will your mother be escorted home from the chapel?'

'Godley Greep will make sure she gets back safely. Why? Do you think there's still someone out there?'

'I don't know, but we must all be very careful. We won't tell your mother about my suspicions, I don't want her alarmed. I'll go out and scout around in a while.'

'I'm glad you're here, Sol. I feel safe.'

'I never want you to be scared, Amy.'

They gazed and gazed at each other. Nothing else on their minds but each other. Eyes locked to eyes. Eyes dropping to lips then back to eyes. As if drawn by an invisible thread they leaned closer and closer, until their lips met. Soft, tender contact. Firm skin

273

on velvety flesh.

'I shouldn't have done that,' Sol said. But he pulled her round the last little space of the table to him, hauling her into his arms and finding her mouth again.

The world seemed to ignite for both of them. Amy's mouth was as willing and needy as his, her arms clinging to his body as vehemently as his were to hers. He kissed her in a way that was designed to get to know all about her. He wanted every drop of her. The very essence of her. She was an eager participant in his quest. A slave to him. She pressed into him, using her lips to his as if she had done these perfect, awesome motions with him a thousand times before.

In one continuous motion Sol got them to their feet. They went on kissing. Releasing their mouths for an instant so they could repeat the demand in different ways. They disentangled their arms only to wrap themselves up again and again. Sol pushed her gently until her back was against the built-in cupboard. Keeping his hands either side of her face, he stared at her for a second. Her eyes were in a fever. She was gasping for breath. So was he. He ran a path of tiny hot kisses along her upper lip and then her lower lip. When he drew his head away she yanked it back, demanding more of him. He studied her for a second. Then he began kissing her in a new way. Tasting her, inviting her to taste him, and she did so, entering into a new dimension of glorious energy leaching kisses.

He kissed her all over her face, holding her with his hands on her waist for she had no strength left to stand firmly. No will of her own left, except to enjoy this shower of exquisite sensations. He nuzzled his mouth along her chin, nibbled on her ear lobes, sending her into a frenzy of rapture, filling her with heat in the very pits of her being. She thought she was about to die and be blasted into some form of new life, all at the same time.

He was trailing tiny wet circles all the way down her neck, kneading his hands on her hips. She was petrified with pleasure as he made the journey from the base of her neck and down over the stuff of her bodice until he reached the peaks of her breasts. His lips were pressing over the material yet felt they were pressing over her flesh too. She thought she would explode. She let out an enormous needful sigh.

The dogs started barking. They were outside and they were making a din of urgent yapping. 'No,' Sol groaned as if in the greatest anguish of his life. His hands were trembling when he took them off her. He was shaking when he moved back from her. The expression he put on her was full of pleading, 'Amy...'

'Y—you go and see...' she said, struggling to find breath, to handle the crop of bittersweet emotions. 'Be careful. I'll check on Hope.'

He turned swiftly, pushed the heaps of money flat, slid the top of the table back into place, then snatching up the gun used for shooting rabbits, which he'd been keeping handy in the cupboard, he went out.

Amy barely found the momentum to climb the stairs. She was praying that Sol would meet no danger. If it was her father out there, why couldn't he have picked a different time to come? She could almost hate him if it was him. She didn't know what would have happened, how far she would have let Sol go, but she felt horribly cheated. The intense, utterly delicious awakenings she had known was replaced with an aching so acute she felt that every nerve in her body was being torn to shreds. And she had an agony of need and hopes plaguing her heart.

Hope hadn't stirred. She smoothed the blankets over the tiny body and ran a finger over her soft face. Hope was warm and well. She left the room. She longed for Sol to come back. She missed him terribly. In compensation she went into his room. He kept few of his things in it but part of him was in here. She picked up his discarded work shirt, which was cast aside for her or mother to take away for laundering, and she breathed in a deep breath of him, the spirit of him, and clutching it to her body, she went to the window. The room was at the back of the house, and she stared through the darkness, hoping to see him and not an intruder.

Moments later she heard Sol coming inside and locking the door. She should leave here and go downstairs. At all costs she mustn't stay in his bedroom. It was wrong in every way. He called her name, softly. She didn't answer. She put the shirt on a chair, moving until she was just inside the doorway. He was climbing up the stairs. He peeped into the nursery. She had time to get out of here. To go downstairs, ask him what had caused the commotion. To try to bring things back to how they had been before they'd kissed. Again came that strange suffocating, yet not frightening feeling, of being consumed by something beyond her control.

He was there in the doorway. She put her hand out indicating the window. She tried to point to it but her arm wouldn't go straight, it was all crooked up. 'I was just looking to s—see...'

'I think it was a fox.'

He stepped into the room and shut the door.

Amy swallowed. It was almost pitch black. Sol touched her arm. A brief touch. Every edge of every nerve in her body leapt alarmingly, but it was something she relished. He was little more than an inch away. She reached out and her hand brushed against his. He gripped her fingers. She squeezed back.

He let her go and moved away and lit a candle. She turned to him. He came back to her. Stood in front of her. He picked up her hand and brought it to his face. He kissed her palm, making the act of devotion last and last. She reached up and stroked his cheek, then ran a fingertip down over his chin and neck and on to his chest.

Then they were reaching for each other, searching for each other's lips, and they instantly reached the place where they had been interrupted. Amy was powerless again, eaten up by the wonderful strange weakness. She could only respond feverishly to his kisses, to his touches, and give them back in equal frantic measure. With a heady willingness, she allowed him to unhook the hooks and unlace the laces of her dress. While smiling into her eyes, he nudged the sleeves down and down over her arms and pulled them free of her hands. Then he was kissing her again. He lifted her up and carried her to the bed, kissing her all the way. He held her, hovering over the bed, pushing hard with his mouth on hers. The frenzy was on Amy again, and she knew he was in the same grip. There was a burning inside her, a need she had to have seen to. She sighed, she moaned softly.

His breath coming in gasps he laid her down on the bed. He pulled her chemise down off her shoulders, lower and lower, to present himself with her perfect figure. He kissed the exquisite mounds of her breasts, teasing her there, tasting her, devouring her. While doing so he was lifting her petticoats, preparing himself. He moved his hand down to her. Amy let out a soft cry. He positioned her, then himself. She felt his weight, then he took his weight on his forearms. He was gentle. The gentleness turned into a searching, then came a pressure, and an invading.

By instinct she moved to help him. The whole of her being was alight. She was utterly aroused, inflamed by so much longing, without fear or caring, and she arched her back to meet him. He accepted her gift and found her fully. There was pain for Amy, but it was wired with the finest of sensations, so infinitely superb, experiences akin to something supernatural.

Joined, entwined, as one, they went on and on, into new worlds, into havens, reaching out, passing destinations and starting all over again. It could have been an age, out of time itself, then Sol reached for her hand, laying her arm at a curved angle above her head. Threading his fingers through hers, contouring his arm gently along hers, he released her lips and came to a shuddering halt, gasping and moaning. Amy had not the knowledge that his intense arousal meant it was all done quickly for him, that he'd had no way of holding himself back. His release had been unstoppable. But the beauty for him was not a disappointment for either of them. The beauty of completion for him turned into the beauty of resting inside her for a while, glorying in the aftermath of his climax, glorying in having taken her, and to being still within her. He felt he was about to weep in ecstasy. He gazed down on her. Her lovely face was aglow in the candlelight. Perfect. Breathtaking. Astonishing. So utterly beautiful.

Amy lay in the wonder of him. He was inside her, above her, all around her. She had

279

given him her most sacredness. He was looking at her, as if in wonder, as if seeing something unique and glorious for the first time, and she knew it all meant so much more to him than a passionate encounter. The gasps, the panting in him, were subsiding. He was making tiny movements, gentle jolts with his body, and he was filling her being with new and wonderful ecstasies. He was so handsome. Masterful. Loving. He lowered his head and brushed her lips with his. It was to be tenderness now. After the urgency, the writhing, the tremendous chanting for fulfilment, this time it was lingering, and agility and grace.

Sol took himself away from her and he made a delicacy of her body. In heaven and on earth was there anything as fine and beautiful as a man and a woman making love, giving themselves over to the other completely? Amy thought. They went on honouring together, discovering together. Reaching for the other one, giving and receiving in delight. Joining in the exploration. Unafraid. Giving enchantment. Little by little he was building up something inside her. She felt it fan out and take her away and sweep her back in dizzying, almost tortuous sensations. She longed for the end of it, for it was going to be such a magnificent end, yet she wanted him to go on forever giving her elation, giving her fire, giving her bliss. Then she was taken to the unstoppable, and it was she who was gasping, and crying out, and panting, and floating away and away.

Sol gave her no time to lie and linger over the glory. He took dominance of her again. She encountered him again. This time he moved with all his power and she gave over all she could, and more. He held on to her and she clung to him. They rocked and gyrated. Making ever new ascendancies, and just as the last pinnacle was about to be reached, he used his skill to waver, just for that ideal moment, then he took her soaring again. The climbing went on and on. Amy loved him in perfect motion, in perfect timing. Together they were one entity, a beautiful being. Then she heard herself crying out. It was happening again. The rise towards the fantastic finish. He was taking her there. And she could hear his sighs, and she knew she was taking him to the same heavenly place. Nearer and nearer. Soon. Soon. Nearer. Nearly to eternity. They reached that special place together. Going on, going on ... Raptures. Crying out, clinging together. As one.

Then they were falling. And the falling away was as wonderful as the passage had been going up. Finally, they were still. Spent. Lying side by side. Hand in hand. Eye to eye. Smiling. They didn't have to tell each other they were in love. Had fallen in love. Deeply and irrevocably in love.

If she died this minute she would take his love with her through all eternity. If from now on she lived in poverty and was shunned by the rest of the world, it wouldn't matter as long as she was with Sol.

Sol held her as if afraid he might lose her. This wondrous time had changed his life. Forever. All that he thought he would do was suddenly lost. But if he'd never known this time with Amy, he would have lived as a man on a pointless journey until death. If he never experienced loving with her again, he was a man of nothing, forsaken. He was lost. Lost to loving Amy.

Twenty

A procession wound its way to the upper floor of Wellspring House. After all the weeks of renovation and extension, the dust covers had been removed, and any remaining dust ruthlessly eradicated. Only smells of paint and base oils hinted that the house had undergone a major upheaval. Following on after Phoebe's swaggering wake was Michael, with the small, soft, white hands of Cecily and Jemima's inside each of his own. The governess, of delicate and distant disposition, the youngest daughter of an unnoteworthy clergyman, tripped along at the rear.

Michael was swinging the hands of the two girls, a sign of the affection he held for them. Like him, they were enjoying it here away from the less restrictive confines of the big house, and despite him seeing little of them, by choice of his obsession with the family history, the bond between the three was steady and unbreakable. He had been glad his father had shunned the girls, that way the old bully hadn't frightened them or brought them down. Cecily and Jemima, who had celebrated birthdays in August and September, and were now six and five years, were his little sweethearts. They were of keen mind and eager spirit. Cheeky little jesters. Something Phoebe sought to suck out of them and something he was delighted to observe was quite impossible. He wouldn't have allowed it anyway, not to the pair of gorgeous cherubs, dressed in black satin, in mourning for their grandfather, but with sugar-pink ribbons round their waists and in their white-blonde, bouncy ringlets.

'You'll like our new nursery, Papa,' Cecily chirruped, with a little skip in her step. Usually, Phoebe would have been on to the breach of correct bearing, but she was too animated in her approval of the improvements – refinements, she called them – of the once dour old house, to notice her daughter's crime. The daydreaming governess Frances Durrant seemed to rarely notice such lapses, besides which, Cecily and Jemima, even for their young years, were too quick in concealing. The intelligence of the girls meant they had acquired a governess earlier than most daughters of the gentry, something Phoebe was proud of and never failed to boast about. 'It has rugs on the floor with our favourites from nursery rhymes.'

'Has it, dearheart?' he swung her hand higher and higher, with a conspiratorial wink, while aiming a wicked look at Phoebe's ramrod straight back. 'How wonderful. Whose suggestion was that?'

'Not Mama's.' Cecily's tone was proof of the shortage of respect she had for her fussy mother. 'It was Mr Laketon's. It's what Jemima and I call him. He said the rugs could become quite the thing, and his family has started to make them to order. Mama agreed with all he wanted us to have.'

'Good heavens,' Michael murmured to himself, as they reached the newly white-painted door. Phoebe agreeing with anyone, let alone a tradesman, and not endeavouring to gain maximum control, was positively shocking. She had been distracted of late and had not burned his ears with her usual nagging. Well done to Laketon Kivell. Michael had left all the decisions on the house to Phoebe. He had spoken to Kivell only a couple of times, and while confident of his expertise, he had thought him a fellow of furtive and brooding undertones. He hoped Kivell's transfer up to the big house wouldn't mean that his wife would revert to the norm. *Why can't you be more like Tara?* he glared at her as she turned the glass doorknob and disappeared into the room. No. There was no one like Tara and he didn't want there to be.

'Close your eyes, Papa!' Jemima trilled,

dancing about at the end of his hand. 'I want you to guess what colour our wallpaper is.'

He obeyed her and entered the little room as a happy captive. The girls took him in. He was aware of the light and was pleased his girls wouldn't have to play and learn in dark surroundings and he could feel polished floorboards under his feet, presumably easy to mop clean. The girls tugged on his hands for his guess. He could feel their excitement and he loved them for it. 'Let me think. Is it purple?'

'No!' Both girls cried together.

'Really Michael,' Phoebe tutted.

He ignored her. He always did nowadays. When he wasn't about his research or estate business, he thought about Tara. They talked most days. She had told him about her charitable hopes for Meryen. 'I've suggested to Joshua that we build a school and pay the penny a week for each child. I would have had a teacher to put in place, in my friend, Miss Amy Lewarne, but sadly she has great concerns.'

'I think a few rudimentary lessons for the children an excellent idea, Tara,' he'd replied. It was a lie. He saw no use for education for the brats of the lower orders, it was a waste. The few that shone and might become engineers or something could be sponsored privately. 'In fact it's the family's duty to be going forward along these lines. How did Joshua respond?'

Tara had seemed annoyed, 'He offered no

objections but I felt he wasn't really interested. I suppose he feels it gives me something to do.' Tara occasionally entertained or went off to fine houses but she never mentioned the ladies she met. She had told him all about her friend, the carpenter's daughter, at Chy-Henver, and her worries for her future.

'I'd be interested in meeting Miss Lewarne and her mother when they arrive for your first committee meeting,' he'd said, as if it was as important a matter as a proposed bill in the House of Commons. Phoebe intended to be at the meeting – there was no way she was going to be left out, even though she had expressed her distaste at mixing with a tradesman's family. He'd take his wife to task if she made things difficult for Tara.

Michael attended to Tara's every word, he took in her unblemished, milk-white skin, her exquisite fairness, her gentle femininity. She had the freshness, the promise and splendour of youth. A woman, although not quite a woman. He couldn't quite define why he sensed this. It must be her wonderful innocence, the little ways she was beguilingly unsure. There wasn't the slightest hint of artfulness in her. She never raised her voice. As each day passed she brought more harmony to Poltraze. She was immensely kind and caring. The servants were devoted to her, falling over themselves to please her. That was no wonder. Anyone who gave her a second thought would be devoted to her. *The house liked her.* Another enormous plus in Michael's mind.

Recently he had come to notice in a mirror that he had a special smile for her. He had watched her as she interacted with others, and it had thrilled him to be rewarded with the knowledge that she also kept a particular smile reserved just for him. 'It's good to have you as my friend, Michael,' she had remarked to him yesterday. 'If my conversation doesn't include the hothouses or the best types of soil Joshua doesn't even bother to listen to me above five minutes.'

'Then Joshua is a fool,' he had turned his deepest smile on her. 'And I am honoured to be your friend, Tara.' How he wanted to be so much more. Joshua was more than a fool, he was in the way.

'Guess again, Papa,' Cecily urged.

Michael peeped through an eyelid. 'I think, actually I'm pretty sure, darling, it's yellow, blue and pink, with tiny rosebuds.'

'Yes, yes, clever Papa!' The girls danced round him.

Phoebe tapped a foot. 'Miss Durrant, bring Miss Cecily and Miss Jemima under control at once. There must be no more of this unruly behaviour.'

A light seemed to flip on in Frances Durrant's unremarkable eyes and she floated out of her daze. 'Yes, Mrs Nankervis.' The governess clapped her hands once. 'Now girls, be perfectly still.'

Michael was amazed when his daughters

dropped their flailing arms and stood side by side, perfectly to attention. Then he had it. Miss Durrant might seem sleepy but she and the girls were in collusion. How very clever. There was, no doubt, an arrangement of some kind, that if the girls appeared totally obedient to her she would turn a blind eye to their bubbly characters, and in turn the girls would leave Miss Durrant to her own private world. As long as Cecily and Jemima learned their lessons, minded their manners, and turned out as fine young ladies, he had no disagreement with this. He glanced at his po-faced wife. Joshua wasn't the only fool who was unaware of all that went on in regard to those to whom they were closest.

'That's better,' Phoebe said sharply.

'Well done, Miss Durrant. Well done, girls,' Michael's voice was steeped in approval. Phoebe had reservations about Frances Durrant. He made it plain the governess was permanently in place.

Phoebe gave Michael a long look. 'I take it you like the room? What Kivell and his labourers have done here?'

'Absolutely, my dear. You are to be congratulated on the outcome of the whole house.' He would order a gold bracelet, as a thank you gift, Phoebe deserved that much. He began to turn away. 'Well, girls, Papa is going up to the big house. Enjoy your new realm.'

'Come again soon,' Cecily and Jemima chorused in unison, like a pair of delectable angels. They adored his indulgent, non-critical manner and readily forgave his long absences.

He was out of the room and pattering down the stairs. Would Phoebe come hurrying after him, to harangue him over something trivial, now the house was in order? He got to the bottom of the stairs and was in the hall, now parquet floored in the latest style, taking his coat, hat and gloves from the senior house-maid before he took a wary glance upwards. The staircase was empty. Brilliant. He was off and out, and he'd stay over for the next two nights under his brother's roof. If providence was really kind to him, Joshua would also spend a night or two away from home and he would be able to dine with Tara alone.

'Yes, Miss Durrant,' Phoebe said, taking easy strides about the nursery. 'Mr Kivell has served us very well here. I'll leave you to the girls' alphabet lesson. Bring them down to me at five o'clock.'

She went to her boudoir, a scrap of a room tagged on to the master bedroom, a small space but one that was important to her. Laketon Kivell had recommended he section it off to give her a little domain all of her own. It gave her a sense of esteem while everything her neglectful husband, and all at Poltraze, did was designed to denigrate her. Laketon Kivell had discussed with her, at length and in exact details, all the schemes to smarten and make her new home as comfortable as possible. Walls had been knocked down to turn cupboard-sized rooms into ones of significance. She had a drawing-room where many ladies in full swinging skirts could gather without fear of encroaching on carpet space. The cheap murky glass of the windows had been replaced by the finest glass, the windows themselves greatly enlarged in width and depth. A conservatory, a most desirable acquisition, had been added, and he had brought vines and seedlings of his own to start her off on what he had promised to be a supreme collection of exotic specimens. He had talked on and on about the plants and how vital it was to keep them at the right temperature. He called himself a perfection-ist, and she was sure it was a ploy to lengthen the job and impress Joshua, who always seemed to be about the place.

She reclined on the pink and white striped, watered silk couch. Here she was, within beauty. The wallpaper had a Japanese design of fantastic birds with impossibly long tails, and chintz and frothy sweeps of scalloped lace adorned the windows. Matching cush-ions were finished with golden tassels. Copies of the New Monthly Belle Assemblee and other fashion magazines lay in perfect arrangement on a tasteful small table. The fireplace had a register grate, and tiles that built up a picture of flaunting birds, and a creamy marble surround. There was a fluted silver bonbon dish. She took one and bit off a tiny nibble and thought about the carpenter.

Laketon was a very good looking man. Tall,

strong, manly but not uncouth. He always smelled clean, his chin shaved close, without the awful adornment of fashionable side whiskers, and he combed his thick black hair as neatly as a barber. When he was in consultation with her he wore a fine suit, and a tie with a stud in it that could be none other than a diamond. He could be mistaken for a gentleman. His hands were expressive, and when he was describing something, whether the shape of a piece of furniture, an extension, or a flower, or a tree, he waved them, and flicked them, and circled them, in slow flowing movements. He held great attraction and an affair with him would be appealing if not for something unwholesome about him. He pretended patience, but she had heard him shouting and swearing at the Kivells who worked with him. She had a feeling he'd go to any lengths to get his own way. He had done well with the house. Phoebe stared round her room. Her *tiny* room. It was like a room in a doll's house. She threw the dish of bonbons at the fireplace where it hit a porcelain figurine and smashed it to pieces. She had given the Dower House a new name, it now had many fine, modern features, but it didn't alter the fact that she and her daughters had been thrown out of their grand home, their places in society lowered. Damn Michael. She had been cheated, made to feel unworthy all her married life. Damn Joshua and Tara. If she could find a way she would bring them all down.

★ ★ ★

Amy put down scraps outside the back door for the dogs. Stumpy and Rip came barking in anticipation. She walked away from them and faced the workshop. Sol came out to see what the ruckus was about. He stood motionless, a tall and proud figure, like some magnificent animal. Apart from the wind tugging at his hair he was like a statue. She might have been one too, so motionless was she. But emotion raged inside her. She knew it did for him too. For they were utterly connected. The hundreds of yards distance between them fled away and it was as if they were entangled lovingly in each others' arms. It was only hours ago when she had lain in his bed with him. A lifetime ago. An instant away. The imprint of him was on and in her body. Her lips tingled from the wonderful kisses they had shared secretly on the landing this morning, while listening for her mother approaching. One of them should break away. He had work to do and she had to go to the shops, but both were reluctant to break the wonderful spell.

It was going to be just about impossible to keep their relationship, their love, to themselves for long. Their every glance would betray them. It was impossible not to touch and linger and bide with each other. They had not spoken about the future, they were content to just let the next course happen.

'I've written out the shopping list, Amy,' Sylvia called from within.

She reached a hand out to Sol and he did so to her. Then she went indoors and put on her cloak and bonnet. The quicker she got through this the quicker she could join Sol in the workshop.

The second she had shut the front gate, Sylvia marched to the workshop. 'Sol. A word if you please. Now! Outside.'

Jowan looked up from where he was fixing a length of wood into the vice. 'I'll have none of your cheeky lip,' she nipped him off before he could utter a syllable.

Sol followed her to some distance away. She kept her back to him. He could see she was simmering with indignation and wrath. He knew what this was about. He came round her, looked down on her. He waited, trying to keep his expression free, but a guilty flush spread over every dimension of his face. She was having trouble articulating the words she wanted to say. 'Mrs Lewarne...'

She gazed at him for a moment from eyes that were so like Amy's, eyes that were brimming over with fury, and he braced himself to witness it unleashed. 'I'm not a fool! I know what's happened. I've packed your things. I want you out from under my roof today. If I wasn't depending on you and your reprobate brother then I'd turn you out of the workshop this instant. It's up to you if you stay or not, but I won't have you inside the house. Any meals can be brought to you. And Amy will no longer work alongside you!' Now she was letting rip her voice rasped bitter and full of courage.

Sol knew she was itching to slap his face. He shifted about. 'I'm sorry you are upset, Mrs Lewarne. Of course, I understand why. I do love Amy, she means more to me than—'

'Just another conquest?' Sylvia cried, growing ever darker in countenance. 'Don't you dare try to sweet talk me! My daughter is young and vulnerable. She was there for the taking and you took her. And I am as much to blame. I shouldn't have left the pair of you alone so often and certainly I should not have gone out last evening – the devil has many a trick to lull the faithful into false security. He's the father of all lies, and you have lied your way into Amy's heart and more. You had better pray to whatever god you believe in, Sol Kivell, that you have not left her in disgrace or you'll be wishing you were facing the hounds of hell rather than what I'll do to you! I lived with a weak husband for nearly twenty years and it left me a weak woman. Not any more! I'm taking charge of my family from this day forward. What I say goes. Do you understand?'

'Yes, I do.' Sol had never thought he would be reduced to the rank of a trembling miscreant, eager to make recompense, but he was, and by a normally mild mannered, middle-aged woman. 'Mrs Lewarne, let me try to reassure you that I would never harm Amy. Please believe me when I say I love her. That I want to be with her always.'

'To marry her, you mean?' Sylvia's voice

verged on mocking.

'Yes, one day.'

'You might believe you mean that now, and that you love her. Amy's not the usual sort of girl you've been involved with.' Sylvia's anger did not seep away, and added to it was a deep distress. 'You can't be trusted. You're going to break her heart. Whether you go off now or some time ahead, you'll leave her stranded in some wretched limbo, for I know my girl, she'll never love another, and looking at you, I can see only too well why any girl would have her head turned. I shall never forgive myself for her fate. I should have known better than to allow you to remain here after you threw my husband out. It would have been better if Amy and I had given up this place and went to work as bal-maidens.'

An unbearable pain was building up inside Sol's heart. He had to make this woman listen to him, to understand. 'Mrs Lewarne, I understand the way you feel, but I swear that if I travelled the whole world and discovered everything there was in it, and if I achieved all that mankind was ever capable of, it would be pointless to me without Amy in my life. Don't turn me out. Let me go on turning round the business. Please, give me a chance to prove that I am a man of honour, and that I really do love Amy and would never do anything to hurt her.' He reached for her hand and clasped it tightly. He had to make her see that loving with Amy had reached him too in the place that meant he could never love another.

'Grandmama Tempest says that fate and God takes us on many journeys. That it's up to us which attitude we take as each step unfolds. I have challenge enough at the moment doing right by you, Amy and Hope. As for the future, I can't see it would be anywhere for me that Amy wasn't. Come to Burnt Oak with me now. I'll ask my father's permission to marry. He won't say no. I'll marry Amy tomorrow.'

Sylvia disengaged her hand. 'Of course your father wouldn't refuse his permission, if he saw it as a way of getting his hands on this family's property. There will be no question of me giving permission to Amy to throw her life away. You will have to prove to me that you really do know your own mind, before I do. You say you'll stay and work, and you are entitled to do so until you have recovered the money you have put into the business. I'll bring the croust in ten minutes.' She walked away from him, graceful and proud.

Amy was on her way back home, her basket laden with things from the general stores, the butcher and the baker. Few people spoke to her in as friendly a manner as in the old days. It was because of Sarah. After chapel the previous Sunday people had been calling Sarah a slut. In her anger, Amy had tried to shame them, 'The Lord goes out and searches for the lost. Sarah was a member of our flock. She's young, barely past sixteen. No one's got the right to judge her so harshly.'

She had met up with Molly Pentewan

outside the baker's, and had been blanked, at first, for a different reason. Then the woman, her back bent over by mine work, had remarked, 'Buying in your bread now, are you? Well, I suppose you and your mother have no time for proper things now you're entertaining Kivells.'

'We're trying to keep ourselves afloat, the best way we can, Mrs Pentewan,' Amy replied patiently. Her newfound love for Sol made it impossible for her to be brought down today. 'My mother has a new baby, she hasn't the time or the energy to do everything in the house.'

'Then you should be spending all your time inside it, not acting like a man in your father's workshop.'

'There's nothing wrong in good, honest work of any kind, don't you think? The Lord helps those who help themselves.'

'Think the Good Lord is helping the Kivells, do you?' Molly Pentewan had shouted. Amy's determined brightness was obviously annoying her. 'They're helping themselves all right, to trade that doesn't rightly belong to them and to the village girls.'

Amy had coloured up, afraid that the woman would see that she had been with Sol.

'In that devil Titus Kivell's case, the younger the better,' Molly Pentewan persisted. 'I pleaded with Sarah not to take the children to Burnt Oak. I'm afraid he'll tire of her in time and start on Tamsyn. Sarah can see no wrong in him. She says, he wouldn't be marrying her if he was that bad. She's having his baby. Did you know? He's robbed her of everything, including her soul.'

Amy put a hand on her stomach behind the cover of her basket. She could be in Sarah's condition, heading for a rushed marriage. What would her mother say?

She carried on along a quiet stretch, with huge rough boulders, and dips and short rises littered with dead heather, gorse and bracken. She saw nothing, her thoughts again centred on Sol and her hopes for a future with him. She could hardly wait to get back to him.

Suddenly a man, a beggar, reared up at her from behind a crop of boulders and was directly in her path. She screamed and fear rode up her spine. 'If it's money you want, you're welcome to it. There's three shillings in my purse and food in the basket.'

The beggar's stance suddenly drooped and he held out his hands as if helpless. 'Amy, it's me.'

She stared and slowly her fright dissipated. 'Father!' She could hardly believe this quivering spectacle in filthy clothing and greasy, dirt-streaked skin was him, Morton Lewarne, once an upright member of Meryen. Was it he who had disturbed the dogs, and temporarily last night, hers and Sol's passion. 'What's happened to you? Where have you been all this time?'

'Amy, help me. Please, I need your help.' He looked about to fall down on his knees and beg.

She looked behind her and ahead. No one was about. Just in case, she indicated the boulders from which he had sprung. 'We'll talk there. I've got bread and cheese. You must have something to eat.'

In the shelter of the ancient stones, Morton was gorging himself with food. 'I'm in trouble, Amy. Will you help me?' He was like a terrified child, shivering in dread, breadcrumbs falling down his coat, which he snatched up and stuffed into his mouth.

'If I can. You obviously need clothes and money. What sort of trouble, Father?'

'I can't tell you. I need lots of money. Can you get me into the house? I need to get inside. Can you get Kivell away for a few minutes, it's all I need. I swear I mean no harm to your mother. Do what you can, Amy. I don't want her to see me like this.'

'You want the money in your little table, don't you? Sol found it. It's in the den. I'll fetch it for you and the other things. Where will you go?'

'Abroad, on a ship,' he wiped a filthy hand across his mouth. His eyes were bulging with fear. 'It's my only hope. You're my only hope, Amy. Don't let me down.'

'Is someone after you? Is that it?'

'Yes, yes.'

She guessed there was a long and sordid story behind his downfall and distress but she didn't persist with her questions. She was unlikely to get the truth anyway and she didn't really want to know. 'Stay here. I'll be as quick as I can.'

Leaving him with the food, she hurried all the way to Chy-Henver, creeping into the house so as not to alert Sol or Jowan of her presence. Her mother was upstairs, she could hear her cooing to Hope. She fetched the bags of money and put them inside a leather satchel. Most of her father's things had been brought downstairs in case he turned up and demanded his personal possessions. She put together a bundle of his clothes and a pair of shoes, then wetted and soaped a towel, and within five minutes she was out of the house and on the road again.

Morton was hiding behind the rocks and he leapt in fear when she got back to him. 'Thank God. I was afraid you'd tell Kivell.' He looked her over, as if seeking to feed a different starvation. 'Have you brought the money?'

'Yes, all of it.' She handed over the satchel, and he scrabbled to poke inside it, counting the money pouches as if to satisfy himself she had not lied about the amount. Amy felt an overwhelming disgust for him. 'Even if Sol realized what I was doing and he followed me, I wouldn't let him hurt you, Father. I've brought the things you'll need to wash your hands and face.'

'You're a good girl, Amy. *You* haven't turned your back on me.'

She refused to accept the compliment, his second remark was an accusation at her

300

mother. She turned round while he stripped off his rags, and cleaned up and got dressed. 'I'm finished,' he said, his voice firmer. With the satchel over his shoulder, he had a sounder bearing. 'I'll be on my way.'

She wasn't going to let him slip off yet. 'Will you get in touch? Father, what about the business? It's hard for us living with such uncertainty.'

'Kivell's seeing you all right, isn't he?' There was a hard, jealous edge to Morton's tone.

'Yes for now, but he doesn't intend to stay for good.' Saying this aloud, the one thing that blighted her happiness at loving Sol, brought a cutting fear in her heart. Her father going off forever was not really important, the thought of Sol abandoning her to roam the world, perhaps for years, perhaps forever, was unbearable.

'Yah!' Morton scowled. 'You can't trust a Kivell. Thinks himself above me, some sort of saviour to you and your mother right now, but he'll soon tire of it.' Then, for a moment, his twisted expression softened and straightened. 'Don't worry, I'll see right by you, Amy. He won't have the last word.'

'What will you do?' she frowned. What could he do in this wretched state?

'Don't look at me like that,' Morton wailed. 'It's not my fault I've been brought down to this.'

Amy stared at him, wide-eyed, 'Whose is it?'

'Toby's!'

'Toby's?' She could barely keep her anger

and resentment in check. 'My poor dear brother? Your son? How could you say that?'

'If he had been the sort of son a man deserves, a son to be proud of, one who would take over one day all that I'd built up, to look after me in my old age, then I wouldn't have succumbed to temptation.'

Unable to speak, for fear she'd say something as horrible as what she'd just heard, wanting to smite the self-pity off her father's face, she clamped her mouth shut and looked down at the ground. She could not bear to meet his eyes a moment longer.

He moved away. 'Goodbye Amy.'

She stayed frozen.

He didn't go far before halting and calling again, 'Goodbye. Amy!'

She knew it was important, vital to him, that she replied in kind. She wanted to deny him his last act of selfishness, but an instant later she called to him, 'Goodbye Father.'

And off he went, the father who had never given her a single embrace of affection. Her anger waned and she saw him as the most pathetic of individuals.

Once more, she set off. To face her mother's reaction over her giving away the money that would have helped them greatly towards stability. To Sol, and whatever the future might hold with him.

Twenty-One

Amy and Sylvia were on the way to Poltraze in the Nankervis carriage, which Tara had sent over to fetch them. Neither of them really wanted to go. They did not mention it, but each knew the other's feelings. What had seemed a good, even thrilling idea, at the time of Tara's visit, now seemed unwise and even foolish. How could they hope to fit in with ladies of higher birth, in a grand drawing room? Amy and Sylvia could say a lot to comfort each other, they could have come up with a scheme to let them off this without hurting Tara, but Sylvia spoke only to Amy when absolutely necessary.

It was two weeks since Sylvia had banished Sol from the house. She had torn into Amy for being intimate with him, sobbing out her disappointment and hurt over what she saw as a betrayal of her Christian mothering. Amy had taken the chastening silently, but in the light of whom she had just seen that day, she'd cried, 'After all that's happened it hardly seems important.'

That had brought Sylvia's indignation and red-hot anger to a head and she had looked as if she'd wanted to slap Amy's face. 'You won't

303

feel like that if he's put a baby inside you!'

'We're in love, Mother. Sol would stand by me. He's standing by all of us and he doesn't have to. The last thing he'd do is run out on me if we were to have his child.'

'That's right, Mrs Lewarne,' had come Sol's quiet, firm voice. He had dared to put his head round the door. 'I told you the truth about my feelings for Amy. I'm in love with her. I'm sorry for all this distress to you. I shall honour your decision and move out today. Now I'm about to start work up at the big house I don't need to be here often. Perhaps we could have a weekly meeting to discuss business matters.' He'd flashed Amy a deep, wonderful look that put across the depths of his love for her. It had reassured her. Told her to be strong, to be patient. The breath had caught in her throat and her eyes had widened as she'd sent back all her love and trust to him. Then he'd become detached and serious, and held up a scrap of clothing. 'Stumpy's just come back with this. I recognize it as being part of one of Morton's shirts. It's ragged and dirty. It must have been him who was hanging about the place last night. He can't be far away. I'll take the dogs and root him out. See what he's up to.'

'My dear God,' Sylvia breathed. 'He must be starving, desperate, to come back in such a state. Find him. If he's hurt, bring him here. He's still my husband. I still owe a duty to him. He must have need of money. He must be given some.'

'There's no need for you to go, Sol. Or for you to worry about doing anything, Mother,' Amy said. 'I've not long left him. That's what I meant when I said the situation between Sol and me doesn't seem so important.' She told them what had happened, what she had done.

'And your father's gone for good? And he has all that money?' Sylvia's tone was hushed. She was shaking with emotion.

'I thought it was the right thing to do, Mother.'

'Yes. Money was all he ever really wanted.' Sylvia went outside and stared at the workshop. Amy and Sol followed her. 'So, it's all over. My marriage. All those years of building this up. He could have come back and started over again. He could have found the courage. He didn't want to. He didn't want me. Or his daughters. Amy?'

'Yes, Mother?'

'Did your father ask about Hope?'

'No, I'm afraid, he didn't.'

'Is there anything else I should know?'

Amy couldn't tell her that Morton had blamed Toby for his downfall. It would be cruel for her mother to have to bear that. 'He said he'd make it up to me.'

'But not to me. Well, he would never do that. Did you believe him?'

'Of course not.'

'I could go after him,' Sol had said. 'Ask him to sell the business to me, for an honest price. I haven't got enough money of my own but my grandmother would willingly lend me the rest. That way, the future would look quite settled.'

Sylvia whirled round. Sol was close to Amy – at one point he had mouthed to her, 'I'll make it all right,' – and they had moved hastily to put distance between them. Sylvia's usual gentle face was a mask of bitterness. 'No! I forbid it. I will not put more money into that man's pockets to waste on drink and whores. And I will not be beholden to you, young man. You may believe your fine and noble sentiments now, but you are a Kivell, son of the dark-hearted.'

'Mother! How could you?' Amy gasped.

'Because of life's cruel experiences, that's how. I believed your father when he said we would have a good life together. We did, or so it appeared for many years, but it was a sham. Then his rotten ways sent Toby off to his death and he didn't cry one tear of sorrow or remorse. He let Titus Kivell send his son here.' She pointed at Sol. 'You may not own your father's evil ways but I feel the restlessness in your soul. Staying here, marrying Amy, would end up stifling you, and your resentment would turn you into some sort of copy of either your father or my husband. No, I will only put my trust in God from now on. If it's His will that I end up in the gutter, so be it.' With a proud lift of her head, but also seeming about to disintegrate, Sylvia went back inside.

Amy and Sol gazed at each across the few

306

yards of ground. Dare they grasp a few words, a few seconds together?

'Amy!' came her mother's shout.

Shaking her head, her hands up to her face, almost in despair, Amy ran inside, leaving Sol alone.

The kitchen was empty. Amy felt empty, desolate. Sol had offered a way out of the family troubles and her mother had tossed it away. She heard Sol ride out of the yard.

Sylvia came into the kitchen with Hope. 'Gone off already, has he?'

'He'll come back. You can trust Sol. You were far too hard on him. There's something I want you to know. I'm going to tell Sol he must go off on his travels soon, do what he's always wanted. I'm not going to be responsible for tying him down. I believe him when he says he loves me. I'll wait for him, no matter how long it takes. After I've told him that I promise I won't try to see him alone.' She'd glanced at her tiny sister. 'Hopefully, there will be no new baby. My babies can wait until years into the future.'

Now, Amy was glad it was raining hard as they rattled along in the carriage, it meant that no one was likely to be out in the village and they wouldn't be seen. The last thing she wanted was for anyone to think they thought themselves to be going up in the world, when in truth they were nearing the bottom. 'Are you nervous, Mother?'

'Of course,' Sylvia answered stiffly, across from her on the plush, buttoned seats.

Amy sighed and stared down at her gloved hands. It was dreadful, living like this, her mother so remote, treating Sol like an outcast. If she left the house to hang out washing or feed the hens she was monitored by her mother. It was unnecessary, she intended to keep her word and not seek to be with Sol alone. When she had told him he should think about setting a date for his travels, that she would wait for him, he had smiled, a special, love-bound smile for her, and said, 'We'll leave it all to fate.' It had heartened her so much, and she and Sol kept in communication by letters, she slipping them inside crevices in the garden wall, he leaving them near the hen-house. Alone in her room she read his letters again and again, and at moments like this, when Sylvia was frosty, she clung to hopes for a happy future.

'Mother,' she dropped her voice to a whisper as they left the village behind and turned into Bell Lane. 'You'll be relieved to learn that nature has paid me a visit. There will be no baby.'

Sylvia let out a loud breath. 'I am relieved. Are you?'

'Yes. I don't want a reason for Sol and I to marry quickly.' A tiny part of her had lied, but she most wanted to prove Sol's love for her was real. He wrote in his letters that he was working hard to get her mother to trust him.

'I'm glad to hear it, Amy.'

With Sylvia seemingly a little softer towards her, Amy tried some conversation. 'I wonder who these ladies are that Tara mentioned in her last letter. We're going to be out of place there, don't you think?'

'Take heart,' Sylvia gave her a half-smile. 'We don't look too bad a sight in our best clothes. If it's too awful, I'm sure Miss Tara will understand if we don't go again. At least, we'll get to see inside the big house. It's something I've always wanted to do.'

Amy became aware of the excitement in her mother and she was glad she had this respite from their troubles. 'We're not doing too badly, are we? I mean, the squire's paid in advance for Sol's work on the new boathouse. It's unusual. Perhaps Tara had a word with him.'

'Well, in her letter she wrote that the squire is taking a personal interest in all that Sol does.'

'He's not so bad, Mother.' Amy bit her lip. Could she bring her mother round to relaxing some of Sol's banishment?

'Not so bad, but only in some ways.' Sylvia would not relent. Amy had to go on hoping she would.

They were shown into Poltraze by the butler, whose dark suit of clothes was of better quality than the most well off merchants in Meryen. Stocky and thin, aging, yet well postured, he did not so much as glance at them as he ordered a maid to take their cloaks. Amy peered about, as Sylvia was, trying to see everything. The great staircase and the gallery above seemed to go up and up. Did they hit the clouds? They saw for themselves they were no rivals for the sky as they were led up the stairs to the drawing-room.

'Mrs Lewarne, and Miss Lewarne, ma'am,' the butler intoned just inside the double doors.

'Thank you, Fawcett.' Tara got up from her chair to meet them, all smiles, looking like a creature from a fairytale in a royal blue velvet two-piece gown, a scrap of white lace on the crown of her hair. 'Amy! Mrs Lewarne. Thank you for coming. Do sit and make yourselves comfortable either side of me. You are the last. Let me introduce you to every-one.'

Chairs and sofas had been arranged in a circle but to Amy and Sylvia the ladies seem-ed at some distance from each other. Tara sat in a graceful sweep of skirts and Sylvia and Amy copied her, both self-conscious and trying not to show it. There were six of them in all. Tara started with the lady of smug appearance across the flowing wool carpet from her. 'This is my sister-in-law, Mrs Phoebe Nankervis.'

'How do you do,' Phoebe said, with her cut-glass accent at its most nasal.

'And Mrs Anthea Nankervis, wife of my husband's second-cousin, the Reverend Clarence Nankervis, vicar of Meryen.' Tara gave the full details, thinking it unlikely Amy and Sylvia knew anyone from the church, as they were Methodists.

310

Anthea Nankervis was white-haired, plump, and a bit vague. 'Good afternoon to you.'

'And the final lady is Mrs Dorcas Keast, wife of Poltraze's steward. I think we represent a fairly broad spectrum of those residing in and involved with Meryen.'

They drank tea from brittle looking cups and Amy and Sylvia feared they would easily break, and they ate the fancies as delicately as they could, hoping it was in the correct manner. Tara brought up the ideas put forward on the day she had gone to Chy-Henver.

Dorcas Keast had an ordinary accent like Amy's and Sylvia's, but unlike them she didn't appear overawed by the occasion. Rosy cheeked from an outdoor life, she pushed her tongue into the corners of her mouth to free cake crumbs. 'I've got five young'uns, ma'am. A bit of schooling would do 'em good.'

'And there is to be a doctor in the village,' Tara said proudly. 'It's a long way to go to St Day to fetch a doctor in an emergency. I've got my husband to agree to provide a fund to pay the costs of deserving cases.'

'Doctor? Doctor?' Anthea Nankervis screeched when confused. 'What's this?'

'A doctor,' Tara said patiently. She wanted more useful women on the committee, but it would be unthinkable to exclude the wife of the parish vicar. 'Hopefully we'll secure someone for the post soon. A suitable house is being found on the estate for him.'

'Deserving cases, Tara?' Phoebe said curtly. 'That will be just about everyone in the

311

village.' She hated being part of this ridiculous meeting and was furious that money was to be allocated to the rabble while she had to endure the embarrassment of existing in a poky house. 'Has Joshua agreed to a site for this school?'

'Yes, it will be built at the entrance to Bell Lane,' Tara said proudly. 'Things are progressing well since I first spoke to Amy and Mrs Lewarne.'

Both Amy and Sylvia flushed when all eyes fell on them. Sylvia ventured to speak, 'Things are getting better in the village. The constables ordering those of the most unfortunate habits to clean around their homes has stopped the cholera taking a hold.'

Phoebe wrinkled her nose in distaste. What a subject to bring up. Why should she have to endure the presence of two such unsuitable women? Tara would make the Nankervis name one of scorn. 'I should think so too. If people make their own problems they deserve to receive a worthy fate.'

'The deaths of children can never be seen as worthy,' Amy said curtly. Phoebe Nankervis had barely made eye contact with her or her mother, making it obvious she thought them beneath her.

Phoebe made a face, conveying she cared nothing of her opinions.

'Have I seen you in church?' Anthea Nankervis screwed up her furrowed face as she studied Amy and Sylvia. 'Where did you say you come from?'

'We're from Meryen,' Amy replied. 'We don't go to church because we're Methodists.' She knew that wouldn't go down well, she might as well have said she and her mother were convicted criminals.

'Methodists indeed!' Anthea Nankervis put her bonneted head up a huff and refused to say another word.

Tara shot Amy and Sylvia a look of apology. She had been naive to think women across the social divide could mix amiably, and she was angry that it was those on her side of this chasm who were behaving rudely. 'To move on to something else. I've been thinking we could make scented gifts, lace items, cloth picture frames and that sort of thing. We could have a sale of work to raise money for our own poor fund.'

'Oh, really, Tara,' Phoebe snickered. 'You can't seriously expect me to do that sort of thing! Who will benefit from this poor fund?' She aimed her cold eyes straight at Sylvia. 'Deserted wives? We must be careful that those who purport to struggle aren't already receiving help from an unusual source.'

Amy opened her mouth to return with something equally hard, in the hope of putting the beastly woman in her place. Sylvia was wiser, she knew that was impossible. Phoebe Nankervis was a bitch and would always come off the superior, and she wasn't going to have Amy making a fool of herself. She said coolly, 'We are not dull-witted. We shall know who genuinely needs help and where it will be met with humble gratitude.'

Dorcas Keast grinned at Sylvia. 'Quite right.'

Tara called the meeting to a halt. There was nothing more to be accomplished today and she wanted to spare Amy and Sylvia any more unpleasantness. After glaring at Phoebe, she rang for Fawcett to see her, Anthea Nankervis and Dorcas Keast on their way.

'I'm so sorry you were put in an uncomfortable position,' Tara said, as she descended the stairs with Amy and Sylvia.

'I wasn't expecting to feel comfortable, Miss Tara,' Sylvia said graciously. 'This is no place for Amy and I. We shall be glad to work for the committee behind the scenes, if that is agreeable to you.'

'I understand,' Tara said sadly, remonstrating with herself for being thoughtless in the first place. 'I still may call on you occasionally?' She would so like to talk to Amy alone. It was plain there was some great sadness upon her. She was withdrawn, distracted.

'We'd be honoured,' Sylvia said. She refused the carriage home. It had stopped raining and she said she and Amy would enjoy the walk.

'What did you think of the place?' Sylvia asked, when they were out of Poltraze's magnificent grounds.

Amy had been thinking about Sol being there, working somewhere on the boat-house. 'There's a lot of grandeur but our home is far more comfortable.'

'I'm glad we'll never be subjected to that

314

dreadful sister-in-law of Miss Tara's again. I don't envy her living close to such people. Dorcas Keast seemed a good woman.'

It dawned on Amy that Sylvia was being bright and chatty. When she linked her arm through hers and talked about putting together a few gifts for Tara's sale of work she was heartened to know she had been forgiven. It would give her something wonderful to write to Sol about.

Phoebe had gone only a little way home when she ordered the groom to turn the trap round and return to the big house. She had been rude to Tara's unrefined acquaintances and rude to Tara herself. She would not gain an improvement in her circumstances if she made Tara hate her. There was nothing for it but to go back and eat humble pie.

Sol had constructed the planked walls of the boat-house and put in the two long windows and hammered on the felt roof. He was sizing up shelves for storage when he saw he was about to be joined by the squire, a not uncommon occurrence, unfortunately. He wasn't about to stay in a confined space with Joshua Nankervis and he went outside into the cold winter air. 'Ah, I was hoping to see you today.'

'You were, Sol?'

Sol winced as the other man's face lit up. His interest in him today, however, could be used to make a very practical gain. He produced some papers from his inside jacket pocket. 'I've been going over the Lewarne accounts books and I've come across some outstanding dues to Morton Lewarne commissioned by your late father.' It hurt to do so but he turned a flirtatious smile on Joshua. 'Would it be an imposition to ask you to settle these? I have the Lewarne women's interests at heart, you understand?'

'Oh, indeed, give them to me and I shall instruct Keast to ensure the bank is given appropriate notification forthwith.' Joshua was ecstatic. It would give him an excuse to present Sol with the cheque. 'The Lewarne ladies have just left the house. I hope their meeting with my wife was satisfactory.'

'Yes.' Sol's mind was on getting the bills paid. It amounted to over five hundred pounds. Morton had obviously been too cowardly to ask for payment off the estate, but it was a good thing he'd kept meticulous details. Amy and Mrs Lewarne had thought it a waste of time presenting the bills now, but now he had pulled it off it might help him go up in Sylvia's estimation. He hated seeing Amy downcast, because of him, because of their loving.

He had gone against Sylvia's wishes the day she had bawled him out and had left Chy-Henver to track Morton down. Morton must have flagged down an ore waggon or a carrier and got away, for even with the dogs, Sol had failed to locate him. He would have got Morton to agree to sell Chy-Henver to him, and kept it a secret, ensuring Amy, her mother

316

and baby Hope always had security. But it hadn't been fate's way for him to find Morton. Things must go on as they were, not an altogether bad situation, for he got to see Amy most days.

Joshua offered Sol one of his father's cigars. It never failed to delight him that he had inherited the old man's well stocked tobacco cupboard, the contents of which he kept from Michael, and even Laketon. Sol took one, and the two men smoked and looked at the boathouse. 'It's coming along well. I do so like the ornamental finish. I'm very pleased with what you're doing.'

Sol allowed him to engage him for twenty minutes. 'Well, if you'll excuse me I'd better get on.'

Joshua left him, trying not to show how reluctant he was to do so. He climbed the steps up the bank and was set upon almost at once by a figure sweeping out from behind a clump of trees. 'I saw you together. You can't keep away from him, can you?' Laketon grabbed his arm.

Joshua tried to pull free but Laketon had him in a strong grip. 'I am allowed to see how the work on my estate is progressing.'

'You're not allowed to favour someone's presence on it. I'm not a fool. I've seen the way you look at him. Why do you persist? Sol would never reciprocate your attention.'

'It makes a change from someone who's too clingy. Laketon, you let your jealousy run away with you.' Joshua was angry but he was also nervous. Laketon had always been demanding, seeking reassurance that there would never be anyone else, and he'd always made threats that he'd never let him go. Sometimes when he was in one of his jealous moods his eyes shone in a dreadful way. Joshua knew it was to frighten him, to control him, and it worked.

'Promise me you won't go near him again.'

'I will not.'

Laketon shook his arm, then squeezed his hand around it tight, and tighter, until it hurt. 'Promise me or I'll make you and him sorry. I never let anyone get in my way. You know that.'

'So you say.' Joshua thought to demand that Laketon let him go but they were in shouting distance of Sol and he was suddenly afraid Laketon would make a scene. 'Listen, it's only ever you I have on my mind. If it makes you happy I'll keep away from everyone else. Now let us spend a little time together.'

'Very well, but take warning...'

Vexed with Phoebe's and Anthea Nankervis's mean attitude towards Amy and her mother, Tara went for a walk to clear her head. She wanted to tell Joshua about the meeting and knowing how most days he liked to observe the restoration work she strolled the way of the boathouse. From a distance, she saw him talking, or rather, he seemed to be arguing, with Laketon Kivell. He gave Laketon Kivell too much sway, the carpenter shouldn't be allowed to make so free with the grounds. Goodness! Kivell had Joshua in his clutches. Tara could hardly believe her eyes. Kivell seemed to be threatening him. Why wasn't Joshua railing against the fellow? He should order him back to work. He should dismiss him.

Then they were making for the trees. Tara gasped in horror. They were...

She ran. It explained a lot, everything in fact as to why Joshua wasn't a proper husband to her. Tara didn't realise that she wasn't the only Nankervis wife who had witnessed the scene. Coming from a different direction to find her, Phoebe had not noticed Tara either. Phoebe hurriedly withdrew. She was not as horrified as Tara. It was a shock to find out her brother-in-law's secret but it was one she was delighted to have discovered. She would use it.

Tara slowed down when she got to the house, and after relinquishing her outdoor clothes, she forced herself to make a dignified walk to the library. She opened the door and went in, closing it behind her. She faced Michael. She had hoped to be calm but she was trembling, her chest was heaving, and her breath was coming in horrified little gasps.

Michael shot up from the long library table. 'Tara! What is it? You appear to have had a terrible shock.'

'I—I...' She felt dizzy and swayed on her feet.

He reached her quickly and next instant had his arms about her. In her distress she

319

threw her arms around his body and clung to him. 'What is it? Tell me?' He held her so he could look into her face. Her lovely face. Pink and flushed and frantic. She wasn't frightened, nothing had scared her. She must be angry. 'Has someone upset you?'

'Yes. Offended me deeply,' she said in a gasp of a voice. 'First Phoebe and then Joshua.'

Michael couldn't be more rapt. His wife and brother had opened a way for him to get closer to Tara, as he'd hoped to do for so long. 'Forget them. You're with me now,' he said in the gentlest tone.

'Yes.' She kept her arms about him. She didn't want to let go. She needed his strength. His understanding. His quiet, pleasant ways. He was gazing at her so kindly, and more. She saw desire, something she'd never see kindled in her husband's face. She had the most wicked of thoughts. She would never have a child, an heir to Poltraze, with Joshua. She was doomed to float about the place with nothing of real importance to do. She wanted a son, to breed the Radical she'd first hoped for on the night of her engagement. His brother had already sired a son ... Michael was staring at her lips, smiling into her eyes. He wanted her. It was good to be in his arms, to be held by a man who desired her. She was filled with sensual need.

When he lowered his head to place his mouth on hers she met the kiss with equal keenness. He drew her to the end of the

320

room, deep within its shadows. 'Tara, you're so lovely,' he murmured.

She didn't speak. She didn't think. All she knew was this great longing to become a woman, to be taken by him, to be used and to use. Moments later, against shelves of musty old books, she cried out in pain and triumph.

Twenty-Two

Sarah was taking lessons with Tamsyn, Arthur and the Kivell children to read and write. She was also learning a little geography, history, Holy Scripture, and even science. She grasped everything swiftly, impressing her new mother-in-law, one of her teachers, with her ready, intelligent mind. Her favourite lesson was dancing, and with a fascination for music she was learning the pianoforte and the flute.

She didn't miss the village or the mine at all, but she missed Amy. Amy was prohibited from coming to Burnt Oak, and Sol, subdued and serious, was living back at home. From Jowan she had learned that Mrs Lewarne had thrown some very harsh words at Sol. Something must have happened between Amy and Sol, they had either got too close for Mrs Lewarne's liking, or Sol had tried to have his way with Amy. Sarah thought it might be the latter – Sol would have a great sexual appetite if he was anything like his father, yet it was easy to see that Sol had a great affection, at least, for Amy. Whatever the reason, it had meant Amy had not attended hers and Titus's wedding.

'I'm thinking of going over to Chy-Henver today,' Sarah informed Tempest, as she helped tidy up the music room after a lesson about Samson and Delilah from the Bible. She likened Titus to Samson, he was big and strong and long-haired, but she would never be a betrayer like Delilah had been. Titus was not an honest, misguided man like Samson, but he was brave, he had a kind side, and she would always love him no matter what he did. 'I'd love to see Amy again. Do you think Titus will mind?'

On most occasions when Tempest talked to Sarah, she studied her face closely. 'It should be all right but don't stay long. Titus will want you to show him you're settled as his wife. I'll pack a basket for you to take, something from the kitchen, and a little gown I've made for baby Hope. If you give me a moment I'll write a few lines to Mrs Lewarne, asking her to be so kind as to accept the gifts.'

Tempest was kind to Sarah but she never particularly sought her company, which was hurtful to Sarah because she was sure Tempest, who had prompted her to relate all she knew about Amy, would behave otherwise if it was Amy who was here. In view of Tempest's supposedly supernatural powers,

322

and as the head of her family, Sarah was in awe of her, usually too nervous to ask her any questions, but today she found the boldness. 'Has Sol had a falling out with Mrs Lewarne and Amy? Has something gone wrong with him working there?'

'Sol and Amy have fallen in love,' Tempest answered at once, surprising and delighting Sarah with the confidence. 'Mrs Lewarne has concerns. She doesn't realise that she can't deny them their destiny.'

'Did you see it? You know...?'

'I did.' It was a simple matter of fact to Tempest. 'I've had the sight since a child. I wish I'd seen my own fate. I'd never have ventured out the day of my kidnapping. But I would never have had Sol in my life. Sometimes even the worst situation throws us compensation.'

'Did you see that I would meet Titus?'

'No, not before it happened, but the instant I saw you, Sarah, I knew it had been inevitable. You are very young and beautiful.' Again came the searching of Sarah's face.

Sarah found it unsettling and she had endured enough. 'Why do you keep staring at me, Mama Tempest? Do you see something? Is it my baby?'

Tempest reached out and put a light touch on Sarah's shoulder. Sarah felt a tingling there, she looked at the elegant hand and then into Tempest's steady gaze, and she knew, with a sense of great comfort that she need never be afraid of her mother-in-law.

This woman may have owned up to murdering her husband, but she would not ill-wish anyone who didn't deserve it. 'Sarah, what makes you think you're having a baby?'

'Well, I don't know really,' she stumbled, reddening up, for she felt silly. 'I've never had monthly courses. A lot of bal-maidens don't. It's believed to be something in the water from the mines that girls are exposed to. I could just be late coming into full womanhood, but I could be pregnant though.'

'I can always tell by looking into a woman's face if she's pregnant. Sarah, I see no signs in yours.'

'Oh! Titus will be disappointed. He wants another son. At least four children with me.'

'I could be wrong,' Tempest smiled, but she looked grave. 'Don't mention anything to Titus yet. If you didn't conceive before the wedding, as he'd thought, there's no reason why it couldn't have just happened. You run along, dear, and get ready to go to Amy. I'll meet you in the hall.'

Tempest asked Eula to see to the gifts then she stationed herself, hands pressed firmly together, at the foot of the stairs. Titus hadn't left Burnt Oak today, and during the afternoons he was home he took Sarah up to their bedroom. Sure enough, inside he came, about to search for her. He raised his thick black eyebrows at seeing his mother's uncompromising stance. 'What's wrong, Mama?'

'Nothing. Sarah's going out, and I'm here to see that you don't hold her up.' Tempest

324

exuded total authority.

Titus, who was afraid of no one but his mother, in fear that if she could kill his father, she might ill-wish him, never argued with her. He always endeavoured to earn the love and respect that he'd never had from her. He had tried to understand that as her first-born, raped by his father, it was inevitable that she'd hate him too, but it was a constant source of hurt to him. It made him feel small. It made him lash out at others and seek ways to be seen as important, it made him need to be in control. 'I'm not about to stop her.'

'Good.' Tempest thanked Eula when she brought the laden basket.

'Where's she going?'

'To visit her friend, Amy. Her only friend, thanks to you.'

'She has new friends now. As much company as she wants. As my wife, she's a respected member of our community.'

'She's respected because she's a nice girl, just like Sol's poor mother was, and unlike your two mistresses, who tried to rule the roost with you. I like Sarah. Do not hurt her. Ever. Do you hear me, Titus?'

'Loud and clear, Mama,' he said with a liberal amount of bitterness. Her interference in his new marriage, spoken in front of a smirking Eula, the sister who had no love for him either, meant it would be spread round the whole family by nightfall. To save face, he said, 'I wouldn't dream of doing my darling Sarah harm. I adore her. Ah, look, here she comes.'

As she met his appreciative gaze on the top stair, Sarah was a radiant vision in a sea-blue plaid outfit and matching bonnet, her hands inside a fur muff. Titus ran up to her and escorted her down. He took the basket from his mother. 'I'll drive you over to Chy-Henver, my darling,' he said. 'My wife goes everywhere in style.'

'What time do you want to leave there?' Titus said, as the trap jolted along the bumpy wintry road, putting a possessive hand on Sarah's leg. 'I'll wait in the Arms and come back for you.'

Sarah was thrilled over his loving concern but she wouldn't take advantage of it. 'I expect Amy is very busy, so I won't stay long. Would an hour and a half be all right?'

'Anything you say, my love.'

He didn't say another word until they reached Meryen. 'If anyone here turns their nose up at you...'

Sarah realized he was in a black mood. She glanced at him. He was staring from side to side as they passed the houses and shops. Looking for people. Looking for trouble. She had heard that minor accidents had happened, away from the mine, to the balmaidens Bess and Mary, who had humiliated her. Titus had to be responsible for both occasions. It must be her fault he was now angry. She should have mentioned it to him first. He was her husband and would be bound to want to know her plans. She offered up a quick prayer. *Please don't let there be anyone about.* Until this, she had been blissfully happy with him, in her fine warm clothes, cared for and cossetted.

'I won't go out again without telling you first, Titus.'

He made a gruff noise under his breath. Nothing more.

Sarah kept a few moments of crestfallen silence. 'I don't have to go there now. Perhaps we should turn round and go home.'

'You've got no choice today!' he thundered. 'Mama Tempest will want to hear about those blasted Lewarne women. She wants Sol to marry the damned girl some day. Well, that's one wish she won't be getting!'

Sarah's prayers were answered. There was no one to be seen in the village. Now she prayed Titus wouldn't show his ill-humour at Chy-Henver.

Sol was in the workshop. The squire was holding a shooting party and wanted no noisy work in the grounds disturbing his guests. Hearing a trap pull up he came outside expecting to see a customer and was amazed to see his father helping his young stepmother to alight.

Amy had heard the arrival and on seeing Sarah she ran outside in her apron. Her eyes met Sol's, and at the same instant they broke away. An automatic occurrence between them now, and one that always felt horribly unnatural.

Her mother was upstairs feeding Hope.

327

With her room at the front of the house she wouldn't be looking out, so Amy looked at Sol again, giving him the warmest and deepest of loving smiles. He did the same to her. Witnessing their love helped lift Sarah out of the misery of this being her only visit here as a married woman. Should she be worried about Titus's threat that he'd never allow Sol and Amy to marry? She decided to forget it. Sol was strong, he wouldn't let Titus ruin things for them.

Sylvia had heard the trap stop outside on the road. Hope was dozing at her breast and she eased her away and laid her in the cradle. Then she went down to see who had come. It was the first time she had seen Titus Kivell at close quarters and it was something of a tummy-wrenching shock. In some ways he was a handsome man, but very much a brute with his scars and natural aggression. How could Sarah have not seen that? It was frightening how easily the cunning man had exploited her, but here she was, gazing at him as if he was some divine being. Yet when Sylvia looked at the well-dressed girl again she saw something else, a nervous eagerness to please him, and the beginnings of fear. Sylvia would have ordered Titus Kivell away, or at least made it plain he wasn't welcome, but she must consider Sarah.

'Sarah, how lovely to see you,' she said. 'Good afternoon, Mr Kivell.'

'And to you, Mrs Lewarne,' he replied, conversationally. He put his hands on Sarah's shoulders and pushed her forward slightly. 'Sarah was wanting to visit Amy, her friend.' This was put in a confrontational manner.

'She is always very welcome here,' Sylvia said, then because she felt there was no other choice. 'Would you both care to come inside for tea?'

Amy, Sol and Sarah looked at him for his reaction; he hadn't expected that. *Good for you, Mum*, Amy thought. Sol was ready in the event his father caused trouble. Sarah sighed with relief. Titus couldn't complain he was being shunned here. Perhaps he'd change his mind and let her come again.

Titus was all gracious smiles. 'Thank you indeed, but I'm sure you ladies would prefer to tittle-tattle without my company. I'll have a word with Sol, and see how Jowan's work is coming along. Sarah, beloved, enjoy your afternoon.' That should unseat the comely Sylvia Lewarne a little off her moral high horse. He preferred much younger women, girls on the threshold of life, but he enjoyed the sight of a nursing mother. In a few months Sarah would be the same, and at her most beautiful.

Sylvia ushered the girls inside, with actions as if gathering them into her arms to protect them from the despicable devil.

The instant the back door was shut, Titus turned on Sol. 'You could have owned all this by now, not behaving cap in hand to that bloody hoity bitch! You listen too much to your grandmother. She's turned you into a

329

goose. So has that girl! I saw the way you looked at her. What's the matter with you? There's women aplenty to see to a man's needs but you're hankering over a wench who don't amount to much. I don't feel the slightest pride in you anymore.'

It was all designed to insult, to injure and enrage. Sol peered levelly at his father. He gave an upward lift of his head, then in a voice that dismissed and mocked, 'I don't give a tinker's cuss what you think of me.' He walked away.

'Don't you dare turn your back on me!' Titus strode after him and made to whirl him round and put a raised fist to his face.

Sol faced him before he could execute his intentions. 'Clear off, Father. The extent of your manhood these days is to control some unfortunate girl and to bully everyone else. You don't do a thing that's useful. You may mock me over Amy but you'll never know the real meaning of love. That makes you the smallest person I know.'

Titus looked as if he'd been delivered a devastating blow to the roots of his soul, as if he had imploded. With his fists balled like lumps of iron he raised them to the level of Sol's eyes. 'I could kill you for that! I've done it for less.'

'It doesn't make you a man.'

Rattled beyond anything he'd ever had to deal with before, Titus thought hard to save face. Sol was a young man who seemed to be going nowhere in life, settling for so much less than he could achieve, yet he was calm, in total charge of himself. 'Bastard,' Titus uttered. 'Don't speak to me again until you apologize.'

He stalked to the trap, turned it round in the yard and drove off to the Nankervis Arms. He wasn't going to win an argument with Sol. The more he said, the more he was being made to look a fool. He would not let Sol get away with it. Liked it at Chy-Henver, did he? Playing the chivalrous knight? Well, how would he feel if the pathetic little business was taken away from his little love? Titus knew people, lawyers who could be paid for falsifying documentation. In a few days he'd have the Lewarne women out on the street, then his high and mighty son would have to support them, have them as a burden, tied down and trapped for the rest of his life. Why hadn't he thought of it before? Morton Lewarne was never going to show his face in Meryen again. The authorities were looking for him in connection with Marcie Dunn's murder, her body discovered four days after the last time Morton was seen in her shack. Morton had not given his real name at the Wayfarer's Inn, but the description of Marcie's lover had put Titus on to his true identification. Wherever he was he'd not come forward and reveal himself now. Yes, Titus grinned to himself, picturing the weeping and bewilderment he was about to invoke. In a few days' time, he'd put an official letter into Sylvia Lewarne's pious hand, informing her that her husband had sold him all the property of Chy-Henver for a very reasonable price. In reality, *nothing!*

His spirit lifted a little by his vindictive scheme, and to provoke more good will in the village, he kept Dilly Trewin busy by throwing enough coins on the bar to buy every drinker enough ale to last the entire afternoon. However, as he called on Lizzie's able services, he had to pay her twice the usual amount to take his wrath out on her. And when he got Sarah home...

Twenty-Three

Joshua was on his way to the west wing. Laketon was so demanding it was necessary to make a call there first thing every morning. Sometimes he was a pain, but he did love him and he felt bad about his fascination with Sol. He hadn't gone far when he was pounced on by Phoebe. 'I'd like a word with you, brother-in-law.'

He didn't like the smug gleam in her eyes. 'What about? I'm in a hurry, Phoebe.'

'I won't keep you long. I've got a list to give you.' She thrust out a long sheet of paper.

'What do you mean?'

'Oh, I've spent a while scrutinizing my home. It's still too humble for my taste. I want everything I've written down and I want it within a month.'

Frowning, Joshua glanced at the paper. It was packed with writing. Next instant he was shouting. 'You want further extensions? A pool? And a whole new wardrobe and two thousand a year of your own? You've taken leave of your senses, woman. Does Michael know about this?'

'No. As far as he will know, you've ordered the additions to Wellspring House out of the kindness of your heart.' Phoebe smiled the most self-satisfied of smiles. 'But he might be told, Joshua, and the rest of the county, about your secret.'

'Secret?' Joshua swallowed hard. 'What are you talking about?'

'Oh, don't say you'd never thought you and Laketon Kivell would be discovered? You will have to be more careful, Joshua.'

Joshua blanched. 'B—but you can't blackmail me like this?'

'You think very hard about it, Joshua.' Phoebe patted his hand. 'No doubt, you're on your way to see your lover. Ask him what he thinks about it.' She flounced away, singing merrily.

A short time later, Laketon was listening to him with narrowed eyes. 'What are we going to do?' Joshua wailed, rapping on the list. 'She won't leave it at this. She'll demand more and more. Blackmailers do. If she tells anyone we're both lost.'

'We won't do anything.' Laketon replied in

the coldest voice. 'I will.'

'What? What will you do?'

'Don't trouble yourself, Joshua.' Laketon was confident and calm, and Joshua heard the menace in it. 'I'll get us out of this spot of bother. Aren't I always the stronger one?'

'Yes.' It was Laketon's strength, his artfulness, his masterful control that held Joshua to him as a willing prisoner. 'Most definitely, dear heart.'

Laketon smiled a deeply satisfied smile. The most important thing to him was to have Joshua's adoration. 'You go on as you always do. Forget about Phoebe and her vicious little scheme.'

'You're going to frighten her off?'

'Let's say that she won't be causing us any more trouble. Your father's old suite is nearly finished. Come and see. As you never darken your wife's bedroom door anymore, and as I can slip into the house as silently as a mouse, it will do us very nicely.'

Joshua eagerly allowed Laketon to lead him away.

Sol was outside the workshop taking a smoke. Amy came out of the house to shake the breakfast crumbs to the birds. He gave her a small wave, longing to linger and gaze and smile at her. Amy lifted her hand in return, but after a moment she and Sol broke away and headed back to their respective places.

Sylvia was watching from a window. The young couple were working hard not to

334

compromise their promise to meet and carry out an affair. Sol toiled away long hours and had gained the respect of the merchants and the traders Chy-Henver did business with and none were pressing for overdue payment. Sol was an honest young man, diligent and clever, and thoughtful and kind. It was known round the village he no longer spent time with loose women. It seemed he really did love Amy. And Amy really loved him. It sang out of her every second of the day. She'd sigh and brood and look downcast, but she wasn't rebellious or complaining, nor did she sneak about trying to see Sol alone. She'd had a lot to put up with but she'd shown, like Sol, a high level of maturity.

She watched Amy warm her hands at the slab. 'I was wondering if Sol and Jowan would like to come inside for their dinner today.'

Amy twirled round. 'Mother...?'

'Well, it's a bitterly cold day.' Sylvia pretended disinterest, while folding dried linen. 'They both work hard. Doesn't seem right to deny them a bit of warmth and comfort.'

Amy allowed herself a small hopeful smile. Was her mother thawing towards Sol at last? 'They'll both be glad of that.'

'Why don't you run along and tell them?'

'Really?' Amy was halfway to the door then hesitated.

'Yes, my love,' Sylvia said. 'Go and tell Sol.'

Amy was on the verge of an excited dance yet still hardly dared to believe this was the best of news. 'You mean it?'

Sylvia waved her hands at her. 'Off with you then. I've kept you apart for long enough. I'm still concerned about Sol going off to travel but he's proved he can be trusted. I'm sure he'll do right by you.'

'Oh Mother!' Months of despair fell away from Amy and she ran to give Sylvia a hug.

Amy raced to the workshop. Sol looked up in surprise, then he saw her excitement and elation and he knew this wasn't going to be anything snatched or stolen. She ran straight into his arms. They were facing happiness at last. Jowan left them alone. Outside, he took a letter from the post boy and carried it to the house.

Titus had also received a letter. Sarah could see it gave him much satisfaction. She prayed it would put him in a good mood. No matter how many signs she hoped to see in her body to indicate pregnancy, morning sickness, or swollen breasts, or mood swings, there were none, and Tempest had looked at her again today and had sadly declared she saw nothing. It might mean she was barren. Some balmaidens were. It might simply be it was taking her longer to conceive, but Titus was unlikely to have the patience. He didn't show as much kindness towards her now, except when his mother was there when he would speak sweetly. He showed Arthur and Tamsyn no interest at all and didn't like them anywhere near him. He wouldn't allow them to eat at the same table and he bawled at them if they made the smallest noise or got in his way.

'I don't like it here anymore,' Tamsyn had sobbed last night when Sarah had tucked her up in bed. 'Titus hit Arthur really hard for leaving a book on the stairs. He'll hit me next.'

'But we have so much more here now,' Sarah had tried to soothe her.

'I'd rather be with Aunty Molly,' Arthur had said aggressively. The Kivells were showing a softer side in the village but many were still fearsome and the children apt to fight. The children of Titus's two common-law wives saw Arthur and Tamsyn as usurpers and bullied them. 'We never get to see her any more. I prefer the children at the mine. Life was hard but at least we belonged there.'

'Things will get better soon,' Sarah had said, but she knew she might be unable to keep her promise. If Titus wasn't watching her, he'd demand a detailed account of everything she did, even what she thought. He picked at her ways, saying she should make more effort to be genteel like his mother. Never a day went by but he wanted intimacy. If he got back late he'd wake her in the middle of the night. Sometimes he was rough, like the very first time, and he'd hurt her, but as he didn't take criticism she dared not mention it.

She was standing side on to Titus. He was staring at her, as if analyzing her, puzzled, as if he was angry with her but didn't know why. Then he looked as if he'd worked it out and was even more bewildered. Sarah grew uneasy. He cried out. She leapt in shock. Tried to stay calm but she knew what this was about, 'What's the matter, dear?'

'Come here!' he thumped his hand down on the dining room table, where he was sitting, having demanded a late lunch.

She froze. 'Why? Have I done something wrong?'

'I don't know. Have you? Come here, I say.' He was up and on his feet, waiting for her to obey his order.

She went near to him on trembling feet. His face was as dark as night. When she got close enough, he yanked her sideways. 'Your body is flat! You should be showing by now. Have you miscarried and not told me?'

'It—it's not that,' she gulped. How was she going to tell him the truth? Make him understand?

He placed a hand tight around her chin and breathed at her. 'What is it then?'

'Well...'

'Well? Well? Well bleddy what? Speak for God's sake!' His hand squeezed cruelly.

'You're hurting me!'

'Are you pregnant or not? Tell me the truth or I'll shake it out of you.'

Her eyes were stung with tears of pain and fright. 'I don't think I ever was pregnant. You see I don't get courses like other girls. I made a m—mistake.'

'You made a mistake!' he roared. 'No, it was me who made a mistake. You married me

338

falsely. You're barren. No use to me at all, you lying little bitch!' He struck her violently across the face.

Sarah's head was swung round at a right angle. She screamed in agony. He had a vice-like grasp on her shoulder and he struck her again, and she screamed again.

He shook her as if she was a rag. 'Do you think I invested all that time and money in you for nothing? If you can't give me children then I've no use for you. I want back everything I've given you. Then you can get out of my house. Get out of my life! And take those disgusting brats with you.'

Hearing her screams, Tempest rushed into the room. 'Titus! Get away from her. I told you what would happen if you ever hurt Sarah. A curse on you.'

'What?' In an instant his wrath and confidence evaporated. 'Take it back.'

'No. Never.' Tempest said, shielding Sarah with her own body. 'You're rotten and you're evil. I should have killed you the same day I killed your father, put an end to another devil's heart.'

'Don't say that, Mama.' Sarah was shocked to see him scared, actually weeping, pleading with his mother with outstretched hands. 'You can't mean that. Take it back. Take it back!'

'It's you who will leave this house for good if you don't change, Titus. You can leave it now. I don't want to see you for several hours.'

'Mama! Take back the curse.'

'Get out of my sight!' Shaking in fury, Tempest pointed to the door.

He strode out, his head up, but he was quivering and his face looked haunted.

Tempest took Sarah to sit down. 'I was afraid this would happen when he found out there was to be no baby. Are you badly hurt?'

Sarah shook her head. 'Can you really curse people?'

'It won't hurt him to believe so until he calms down, which might take several days.' Tempest stroked her hair away from her burning face. 'Sarah, I'm going to have to get you and the children away from here, and then we'll have to decide what to do. Do you want to continue as Titus's wife?'

She hung her head miserably. 'I could stand it if it was just myself, even the worry if he was going to get angry and hurt me. I do love him, you see. But I don't know if it's right to let Arthur and Tamsyn suffer too.'

'I'll get someone to take you to a hotel at Redruth. In a few days I'll come to you. Sarah, you are a Kivell wife, and whatever you decide you can rest assured that you will always be under Kivell provision.'

The letter addressed to Chy-Henver was for Amy. Jowan gave it to her after she and Sol had reluctantly unlocked themselves from a series of passionate embraces. 'How unusual.' She turned the wax-sealed envelope over and over in her hand. 'It can't be from Tara, she always sends letters over by hand. I'd better open it in front of Mother. It's the polite thing to do.'

A horse came charging into the yard. Jowan peeped outside the workshop. 'Sol! It's Father, and by the look of him it's trouble.'

Moments later, Titus had an audience of all those there. He thrust his letter and a document at Sylvia then leered at the gathering. 'See this, woman? It's your notice to quit! I managed to track down your husband and this says that he's agreed to sell me Chy-Henver, all of it, down to the last speck of sawdust. I want everyone here off the property within the hour or I'll toss you out as trespassers.'

Before Sylvia could respond, Sol hurled at him, 'Do you really think we'll accept that as a bona fide document? You've got someone to produce a forgery. It's the sort of level you'd stoop to.'

'Think what you damned well like!' Titus stormed, balling his fists, looking as if he wanted to tear Sol and everyone else apart. 'It says I'm the owner of this shabby little place and I can do what I like with it.' He began to mock. 'Which is to close the business down. It could have been yours, Sol, but you've turned your back on me so it'll belong to no one. I'll burn it down!'

Amy had taken a few steps away. She ripped her letter from the wax and read the contents. She gasped in shock, hardly believing what she was reading. Then she faced Titus. 'Well,

341

it's very strange that you should have a letter on the same day as me from a lawyer. This says Chy-Henver had been handed over to me, by my father.' She waved a document in front of him. 'See here? That's my father's signature.'

Crumpling Titus's script in her hands Sylvia threw it down in the dirt. 'That's all your deeds are worth, Titus Kivell. Now get off – my daughter's land.'

Titus looked as if the last breath had been knocked out of him. Alarming pains shot through his limbs and through his chest, as if great weights were crushing him. 'I'll make you all pay!'

'Pay for what?' Sol cried. 'What have any of us ever done to you? You seek revenge where none is just. You'll suffer all kinds of hell for this.'

Titus recalled his mother's curse. He had trouble getting his breath and he felt about to die. He staggered on his feet, his hands to his throat, terrified for the first time in his life. 'Help me...'

'Don't be pathetic,' Sol said, walking towards him, making him back away. 'You're all finished up, Father. Your rotten schemes will frighten and intimidate no one any more. Go home and settle down and wait for old age or you'll end up like your old friend, Darius Nankervis, and suffer some kind of terrible fate.' Sol knew the exact words to say to humiliate and torment him.

Jowan fetched Moonlight, his father's mare.

Gripped in the fear that his mother ill-wishing him was working and he was about to die Titus grabbed at the reins, missed them, then scrabbled about until he succeeded. Even in his horror, he was aware of the others standing back and watching him dispassionately. It hit him like a bolt from hell how his sons held no respect for him. Somehow he got up into the saddle and kneed the mare to walk away. He headed off for the moors, his only thought that if he was to die a horrible lingering death he wanted no one to be watching him.

'Well,' Sylvia said. 'Your father came through for you, Amy. He actually kept his word. Does the letter say where he is?'

Amy searched her mother's face for signs of upset but she was calm and even seemed pleased. 'It says that by the time I receive this he'll be somewhere overseas and that he'll never contact us again.'

'It must be a relief to have the ownership of Chy-Henver settled at last, Amy, Mrs Lewarne,' Sol said, slipping his hand around Amy's.

'It is,' Sylvia said. 'Sol, do you think your father will come back and cause trouble?'

'I'm afraid that's a possibility. He's always been a vindictive man.'

'Then if it's all right with you, perhaps you'd like to move back in again until we're sure all will be well. I shall be keeping a wary eye on you and Amy.'

Amy was ecstatic. Within one morning everything in her life had changed for the

343

better. She linked her arm through Sol's.

'I'd be honoured to, ma'am. I'd like to talk to you about Amy and I getting engaged,' Sol said, daring to slip an arm round Amy's waist.

'Don't you think that's looking a little too far ahead? You have plans that don't include Chy-Henver,' Sylvia said, although she was smiling.

'Not at all. The future starts here, and whatever happens, wherever I may be, Amy will be part of it.'

Sylvia gazed at Jowan. 'Well, you are training a resourceful craftsman in your brother there. That was what I was hoping to hear, Sol. And as you often say yourself, what will happen, will happen.'

That same morning, over at Poltraze, Tara was reading something, not a letter or a document, but her diary. She closed it, locked it, then pattered down the stairs and went to the library. To Michael. She spent part of most days with him. Sometimes they worked on the family records together. Often they made love. With Joshua having abandoned the marital bed for good, and with him out most nights, it was easy for Michael to take his place. Tara didn't love Michael but she was fond of him, she enjoyed making love with him, he had just the right amount of gentleness and virility to suit her needs. And now she had something to tell him. She was with child. It was really too soon to be certain but her cycle had always been regular to the day, and while being a week late, she had been sick these last few mornings, and she just knew she was pregnant.

Phoebe was alone in her boudoir, but this time she wasn't in a foul mood over Michael's neglect. She had made a copy of the list she had forced on to Joshua and she reclined on the couch with it, stuffing herself with bonbons, crowing over what she was to get out of him. Two thousand a year was a little ambitious but she'd settle for one thousand, and Joshua would feel less strained and pay up all the more easily. He had no choice, otherwise he would have to face public shame. It would be good to throw this truth into Tara's pious, smug face, but that would not serve her purposes. For years her life had been so much less than she deserved, the next additions to her home and the money would go a little way to compensate her. She would be able to afford to travel, get away from this boring unfulfilled life, indulge herself with some attentive lovers.

Her mouth felt suddenly dry and she ran her tongue round it. The sweetmeats were rather bitter. She'd make a complaint to the confectioner. A horrid dragging feeling started up in her stomach. She hoped she was not about to be sick, not while she had something at last to celebrate.

The door opened. 'I didn't ring,' she assumed it was a maidservant. 'But now you're here you can bring me some fresh water.'

'Good evening, Mrs Nankervis.'

She recognized the voice with some fore-boding. She tried to get up from the couch but her legs were crying out with painful cramps. 'Laketon Kivell! What do you want?'

'Nothing in particular. Just a bit of a chat and to watch you.'

'You've come about my demands. You can't threaten me in my own home. I won't change my mind. Joshua will have to pay up.'

Laketon was immaculately dressed. Lifting his coat tails, he sat across from her. He gazed about the room, admiring his handiwork, then stared at Phoebe with a peculiar smile.

She was feeling more ill by the second, a strange throbbing had started in her head. 'Get out!'

'You're an intelligent woman, Mrs Nan-kervis, but you don't see what's going on in front of your eyes. Did you know your husband is bedding Joshua's wife?'

'Liar! You're only saying that to get back at me.'

'Oh, but he is. I've seen them together. It suits me very well. It means I have Joshua all to myself, and that's a good thing for Tara, because I won't share him. I remove anyone who gets in my way to enjoy him, like Estelle Nankervis and the blustering squire. He'd have found a way to unsettle Joshua even all the way up in London and when Joshua's anxious he's not so much fun.'

Phoebe was open-mouthed and horrified. 'Are you saying you murdered them?'

'Yes, and Jeffrey Nankervis. You weren't the

346

first to discover Joshua and I. The boy was an arrogant prig, but like you he was foolish. He confronted me and laughed at how he intended to tell his father. So he had to die, and he made such a fuss when he realized he was to end up in the pool. He was already dead when my cousin came across him. Titus thought it the most enormous fun to lie that he'd tried to save him.'

'Please, I won't say anything.' Phoebe knew it was a useless plea. Laketon Kivell was a cold-hearted killer, as pitiless as the grave. Her heart hammered, her throat felt as if it was drying up. She wanted to get away from him but was frozen in fear, her body relentlessly petrifying. 'What ... are you ... going to do to me?' She had terrible difficulty getting the words out.

'Do to you? I've already done it. I knew you had a passion for bonbons. Didn't you think they tasted rather strange tonight? I coated them with an extract from a root of a rare plant from the jungles of Borneo. The natives use it to paralyze their victims. It's rather cruel Phoebe, for there's no antidote and it takes a long time for someone to expire. The medics and the authorities will see you've been poisoned, they'll be puzzled, but they'll probably put it down to you touching something in your conservatory and eating without first washing your hands.' He looked at his pocket watch and stood up, slipping the remaining bonbons carefully into a leather bag he produced from his pocket. 'Well, I must be away and tell Joshua his worries are at an end. I'll leave you to it. Good evening, Mrs Nankervis.'

'Arghh.' The power of speech had left her. To add to her horror and terror Phoebe knew Kivell hadn't gone yet. As he'd said, he'd come to watch her, watch and enjoy every last moment of her fear and agony.

Twenty-Four

Tempest had an unusual visitor to her sitting room. 'To what do I owe this questionable pleasure?' She didn't ask Laketon to sit down, but he looked as if he wouldn't accept an invitation anyway.

'I've come as a matter of some small respect to you as you're the head of this family,' Laketon said in clipped tones. 'I'm moving out of Burnt Oak.'

'I'm not at all sorry to hear that.' Tempest indicated the door. 'I hope you'll never feel the need to return.'

'You'll get your wish, ma'am,' he replied most respectfully, but his eyes were sharded and cold. 'I'm giving up the carpentry, so there'll be no rivalry for your favourite, for as long as Sol wishes to continue with it, that is. If he's wise, he'll form a partnership with the

348

young trainees here and the girl at Chy-Henver. One business, to take on all the work hereabouts. It will consolidate the Kivell attempts to fit into the wider community very nicely.'

'Sol might well think the same as you,' Tempest nodded with approval. 'What will you do?'

'Ah, you are keen to know if I offer anyone here a threat. The thing is, there is much jubiliation at the big house. The squire's wife is with child.' He appeared consumed with joy.

'A nice change from the sudden deaths there. So the young lady Tara has a lover. Is your lover as pleased about the child as you are?' There was nothing Tempest did not know about Laketon.

'Joshua is ecstatic. He realizes it must be his brother's. Now Michael is widowed it means we may all go about our lives with perfect ease. I shall be living in a very pleasant cottage on the estate and I shall be taking charge of the gardens.'

'And the squire may truthfully raise a Nankervis without fear of slights to his masculinity. I am pleased to hear the squire's wife will not be in your way and will be able to live long and well.'

'As one murderer to another I'm heartened you see things that way, ma'am.' Laketon smiled the smile of an angel, emphasizing his good looks, but it spread chills through every fibre of Tempest's bones.

'Our circumstances are completely different. I killed for my survival.'

'Whatever one does it all amounts to the same, to bring one's own happiness, even in my cousin Titus's case. I am not sorry to be leaving here now he's skulked back home, having realized after a few days of unnecessary terror that your ill-wishes have absolutely no power over him.'

When he reached the door, Tempest said, 'Don't be too sure about that.'

Laketon paused, reflected, then shook his head. 'Never on this earth. And now I bid a last goodbye to this little world here.'

One person was leaving her home but Tempest was expecting the arrival of many others.

'I hope you're not as nervous about coming here as you were on the way to Poltraze,' Amy said to Sylvia. They had arrived at Burnt Oak, and Amy was buzzing with excitement and joy, for there was to be a celebration here to mark her betrothal to Sol. The music room in Morn O' May was about to bustle with people and resound to music and dancing and feasting.

Sol led the women inside and introduced Sylvia to his grandmother.

'I'm so glad you've brought the baby, Mrs Lewarne. I've so wanted to meet little Hope,' Tempest said. 'This is a day I've waited to see and one I'm glad I didn't have to wait long for.' The women went off, chatting as if they'd known each other for years, their abusive husbands giving them something in common.

An open invitation had been given to the village and over twenty inhabitants, including the Greeps, those eager to gain trade and the plain nosy, filed into the music room, exclaiming at how grand but homely the house was. To loud and merry fiddles, flutes and drums, the gathering danced and laughed, and with suspicions and grievances on both camps set aside, all were having an enjoyable time.

Amy and Sol danced with no one but each other. She gazed at him adoringly. 'It would have been good if Tara and Sarah were here, but they can't be, of course.'

'Tara Nankervis has found her own happiness, and hopefully, one day, somehow, Sarah will find hers.' Sol kissed her. 'I love you. It's strange that we'll not live here as man and wife, now that you've agreed to me putting money into the business and us forming a proper partnership at Chy-Henver.'

'Do you mind?'

'No. When the time is right we'll go off and see the world. Together.'

Amy beamed all her love to him. This was a perfect day, the perfect place, with his family and people from the village, to witness their promises to share their future. She twirled and laughed in Sol's arms to riotous country music. In spite of all the noise there was a sense of peace. Something caught her eye in one quiet corner and for a moment she was sure she saw Toby there. In her heart she called to him. He answered her, and it was more than an echo, something she could cherish and keep forever.

Sarah slipped unseen into Burnt Oak and made her way up to the bedroom she had shared with her husband. Titus was lying on the bed, unwashed, unshaven, drinking, scowling at the sound of the merrymaking below. When the door opened, thinking someone had come to encourage him to clean up and take part in his son's engagement party, he made to throw the glass at the intruder, to swear at being disturbed. He sat up on seeing Sarah, nervous, brave, and so beautiful.

'What the hell are you doing here?'

'I was sent word that you'd come back. How are you, Titus?' She could see for herself, he was as angry as hell and as bitter as gall.

'Why should you want to know?' he sneered. He hated her, but he was drawn as always to her gorgeous blue eyes, her raven black hair, her tender body. And her youth.

'I'm your wife. I meant my vows. I love you, Titus. I've come to ask if you want me. If we can try to make our marriage work.' She held out her hands to him, then wrung them together, afraid of him, yet wanting to go to him, wanting to look after him. Even though he was hard and heartless, and even though he had hurt her and probably would again if he took her back, she really did love him and she wanted to do everything for him.

'Sweet, young, beautiful Sarah.' He put his glass down and beckoned to her. 'Come to me.'

On shaky feet she obeyed. Titus reached out and brought her down on the bed with him. He rested the top half of himself over her. She felt his weight like a heavy boulder. She was trapped, but even though she was scared it was an entrapment she wanted. He stroked her face, a gentle touch. She prayed she'd have his touches for the rest of their marriage and he would keep them gentle. 'My mother wouldn't tell me where you were. I suppose she told you to go on with your life and forget me.'

'No, she came to me at the hotel at Redruth and she told me to follow my heart. That's what I'm doing, Titus. That's why I'm here.' Sarah had lied. Tempest had begged her to keep away from him, saying, 'Try to look on what has happened as a blessing, Sarah. It could mean not having to endure years of abuse, of feeling that if you had to go through one more day of it you'll go mad. Of wishing you were dead or never been born.'

'But Titus had a right to be angry with me.' After the hurt, shock and shame, she had thought about the facts of her brief marriage every minute she'd spent alone. 'I lied to him. I let him think I was pregnant. I should have told him the truth right from the start.'

'But don't you see, my dear, you've done nothing wrong. Nothing was your fault. You

353

shouldn't have had to wonder if you were pregnant. Titus manipulated you right from the beginning. You were just a child. No husband has the right to treat his wife so cruelly.'

'But he's been good to me. I had nothing before I met him. I was depressed. I know what it's like to wish I was dead. I wished it nearly every day. Titus did more than rescue me from the moor. He gave me confidence and dignity.'

'And where is that confidence and dignity now, Sarah? How long do you think you'll retain it if he takes you back, because if he does it will be to spite you, to torment you. Is that what you want Tamsyn and Arthur to see at Burnt Oak?'

'At the moment they think things will be better if we went back to how things were before, but they'd receive no education, they'd go cold and hungry. We don't even have a place to live in the village anymore.'

'But it need not be like that. I'd see you're all well. I'd find you somewhere pleasant and safe to live and ensure you have all you would ever need. Think about it, Sarah. You owe it to yourself to have a good life.'

'You could do that for Tamsyn and Arthur. Aunty Molly could go with them, they'd all like that. She's got enough years left until the children are grown. But I owe Titus my loyalty.'

'Oh, Sarah,' Tempest had grown exasperated. 'Why can't I make you see? You owe him

nothing. He'd only destroy you. I never allowed my husband, Garth, to condition me into
believing I deserved to be ill treated. The day
I shot him he beat me to within an inch of my
life. I sometimes feel guilty for taking his life
but I don't regret it. He was going to start on
Eula, you see, in the bedroom. I've never told
anyone that, I never intended to, but I want
you to know this to save you, and perhaps
Tamsyn too. She's a pretty little girl, Titus will
notice this in a few years time. How would
you feel if he replaces you with her? He'll tire
of you anyway, he throws away all his women
when they leave the flush of youth. Sarah,
don't throw your life or my words away. You
have a chance to start a new life. Don't make
the wrong decision.'

Quietly, with the utmost conviction, Sarah
had said, 'But there is one big difference to
your situation and mine, Mama Tempest. You
were kidnapped and raped and forced to
marry. I love Titus and I gave myself to him
willingly and I was so happy to be given the
chance to marry him. I love him, I can't help
it, but I do.'

It was that love, and the lonely days and
nights of missing him that had brought her to
him now. She'd do anything for him. She
would never disobey him. If he gave her
another chance she'd work every minute of
every day to please him, and he would have
no cause to be angry with her, so he'd never
have a reason to hurt her. She would prove
Tempest wrong, somehow she would.

'Aren't you a little bit glad to see me, Titus? Didn't you miss me at all?'

Titus stared at her. He pressed a hand down hard on her stomach. 'Miss you? A conniving little barren bitch who'll never have a child of mine inside her.'

She put a hand up to his shoulder. 'But there's still a possibility I might have a baby one day. It's not been unknown among the bal-maidens to have my problem but go on to give birth. Now I'm away from all that my body might put itself right.'

He thrust her hand down, shoved it under her body, and with his weight on her it was trapped there. 'And I'm supposed to wait until that might happen, am I? You married me falsely, Sarah. No one lies to me and gets away with it.' He stroked her face again, this time digging in the side of his nail, leaving a sore red mark. 'Thought yourself lucky when I came along, didn't you? You used me. I hate that. I hate you for it. And you think you're an innocent, a sweet young bride, but you're not, Sarah. You're a whore. You took everything you could get from me and paid me for it with your body, just like Lizzie at the inn. You trapped me into wedlock, but no one makes a prisoner of any kind out of me.'

'Please Titus, I never meant any betrayal to you.' Sarah was frightened, it was an effort not to scream for help, but her feelings for him were greater even than that. 'I gave myself to you out of love, only love. I've come to you in good faith, to offer you my love. I

356

love you. Let me love you and look after you.'

Titus laughed, an eerie, evil sound, and he swore profanely. 'There's no such thing as love in this world, you silly bitch! Only power and procreation and having a good time. Don't say another sickly word. I can't bear the sound of your sugary voice. And don't look at me! I hate your eyes, no matter how beautiful they are because they look at me from your pathetic heart.' In one furious yank he ripped away the front of her dress. Sarah screamed in fear and pain. She tried to plead but he smacked her face hard. 'I said don't look at me!'

She closed her eyes, shaking and moaning in fear.

'I'm going to punish you, Sarah. Really enjoy myself. You can scream again if you like. With all that racket going on downstairs no one will hear you. Then I'm going to take you for a ride on the moors, just like when we first met. But this time I'll be coming off it alone. You're going down the first old mine shaft or deep marsh we come to. I'll be free again, free to marry a girl I'll wait for to be at least seven months pregnant and who'll give me many more babies. And one day, no matter where she might be, I'll go after your little Tamsyn and I'll give her a baby. How do you like that idea, Sarah, you barren bitch? Kivell blood mixed with Hichens blood at last?'

He was on top of her, tearing away her skirts. Sarah lay helpless beneath him, sick over what he'd said, terrified for herself and for Tamsyn in the future. He was hurting her, about to brutalize her. She should have listened to Tempest. Turning her head to look up at her husband she saw him for what he really was, a cruel evil bully, a savage, a madman.

'Get away from her Titus! I've got a gun! I shot your father and I won't hesitate to do the same to you,' Tempest shouted at her highest pitch.

Titus rolled off Sarah and smoothly covered her up. The change in his terrible harsh features was swift, he was smiling sheepishly, almost innocently. 'Mama,' he said in a voice that sounded embarrassed, even boyish. 'What are you doing? You're interrupting a time between a man and his wife. I know me and Sarah might have been noisy, but it's how we like it sometimes. Isn't it, my darling?' He helped Sarah to sit up and was stroking her face, tidying her messed up hair. 'I haven't seen her for a few days, I got carried away with passion. That's how it was, wasn't it, Sarah?' While Tempest glared at him, the shotgun held up to her shoulder in an unwavering grip and aimed at his chest, he whispered in Sarah's ear. 'Tell her it's so, my love. I was upset and I was only punishing you. I went a little too far, that's all.'

'Don't fall for his lies, Sarah. Get off the bed and come to me. Don't be afraid,' Tempest said.

'You've no right to interfere, Mama,' Titus said. 'Sarah loves me.'

'Do you love him that much, Sarah?'

Sarah gazed at her mother-in-law. For all that had just happened she still loved Titus. She couldn't simply turn off her feelings. He was holding her, caressing her arm. 'Sorry, my darling,' he whispered.

'Sarah, he was hurting you. Don't let him hurt you again.' Tempest kept the shotgun steady.

'I'm not worried about myself,' Sarah said. 'Titus, I need to breathe. Let me get up.'

'Then we'll talk? You'll stay with me. We'll sort this all out?' His words purred as if with affection and promise.

Sarah nodded. He let her go. She got up and pushed the tangled hair from her face, holding her bodice to cover herself.

'You heard her, Mama. Put the gun down.' His tone had changed, he was gloating now.

'Sarah...' Tempest's voice was steeped in disappointment. 'If I hadn't come upstairs when I did he might have killed you.'

'He planned to.'

'And you've forgiven him?'

'Yes.'

'See Mama?' Titus crowed, standing up, tall and strident. 'You've no power over me. You can't hurt me with curses or ill-wishes. You won't go against what my dear little wife wants. You're just another weak foolish woman.'

'I can forgive anything you do to me, Titus,' Sarah said. 'I know it's ridiculous and it's pathetic and most people wouldn't understand it. But I won't allow you to hurt Tamsyn. I've always vowed to protect her and I always will. Don't let go of the gun, Mama Tempest. I'm leaving. I'll go far away where he will never find me.'

'That won't ever be far enough, you rotten bitch!' Titus bawled in fury. He made a dash at his mother and managed to snatch the gun from her hands. 'Get over beside her, Mama!'

Tempest moved to Sarah and stood in front of her. 'What are you going to do now, Titus. Kill us both?'

'Yes. You deserve to die too, you've never given me a mother's love.'

'That's because I saw right into your heart the day you were born and saw nothing but darkness and evil. The gun has only one cartridge in it.' Tempest stared into his eyes. 'You can kill me, but someone from downstairs will hear before you can reload. Sarah will be safe, and you'll get what you deserve. No one will bother to save you from a hangman's noose.' She pushed Sarah away so she wouldn't be hit in the blast.

Her steady sight on Titus angered him. 'Don't try your tricks on me. You can't hurt me.' But when Tempest started muttering it unnerved him. 'Stop it!'

'A curse on you, Titus.'

'No!' He aimed the gun at her.

'Titus don't!' Sarah screamed.

He looked from her terror to Tempest's calm resignation. His mother didn't mind dying as long as she could protect others. She

360

loathed him and he hated her for it. She deserved to be punished and he knew how to do it in the way that would hurt her most. 'I'm not going to hurt you, Mama, but...'

He hurtled out of the room and headed for the stairs. 'Is he leaving?' Sarah asked shakily.

Tempest was on to her son's next dire move. 'No. Sol!' She raced after him.

The music was loud, the party in full sway when Titus charged into the room. He had the shotgun hanging from his hand, and at first no one realized he had it with him, but his ugly expression as he pushed through the revellers to where Sol and Amy were, waiting for Tempest to return for the speeches, made his family and the villagers shy away from him and become still and to stare, worried what he'd do. Then the shotgun was seen, followed quickly by cries of horror and calls for the music to stop.

As an unearthly hush fell in the room, Sol saw the danger and he stepped away from Amy. 'What's this about, Father?'

'About many things,' Titus snarled. 'Lack of respect from you, a lifetime of rejection from my rotten mother. Revenge. She's always said you were the one thing that made her life worth living, now let's see how she goes on without you.' Titus lifted the shotgun and took aim at Sol's forehead.

'No!' Amy screamed. 'You can't really mean to kill your own son.'

'Watch me.' Titus's finger moved to the trigger. A look of disbelief and horror flooded

361

Sol's face. His life with Amy was to be over before it had really begun.

'Titus!' It was Tempest. 'Stop or it will be you who dies this day.'

'You don't frighten me anymore, Mama.' He made to squeeze the trigger, but as he did a terrible pain shot up his left arm and his finger wouldn't work. He broke out into a burning sweat and he felt dizzy. The room started to spin and he felt sick. As he wavered Sol hurtled forward and yanked the shotgun out of his hands. Titus fell to his knees, his hands shooting to his chest as he was gripped by the most excruciating pains. 'Mama don't! Mama stop it! I'm sorry.'

Sarah crept up to him and stared down on him from blank eyes. Titus could just make her out. 'Sarah, help me.' She had seen many things in her husband's eyes, confidence and arrogance, and cruelty and hatred in latter days, but now she saw only fear. She saw right into his dark soul and it horrified her. 'Sarah ... you're my wife ... you have to help me.'

Titus had a circle of observers. He peered up from stricken eyes, screaming again and again as agony gripped his chest. Family or villagers, no one was going to help him. No one cared. He couldn't breathe. He panicked. 'Help me! Mama!' She came immediately in front of him. She had given him life and now she was taking it away.

'Titus, you can't fight fate, and Sol's is to have a long life with Amy.'

Hers was the last face Titus saw. On his

back, gripping his chest, his body twisted as the pains contorted him, he breathed his last. Dying all alone.

For several moments no one spoke. Then Godley Greep said, without the reverence usually reserved for the dead, 'Classic case of heart failure, I'd say.'

Tempest knelt and closed her son's eyes. She wiped away a single tear from her own eye. Sol and Amy came to her side. Tempest said, 'He can be taken to his room. I'm sure the coroner will agree with Mr Greep's deliberation. Then he can be buried next to his father. I'm sure everyone will understand if we all quietly disperse and carry on with the celebration another time.' She went to Sarah. 'You can share the children's room tonight and you can all rest easy here from now on.'

'I didn't bring the children with me,' Sarah said, with a tone of cool maturity. The last hour had seen to it that all her illusions were thrown off, and all her hopes gone, except for one. Now she knew where she really belonged. 'They're with Aunty Molly. She said if I come to my senses I can live with her too. Well, I have, and not just because Titus is dead. I should have accepted my lot in life like the other bal-maidens who support their families with pride and without complaint. If I can get work back at the mine it's what I shall do.'

'But you don't have to go back to that, Sarah. I understand why you don't want to live here but let me help you move away and

363

start again.'

'No thank you,' Sarah said firmly. 'I know you mean well, but I'll never take anything again from a Kivell.'

'Good for you, Sarah,' Godley Greep's voice boomed praise. 'You can come back to my tributer team, and if anyone doesn't like it they'll have me to answer to.' A murmur of agreement ran through the villagers present. Sarah had shown pride and repentance in her decision and she had their unanimous approval. 'I'll take you to your aunty's now.'

It was dawn and Sol was up on the hill outside Chy-Henver. Amy went to him. They clung together, gazing over the silent landscape.

'I don't think any of us got much sleep last night. Will your grandmama be all right?' She pressed her face in to his shoulder.

'She'll grieve for my father in her own way.'

'And you, darling?'

'I'll be fine.' It was a typical male answer of understatement. Amy had got close to Sol, as two people in love do, but she was certain he would never disclose how he felt about his father's attempt to kill him and his subsequent death. He leaned round and kissed her lips. 'We'll be fine.'

'I know.' She snuggled into him. Content to be here quietly with him for now. Looking forward to learning more about him. Already on the next stage of life's journey with him.